THE LAST DANCE WAS DEATH'S

He sprang to the ground as they came to a standstill and ran over to the stranded car. For a moment he stood peering in through the window and then without a word wrenched open the door. Campion saw him bending down, his head and shoulders hidden from view in the dark interior.

The next moment a rug came hurtling out and a cry that was not a scream or a shout, but somewhere midway between the two, escaped its owner.

Sock drew back slowly. His face was livid and his young eyes were horror-stricken. He put his hand over his stomach.

Campion sprang from the Lagonda and, pushing past the younger man, peered down into the coupe.

The body lay doubled up on the floor with its legs forced round the controls and its head jammed against the front of the passenger seat. That it was a dead body was painfully apparent. The skull had been battered unmercifully.

Agatha Christie

Death on the Nile
A Holiday for Murder
The Mousetrap and Other Plays
The Mysterious Affair at Styles
Poirot Investigates
Postern of Fate
The Secret Adversary
The Seven Dials Mystery
Sleeping Murder

Dorothy Simpson

Last Seen Alive
The Night She Died
Puppet for a Corpse
Six Feet Under
Close Her Eyes
Element of Doubt
Dead on Arrival
Suspicious Death
Dead by Morning

Elizabeth George

A Great Deliverance
Payment in Blood
Well-Schooled in Murder

Colin Dexter

Last Bus to Woodstock
The Riddle of the Third Mile
The Silent World of Nicholas Quinn
Service of All the Dead
The Dead of Jericho
The Secret of Annexe 3
Last Seen Wearing

Michael Dibdin

Ratking

Liza Cody

Stalker
Head Case
Under Contract

S. T. Haymon

Death of a God
coming soon: Death and the Pregnant Virgin
A Very Particular Murder

Ruth Rendell

A Dark-Adapted Eve
(writing as Barbara Vine)
A Fatal Inversion
(writing as Barbara Vine)

Marian Babson

Death in Fashion
Reel Murder
Murder, Murder, Little Star
Murder on a Mystery Tour
Murder Sails at Midnight
The Stalking Lamb
coming soon:
Murder at the Cat Show

Dorothy Cannell

The Widows Club
Down the Garden Path
Mum's the Word
coming soon: Femmes Fatal

Antonia Fraser

Jemima Shore's First Case
Your Royal Hostage
Oxford Blood
Cool Repentance
coming soon:
A Splash of Red
Quiet as a Nun

Margery Allingham

Police at the Funeral
Flowers for the Judge
Tether's End
Pearls Before Swine
Traitor's Purse
Dancers in Mourning

DANCERS
IN MOURNING

MARGERY ALLINGHAM

BANTAM BOOKS
NEW YORK · TORONTO · LONDON · SYDNEY · AUCKLAND

*This edition contains the complete text
of the original hardcover edition.*
NOT ONE WORD HAS BEEN OMITTED.

DANCERS IN MOURNING
A Bantam Book / published by arrangement with Doubleday.

PRINTING HISTORY
Doubleday edition published September 1937
Bantam edition / January 1984

ISBN 0-553-23880-9

Published simultaneously in the United States and Canada

Bantam Books are published by Bantam Books, a division of Bantam
Doubleday Dell Publishing Group, Inc. Its trademark consisting of the words
"Bantam Books" and the portrayal of a rooster, is Registered in U.S. Patent
and Trademark Office and in other countries. Marca Registrada. Bantam
Books, 666 Fifth Avenue, New York, New York 10103.

PRINTED IN THE UNITED STATES OF AMERICA

OPM   13 12 11 10 9 8 7 6 5 4

This book is for Nerney

1

When Mr. William Faraday sat down to write his memoirs after fifty-eight years of blameless inactivity he found the work of inscribing the history of his life almost as tedious as living it had been, and so, possessing a natural invention coupled with a gift for locating the easier path, he began to prevaricate a little upon the second page, working up to downright lying on the sixth and subsequent folios.

The book appeared at eighteen and sixpence, with frontispiece in 1934, and would have passed into the limbo of the remainder lists with thousands of its prototypes had not the quality of one of the wilder anecdotes in the chapters dealing with an India the author had never seen earned it a place in the news columns of a Sunday paper.

This paragraph called the memoirs to the attention of a critic who had not permitted his eminence to impair his appreciation of the absurd, and in the review which he afterwards wrote he pointed out that the work was pure fiction, not to say fantasy, and was incidentally one of the funniest books of the decade.

The public agreed with the critic and at the age of sixty-one William Faraday, author of *Memoirs of an Old Buffer* (republished at seven and six, seventy-fourth thousand), found himself a literary figure.

He almost succeeded in looking the part as he sat in his box at the Argosy Theatre, his small bright eyes fixed upon the stage where the three hundredth performance of *The Buffer*, the musical show which had been built on some of the bones of his book, was taking place.

Having seen the show some thirty or forty times, he naturally tended towards the critical, but he enjoyed it nevertheless.

The rest of the audience was not so surfeited. It exulted,

hugged itself and, in the cheaper parts of the house, became a little hysterical.

Even the consciously intelligent element was happy, enjoying a rare burst of spiritual freedom. A Jimmy Sutane-Slippers Bellew show was a recognized intellectual leveller and provided one of those blessed Alsatias wherein the eyes of the moron and the highbrow meet and wink. There were Sutane fans in stalls and gallery; childlike spirits, hid in most unexpected bosoms, followed his angular ecstatic figure in its graceful yet faintly grotesque interpretation of Mercer's music with all the heart-rending pleasure of imprisoned birds observing flight.

It was an occasion, a night to be remembered and recalled with embellishments. A party spirit enveloped the old Argosy and even the florid goddesses above the candelabra in the auditorium seemed to infuse a new enthusiasm into their painted sports.

The various managerial staffs, gay if exhausted, wrestled twice as vigorously as was strictly necessary with the telegrams, the insufferable idiots expecting seats before Christmas, the flowers in ice from Australia, and the expensive and importunate Atlantic phone calls.

The programme girls in their fresh uniforms glanced at the stage with new interest even when Sutane was not upon it, while the orchestra, basking in an unfamiliar sense of security, became almost elated in spite of the new number in the second act.

That disturbing emotional experience, the first night, was a thing of the past. That had been a nightmare with a happy awakening. This, the three-hundredth performance, had the pleasant quality of reality about it. The "House Full" boards appeared to be a permanency outside the doorways in Shaftesbury Avenue and the library order was no longer a matter for prayer.

Mr. Faraday leant forward. His small bear's body in its black-and-white elegance swayed to the fox-trot rhythm of the *première* hit of the show. The amusing backcloth of grotesque faces which Pavalini had designed hung across the back of the stage and habitués in the audience nudged their companions, whispering to them to notice the villainous caricature of the Doremus woman on the croupier's extreme right.

As the light increased the chorus boys appeared in their

2

twenty, fifty and a hundred franc plaque costumes. They came trotting on, more and more and more of them, drilled to automaton perfection, bobbing and clattering in carefully contrived disorder until the suggestion of a shower of counters on a boule table was complete.

The giant roulette wheel in the middle of the stage began to glow, the music softened, and the applause drowned the cue, as it always did, when the audience saw the familiar figure in the suit of white tails leaning on the silver turntable. Then came the cue again and the small, charming voice, which knew all there was to know about putting a song over and little enough about singing, pattered neatly through the first chorus.

> "What's the odds I'm on your number?
> It's a thousand—a million to one.
> It's a cert. It's a twist.
> It's a chance you have missed—
> A thousand—a million to one."

The face was a blur to eighty per cent of those in the theatre, a little white speck in a paper storm of subdued colours, but everybody knew the high forehead, the round mournful eyes, the long duck's-bill nose and the mouth which widened so amusingly into a sophisticated smile.

As the chorus was taken up by the others the wheel began to turn and the tap dance, which had made stage gossip and was likely to make stage history, began for the three-hundredth time. The small white figure with the amazing feet ricochetted and pirouetted round the wooden slats, tapping out its own music with a quality in which mere accuracy merged into the miraculous. Faster, faster and faster! A thousand—a million to one . . . a thousand—a million to one. . . .

The crisis came in a breathless moment. The audience swayed, satiated and exquisitely at peace. The wheel began to slow down, the beat of the pattering feet became sparse, and the tune slurred agonisingly an octave lower. The chorus took up the song again, the lights turned the wheel into a vast zero, and applause, like the sound of wind passing through a cornfield magnified to terrifying proportions, swept down upon the white figure grinning in its midst.

William Faraday turned to the man who sat beside him.

"It's a damned shame, Campion," he murmured, the words rumbling between his lips. "Something's got to be done, my boy. See that with half an eye. Means so much, you know."

Mr. Campion nodded. The roar from the great pleased animal whose vastness filled the theatre, and of which he was so alarmingly a part, made conversation impossible. He sat leaning back in the shadows, the light from the stage catching his horn-rimmed spectacles and the unexpectedly strong line of his chin.

He was not a handsome man. There was a certain vacuity in his expression which counteracted the pleasant angles of his face and lent his whole appearance an indefinable quality, so that those who knew him were apt to find him hard to recollect and impossible to describe.

At the moment Mr. Faraday, who knew him well and had excellent personal reasons for believing in his resource, wondered if he had heard and, if so, had understood him.

"More trouble here, shouldn't wonder," he muttered a few minutes later as the curtain rose on the old-time music-hall scene and the music for the extra number inserted into the show in honour of the occasion began its lazy, insinuating measure. "Don't understand why they want more dancing. Theatrical people beyond me—always were. Never liked this gel in the old days. Too damned highbrow by half. Must be an oldish woman by this time."

He turned in his chair, the shortness of his neck making a rather complete movement necessary.

"Lookin', Campion?"

"Naturally." Mr. Campion seemed startled.

His host grunted. "Here she comes. Could tell you something about her."

The art of Chloe Pye belonged to an earlier age than the inspired patterings of Jimmy Sutane, and Mr. Campion himself wondered why, on her return from a long colonial tour, she should have elected, much less been invited, to attempt a comeback in the midst of such strong competition. He had been a schoolboy when he had first seen her taking up a quarter of the bill at one of the better music halls, her rather mediocre talent helped out by a personality so feminine that her gentle seductiveness reached out well over the footlights. Her act had always been the same, a series of little dances each telling a story, each delivered in varying period cos-

4

tume, parts of which were discarded as the performance continued. The mild indelicacies involved were invariably excused by the dictates of the tale. Thus a vision of Chloe in Stuart underwear was archly exhibited under the title "Nell Gwyn Prepares for Court," and Victorian petticoats and the pantalettes in entirety were displayed with equal timid vulgarity in "Morning, 1832."

Her success in the days after the war when modern underclothes had reached an uninteresting minimum was considerable and her turn had borrowed an added glamour by the gossip which surrounded her private life.

In those days promiscuity had still the remnants of novelty and her affairs were eagerly discussed, but today, when the weary business of polyandry was arriving at the end of its melancholy cul-de-sac, her reputation, when it was remembered at all, detracted from rather than enhanced her appeal.

So, too, the return of underclothes in shopwindows and on the familiar bodies of wives and sisters destroyed the attraction of the original idea, and tonight there was no murmur of tolerant protest as petticoat after petticoat dropped to the ground.

"Highbrow?" murmured Mr. Campion, harking back to his host's earlier criticism.

"Historical," explained Mr. Faraday briefly. "Don't see why he put her in. Nothin' to do with the book. They tell me she used to draw. Won't sell a seat now."

Looking at her, Campion was inclined to agree with him. The audience, thoroughly warmed and friendly, was kind, but it was obvious that its mood was anticipatory and it only awaited the return of Sutane and Slippers in their "Round the World in a Four-in-Hand" number, to the tune which Mercer had written one afternoon while Jimmy talked to him and which was now all over two continents.

"Don't like the woman," Mr. Faraday murmured. "Might have thought she was at the bottom of it if she hadn't only just come back to England. Look at her—fifty if a day."

With his eyes on the dark vivacious figure on the stage Campion reflected that he was wrong. Chloe Pye was forty-two and in excellent physical trim. It was her mind, not her body, that was so hopelessly *vieux jeu*.

His companion touched his arm.

"Come behind," he whispered gustily. "Can't stand this.

5

Shouldn't say so, of course. Want your help, my boy. Relyin' on you. Come along."

The Argosy was an old theatre and, true to its type, its backstage accommodation had never received any serious thought. Campion edged through a door which inconvenienced him in height almost as much as it incommoded Mr. Faraday in width, risked his neck by climbing down an iron staircase with a wobble, and came out into a corridor which looked and smelled like one of the less frequently used passages in a riverside tube station.

Mr. Faraday glanced over his shoulder, his eyes brightening.

"Used to come here to see Connie. Before your time," he murmured. "Pretty little woman. Must be old now." He sighed and added with a shy confiding which was almost the whole of his charm, "Still gives me a thrill, you know, this sort of thing. *Vie de bohéme*, lights, far-off music, smell of the grease paint, women and so on."

Fortunately Mr. Campion, who was somewhat at a loss, was spared the necessity of comment. One of the doors a little higher up the corridor burst open and a golden-haired young man in exquisite evening clothes appeared wheeling a silver-plated racing bicycle. He was very angry and the expression upon his face, which was a little too beautiful to be altogether pleasant, was sulky and absurd.

"It's all very well for you to behave revoltingly, Richards, but I can bring my bicycle where I like," he said over his shoulder. "You know it as well as anybody."

"I'm sorry, Mr. Konrad." A harassed uniformed man with weary eyes and an untidy moustache came out of the door. "Mr. Webb told me himself to see nothing of the sort come into the theatre. There's not enough room for the artists, let alone you bringing in bicycles."

"But Miss Bellew brings in her great Dane." The young man gripped his machine with something approaching ferocity, but the doorkeeper spoke with the obstinacy of old authority.

"Miss Bellew is a principal," he said heavily.

The boy with the bicycle stiffened as the colour rose slowly over his face into the roots of his curling golden hair. For an embarrassing moment it seemed as if he were about to cry.

"This bicycle was presented to me by my admirers," he said. "Why should I let pure jealousy on the part of some

6

people"—he shot a waspish glance back through the doorway, presumably at some third person within—"prevent me from showing it to anyone I like? You're making a fool of yourself. I shall certainly speak to Jimmy himself about it. Why don't you keep your eye on the important things that keep happening?"

There was defiance in the last words, as though the speaker deliberately touched on a tabooed subject. A spot of colour appeared in the doorkeeper's grey cheeks and he glanced behind him. Seeing Campion, he started forward angrily, only to fall back reassured at the sight of Mr. Faraday, to whom he nodded. Shaken but still obdurate, he returned to the job in hand.

"Now, Mr. Konrad," he began, laying a heavy hand on the glittering machine, "we'll have this outside, if you please."

The boy with the golden hair relinquished it to him with a contemptuous shrug of his graceful shoulders.

"Oh, it's Uncle William," he said. "Do look here and see what the Speedo Club has insisted on sending me. Isn't it too absurd?"

Mr. Faraday coughed noisily. "Magnificent," he said fiercely and, gripping Campion's arm, he propelled him firmly down the corridor. "I hate those fellers," he muttered in an all too audible undertone. "Called me Uncle William—did you hear him?—impudent little tick! Don't mind it from my friends—rather like it. Used to it. Notice you've dropped it. Don't hesitate, my dear feller. But a worm like that...turns my stomach over, don't mind tellin' you. Golden curls!...Come on, we'll slip into the wings. Know my way about by this time. Want you to see Slippers. Nice girl. No damned nonsense about her. No sex appeal off, though," he added regretfully and coughed again, as if he feared he had betrayed himself.

The "Round the World in a Four-in-Hand" number was at its height as they approached. Over Mr. Faraday's shoulder Campion caught a glimpse of the two figures, so familiar to the fashionable audiences of both continents. Slippers Bellew was a pale gold flame flickering over a twilit stage, while beside her moved Sutane, faithful as a shadow, and contriving by his very sympathy of movement to convey the mute adoration which the song demanded of him and which was so great a part of his appeal.

The roar of the audience at the end was tremendous. The harsh sound swept in on them like a great hot breath, and they stepped back through the crowd of girls and small-part folk coming down for the "Little White Petticoats" finale.

The excitement which is never wholly absent from the theatre, even on the three-hundredth night, forced itself upon Campion and he, too, was aware of the power of the Sutane personality which dominated the house, both before and behind the curtain. He tried to analyse it as he followed Uncle William to the dressing room. There was grace and skill personified in the man, but that alone was not sufficient to make so deep an appeal. It was the sophisticated, amused but utterly discontented intelligence which constituted the real attraction, he decided, an ease and dignity which was yet emotionally unsatisfied—the old pull of the hero in love, in fact.

His companion was still talking.

"Wait for him in here," he remarked, tapping at a door with a One on it. "Wants to see you. Promised I'd bring you along."

They were admitted to a large room, overlit to the point of discomfort, by a stolid young man in a white coat and spectacles with very thick lenses.

"Come in, sir. Glad to see you," he said, conducting the elder man to an armchair beside the dressing table.

Uncle William grunted gratefully and sat down.

"This is Henry, Campion," he said with a wave of a pudgy hand. "Good feller, Henry."

The young man beamed and set a chair for the other guest. He managed to convey at once that he was not at all sure if he was behaving like a first-class manservant but thought that there was a very good chance that he was.

"A nice drop of whisky, sir?" he ventured hopefully.

Uncle William looked interested. "Good idea," he said consideringly and Henry coloured as if he had received a compliment.

While the decanter was forthcoming Campion had leisure to observe the room, which displayed three different influences in sharp contrast. There was the florid taste of the original furnisher, which ran to Turkey carpet and a day bed with gilded legs; the somewhat militaristic neatness and a feeling for gadgets as expressed by the bar concealed in an old gramophone cabinet, which was obviously Henry's contribution; and something else, not so easy to define. Apart from a mass of papers, photographs and telegrams mostly, there were several odd indications of Jimmy Sutane's personal interests. Two or three cheap mechanical toys lay upon the dressing table beside a box of liquorice all-sorts and a bunch of white flowers, while on a shelf in the corner sat a very nice white Hotei and a tear-off calendar, complete with an astrological forecast for each day of the year.

Uncle William sat back in his chair, the bright lights glinting on the double row of near-white curls at the nape of his plump pink neck. He looked worldly and benign, and somehow bogus, with his watery blue eyes serious and his expression unwontedly important.

"Well," he demanded, "anythin' new?"

Henry paused in the act of laying out a suit but did not turn round.

"It just seems funny to me, sir," he said sulkily. "Miss Finbrough may take it seriously but I don't."

"Miss Finbrough, eh?" Uncle William cleared his throat. "Things have to be pretty bad for her to get the wind-up, I should think."

"You'd say so, sir." Henry was deliberately noncommittal and still did not turn round.

The elder man was silent for a moment or so.

"May be nothin' in it," he said at last.

Henry swung round, his face red and unhappy.

"Theatrical people aren't like ordinary people, sir," he burst out, blushing with shame at his own disloyalty. "I'm new to it and I notice it. They're *theatrical*. Things mean more to them than they would to you or me—little things do. There's not a nicer gentleman than Mr. Sutane anywhere; no one's denying that. But he's been in the theatre all his life and he hasn't been about like an ordinary person. Suppose little things do happen now and again? Aren't they always happening? Being in the theatre is like living in a little tiny village where everybody's looking at everyone else and wondering what they're going to be up to next. It's small, that's what it is. And Miss Finbrough . . ." He broke off abruptly. Someone turned the door handle with a rattle and Jimmy Sutane came in.

He stood for a moment smiling at them and Campion was

9

aware of that odd quality of overemphasis which there is about all very strong personalities seen close to for the first time. Confronted suddenly, at a distance of a couple of yards, Sutane presented a larger-than-life edition of his stage self. The lines of his famous smile were etched more deeply into his face than seemed possible in one so thin, and the heavy-lidded eyes beneath the great dome of a forehead were desperately weary rather than merely tired.

"Hallo, Uncle," he said. "This Mr. Campion? Awfully good of you to come along. God, I'm exhausted! Henry, give me a drink. 'Fraid it's got to be milk, damn it."

The pleasant boyish voice was unexpectedly resonant, and as he closed the door and came into the room the place seemed to have become smaller and the walls more solid.

While Henry brought a glass of milk from the bar cupboard and assisted him out of his clothes and into a dressing gown there was a constant stream of interruptions. Excitable dinner-jacketed figures put their heads in, apologised and disappeared. More notes and telegrams arrived and the phone bell clamoured incessantly.

Campion sat back in his chair in the corner and watched. After the urbanity of his greeting Sutane seemed to have forgotten his guests. There was a nervous tension, a suppressed excitability, about him which had not been noticeable on the stage. He looked harassed and the nervous force which exuded from him like vibrations from a dynamo was not directed at any one thing but escaped abortively, creating an atmosphere which was uneasy and disquieting.

A minor climax came when he turned on an unsuspecting newcomer who was pushing the door timidly open and sent him scuttling off with a passionate protest.

"For God's sake, Eddie!—give me ten minutes..."

The explosion embarrassed him and he grimaced at Campion, his temporary audience.

"I'm going to pieces," he said. "Henry, get on the other side of that door and put your back against it. Tell them I'm saying my prayers. Unhook the phone before you go."

As the door closed behind the obedient dresser he turned to Campion.

"Come down tomorrow, can you? I've got conferences and things about this *Swing Over* show for the Orient, but Sunday is more of a breather than any other day. I don't know what

10

you'll think of it all. Something's going on; I know that. This fat ass here says I've got persecution mania... my hat, I wish I had!"

He laughed and, although the familiar gaiety was there, the man watching him saw suddenly that it was a trick of line and feature rather than an expression of genuine feeling. It was typical of him, Campion reflected. His very skin and bone was make-up. The man himself was within, intelligent still but different.

"It began with the 'House Full' boards," Sutane said slowly. "Someone stuck 'Last Week' slips across them. That was irritating but it didn't mean anything. Then, as far as I remember, there was an outburst of the bird in the gallery one night. It was a claque and the rest of the house was annoyed. That didn't matter in itself but little paragraphs about it got into the Press. I put Sock Petrie onto it at once and he traced one or two of them to phone calls put through the same night."

He paused.

"It's nothing much to talk about, I know, but it's been so continuous. We've had to put fresh glass over my photograph outside almost every other day. Someone smashes it regularly. Never a trace of him. There have been dozens of other trivial little things too; nothing in themselves, you know, but alarming when they mount up."

His dark eyes grew sombre.

"It's now that it's spread out to our place at home that it's getting me down. Finding strangers in the garden with silly excuses and that sort of thing."

He broke off lamely and turned to the elder man.

"That woman Chloe Pye is going down there tonight," he said. "She says my wife asked her and she's going. I told her I'd rather she didn't, but she laughed at me. Can't chuck her out, can I?"

Uncle William made a deprecatory sound and Mr. Campion retained his habitual expression of polite interest. Sutane paused and reddened suddenly under his grease paint.

"I'm damned if it's all coincidence!" he burst out. "You come down tomorrow, Mr. Campion, and see how it strikes you. It's getting on all our nerves, these little petty digs at me. There was a rumour all over the place last week that I'd torn a muscle in my arm. Nine different people rang me up in one morning to sympathise."

His voice had an edge to it, and his long fingers drummed on the glass top of the dressing table.

"It doesn't matter so far," he said, "but where's it going to end? A reputation like mine, which depends on good will, can get pretty seriously damaged by a campaign like this. Yes?"

The final word was addressed to the doorway, where an apologetic Henry stood hesitating.

"It's Mr. Blest," he ventured, "I thought . . ."

"Blest! Come in." Sutane seemed relieved. "You know Mr. Faraday. Mr. Campion . . ."

Ex-Inspector Blest grinned and nodded to the tall figure in the corner.

"Evenin'," he said. "Didn't expect to see you here, Mr. Campion. It's as serious as that, is it? Well, Mr. Sutane, it's all quiet tonight. Nothing to report at all. There's not a word uttered out of place in the whole theatre. Ever since you engaged me to keep an eye on things I've been keeping my ears open, and you can take it from me, sir, there's nothing but friendliness towards you everywhere."

"Is that so?" With a movement so sudden and angry that the detective stepped back involuntarily, Sutane took up a face towel from the table and wiped his cheek. "What about that?"

The four men in the room looked at him curiously. From a point just below the left eye and following the line of the nose to the upper lip was a deep ragged scratch. Sutane ran his finger down it.

"D'you know what that is, Blest? That's the oldest, dirtiest little theatre trick in the bag. A pin in the grease-paint stick. God knows how long it's been there. One day I was certain to work down to it. It happened to be tonight."

Blest was astonished in spite of himself. His round heavy face was crimson and he looked at Henry suspiciously.

"D'you know anything about this?" he demanded. "Who could have had access to your master's paint?"

"Oh, don't be a fool." Sutane's tone was weary. "The show has run for three hundred performances. My dressing room isn't always locked. Hundreds of people have been in and out of here in the last eight months. It's a long pin, you see, and

12

it has been stuck up through the bottom of the stick. The head was buried in the silver-paper holder."

He began to pile cream on his face to get the rest of the paint off.

"Then there's the bouquet," he went on lazily, half enjoying the sensation he was creating. "There it is. A messenger boy handed it in at the stage door just before the show began."

"Flowers?" The ex-inspector was inclined to be amused. "I can't say I see anything funny about that, sir."

He took up the little white bunch gingerly and eyed it.

"Not very grand, perhaps. Star of Bethlehem, aren't they? Country flowers. You've got a lot of humble admirers, you know."

Sutane did not speak and, finding himself ignored, the ex-policeman raised the flowers to his nose and sniffed them idly. His sudden change of expression was ludicrous, and he dropped the bouquet with an exclamation.

"Garlic!" he ejaculated, his small eyes round with astonishment. "Garlic! Hey, what d'you know about that! A messenger brought it, did he? Well, I think I can check up there. Excuse me."

He retrieved the flowers and plunged out of the room with them. Sutane caught Campion's eye in the mirror and turned round to face him.

"It's all trivial," he said apologetically. "Little tuppenny-ha'penny squirts of malice. They're negligible on their own, but after a month or so they get one down."

He broke off and smiled. When he spoke again it was to reveal the essential charm of the man, a charm which was to puzzle and finally defeat an Albert Campion who was then barely in existence.

"It's worse for me," he said. "I've been such a blasted popular sort of fellow for so long." His grin grew lopsided and his eyes were sad and childlike and intelligent.

2

Afterwards, when the tide of circumstance had reached its
flood and there was no telling what were the secrets beneath
its turbulent waters, Mr. Campion tried to remember every
moment of that long and catastrophic day. Details which had
seemed unimportant at the time flitted about in his mind
with exasperating vagueness and he strove to catch at them in
vain.

Yet the whole story was there, so clear to read if only he
had been looking for it.

On the momentous Sunday Mr. Campion went to White
Walls in the morning. On that day Chloe Pye plumbed the
final depth of inconsideration, entirely outclassing all her
previous efforts. This, in itself, was a remarkable feat since
her total disregard for those who entertained her was a
byword among the host of near friends who composed her
circle.

Uncle William Faraday sat beside Mr. Campion in the
Lagonda and pointed out the way with most of the pride of
ownership. It was July and the roads were hot and scented,
cow parsley making a bridal avenue of every lane. Uncle
William sniffed appreciatively.

"Twenty miles from London. Nothing in a car. But feel
you're in the heart of the country. He runs a flat, of course,
but gets down here most evenings. Don't blame Sutane.
Sensible feller, at heart."

He glanced at his companion to make sure he was attending.

"Dear old place," he went on, receiving a nod of encouragement. "You'll like it. Used to belong to his wife's uncle. Girl
wanted to keep it when it came to her and Sutane suddenly
thought, 'Why not?' That music writer, Squire Mercer, who
did the stuff for my show, has a little house on the estate. Had
it for years. Matter of fact, it was at his place that Sutane met

14

Linda, his wife. She was stayin' with her uncle up at White Walls and Jimmy came down to see Mercer. They fell in love and there you are. Funny how things work out."

He was silent for some little time, his old eyes speculative and his lips moving a little as though he rehearsed still further details of Sutane's private life. Mr. Campion remained thoughtful.

"This persecution business has got on his nerves, has it? Or is he always as excitable as he was last night?"

"Always a bit mad." The old man pulled the large tweed cap he affected for motoring more firmly over his ears. "Noticed that as soon as I saw him. Don't think he's very much worse than usual. Of course you can understand it when you see the life the feller leads. Most unnatural... overworked, thinks too much, no peace at all, always in the thick of things, always in a hurry..."

He hesitated as though debating on a confidence not quite in good taste.

"It's a rum ménage for a decent house," he remarked at last. "Don't know what the old servants make of it. My own first experience of Bohemia, don't you know. Not at all what I thought."

He sounded a little regretful and Campion glanced at him.

"Disappointing?" he enquired.

"No, my boy, no, not exactly." Uncle William was ashamed of himself. "Freedom, you know, great freedom, but only in the things that don't matter, if you see what I mean. Very rational really. Like you to meet 'em all. Turn down here. This is the beginnin' of the estate. It's a modern house on an old site. This is the park."

Mr. Campion turned the nose of the car down a flint lane leading off the secondary road. High banks, topped by a chase of limes and laurels so dear to the privacy-loving hearts of an earlier generation, rose on either side. His passenger regarded these screens with satisfaction.

"I like all this," he said. "Since it's a right of way, very sensible. Notice this?"

He waved a plump hand towards a high rustic bridge overgrown with ramblers which spanned the road ahead of them.

"Pretty, isn't it? Useful too. Saves havin' steps down to the road. The house, the lawns and the lake are over here to the

15

right and there's an acre or two of park on the other side. Must cost him a pretty penny to keep up."

They passed under the bridge and came on to the drive proper, wide and circular, leading up to the house. Campion, who had entertained misgivings at the term "modern," was reassured.

Standing on high ground, its wide windows open to catch a maximum of sun, was one of those rare triumphs of the sounder architects of the earlier part of the century. There was nothing of the villa in its white walls and red-tiled roof. It possessed a fine generosity of line and proportion and succeeded in looking somehow like a great white yacht in full sail.

"French-looking," commented Uncle William complacently. "Take the car through into the yard. Like you to see the stables."

They passed under the archway of the stable buildings on the left of the house and came into a brick yard where several cars were already parked. Apart from Sutane's own black Bentley there were two small sports cars and one remarkable contraption of considerable age on which a young man in overalls and a cloth cap was at work. He grinned at Uncle William.

"It's back again, sir," he said. "Universal joint gone this time." He nodded to Campion with impartial friendliness, indicated a parking spot, and returned to his work.

"See what I mean?" said Mr. Faraday in one of his disastrous asides. "No formality in the whole place. That's Petrie's car he's at work on. Feller they call 'Sock.' Can't quite understand him. Like your opinion."

As they emerged from the archway Mr. Campion became aware of a certain hesitation in his companion's manner and, looking up, he saw the cause coming down the drive towards them. It was Chloe Pye.

She was dressed in a small white swim suit, high-heeled shoes and a child's sunbonnet, and managed to look every one of her forty-odd years. Off the stage she, too, presented some of that self-exaggeration which had been so noticeable in Sutane. Her body was hard and muscular and one saw that her face was old rather because of the stuff it was made of than because of any defect of line or contour. She was swinging a long bright scarf and carried a book and a deck chair.

16

At the sight of the visitors she threw the scarf round her shoulders and stood hesitating, arch and helpless.

"How providential!" she called to Uncle William as soon as he was within earshot. "Come and help me, darling."

Mr. Faraday bustled forward, self-conscious and incompetent. He raised his cap to her carefully before taking the chair.

"And who's this?" Chloe Pye managed to pat Uncle William's arm, hand him the chair and indicate that she was waiting for his companion to be introduced all in one movement.

Campion came up and was conscious of pale green eyes, a trifle too prominent, which looked up into his face and found him disappointing.

"They're all in the house," she said. "Shop, shop, nothing but shop the whole time. Shall I have the chair under the trees, Mr. Faraday? Or do you think it would be better by the flower bed?—that one over there with the silly little red thingummies in it."

It took some little time to get her settled and themselves out of the reach of her tenacious conversational openings, but they broke away eventually and once again headed for the front door.

"You won't believe a word they tell you, will you?" she shouted as they reached the path. "They're all quite mad, my dears. They're just seeing insults on all sides . . . Tell somebody to bring me some ice water."

The front door stood open and from it came the sound of a piano. The unsuspecting Mr. Campion had just set foot on the lowest step when there was a roar above him and a gigantic Dane, who had been sleeping on the mat just inside the hall, leapt down, his neck bristling and his eyes uncompromisingly red.

"Hoover!" protested Mr. Faraday. "Down, sir! Down! Somebody call the dog!"

The thunderous barking shook the house and a woman in a white linen coat appeared in the doorway.

"Lie down, you little beast," she said, hurrying down the steps and cuffing the animal with a broad red hand. "Oh, it's you, Mr. Faraday? He ought to know you. Get back, Hoover. Go in and watch your mistress."

The authority in her voice was tremendous, and Campion

was not surprised to see the brute cower obediently and slink into the house, his tail drooping.

The newcomer came down another step towards them and suddenly became a much shorter, stockier person than he had supposed. She was forty-five or so, with red untidy hair, a boiled pink face and light eyelashes. Campion thought he had never seen anyone more self-possessed.

"He's working in the hall," she said, lowering her voice and giving the personal pronoun a peculiar importance. "Would you mind going round through the sitting-room windows? He's been at it since eight o'clock this morning and hasn't had his massage yet. I'm waiting to get hold of him."

"Of course not. We'll go round at once, Miss Finbrough." Uncle William was deferential. "This is Mr. Campion, by the way."

"Mr. Campion? Oh, I'm glad you've come." Her blue eyes grew interested. "He's depending on you. It's a thorough-going shame. Poor man, he's got enough worry in the ordinary way with this new show he's producing without having all this trouble. You run along. He'll see you soon."

She dismissed them with a finality that would have daunted a newspaperman. It had done so, of course, on many occasions.

"An extraordinary woman," confided Uncle William as they went round the side of the house. "Devoted to Sutane. Looks after him like a nurse. Come to think of it, that's just about what she is. Went in the other day and she'd got him on a mattress, stark as a plucked chicken, pummellin' the life out of him. Henry, the feller we saw last night at the theatre, is terrified of her. Believe they all are. Wonder if we'll get in here."

He paused outside a pair of very high french windows which gave out onto the terrace on which they stood. Here, too, there was music, but softer, the beat less insistent than the other which still sounded faintly from the hall. It ceased abruptly as a man at the piano caught sight of the visitors, and a voice so slovenly that the words were scarcely articulated welcomed them in.

Campion followed Mr. Faraday into a large light room whose original style of decoration had followed a definite modern scheme embracing pearl-grey panelling and deep, comfortable black chairs, but which now resembled nothing

18

so much as a playroom devoted to some alarmingly sophisticated child.

Temporary tables ranged round the room supported piles of manuscript, sheaves of untidy papers, model sets, and whole hosts of glossy photographs.

In the center of the polished floor was a baby grand and behind it, nodding at them, sat the man who had spoken. He was an odd-looking person; yet another "personality," thought Mr. Campion wryly. He was extraordinarily dark and untidy, with a blue chin and wide bony shoulders. The jut of the great beak of a nose began much higher up than usual so that his eyes were divided by a definite ridge and his mild, lazy expression sat oddly on a face which should have been much more vivid.

He began to play again immediately, a mournful little cadence without beginning or end, played over and over with only the most subtle of variations.

The other two people in the room rose as the newcomers appeared. A large rawboned person who could only be described as disreputable disengaged himself from the chair in which he had been sprawling amid a heap of newspapers and came forward, a pewter tankard in his hand. He shook himself a little and his creased woollen clothes slipped back into some semblance of conventionality. He was very tall, and his cheekbones were red and prominent in his square young face.

"Hallo, Uncle," he said. "This is Mr. Campion, is it? Sorry James is so very much engaged, but it can't be helped. Sit down, won't you? I'll get you some beer in a minute. Oh, you won't? All right, later on then. Do you know everyone?"

He had a pleasant but powerful voice and a natural ease of manner very comforting to a stranger. His black hair was strained off his forehead and appeared to be plastered with Vaseline, while his small deep-set eyes were sharp and friendly.

Uncle William plumped himself in a chair and looked at Campion.

"This is Sock Petrie," he said in much the same tone as he might have pronounced "Exhibit A." "Oh, and this is Eve. Sorry . . . I didn't see you, my dear."

He struggled to get up out of the low chair and was defeated.

A girl came forward to shake hands. She was obviously

19

Sutane's sister. Campion had never seen a resemblance more clearly marked. He guessed that she was seventeen or eighteen. She had her brother's arched brows and deep-set, unhappy eyes, as well as a great deal of his natural grace, but her mouth was sulky and there was an odd sense of resentment and frustration about her. She retired to a corner immediately after the introduction and sat very still, her thin body hunched inside her plain cotton dress.

Sock glanced round.

"Let me present Squire Mercer," he said. "Mercer, for God's sake shut up a minute and say how-d'you-do."

The man at the piano smiled and nodded at Campion, but his fingers did not cease their endless strumming. He looked pleasant, even charming, when he smiled, and his eyes, which were not dark, as they should have been, but a light clear grey, grew momentarily interested.

"He's just a poor bloody genius," said Petrie, flopping down among the newspapers again. He splashed his beer over himself as he swung one huge leg over the arm and exhibited a runkled sock with an inch or so of bare leg above it. The visitors got the impression that Mercer's lack of hospitality embarrassed him.

Campion found a chair and sat down. Petrie grinned at him.

"Furious activity mingled with periods of damn-all, that's what this life is," he remarked. "What d'you make of this last business? Had time to consider it at all?"

There was a weary sigh from the corner.

"Must we go all over it again, Sock?" Eve Sutane protested. "Silly little odds and ends of rubbish that don't mean anything. They're all so petty."

Petrie raised his eyebrows.

"That how you see it, poppet?" he said. "It's getting James down, I can tell you that, and it's bad for his reputation. I haven't handled his publicity for five years without being able to say that definitely. It's happening from the inside, you know, Campion. That's the annoying part. . . . Mercer, must you keep up that same silly little tune?"

The song writer smiled contentedly.

"It's a funeral march for a dead dancer," he said. " 'Mutes in Dance Time.' I like it."

"Very likely. But you're giving me the pip."

20

"Then go away." There was unexpected fury in the tone and it startled everybody.

Petrie reddened and shrugged his shoulders.

"Go ahead."

"I shall."

Mercer continued his strumming. He was quiet and happy again, lost, it seemed, in his own private and particular world.

Petrie returned to Campion.

"There's a par in the *Cornet*," he said, "and another in *Sunday Morning*. Look at them."

He took out a wallet which would have disgraced a lie-about and extracted two ragged scraps of newspaper. Campion read them.

GARLIC FOR THE STAR

was the *Cornet*'s heading.

There are many feuds in stageland. Once a star, of whatever magnitude, becomes really unpopular there is never a shortage of people anxious and able to let him know it. Among the tributes handed over the footlights at a certain West End theatre last night was a little bunch of white flowers. The star took them and pressed them to his nose. Only a long training in the art of self-control prevented him from flinging the bouquet from him then and there, for the white flowers were wild garlic. Somebody disliked him and chose this graceful way of saying so.

Sunday Morning treated the matter in its own way.

DANCING WITH TEARS IN HIS EYES?

Who was the joker who sent Jimmy Sutane a bunch of garlic on the three-hundredth night of The Buffer? *It could not have been a comment on his work. Jimmy's flying feet don't need encouragement of this sort. Maybe he made someone cry and they wanted to return the compliment.*

"I can't get a line on these until the Press boys get back to work." Sock retrieved the paragraphs. "But you see what it

21

means. Someone turned that information in early. It was the end of the show when James told that ass Blest about the flowers—far too late to make these rags. That leaves Henry, who I'd pin my shirt too, Richards the doorkeeper, who is beyond suspicion, and, of course, the chap who sent 'em." He paused. "The information reached these blokes by phone. Any other paper would have rung up for confirmation, but these two print anything. The *Cornet* left out the name and *Sunday Morning* got round the libel with a compliment—not that they care for libel. If they don't get five actions a week they think the rag's getting dull."

He grimaced and replenished his tankard from a bottle behind the chair.

"It may be all poppycock but it's damned unfortunate," he said. "If it came from outside it might be one of the poor lunatics who badger stage folk until some merciful bobby locks 'em up, but when it's from inside, like this, there's genuine malice in it and it's not so funny."

Mr. Campion was inclined to agree with him and his interest in the affair revived. Sock Petrie breathed an atmosphere of worldly common sense.

"Is Sutane likely to have any enemies?" he enquired.

Mercer cut in from the piano.

"Jimmy? Oh, no, everyone likes Jimmy. Why shouldn't they? I mean, I do myself, and I shouldn't if he wasn't a good chap."

The words were articulated so carelessly that the sense was only just clear. Campion glanced at him curiously, looking from some hint of sarcasm in the remark. He met the light grey eyes directly and was astonished. Mercer, he saw suddenly, was that rarity in a modern world, a simple literalist. His face was bland and innocent; he meant exactly what he said.

Sock smiled into his tankard and afterwards caught Campion's eye.

"There's a lot in that, Mercer," he said, and there was more affection than patronage in his tone.

The man at the piano went on playing. He looked calm and happy.

A shadow fell across the threshold and Uncle William sat up abruptly.

"Ice water," he ejaculated guiltily and Petrie groaned.

Chloe Pye came into the room, conscious of her figure and

22

ostentatiously annoyed. She ignored both Campion and Uncle William, who had struggled out of his chair at great personal inconvenience to meet her, and spoke plaintively to Eve.

"Would it be too much trouble for me to have some ice water? I've been sweltering in the garden for hours."

"Of course not. I'll send for some, Chloe." The girl pressed a bell push in the panelling. "By the way, this is Mr. Campion. You know Uncle William, don't you?"

Miss Pye regarded the strangers with open hostility. Her lips were petulant and, Campion was amazed to see, there were actual tears in her eyes.

"We met in the drive," she said and, turning her back on them, leant on the piano to talk to Mercer.

It was an odd little display and Campion, whose experience did not include many women of forty who dressed and behaved like sulky six-year-olds, was a little shocked. He felt elderly and out of his depth.

An unexpectedly correct manservant appeared in answer to the bell and was dispatched for the water. When it came Miss Pye took it modestly.

"I hate to be so much trouble," she said, making big eyes over the rim of the glass, "but poor Chloe was t'irsty. Move up, Squire darling. She wants to sit on the music bench too. What are you going to play for me?"

Campion, who had expected a minor explosion, was relieved to see Mercer make room for her. He was not pleased but did not seem to be disposed to make a fuss. The woman put her glass down and thrust an arm round his shoulders.

"Play some of the old songs," she said. "The ones that made you famous, sweetheart. Play 'Third in a Crowd.' It makes me cry whenever I hear it, even now. Play 'Third in a Crowd.'"

Mercer appraised her with his frank eyes.

"But I don't want to make you cry," he said and played again his little half-finished melody, which was beginning to irk even the iron nerves of Mr. Campion.

"Don't you, darling? You are sweet. Play 'Waiting' then. 'Waiting' reminds me of happy days in the sun at Cassis. Or 'Nothing Matters Now.' 'Nothing Matters Now' was pure genius, pure, unadulterated genius."

Mercer, who seemed to accept the tribute without surprise

or embarrassment, played through the chorus of the song, which had captured the great hairy ears of the unfastidiously musical a few years before. He guyed it gently but without bitterness and when he had finished nodded thoughtfully.

"One of the better of my Wurlitzer numbers. Pure Vox Humana," he observed.

"You're not to make fun of it," protested Chloe. "It's got the sexual urge, or whatever they call it. It grips one in the tummy..."

"Whether it makes one sick or not," put in Petrie. "How right you are, Miss Pye."

"Oh, Sock, is that you, darling? I saw a heap of smelly old clothes in the chair. Don't interrupt me. We're getting off quietly. Play something else, Squire."

Eve rose to her feet.

"Lunch in half an hour if it's not postponed," she said. "I'm going to wash."

She slouched off and Chloe looked after her.

"Like Jimmy, but no lift—no lift at all," she said. "An odd little face, too. Squire, I'll play you one of your own songs that you've forgotten. Get your hands out of the way."

She wriggled closer to him and began to play a melody which was only faintly familiar. It had been popular in the early post-war days, Mr. Campion fancied. The name came back to him suddenly—"Water-Lily Girl."

"Corny old stuff," said Mercer. He seemed a little irritated.

"No, you're to listen," Chloe was insistent. Over the piano's broad back they could see her looking up into his face while she played the song execrably, separating the chords and lingering sickeningly on each sentimental harmony.

She went right through the tune, playing the verse as well as the chorus. Mercer seemed to have resigned himself, but when she had finished he edged her gently off the seat and went back to his little half-born melody.

Miss Pye walked over to Sock and perched herself on the arm of his chair. She was still angry with Campion and Uncle William, it seemed, for she ignored them pointedly. Sock pulled her down onto his knee.

"What a nasty little girl," he said, managing to convey that he was a man of experience, that she was a nuisance, and that while he knew perfectly well that she could give him at least ten years she was a pretty little female thing and he forgave

24

her. "So precipitate," he continued. "You met us all for the first time last night and now here you are crawling all over us in a bathing suit."

Miss Pye got out of his arms and settled herself on the edge of the chair again.

"You're rude," she said. "Jimmy and I are old friends, anyway, and I met you once at the theatre."

"That's no excuse." Sock was only partially playful so that the scene was not without its embarrassment. "That is Mr. Mercer, the composer, you've been talking to over there. He's a bachelor and a misogynist. He saw you for the first time late last night. If you work too fast you'll give him blood pressure."

Chloe laughed. She was childishly excited.

"Squire, shall I?"

"What? Sorry, I wasn't listening."

"Shall I give you blood pressure?"

Mercer blushed. His dark face looked odd suffused with sudden colour.

"I don't think so," he said carelessly and began to play loudly, making an interesting addition to the tune at last. This development seemed to absorb him and came as a blessed relief to everyone else in the room.

Miss Pye became dignified with a lightning change of mood which comforted Uncle William, who had been watching her with growing dismay. She left Sock and walked across to the window with conscious grace.

"Jimmy has quite a charming estate, hasn't he?" she remarked. "I do think surroundings have a definite effect upon one. He's losing all his old *joi de vivre*. Here comes Mrs. Sutane. Poor woman, she's not used to you all yet, even now, is she? How long have they been married? Seven years? I like her. Such an unassuming soul."

Footsteps sounded on the path, and Mr. Campion rose to his feet to meet his hostess and the only woman of whom Chloe Pye had ever publicly approved. He never forgot the moment. Long afterwards, he remembered the texture of the arm of the chair as he put his hand upon it to pull himself up, the formation of the fat cumulus clouds in the half oval of the window, and a purely imaginary, probably incorrect, vision of himself, long and awkward, stepping forward with a foolish smile on his face.

25

At that point his memories of the day and the chaotic weeks which followed it became unreliable, because he never permitted himself to think about them, but he remembered the instant when Mrs. Sutane came into the living room at White Walls because it was then that he gave up his customary position as an observer in the field and stepped over the low wall of the impersonal into the maelstrom itself and was caught up and exalted and hurt by it.

Linda Sutane came in slowly and as though she was a little shy. She was a small gold girl trimmed with brown, not very beautiful and not a vivid personality, but young and gentle and, above all, genuine. With her coming the world slipped back into its normal focus, at least for Mr. Campion, who was becoming a little dizzy from close contact with so many violent individualists.

She welcomed him formally in a comforting voice, and apologised because lunch was going to be late.

"They're still so busy," she said. "We daren't disturb them. Besides, no one can get into the dining room. There's a piano across the door."

Sock Petrie sighed.

"I am afraid we all disorganise your house, Mrs. Sutane," he said.

He spoke with genuine regret and it was the first intimation Mr. Campion had of the curious relationship between Linda Sutane and the brilliant company which surrounded her husband. It was a perfectly amicable arrangement based on deep respect on both sides, but kept apart by something as vital and unsurmountable as a difference in species.

"Oh, but I like it," she said, and might have added that she was profoundly used to it.

She sat down near Campion and bent forward to speak to him.

"You've come to see about all the trouble?" she said. "It's very kind of you. I hope you won't decide that we're all neurotic, but little things do get round one's feet so. If they were only big obvious catastrophes one could get hold of them. Sock showed you the paragraphs? Don't mention them to Jimmy. It makes him so angry and we can't do anything until the newspaper people get back to their offices."

Chloe cut into the conversation.

"Don't say you're going to start in on it all over again," she said plaintively. "Ever since I've come to this damned house I've heard nothing but 'persecution,' 'practical jokes,' 'someone's making fun of Jimmy.' Don't you let it get you down, my dear. Actors are like that. They always think someone's after their blood."

Mr. Campion looked up into her face, which was so distressingly raddled on that strong, trim body, and controlled a sudden vicious desire to slap it. The impulse startled him considerably. Linda Sutane smiled.

"I think you're probably right," she said. "Mr. Campion, come and see my flower garden."

She led him out onto the terrace and into a formal old English garden, walled with square-cut yews and ablaze with violas and sweet-scented peonies.

"I ought not to have forgotten she was there," she said as they walked over the turf together. "Naturally she doesn't find it interesting, but someone must tell you all about it or you'll be wasting your time. This is a very difficult house to get anything done in in the ordinary way, but just now, while they're all at work on this *Swing Over* show, it's worse than usual. You see, *The Buffer* has been such a great success that Jimmy and Slippers are anxious not to leave it. They were under contract to do *Swing Over*, though, and finally they came to an agreement with the Meyers brothers whereby Jimmy produces it and goes in on the business side and in return they let him out personally. Unfortunately negotiations took such a long time that they're late with production. They've got the principals here now, rehearsing. That's why Jimmy couldn't see you at once. They had to work in the hall because of the stairs. Ours are particularly good for some reason or another. Jimmy had them copied for *Cotton Fields* last year. I think you ought to know all this," she added breathlessly, "otherwise it's very confusing and you might think us all mad."

He nodded gravely and wondered how old she was and what her life had been before she married.

"It makes it clearer," he agreed. "What do you think about the business—the trouble, I mean? It hasn't actually touched you personally, has it?"

She seemed a little surprised.

"Well, I've *been* here," she said dryly. "We may have imagined most of it. We may have thought all the odds and

27

ends of things were related when they weren't. But a great many irritating things have happened. There are people in the garden at night, too."

Campion glanced at her sharply. She had spoken casually and there was no suggestion of hysteria in her manner. She met his eyes and laughed suddenly.

"It's ridiculous, isn't it?" she said. "I know. I've been wondering if I live too much alone or if the hypersensitiveness of the stage is catching. But I assure you there are people in this garden after dark. Plants are trampled in the morning and there are footmarks under the lower windows. The servants get unsettled and I've heard whispers and giggles in the shrubs myself. You see, in the old days when my uncle was alive—I used to come and stay with him sometimes—the village policeman would have been warned and he would have watched the place, but we can't do that sort of thing now. When a man's name is part of his assets he can't afford to do the simplest thing without taking the risk that it will be seized on, twisted and made into an amusing story, so we just have to sit still and hope it all isn't true. That's not fun, with Jimmy in his present nervy state. He's beginning to feel it's a sort of doom hanging over him."

She spoke wistfully and Campion looked away from her.

"It's all rather indefinite, isn't it?" he said severely. "Mercer tells me Sutane has no enemies."

She considered. "I think that's true, but Mercer wouldn't know if he had. Mercer's a genius."

"Are geniuses unobservant?"

"No, but they're spoilt. Mercer has never had to think about anything except his work, and now I don't think he's capable of trying to. You don't know everybody yet. When you do you'll find you know them all much better than they know you."

"How do you mean?" Mr. Campion was startled.

"Well, they're all performers, aren't they? All mild exhibitionists. They're so busy putting themselves over that they haven't time to think about anyone else. It's not that they don't like other people; they just never have a moment to consider them."

She paused and looked at him dubiously.

"I don't know if you're quite the man to help us," she said unexpectedly.

"Why?" Mr. Campion did his best not to sound irritated.

"You're intelligent rather than experienced."

"What exactly do you mean by that?" Campion was surprised to find himself so annoyed.

Linda looked uncomfortable.

"I don't mean to be rude," she said. "But there are roughly two sorts of informed people, aren't there? People who start off right by observing the pitfalls and the mistakes and going round them, and the people who fall into them and get out and know they're there because of that. They both come to the same conclusions but they don't have quite the same point of view. You've watched all kinds of things but you haven't done them, and that's why you'll find this crowd so unsympathetic."

Mr. Campion regarded the small person at his side with astonishment. She returned his glance timidly.

"It's all very upsetting," she said. "It makes one rude and unnecessarily forthright. It frightens me though, you see. Do help us out if you can and forgive me."

Her voice was quiet and had the peculiar quality of capitulation. Mr. Campion nearly kissed her.

He came so near it that his common sense and natural diffidence combined, as it were, to jerk him back with an almost physical force only just in time. He stared at her, frankly appalled by the insane impulse. He saw her dispassionately for a moment, a little yellow-and-brown girl with a wide mouth and gold flecks in her eyes. All the same, it occurred to him forcefully that it would be wise if he went back to London and forgot the Sutanes, and so he would have done, of course, had it not been for the murder.

3

Chloe Pye tied a long red silk skirt and a kerchief over her bathing dress in honour of lunch, which was served with obstinate ceremony on the part of the servants at a quarter to four.

The two visiting stars had departed with apologies, already two hours late for other appointments, and Ned Dieudonne, Sutane's invaluable accompanist, had been given a drink and a sandwich and bundled off to return the borrowed score to Prettyman, in Hampstead, who was doing the orchestrations.

The rest of the party ate hungrily. Apart from those he had already met, Campion noticed only two newcomers at the table: the young man with the golden curls whom he had last seen fighting with the doorkeeper over a silver-plated bicycle, and the incomparable Slippers Bellew.

Slippers was a nice girl. As soon as he saw her Campion understood Uncle William's regret. In her short white practice dress, her warm-yellow hair knotted high on the top of her head, she was about as alluring as any nice healthy child of twelve. She, Sutane and the golden-haired boy, who turned out to be Benny Konrad, Sutane's understudy and the young man in the "Little White Petticoats" number in *The Buffer*, ate rather different food from the rest of the gathering and drank a great deal of milk.

Sock Petrie did most of the talking, skilfully keeping Chloe Pye occupied so that her attention was diverted from Mercer, whom she was inclined to tease.

Campion sat next to Sutane, who talked to him eagerly, his thin mobile face reflecting every change of mood and lending every phrase an emphasis quite out of keeping with its importance.

"We'll snatch half an hour after this," he said, "I've got Dick coming down at half past four with a fellow I've got to meet. The chap wants to put some money into *Swing Over*, so we mustn't discourage him, bless his heart. Has Linda told you about the trouble down here?"

He used his hands as he talked and Campion was reminded again of the dynamo simile. The nervous force the man exuded was overpowering.

"I heard about the people in the garden at night, but that might be just inquisitive villagers, don't you think? You're an exciting household, you know, to a quiet country community."

"It might be so." Sutane glanced out of the window, his eyes, which seemed to be nearly all pupil, dark and resentful. "We're too near London," he declared suddenly. "It's convenient, but there's a suburban note about the place. No one seems to realise we have work to do."

He paused.

"I hate that," he said vehemently. "You'd think they'd use their heads."

Mr. Campion was silent. He thought he understood this part of the situation. He knew something of country life and the social obligations which certain houses seem to carry as though they had a personality quite apart from their owners. He imagined a bored community, in which every member had at least a nodding acquaintance with every other, thrown into a state of chattering excitement by the knowledge that a national hero was coming to join it, only to be disappointed and irritated to find that the celebrity retained his inaccessibility and merely deprived them of one of their woefully few houses of call.

He glanced down the table to where Linda sat, flanked by Uncle William and Mercer. She looked up and caught his eye and smiled. Campion turned back to his host.

"I thought I'd go..." he began, but Sutane interrupted him.

"You stay here a day or so. I shall feel happier if you do. What I want to know is this: how much of it is my nerves and how much real mischief?... Good God, what's that?"

The final words escaped him with a violence which silenced all other conversation.

Campion, who was sitting with his back to the window, glanced over his shoulder and saw the phenomenon. Coming slowly down the drive, with a dignity befitting its age, was a large Daimler, *circa* 1912. It was driven by an elderly chauffeur in green and carried a very youthful footman in similar uniform. Behind it came a Buick also chauffeur-driven, and behind that again a taxicab. In the far distance yet another car was discernible.

Sutane glanced at his wife questioningly. She shook her head. She looked positively frightened, Campion thought.

Meanwhile, the Daimler was depositing its passengers: a resplendent old lady and a willowy girl.

The peal of the front-door bell echoed through the house and the Dane, who had been asleep under the table, got up and began to bay. Slippers quietened him after some little time, and an ominous silence fell over the room, while from

31

outside in the hall the murmur of voices and the patter of feet upon the polished floor came in to them.

Presently, just as other cars appeared in the drive outside, another sound, an undignified lumbering noise, was added to the chatter. Slippers giggled.

"That's the piano," she said. "We moved it across the drawing-room door. There wasn't time to get it back. Jimmy, you told Hughes not to bother."

Sutane pushed back his chair. He was suddenly and theatrically furious.

"Who the devil are all these damned people?" he demanded. "What the hell are they doing calling in here? God! There's millions of them!"

Benny Konrad laughed nervously.

"Doesn't anybody know them? How marvellous! Let's all go out and fraternise."

"Shut up!" Sock Petrie was frowning, his deep-set eyes fixed anxiously on Sutane.

The star was trembling and his long fingers gripped the back of his chair.

The door behind him opened softly and the elderly man-servant who had conducted the meal came in. He was red and flustered.

"A great many people have called, sir," he began in an undertone. "I've put them in the drawing room, and one of the maids is opening the double doors in the living room. Would you wish me to serve tea?"

"I don't know." Sutane glanced at his wife helplessly.

Linda rose. "It's cups, I suppose. Cups and cake, and milk of course. How many people have come?"

"About thirty at the moment, madam, but..." The old man glanced down the drive expressively. Another car pulled up and a group of excited young people got out.

"Oh, well, do what you can." Linda sounded resigned. "There's a case of sherry in the pantry; that may help. Hughes, is there anybody you know?"

"Oh, yes, madam. There's old Mrs. Corsair from the Towers, Lady Gerry from Melton, Mr. and Mrs. Beak, Miss Earle—they all called on you, madam." He managed to convey a gentle reproach. "I'll go and attend to them. Will you come?"

The girl glanced down at her brown cotton dress.

"Yes," she said at last. "Very well."

32

She hurried out after the butler, looking, Mr. Campion thought, like a very small ship going into battle.

Chloe rose. "We ought all to go and help her," she said, not without a certain relish. "Who are all these people, Jimmy? Your local audience?"

Sutane ignored her. "The cheek of it!" he exploded. "To come to one's house in hordes when one's got work to do!"

Mr. Campion coughed. "They've been asked, you know," he said gently. "People don't turn up by the hundred at four o'clock precisely without an invitation."

"God bless my soul!" said Uncle William.

Benny Konrad squeaked. "It's a dirty practical joke," he ejaculated. "I say, someone's got their knife into you, Sutane. What are you going to do?"

"Disappear," said Jimmy promptly. "It's hard on Linda, but I've got a business conference in twenty minutes."

"I say, old boy, I shouldn't do that." Sock's voice was quiet but very firm. "Bad publicity, you know. It's a swine's trick but you'll have to make the best of it. Both you and Slippers *must* appear. Go out and say pretty things. Explain you've been practising and that's why you're in these clothes. It's absolutely the only thing to do. We'll all back you up."

Sutane stood irresolute.

"It's a damned imposition."

"I know it is, but what can you do?" Sock was appealing. "Once someone realises that the whole thing is a hoax the story will get out and it'll make good reading. Do go along, there's a good chap."

Slippers, who had a kindly feeling for Sock, linked her arm through Jimmy's.

"Come on, loov," she said. "We'll make our entrance."

"Will they applaud?" murmured Benny and giggled.

Sock kicked him gently and he grew red and, ridiculously, raised a hand to hit back.

Mercer came over to Campion and Uncle William.

"I suppose they've got all three pianos?" he said. "Do you know?"

They looked at him in surprise and he frowned.

"They're bound to use all the rooms. I'll go home. It's only across the park."

He opened a window and swung himself out into the drive, much to the astonishment of some new arrivals who all but

33

ran him down. He stepped aside and scowled at them ferociously and the last Campion saw of him was his short top-heavy figure striding off across the park.

Chloe Pye peered at herself in a compact mirror.

"Will I do?" she said to Uncle William, and, on receiving his startled nod, plunged out into the hall.

The party, as a party, was the fiasco its perpetrator had evidently planned. Any house is uncomfortable when strained to the uttermost limits of its capacity, and thirteen bottles of amontillado and forty cups of tea, including six kitchen mugs, will not, in these degenerate days, satisfy the five thousand. The furniture was in the way and the empty beer bottles, the relics of Sock's morning refreshment, did not grace the living-room piano where a thoughtful guest who had stepped amongst them placed them for safety.

All these were minor disasters, however, compared with the real misfortune of the afternoon. As he was jostled to and fro among the crowd Mr. Campion made an interesting discovery. The company was mixed by a hand that pure ignorance could scarcely have directed. The snobbish distinctions which are the whole structure of any country society in England had been deliberately flouted. Campion was inclined to suspect a telephone directory as the source of the selection. The upper stratum had come because it had called and been called upon in return and was therefore technically acquainted with the Sutanes; the others were simply those who had been gratified to receive an invitation from a celebrity. Since the one fraternity waited on the other, for the most part, in the way of trade and were therefore well acquainted, it was a particularly unfortunate mixture.

Altogether it was a disastrous gathering.

A man called Baynes, who appeared to be a councillor from some borough unstated, since the two excited young women who accompanied him persistently addressed him by that title, was inclined to be noisily friendly, but the remainder of the gathering was stiff and mulishly uncomfortable.

Chloe's bathing dress was not a success, in spite of her crimson skirt, and her brush with the old lady who had been the first to arrive provided an unhappy five minutes for all within earshot.

Sutane did his best, but his entrance with Slippers instead

34

of his wife, which was the purest accident, was not forgiven him.

Campion saw him standing at one corner of the room, slender and excitable, talking gracefully to people he did not know, with Sock at his elbow lending moral if not sartorial support.

Linda was even less fortunate. A great many of the visitors were her own country kind and they believed that she had deliberately embarrassed them. Campion saw unwonted colour in the small face with the wide mouth and the eyes with gold flecks in them, and was profoundly sorry for her.

Uncle William strode about manfully and made conversation of a somewhat sporadic and explosive kind, addressing his remarks to anyone who did not actually scowl at him, and Eve did her sulky best.

It was a harrowing experience for all concerned. The cars began to leave. The called-upon departed in a measured rout; the others followed, taking their cue from their leaders.

Finally only the councillor remained and even his friendliness vanished when Sutane, his brittle nerves breaking beneath the strain of an hour's acute embarrassment, told him brusquely not to call him "old pal."

As the last car vanished down the drive with its cargo of nettled guests Linda sat down abruptly in an armchair and blew her nose. Sutane stared at her.

"We'll sell the damned place," he said.

She shook her head. "They'll get over it in time."

"So I should hope." Sutane was contemptuous. "Good heavens, they must have seen we were taken by surprise. Surely they don't imagine anyone in his right mind would ask two hundred people to tea one Sunday afternoon and provide them with forty cups between them?"

Linda looked up.

"They think *we* might," she said. "They've always suspected we were a little queer and now I'm afraid they're convinced of it. The trouble is they think we're rude as well. They've gone home thinking it was just slackness."

Sutane remained looking down at her, his face growing dark. In common with many members of his profession, he had a strong streak of the snob in him, and her suggestion was both distasteful and convincing. He turned to Campion.

"Now am I imagining things?" he demanded, his voice

rising. "It's got to stop, I tell you! It's driving me off my head. It's got to stop."

"Jimmy old man, I told you four-thirty."

An injured voice from the doorway interrupted the outburst and Campion, glancing up, saw a little man with a tragic, ugly face hesitating on the threshold. Everything about him was tiny but very masculine. His hands were coarse but minute and his chin was as blue as Mercer's own.

He came quickly across the room and spoke in a low and confidential tone, which Campion afterwards discovered was habitual with him.

"I didn't know you were having a tea fight. We arrived in the middle of it and I took Bowser straight up to the den. He's a busy man, Jimmy. Come along."

Sutane sighed with exaggerated weariness and grimaced at Campion with a flicker of his old charm.

"I'm coming," he said and they went out together.

"That's Poyser, Jimmy's manager," murmured Sock, lounging across the room to Campion. "This is a bit of bad luck, isn't it? He was nervy enough already. It's got to be stopped somehow."

Campion nodded. He was standing by the chair in which Linda sat and his long angular form shadowed her. He looked down and spoke apologetically.

"I seem to have been here a long time and done nothing of the faintest use to anybody," he said. "D'you know anyone who came this afternoon well enough to take into your confidence? If we had one of the invitation cards which were presumably sent round we might be able to locate the printer, or at least find out when they were sent and where from."

"No, there was no one," she said stiffly. "I recognised two or three people who called on us when we first came, but the rest were complete strangers."

Sock grinned. "They knew each other all right, didn't they?" he said. "There were some pretty sizzling remarks floating around."

"I heard them." The girl looked up at them and they were embarrassed to see tears in her eyes. "I'll go and talk to the kitchen," she murmured. "I'm afraid there may be a minor crisis down there."

As the door closed behind her Sock thrust his hands in his pockets and smiled wryly.

"Poor old girl, she's rattled," he said. "But we can't do anything. That idea of yours would be perfectly sound in the ordinary way, but you see the difficulty in the present case. These good people, whoever they are, can chatter among themselves about the funny actors, but they can only say the place was in a bit of a mess and there wasn't enough food to go round. But once the hoax story gets out it makes a little news par, doesn't it? See what I mean?"

"It seems a bit hard on Mrs. Sutane."

The other man looked at Campion curiously.

"Quite a lot of things are hard on Mrs. Sutane," he observed. "You'll notice that if you stick around."

A cold meal was served at half past eight, at which no mention of the incident of the afternoon was made, out of deference to a solid, frightened-looking person called Bowser who sat between Sutane and his manager and kept his eye on his plate.

Mercer, who had appeared again as soon as the coast was clear, made several attempts to bring up the matter, in which he was assisted by Chloe, who was in mischievous mood, but they were both restrained by the able Mr. Petrie.

Dick Poyser carried Sutane and his guest off again after the meal. Like most people directly concerned with the management of money, he had a curious preoccupied mannerlessness, as though he and his mission in life were somehow sacrosanct and privileged. He did not speak to anyone outside his two charges and ignored his hostess completely, yet there was no deliberate rudeness in the man.

After the meal Campion cornered Uncle William.

"Leave, my dear fellow?" The old man was aghast. "Of course you haven't made any progress yet. Haven't had a moment. No, no, wait a little while. Must see Sutane before you go, anyway."

He stumped off, anxious to avoid further conversation.

Campion sat down in a corner of the living room. There was a restlessness in the big house which had nothing to do with noise. Outside, the garden was warm and scented, a light wind playing in the lime trees.

On the lawn below the terrace he could see Chloe walking

37

between Petrie and Benny Konrad, and her high thin laugh came up to him every now and again.

The others had disappeared.

He sat there quietly for a long time until the yellow light died on the treetops and the colder shadows of the approaching night swept over the garden.

Once he heard voices in the hall and the closing of doors, but then all was quiet again. He lit a cigarette and smoked it thoughtfully, his long thin hands loosely clasped across his knees. He was angry and dissatisfied with himself.

The hand on his sleeve and the voice so passionate in its enquiry startled him considerably.

"What's your name?"

It was a child in a big old-fashioned overall. She was not pretty but her plump face was eager and flushed with excitement, and she had round eyes with startlingly familiar gold flecks in them.

Mr. Campion, who was a little afraid of children, regarded her with something akin to superstition.

"What's your name? Tell me your name!"

Her demand was vehement and she clambered over the chair towards him.

"Albert," he said helplessly. "Who are you?"

"Albert," she repeated with satisfaction. Having attained her objective she was now inclined to shyness as violent as her first overture had been. She wriggled away from him and stood hesitating. "Albert's a dog's name," she said.

"Who are you?" he repeated and wondered at his dislike of her.

She stared at him as if she guessed his antagonism.

"I'm Sarah Sutane. I live here. I'm not allowed to talk to you or anybody, but I want to. I want to. I want to."

She flung herself sobbing into his arms and rubbed a wet unhappy face against his tie. He sat her up on his knee, doing his best to look as if he were not pushing her away from him, and felt for a handkerchief, which seemed the moment's most pressing need.

"How old are you?"

"Six."

"Sarah." Miss Finbrough and a woman in nurse's uniform appeared at the french windows. "I'm sorry, Mr. Campion. She ought to be in bed. Come along, child, do. She ran away

38

just before bedtime. Where have you been hiding? In the garden?"

Sarah shrieked and clung to her link with the outside world, who rose, embarrassed and dishevelled. In the end the nurse took her and carried her off, kicking. Her angry screams echoed faintly and more faintly as a succeeding procession of doors closed after her. Miss Finbrough raised her eyebrows.

"She's a nervy child," she said. "Still, what can you expect? She wants other children to play with. She's lonely, but you can't have the place overrun with kids. It's not like an ordinary house. D'you know I haven't been able to get hold of Mr. Sutane all day?"

"Doesn't Sarah see anyone?"

"Oh, well, she sees her mother and her nurse, and me. Her mother spoils her, but she agrees with Mr. Sutane that she can't run loose among the guests. She'd get spoilt and precocious and pick up I don't know what words. Mr. Sutane has a horror of her becoming what they call a stage child. I keep telling them she ought to go to boarding school."

"At six?"

"That's what her mother says." Miss Finbrough showed her impatience. "Still, if a child's got an overworked genius for a father it's got to take the consequences."

Mr. Campion felt his usual urbanity deserting him.

"You're a little hard, aren't you?"

"Hard? Have you seen him dance?" The plain woman's face was flushed and her eyes were bright. "You can't expect *him* to upset his health, filling the place with children." She checked herself. "Mrs. Sutane's out in the garden looking for the child," she said. "It would run away just when we were so upset already. I wonder if you'd mind telling her?"

Campion went out into the dusk. On the lower lawn he encountered Chloe and Sock Petrie, who was carrying a portable gramophone and a case of records. The woman was excited, he noticed. The twilight softened her face and her eyes were brilliant.

"I'm going to dance by the lake," she said. "This warm, passionate, *exulting* night!"

She threw out her arms to the opal sky.

Petrie scowled. "I'll put on a couple of records for you and

39

then I've got to have a look at my bus," he said ungallantly. "She's got to get me to town tonight, poor old trumpet."

Chloe laughed at him.

"So you think," she murmured.

"So I damn well know, my dear," he retorted. "Hullo, what's Donald Duck want?"

Benny Konrad sprinted across the lawn towards them rather too consciously like a young faun.

"I say, Sock, Sutane's gone," he began with a hint of relish. "Yes, he took a fancy to one of the guests who came today and he's gone tearing off in the Bentley to see him. After his invitation card, I expect."

Sock put down the gramophone and swore.

"He would," he said finally. "Oh, my God, he would. Here, Benny, take these blasted things and go and put on records for Chloe. I'm going round to the garage to see if Joe knows where the lunatic's gone."

"I think you're insufferable," said Miss Pye to his retreating figure and spoilt the dignity of her reproach immediately afterwards by shouting: "Come back when you've finished!"

Sock did not reply and Benny picked up the gramophone.

"I'll dance too," he said. "I say, what was the matter with Eve?"

Chloe turned on him with unexpected interest.

"When?"

"Just now. After food. She was crying divinely, all alone under a little rosebush. When she saw me she ran away."

"Where to?"

"I don't know. Up to her room, I suppose."

He giggled and for an instant Chloe Pye stood irresolute. Then she shrugged her shoulders.

"Be careful with the records," she said.

Albert Campion went on his way to find Linda. She was in the park. He came on her as she stood shouting for Sarah in a small, appealing voice.

"Please, darling, come out! Sarah pet, come out. Please come out for Mummy."

He dropped into step beside her.

"Sarah's in bed," he said.

She turned to him with relief and he was gratified to see welcome in her eyes. They strolled back through the garden to the house and sat on the terrace talking until it grew dusk, when they returned to the morning room, too engrossed in each other to notice the continued absence of the others.

Campion was not conscious of the time. His carefully trained powers of observation were temporarily in abeyance. He had ceased to be an onlooker and was taking part. He was extraordinarily happy. His good conceit of himself grew. He felt capable and intelligent and he talked with all the old animation of his early youth. All trace of vacuity vanished from his face and his eyes became alive and amused.

Linda was sparkling at him.

As they talked of the disastrous party of the afternoon the affair began to present its purely humorous side and a frankly hilarious note crept into their consideration of the entire problem.

They were each aware of a new sense of freedom and discovered together, as they paid each other the irresistible compliment of complete comprehension, the most delightful and the most dangerous quality of mutual stimulation.

The rest of the household and their weary, worried and excitable personalities were forgotten. It was a long and supremely satisfying evening.

The inevitable ending of such a spring dance came when neither of them expected it. He looked across at her and grinned.

"This is very good," he said.

She laughed and sighed and stretched herself like a small yellow cat.

"I'm very happy."

"I believe you are," he murmured and got up lazily with every intention of kissing her. It was a completely casual, unpremeditated movement, arising naturally out of the un-selfconscious exuberance of his mood, and he was halfway across the rug towards her when the world returned to him with a rush and he became acutely aware of himself and who and what and where he was.

For the second time that day he was seized by a sudden terror that he had gone completely out of his mind.

He shot the girl a startled glance. She was looking at him gravely. The gaiety had died out of her face and a faint bewilderment had taken its place. It occurred to him that she had shared his experience. She rose and shivered a little.

"I'll go down and see if I can cajole some coffee out of the

41

baleful company in the kitchen," she said lightly. "They're very much on their dignity after the fiasco this afternoon. I've done all I can. They've had their wireless on all night, which is against the rules on Sunday when Jimmy's at home—you can hear it, can't you? They've got a passion for military bands and they've been bribed with port and sweet words. Yet Hughes gave me notice this evening. He's outraged, poor dear. I'm doing my best to woo him back. I can't lose him. He was with my uncle."

She went out quickly, closing the door softly behind her.

Left to himself, Campion stubbed out his cigarette and passed his hand through his sleek fair hair. Resentment not untinged with amusement at the utter unreasonableness of his own hitherto decently controlled emotions consumed him.

"It doesn't happen," he said aloud and looked round guiltily, terrified lest he had been overheard.

The cry across the park came so faintly at first that only a part of his mind was aware of it, but as it was repeated, growing steadily in volume and insistence, it burst into his thoughts with the force of an explosion.

"Come, damn you! Somebody come! Come at once! Where is everyone? Somebody come!"

At the moment that Linda stepped back into the room the thudding feet came pounding onto the terrace and Sutane, his face livid, appeared at the open windows. Even then his sense of the theatre did not quite desert him. He paused and stared at them.

"I've killed her," he shouted. "Oh, my God, Linda, I've killed her! I've killed Chloe Pye."

4

There are moments of acute sensation before the mind gets to work again when shock is no more than a feeling of physical chill, and at these times the details of one's surroundings are apt to take on a peculiar vividness.

Linda became aware of the untidiness of the brightly lit room, of Chloe's red handkerchief folded neatly on the piano with her book upon it, and of Campion's long, dark, suddenly important back as he stood arrested, half turned towards her husband.

Then there were footsteps in the hall behind her and Sutane's manager, Dick Poyser, his sad eyes inquisitive, came in.

"I heard a noise," he said. "What's the matter, Jimmy?"

Sutane stepped into the room. He was a little unsteady on his feet.

"I've killed Chloe . . . she chucked herself under the car."

"For God's sake, shut up!" Poyser looked round him involuntarily and his thought was as evident as if he had spoken it. "Where is she?" he went on, adding instantly: "Anyone see you?"

"No. I was alone." Sutane shook his head as he spoke, his naïveté almost childlike beside the other man's authority. "She's down in the lane on the grass. I put her there. I didn't like to leave her in the road. The car's there, too, because of the lights. I couldn't leave her in the dark. I cut across the park."

"Sure she's dead?" Poyser was staring at him in horrified fascination.

"Oh, yes." The light pleasant voice was dull. "The wheels went clean over her. It's a heavy car. What the hell shall we do?"

There were other movements in the house now and Mercer's voice, lazy and inarticulate as usual, sounded from the little music room across the hall. Uncle William's characteristic rumble answered him. Poyser turned sharply to Campion.

"Are you something to do with the police?"

"No." Campion glanced down at him curiously.

"Thank God for that!" His relief was heartfelt. "We'll go down. Where did it happen, Jimmy? Give him a drink, Linda. Pull yourself together, old boy. Steady now, steady."

"I should phone for a doctor and the police at once." Mr. Campion's quiet impersonal voice cut into the conversation.

"Why the police?" Poyser pounced on the word suspiciously.

43

"Because there's been an accident. It's the rule of the road, to start with."

"Oh, I see..." The little man looked up, a faint smile which was both knowing and appreciative twisting his mouth. "Yes, of course. I forgot that. Linda, that's a job for you. Give us three minutes to get down there and then phone. First a doctor, then the police. Just be perfectly natural. There's been an accident and someone's hurt. Got that? Good. Now we'll go. Jimmy, you'll have to come, old chap."

Just before he went out after the others Campion glanced back at the girl. She was still standing halfway across the room. Her hand covered her mouth and her eyes were round and frightened. He realised suddenly that throughout the whole scene she had said nothing at all.

As soon as the three hurrying men stepped out into the darkness they saw the pale haze of headlights above the trees in the lane. Sutane was talking. He was excited, but his extreme nerviness of earlier in the day had gone. Campion received the impression that he was watching his words as carefully as he could.

"I told her not to come here at all," he said as they strode over the grass. "I told her frankly I didn't want her here. But she insisted, you know she did. This must have been in her mind all the time. What an incredible trick! On *my* place! Under *my* car!"

"Be quiet." Campion caught the gleam of Poyser's little black eyes as they flickered towards him. "Be quiet, old boy. We'll see what happened when we get there."

They hurried on in silence for a little while. Sutane was breathing heavily.

"I was blinding, you know," he said suddenly. "Didn't see her until I was over her."

Poyser took his arm. "Forget it," he said softly. "We'll get it straight in a minute or so. How do we get through this hedge?"

"There's a gap somewhere. I climbed the bank and forced my way through. It's only laurels."

They came slithering down the high bank to the road, bringing great clods of sandy yellow earth with them. The car stood in the middle of the lane, her engine still running, while behind, ghastly in the faint red glare of the taillight, was something white and quiet on the grass verge. Poyser tiptoed forward, oblivious of the absurdity of his caution. He bent down and struck a match. He stood holding it in the still, warm air until it burned his fingers.

"Lumme," he said softly at last, and the old-fashioned expletive was more forceful than any other he could have used.

As Campion and Sutane came up he swung away from the body and took the actor's sleeve.

"Where was she when you hit her?"

Campion left them. He had a pencil torch in his pocket and now knelt down beside the dead woman with it. Chloe Pye was still in her white swimming suit. She lay on her back on the verge, her head dangling over the grass-grown ditch and her thin body limp and shapeless. The nearside wheels of the car had passed over her chest, crushing her rib cage. There was dirt and considerable laceration of the skin, but very little blood. Her hand was cool when he touched it, but not clammy.

Mr. Campion sat back on his heels. In the darkness his face was blank. Poyser's voice recalled him.

"Have you got a flash lamp there? Bring it here a moment."

Campion rose and went over. The skid marks were easily discernible on the flint road. By the light of the little torch they found the spot where Sutane had jammed on his brakes, and a little farther on the dreadful smother of stones and dust with the pitifully small stain in it where the woman had fallen. Sutane's teeth were chattering.

"She just dropped in front of me," he said. "I didn't see her till she flashed past the windscreen. She chucked herself under the car. I didn't know what had happened until I came back to see what I'd hit."

"It was an accident." Poyser's voice was pleading. "A pure accident, old boy. Where was she standing?"

"Don't be a fool. She did it deliberately." Sutane's voice was exasperated. "That's where she came from." He snatched the torch and sent its beam flickering upward.

Poyser swore because the unexpected sight startled him.

"The bridge . . ." he said, staring up at the rose-hung arch. "Good God, didn't you see her fall?"

"No, I keep telling you." Sutane sounded sulky. "I was blinding. Naturally I was looking at the road, not up in the air somewhere."

"All the same, I should have thought the headlights would have caught her," the other man insisted, still staring up at the leafy span above him.

In the faint light from the torch Campion saw his small face alive with worry and invention.

"That's it," he said abruptly. "That's what happened. I see it now. That's what happened, Jimmy. She saw you coming and waved to you to stop. Probably she leant right over, imagining she was a fairy or a bumblebee or something—it's the sort of crazy idea she might have—and somehow or other she overbalanced and fell under your wheels before you could stop. That's what happened. It'd make it much more simple if you'd seen her do it. You must have seen her up there."

"But I didn't, I tell you." Sutane was obstinate. "I was blinding with my eyes on the road and my mind on those damned invitations. Suddenly something plumped down just in front of me and I slammed on the brakes. There was a sort of jolt and I pulled up when I could and backed the bus down the road. Then I got out and went round to the back of the car and there she was."

"Jimmy"—Poyser's voice was wheedling—"it *must* have been an accident. Think of it, my dear chap, think of the situation. It *must* have been an accident. Chloe wouldn't kill herself. Why should she? She was making a comeback in your show. She was a visitor in your house. She wouldn't deliberately chuck herself under your car. That's the kind of story newspapermen dream about when they're half tight. She was trying to attract your attention and fell over. That's the obvious truth as I see it, and believe me it's bad enough."

Sutane was silent. The vibrations of Poyser's arguments still hung about in the darkness. He shuddered.

"It may have been so," he said with an unsuccessful attempt at conviction. "But I didn't see her, Dick. On my oath, I did not see her."

"All right. But it was an accident. Do understand that."

"Yes. Yes, I do."

Mr. Campion asked if he might have his torch back, explaining that he wished to examine the bridge.

"Good idea." There was an element of conspiracy in the way Poyser thrust the pencil into his hand, and it occurred to Campion that the tactics of businessmen were elephantine capers. He hoped devoutly that the affair would remain a country one and that the astute Mr. Poyser would never be confronted by a metropolitan detective.

He scrambled up the bank again and, forcing his way through the shrubs, found the path without much difficulty. The bridge itself was a much more solid structure than it had appeared from the road. The parapets, although constructed of "rustic" work, were astonishingly steady and were further reinforced by a tangle of American Pillar and wild white convolvulus. The bright red roses looked unreal and somehow Victorian in the artificial light of the torch as Campion examined the hedge of flowers carefully, his discomfort increasing. The creosoted boards beneath his feet told him nothing. The dry summer had left them smooth and barely even dusty.

He worked over the ground with hurried inquisitiveness and at every step his uneasiness grew. Yet it was not his discoveries which so disturbed him. Poyser's voice, carefully lowered to an inarticulate murmur, floated up to him with the scent of the flowers in the warm, soft air. Now and again Sutane answered, his voice clear and irritable.

"It would be like her," Campion heard him admit.

And again, after a prolonged muttering from Poyser:

"Yes, she liked secrets."

At this point another beam of light swung down the lane and came racing towards them. Campion hurried off the bridge and plunged back through the laurels. In view of everything, he was anxious to be present when the police arrived.

He came out through the bushes and slid into the road just as a car came to a standstill within a few feet of him so abruptly that the engine stopped. He saw it was a large Fiat, a few years old, a portly vehicle. The near-side window came down with a rattle and an old voice, slow with the affectations of the educated seventies, the father, as it were, of Uncle William's voice, said sternly:

"My name's Bouverie. Somebody telephoned to my house to tell me that someone was hurt."

"Doctor Bouverie?"

"Yes." The curtness of the monosyllable suggested that the speaker was irritated at finding himself unknown. "Get that car out of the way. You've taken the patient up to the house, I suppose."

47

"No. No, we haven't. She's here." It was Sutane who interrupted. He had hurried forward and now adopted unconsciously the tone of nervous authority which he kept for such of those strangers whom he did not instantly set out to charm.

"Are you Mr. Sutane?"

The voice in the car had authority also, and of the magisterial variety.

"I think I met you at your house this afternoon. Were you driving the car?"

Sutane was momentarily taken off his balance.

"Yes," he said. "Er, yes, I was."

"Ah!"

The door opened.

"Well, I'll take a look at your victim, don't you know."

Campion never forgot his first glimpse of the figure who climbed slowly out of the darkness of the car into the tiny circle of light from the torch. His first impression was of enormous girth in a white lounge suit. Then he saw an old pugnacious face with drooping chaps and a wise eye peering out from under the peak of a large tweed cap. Its whole expression was arrogant, honest, and startlingly reminiscent of a bulldog, with perhaps a dash of bloodhound. He was clean-shaven except for a minute white tuft on his upper lip, but his plump, short-fingered surgeon's hands had hair on the backs of them.

A Georgian tough, thought Campion, startled, and never had occasion to alter his opinion.

He had not seen the doctor at the disastrous party of the afternoon and rightly supposed that he had been one of the many who had come late only to leave almost immediately afterwards.

Sutane remembered him, so much was obvious. His face wore that indignant, contemptuous expression which is always more than half embarrassment.

Poyser, who saw trouble brewing, came forward ingratiatingly.

"It was a pure accident," he volunteered, attempting to be matter-of-fact and succeeding in sounding casual.

"Oh!" The newcomer raised his head and stared at him. "Were you in the car?"

"No, I wasn't. Mr. Sutane was alone. Mr. Campion and I have just come down from the house. We——"

48

"Quite. Where is the patient? It's a woman, you say? Where is she?"

Dr. Bouverie had brushed past the discomfited Poyser and addressed Sutane. His whole manner was truculent and highhanded to an extent which would have been ridiculous or merely rude had it not so obviously sprung from a lifetime of authority. As it was, he was frankly awe-inspiring, and Mr. Campion, who knew the signs, felt his heart sink.

The doctor produced an eighteen-inch torch from his enormous coat pocket and gave it to Sutane to hold.

"In the back of the car, I suppose," he said, advancing upon the Bentley.

"No, she's here." Sutane swung the beam of light onto the verge with a suddenness unconsciously dramatic, and the newcomer, who was growing more like the spirit of rural justice incarnate at every step, paused in his tracks like a startled grizzly. He made a little teetering sound with his tongue, expressing astonishment and, it would seem, disgust.

"Come closer, will you?" he said. "I want the light actually on her. That's a little better. If you can't keep it steady one of the others must hold it."

Poyser took the torch and the old doctor knelt down on the grass, having first assured himself that it was not damp. His whole poise suggested extreme distaste and disapproval, but his square hands were exquisitely gentle.

After a while he got up, disdaining Sutane's assistance.

"She's dead," he said. "You knew that, of course? What was she doing running about naked?"

He pronounced it "nekkit" and the affectation gave the word an odd shamefulness.

"She used to do that," said Sutane wearily. "She's worn a bathing dress all day. What on earth does it matter?"

The old eyes under the peaked cap stared at him as at a curiosity and Poyser interrupted again. He insisted on giving his version of the affair, investing it, in his extreme anxiety to be both lucid and convincing, with a glibness which sounded positively inhuman.

The monstrous old man listened to him until the end, his head slightly on one side. It was a hopeless encounter, Mr. Campion reflected; like a clever fish trying to talk to an equally clever dog, an experiment predestined to end in mutual distrust.

Dr. Bouverie directed his torch at the bridge.

"But if she fell off there by accident, don't you know, she must have climbed out over those roses—an extraordinary thing to do so lightly clad. Ah, here comes the man we want. Is that you, Doe?"

"Yes, sir. Good evening, sir." A police constable, young and remarkably handsome in the uniform which seems to vary between the impressive and the comic, solely according to its wearer's face, swung himself off his bicycle and laid the machine carefully against the bank. The doctor advanced upon him.

"There's been a shocking accident," he said, sounding like an army colonel addressing a favoured subordinate. "The woman either fell or threw herself off the bridge here under Mr. Sutane's car. This is Mr. Sutane. The woman is dead. I shall want the body taken down to Birley and I'll ring up the coroner first thing tomorrow morning and probably do a post-mortem a little later."

"Yes, sir."

The doctor had not finished.

"Meanwhile," he said, "I should like to take a look at that bridge. How d'you get up to it, Mr. Sutane?"

"I climbed up the bank, but there's a gate a little farther along." Sutane's utter weariness was pathetic.

"Then I'll use it. Perhaps you'd be good enough to direct me." The old doctor was brusque and bursting with energy. "Doe, throw a rug over that poor woman and then come along."

Mr. Campion did not join the party. As was his custom when his immediate presence was not necessary, he succeeded in effacing himself. As soon as the policeman's steady steps disappeared down the lane he wandered over to the Fiat and looked inside. The back of the car contained a bag, a folded rug and a wedge-shaped wooden box fitted with small flower containers in little sockets arranged in neat equidistant rows. The rest of the interior told him nothing and with infinite caution he raised the bonnet.

Sutane was the first to return. Campion was standing aimlessly by the Bentley when he came up. Overhead on the bridge there was the murmur of voices. Sutane was trembling with fury.

"Surely that fellow's exceeding his job?" he began in a whisper. "That bobby treats him as though he was God

Almighty. What's it matter to him if she committed suicide or not? Blithering old ass!—he's about ninety."

"Then he probably *is* omnipotent in this district." Campion lowered his voice discreetly. "A personality like that would make an impression anywhere, given time. Look out; he's probably on the Bench."

Sutane wiped his forehead. In the glare of the headlights he looked like one of his own photographs outside the theatre, a fantastic figure caught for an instant in a nightmare world of towering shadows.

"This is the last straw," he said. "It's got to be an accident, Campion. I see that now. Poyser's right. For all our sakes it's got to be an accident. Good God! What did she want to do it for?—and why here?"

"What's happened?" Sock came slithering down the bank behind them, a tousled scarecrow in the uncertain light. "Linda told me something frightful—I couldn't believe it. Jimmy, my dear old chap, what's up?"

They told him and he stood looking down at the rug-covered mound, his shoulders hunched and his hands in his pockets.

"Oh, Lord," he said, something like tears in his voice. "Oh, Lord."

Campion touched him on the shoulder and, leading him a little to one side, made a request.

"The old boy's going to be nasty, I'm afraid," he finished. "He came to the party this afternoon and didn't understand it. I'd go myself, of course, but I want to be here when he comes back."

"My dear chap, anything I can do." Sock's voice was still tremulous. Like many intensely virile men, he was bowled over by emotion of any sort. "I'll be back in a moment. Delighted to be able to do anything I can. I'll tell the others to stay up there, shall I? After all, they can't do much."

He went off, clambering up the bank again, and footsteps down the lane announced the return of the others. Dr. Bouverie was still in charge.

"Unless she was actually standing on the parapet, a thing no woman in her senses would do, surely, I don't see how she managed to fall." The old voice, which was yet so powerful, made the statement for his companions' information. He

51

implied no doubt whatever: he simply did not see how she managed to fall.

"Oh, but she might easily have done that, Doctor. I knew her. She did that sort of thing." Poyser's soothing tone was wearing thin.

"Was she unbalanced? Her costume, or lack of it, does suggest that."

"Oh, no, nothing like that. She was impulsive—temperamental. She might easily have climbed up there to wave to Sutane."

"Indeed." Dr. Bouverie was not impressed. He turned to the constable. "Well, I've finished, Doe. You know what to do. Treat it just like an ordinary accident. You can get some sort of conveyance probably. I shall be at Birley about ten tomorrow morning. Probably Doctor Dean will be with me. Good night, gentlemen."

He climbed into the car and pressed the starter. The Fiat did not respond.

The next fifteen minutes was devoted to the car by the whole company. Any man in an obstinately stationary car seems to be a responsibility to all about him, but Dr. Bouverie in that predicament was a sacred charge. Aware, no doubt, that a god in a machine that won't go may easily degenerate into an angry mortal, he kept his dignity and controlled his temper, but contrived, nevertheless, to appear somehow terrible in the more ancient sense of the word. The tragedy of Chloe Pye's death faded into obscurity for a moment or so.

Sock Petrie's arrival in Campion's Lagonda was nicely timed. As Poyser shifted the Bentley to let the grey car pass, Campion made his graceful suggestion.

"Let me run you home, sir," he murmured. "There's a good man up at the house who will put this right and bring your car along."

Dr. Bouverie wavered. His keen eyes regarded Campion inquisitively and, seeing nothing to dislike in him, he accepted with unexpected charm.

"Extremely civil of you," he said. "It's my own fault. I ought to have got my man up, but he's done a hundred and twenty miles with me today, so I thought I'd let the feller sleep, don't you know."

As they set off down the lane at a sedate pace Campion prepared himself for a delicate campaign.

52

"Excellent roads," he began cautiously. "This is my first visit to this part of the world. I noticed them at once."

"Think so?" A trace of satisfaction in the old voice warmed his heart. "They ought to be. We had the devil of a job getting the authorities to realise that a side road is as important to the residents of a district as the main ways that cater for all these damned trippers who do their best to ruin the country. Still, we hammered it into their heads at last. You're a stranger, you say? Were you at that gathering this afternoon?"

"Yes." Mr. Campion sounded regretful. "A most unfortunate business. The mistake of a secretary. Dates mixed, you know."

"Really? Oh, I see. Thought it curious myself. These Londoners don't understand our country ways. Forgive me, I didn't catch your name?"

Mr. Campion gave it and added that he was a Norfolk man. To his relief they discovered a mutual acquaintance and, as the old gentleman softened considerably, he took heart.

"A frightful accident," he ventured. "Miss Pye seemed in such good spirits all day."

"Ah, indeed. We turn to the left here if you don't mind. How pleasant the clover smells in the dark. Notice it?"

Campion took the hint and played his best card.

"Isn't this a great district for roses?" he enquired, remembering the wedge-shaped box in the Fiat.

His passenger brightened noticeably.

"Finest in the world. I take a little interest in roses myself." He paused and added with an unexpected chuckle: "Twelve tickets out of fourteen at Hernchester yesterday. Five fists for roses, and a cup. Not bad for an old 'un, eh?"

"I say, that's extraordinarily good." Mr. Campion was genuinely impressed. "Do you believe in bone manure?"

"Not on my soil. I've got a streak of the genuine clay."

They discussed roses and their culture for several miles. Even Campion, who was used to strong contrasts, was aware of a certain nightmare quality in the drive. Dr. Bouverie talked of his hobby with knowledge and the passionate interest of a young man in his twenties. The brittle world of White Walls and the stage seemed a long way away.

By the time they pulled up in a darkened village the doctor was engrossed in his subject.

"I'll show you those Lady Forteviots. If you've missed 'em you've missed a treat," he said. "Here we are."

Campion discovered that the dark wall which he had taken to be the side of a rural factory was the front of a bleak Georgian house. A Victorian porch, fastened with solid wooden doors, stuck out into the road at an angle which no modern council would dream of sanctioning.

The doctor rang the bell and bellowed "Dorothy!" at the top of his surprising voice. At the sound a lamp appeared in a window on the first floor and Campion followed its passage through what seemed to be endless galleries, the faint beams flickering through window after window until they disappeared in the darkness directly above their heads. A moment later the doors began to rattle and after a considerable delay wherein bolt after bolt was drawn they clattered open and an elderly woman appeared holding a paraffin lamp above her head. It was a Dickensian greeting. She did not smile or speak but stood back respectfully to allow them to pass. The doctor strode into the darkness beyond the circle of light and Campion followed, very conscious that it was after midnight.

The old man clapped his hands, a sultanic gesture curiously in keeping with his personality.

"Whisky and water in the dining room, and go down to the cottage and tell George I want him."

"He'll be in bed, sir."

"Of course he will, if he's a sensible feller. Tell him to put on a coat and a pair of trousers and meet me in the conservatory. I want to show this gentleman some roses."

"Yes, sir." She set down the lamp and went off into the darkness.

Campion demurred feebly.

"Oh, no trouble at all." The old man sounded like a stage schoolboy out of a Victorian revival. Campion thought he had never seen anyone so gloriously happy. "We're up at all hours of the day and night here. A doctor's life, you know."

He took up the lamp and Campion discovered that the thing he had been half leaning against under the impression that it was the banister head was a full-sized stuffed wolf. He glanced round him and got a fleeting impression of narrow walls covered with cases of stuffed birds.

"Do any shooting?" said his host over his shoulder. "A hundred and thirty-two heads, my own gun, walking alone

54

last October. Not bad, eh? Ten hours of it and then the night bell till dawn. I'm seventy-nine and don't feel it."

He spoke boastingly but obviously without exaggeration.

They went into a small overcrowded dining room whose red-and-gold paper was almost hidden behind execrable sporting oils and yet more cases of wild fowl. The old doctor looked less extraordinary in these surroundings. He stood on the hearth rug, so much a part of his own world that it was his visitor who felt himself the oddity. His host stared at him with professional interest and Campion, who wondered what he was thinking, was suddenly enlightened.

"Can you fight?"

The younger man was surprised to find himself nettled.

"I'll take on anyone of my weight," he said.

"Ha! Go through the war?"

"Only the last six months. I was born in nineteen hundred."

"Good!" The last word was spoken with tremendous emphasis, and there was a pause. Dr. Bouverie looked sad. "I was considered old even then," he said regretfully.

The woman returned with the decanter and glasses.

"George is waiting, sir."

"Very well. You can go to bed now."

"Yes, sir." There was no expression at all in her voice.

Campion sipped his drink and thought of Chloe Pye, Sutane and the newspapers. He supposed he had driven the old man five miles at the most. It seemed a little space to separate such different worlds.

"Now these roses"—the doctor set down his glass—"they're extraordinary. There's not a rose to touch 'em for exhibition, unless it's the old Frau Karl Druschki. They've got the body. That's the important thing in an exhibition rose—body."

He led his guest through a drawing room which was chilly in spite of the heat of the night and appeared from the fleeting glimpse Campion got of it to be literally in rags.

The conservatory was a magnificent sight, however. It was overcrowded but the show of begonias and gloxinias was astonishing. A tall thin depressed figure in a felt hat and a raincoat awaited them with a hurricane lantern.

"Ready, George?" the doctor sounded as if he were going into battle.

"Yes, sir."

They came out into a dark garden which felt and smelled

55

like a paradise but which was, unfortunately, completely invisible. The roses were found, golden-yellow blossoms fading into apricot on long, carefully disbudded stems. Little white canvas hoods on stakes protected them from the weather.

The two old men, the doctor and the gardener, pored over them like mothers. Their enthusiasm was both tender and devout. The doctor put his blunt fingers under a blossom and tilted it gently.

"Isn't she lovely?" he said softly. "Good night, my little dear."

He rearranged the canvas hat.

"You won't see a better rose than that in the county," he boasted.

As they walked back to the dark house Campion took his courage in his hands.

"I suppose it was hitting her head on the road that really killed that woman?" he said.

"Yes, the skull was fractured. You noticed that, did you?" The old doctor sounded pleased. "What I don't see is how she came to fall, don't you know, unless she threw herself over. That's a matter which must be cleared up, because of the inquest. I—ah—I didn't notice any reek of alcohol."

"No, she wasn't drunk," said Campion slowly. "Not technically."

To his surprise the old man followed his thought.

"Hysterical type?" he enquired.

Campion saw his chance. "There's not a great deal of difference between hysteria and what is usually called temperament, don't you think?" he said.

The old man was silent. He was considering.

"I haven't had much experience of temperament," he said at last, admitting it as though it were a fault. "I attended an opera singer once, close on fifty years ago. She was insane. I didn't like that bathing dress this evening. Had she been walking about like that all day? We're forty miles from the sea."

Campion launched into a careful explanation. He did his best to convey Chloe Pye in elementary terms. She was vain, he said; hard-working, physically active, and anxious to appear younger than she was.

"So you see," he finished, "she might easily have climbed

56

the parapet and waved to Sutane, who was looking at the road and did not see her."

"Yes." The old man sounded interested. "Yes. I see that. But if she was sufficiently active to get up there, and was, as you say, practically an acrobat, why should she have fallen?"

It was a reasonable argument but without inspiration. Campion felt sure he must be on the Bench.

"Something may have frightened her," he said lamely. "Her foot may have slipped on the crushed stems."

"But there were no crushed stems," said Dr. Bouverie. "I looked for them. Still, I thank you for your information. The woman isn't so incomprehensible to me now. I shall go over her carefully in the morning. I may find something to account for sudden faintness, or something like that. It's been extremely civil of you. Come and see my roses in the daylight."

He conducted his guest to the door and Campion, stumbling against something in the dark, felt a warm muzzle in his hand. The dog had made no sound from the beginning and he realised suddenly that the two servants had been the same—silent, utterly obedient, and yet friendly and content.

His host stood on the porch, the lamp raised.

"Good night!" he shouted. "Good night!"

Campion drove slowly back to White Walls. The clouds had shifted and the starlight shed a faint radiance on the wide flat fields about him. It was eerily quiet and very much the country. He felt he was travelling back a hundred years.

In the lane he found the doctor's car parked at the side to await the chauffeur's ministrations in the early morning. He drew up and, getting out, raised the bonnet of the Fiat. He found the main lead from the distributor to the coil and connected it again. When he touched the starter the engine turned over obediently.

He got back into the Lagonda and went on. As he saw the graceful white house rising up against the sky he hesitated for a moment, half inclined to turn back and make for London.

A few hours before he had fully intended to pass quietly out of the lives of the two Sutanes as speedily as possible. He never remembered feeling such curious mental alarm and the experience had not been pleasant. Now, however, a situation had arisen which made his presence necessary, a situation wherein to leave was to run away from something more concrete, and therefore less terrible but more important, than his own emotions.

57

Mr. Campion was not a medical man, but his experience of violent death was considerable. Dr. Bouverie, he knew, had seen many car accidents in the last twenty years, so many that he was used to them, and that therefore there was a real chance that a certain vital and obvious fact might escape him.

What Campion had noticed when he had first bent over the body of Chloe Pye, and what he had taken great pains to assure himself had so far escaped the doctor, was the remarkable absence of blood in the road.

Since blood does not circulate once the heart which pumps it has stopped, it seemed to Mr. Campion that there were a hundred chances to one that Chloe Pye had been dead for something under fifteen minutes when her body had left the bridge. In that case, of course, she had neither fallen nor jumped from it.

As he drove into the yard he wondered how she had been killed and who had thrown her under the Bentley. He also wondered if she had deserved to die.

What it did not occur to him to consider was his own unprecedented behaviour in the matter.

5

The hall door stood open and a wide shaft of yellow light zigzagged down the shallow steps to the drive. An atmosphere of excitement, of catastrophe of the more bearable kind, enveloped the whole building. It floated out into the night with the sound of hurrying footsteps on the polished stairs and escaped from the windows with scattered voices and half-heard scraps of conversation.

Campion paused at the foot of the steps, his thin, loosely knit figure casting a long shadow across the path. The sky was clearing rapidly and a battered moon appeared hanging low over the elm avenue on the other side of the lane. It was quite light in the garden. Over on the lawn the deck chair which Uncle William had set up that morning for Chloe Pye looked like a small dark boat on a moonlit sea.

A thought occurred to Campion and he turned down around the side of the house, taking the path to the lake. As he passed the french windows of the lounge he heard Sutane's voice, sharp with nerves, answering somebody.

"My dear chap, how should I know? I've no experience of the woman."

"All right, all right, don't go off the deep end." Poyser sounded exasperated. "I only thought we ought to make up our minds."

Mr. Campion walked quietly away. It always happened, he reflected. As soon as a violent death occurred there was always some authoritative soul on hand to come forward with the inevitable "plan of campaign," entirely disregarding the fact that there has arisen the one situation which is still taken seriously by the community at large.

Love or money can conceal every other disturbing occurrence to be met with in civil life, but sudden death is inviolate. A body is the one thing that cannot be explained away.

As he walked alone between the yew hedges it occurred to him that in an age when all the deepest emotions can be successfully laughed out of existence by any decently educated person, the sanctity and importance of sudden death was a comforting and salutary thing, a last little rock, as it were, in the shifty sands of one's own standards and desires.

He came out of the shelter of the hedge and walked down an incline to the wide stone margin of the water. The little lake was really no more than a large kidney-shaped pond formed by widening the natural bed of a small brook which ran through the grounds. A past owner had planted willows round the stone pavement and the Sutanes had contributed a bathing pavilion.

He found what he was looking for immediately. On the east bank, in front of the pavilion, there was a wide paved platform about twenty feet square, and upon it stood the small black gramophone, the lid still raised.

In the daylight the place had an overgrown, partially neglected air which was not unattractive. Sutane was not extraordinarily wealthy and two good men and a boy provided all the labour he could reasonably afford for the grounds. In the moonlight, however, all the old formal glory conceived by the original designers was magically restored and Campion made his way to the gramophone through a world of ordered grandeur as visionary as any other ghost of the past.

He stood for some little time at the foot of the low step to the platform and looked at the surface closely. It was as smooth and dry as tarmac and about as informative.

Having convinced himself on this point, he approached the gramophone and squatted down on his heels beside it. The record had played until the automatic stop had silenced it. Campion read the title, "'Etude,' Vowis," a silly little piece of experimental trivia barely worth recording. If Chloe Pye had danced to that formless bagatelle he took off his hat to her.

He glanced into the record case and saw that two discs were missing. Looking round for the second, he found it lying on its grey envelope in the patch of shadow cast by the gramophone lid. Its discovery interested him considerably. It was cracked, not in a clean break, but in small pieces, as though a heavy foot had been planted directly upon it. The label was still legible, and he made it out with the aid of his torch. It was Falla's "Love, the Magician," Part 1. Part 2 was presumably on the other side, therefore, and an idea occurred to him. Using a handkerchief to protect his fingers, he raised the record still on the machine. As he had suspected, the third and final part of the Falla piece was on the underside. He raised his eyebrows. Trivial pieces like the "Etude" were frequently used, he knew, as fill-ups when a serious work did not divide into an even number of records, but if Miss Pye had been dancing to the Falla, which was a reasonable thing to do, he wondered why she had played through the "Etude" at all, and where she had been when the automatic stop had silenced its delicate inanities.

He sat back on his heels and looked about him for the other thing he had come to find. A glance told him that his second quest was not to be so simple as the first had been. Scarlet silk, so evident in sunlight, is apt to melt into a black shadow in the tricksy light of the moon. However, Chloe Pye had been wearing a red silk wrap-round skirt to her ankles last time he had seen her alive, and she had certainly not been wearing it as she lay so tragically mangled on the grass verge in the lane. He wondered when and where she had lost it.

It was at this point in his investigations, as he sat silent in moonlight so bright that it seemed strange that it should not be warm, that he first noticed that he was not alone in the garden. Something was moving over the dry wiry grass under the oaks behind the pavilion. He thought it was a dog at first, padding backwards and forwards beneath the trees, until a certain rhythmic regularity in the sounds made him change his mind.

Not wishing to be discovered examining the gramophone, he rose cautiously and stepped onto the clipped turf of the path. The shadow of the pavilion sheltered him and he stood there quietly staring in front of him.

Just behind the bathing house there was a natural clearance between the trees. A wide strip of mossy grass which had been allowed to grow wild ran down to the ivy-grown relics of an artificial ruin. This structure had never been an unqualified success, even in its Georgian heyday, and it now remained a record of the failure of an uninspired British workman to reproduce the half-remembered majesty which his employer had seen upon the Grand Tour. The movement came from the shadow below this ruin, and between Campion and itself the moonlight lay in patches upon the grass, making the turf look like the spread-out skin of some enormous piebald animal.

As Campion watched he could hear the steps distinctly, a slow measured rustling in the darkness.

It occurred to him with something of a shock that it must be two o'clock in the morning at least. The very lateness of the hour seemed to excuse an open investigation and he was just about to walk out of his refuge when a light wind sprang up in the trees, swinging the shadows like clothes on a line.

Mr. Campion stood perfectly still. Among the shadows he had seen a figure. As he stared it emerged into the light. It was a girl and she so startled him that he did not recognise her immediately. She was dressed in a flimsy nightgown with some sort of chiffon coat with floating sleeves over it, and she was dancing.

Compared with the professional standard of Sutane and Slippers her display was painfully amateur. Her movements were not particularly graceful and were without design. But there was an intensity of feeling, an urge for self-expression, which was primitive and impressive.

61

She was intent upon her dance, which appeared to have some half-considered ritual as a motif. Campion watched her running backwards and forwards, bowing and wheeling her arms now above her head, now shoulder-high. He recognised Eve Sutane and was unaccountably relieved. Out here in the warm night air, her draperies fluttering round her and her body taut with emotion, she was a very different creature from the sullen, dull-eyed girl of the morning.

He remembered that she was probably about seventeen. In common with all good neo-Georgians, he had done his share of reading on the one great study of that barren age and knew a little about the psychology of sex. It occurred to him irrelevantly that whereas a Victorian would have seen in this display either an exhibition of sweet, spiritual sensibility or a girl catching her death of cold, he himself received a confused and uncomfortable impression of sap-risings, undiscovered desires and primitive exhibitionism.

He was considering which aspect was really the most satisfactory in the long run when the unusual circumstances attending this particular manifestation of youth returned to his mind with a shock. He wondered if she could possibly not have heard of Chloe Pye's death, and walking round behind the pavilion, he coughed discreetly.

She came sweeping past him as he wandered down the path. At first she evidently intended to ignore him but changed her mind and returned. She looked almost beautiful in her excitement. Her eyes were shining and her mouth, wide and sensitive like her brother's, twisted into a smile whenever she forgot to control it.

"What are you doing here? I thought you'd gone to the doctor's."

Her manner was gauche to the point of brusqueness.

Campion eyed her quizzically.

"He was an exhausting old gentleman. I thought I'd cool off before going in."

"Have you been down here long?"

"No," he lied politely. "I've just arrived. Why?"

She laughed and he could not tell if she was merely relieved or really was as exultant as she sounded.

"We don't like sneaking, snoopy people," she said. "We hate them. Good night."

Turning from him, she ran on down the path, happiness in

every spring of her body and in the tread of her bare white feet.

Campion made certain that she had gone into the house before he returned to the clearing. There he found Chloe Pye's red silk skirt spread out like a prayer mat. Eve had been dancing upon it.

6

"CHLOE PYE DIES TRAGICALLY

"BRILLIANT YOUNG DANCER MEETS WITH FATAL MISHAP

"At a little after ten o'clock this evening Miss Chloe Pye, who only last night had made a successful return to the London stage in The Buffer *at the Argosy Theatre, fell to her death beneath the wheels of an oncoming motorcar. The accident happened at the country estate of Mr. Jimmy Sutane, where she had been spending the week-end. Mr. Sutane, who was driving the car when the fatal incident occurred, is prostrated with shock.*

"And I don't see we can say any more than that, do you? It gives it to them in one. Of course it'll bring them down on us like a cloud of hornets. Still, they'd come anyway."

Dick Poyser looked up from the bureau in the living room and spoke with his fountain pen hovering. Sock, who was lounging behind him, his hands in his pockets, shrugged his shoulders restlessly.

"You can cross out 'The Buffer at the Argosy Theatre,'" he said. "They won't print that. Oh, all right, old man, all right. I'll have it roneo'd and take it round if it'll please you. Some of 'em may even use it. But we're not going to get away with this easily, believe me."

63

Poyser threw down his pen, letting the ink splatter over the finished page.

"Who in blazes said we were?" he demanded, his voice shrill with irritation. "When you've been in this business as long as I have you'll know that if you give a journalist a bit of copy all ready to send down the chances are he'll use it, or at least a bit of it, rather than take the trouble of working the sentences out for himself. You can't dictate to 'em, but you can sometimes persuade 'em, if they don't know you're doing it.

"Besides," he added with great seriousness, "it's all a question of time."

"You're telling me," said Sock grimly as he took up the written sheet.

"Oh, for God's sake!" said Sutane.

He was sitting in an armchair over a fire which Miss Finbrough was coaxing to life. Linda stood forlornly behind his chair and Uncle William sat blinking quietly in a corner, his round pink face a little bluish and his podgy hands folded on his stomach.

The two men by the bureau gave up their wrangling instantly.

"You go to bed, Jimmy," said Poyser. "You've got to keep fit, old man."

Sock looked up, his young face lightened by a wry smile.

"The whole outfit depends on you, James," he said regretfully.

"I'll take him up," murmured Miss Finbrough as though she had been speaking of a child.

Sutane looked round at them all, a flicker of genuine amusement appearing on his sad, intelligent face.

"What d'you think I am?" he said. "Go away, Finny. I'm perfectly capable of looking after myself. I'm not mental. I may be a dancer of genius, I may make a few thousands a year, I may have just killed Chloe Pye, poor girl, but I'm not a goddam kid. Oh, hullo, Campion, how did you get on with the doctor?"

It was astonishing how his pleasant nervous voice could take on such authority. They were all quiet as Campion came in.

The thin young man smiled at them faintly and gave a guarded account of his visit.

"He's not an unattractive old boy," he said finally, trying to

64

sound reassuring. "It was the bathing dress that got him down. Once I'd put it to him that we were all perfectly normal but busy people he began to be much more tractable. He'll perform an autopsy, of course. I—er—I don't think he's quite so set on suicide as he was."

"Good man," said Sutane. "Good man. I appreciate that, Campion. Sock told me about the car. That was amusing. I shouldn't have thought of it on the spur of the moment. You'll have to stay and see us through, you know."

"What's that? What's that?"

Poyser was interested and, much to Mr. Campion's embarrassment, his little subterfuge was explained in detail. He stood by, looking at them all uncomfortably while they discussed the mechanics of the move with schoolboyish satisfaction. It occurred to him then what a pack of children they were, all of them. Their enthusiasm, their eagerness to escape from the main shocking reality, their tendency to make everything more bearable by dramatising it; it was the very stuff of youth.

He glanced at Linda. She alone had reacted to the tragedy in a way he fully understood. As she stood behind Sutane's chair, her arms hanging limply at her sides and her face pallid, she looked exhausted, ready to sleep on her feet.

Sock went out into the hall and came back in a disreputable leather coat. He was as brisk as if he had only just risen.

"Well, I'll get going then," he said. "I'll trot round and see everybody I can find. We can't possibly keep it quiet. We all know that, don't we? But I'll put in a delicate word here and there and I'll come down in the morning and meet the boys when they turn up. You go to bed, Jimmy. Leave it all to us."

He went out and Sutane turned in his chair and glanced at his wife.

"Mercer had better put up these two," he said. "Where is he?"

"I left him in the little music room," said Uncle William, coming to life with a jerk. "I'll go and find him."

He padded across the room and came back with the composer. Mercer glanced round gravely.

"I knew I couldn't do anything," he said, "so I hung about in there to be out of the way. Was that right? What happened? Police gone away?"

"Yes." Dick Poyser closed the bureau. "Yes. They'll be back

in the morning. There'll be an inquest. You'll have to attend that, Jimmy. Would you like to cut out the show for a day or so? Let Konrad take it."

Sutane frowned. "What do you think..." he began unhappily.

Linda interrupted. "It's three o'clock in the morning," she said. "He must sleep. Talk tomorrow."

Miss Finbrough sniffed.

"There's a lot to be said for that," she put in so sharply that Campion looked at her. She was resentful, he noticed, and it occurred to him that she did not like any other woman to give a thought to Sutane's physical well-being, a province which she evidently thought entirely her own.

"Where is Konrad?" Campion enquired.

"Oh, he went to bed." Poyser laughed as he spoke. "Konnie has to have his sleep, whoever gets killed. He's got his rally to think of."

Linda turned to Mercer.

"I wondered if you'd put up Uncle William and Mr. Campion?" she said. "They didn't intend to stay, you see, and there isn't a room ready."

"Yes. I'd like that." Mercer spoke as though the suggestion had been put forward as a measure to spare him any loneliness. "We'll push off fairly soon, shall we? Getting late."

"Good idea," agreed Uncle William. "Think better in the morning." He took Linda's hand and held it. "A terrible thing, my dear," he said. "A terrible thing. But we're here, you know, Campion and I. Do anything we can. You can rely on us. Try to sleep and forget all about it until the morning. Things never seem so bad in the morning. I've noticed that all my life."

It was not an inspired speech but its intention was unmistakable. Linda smiled at him gratefully.

"You're a dear," she said. "Good night."

Mercer looked round him.

"I had a coat..." he began. "No, that's right, I didn't. I'd better take one out of the cloakroom, hadn't I, Jimmy? It gets damned cold at this time of night."

He went out to pick up the borrowed garment and Poyser giggled. Like many very small men he had a curious rattling laugh with a gurgle in it which is usually associated with childhood.

66

"What a bloke!" he murmured. "Well, I shall sleep for a couple of hours and go up in the dawn."

Uncle William touched Campion's sleeve.

"Come on, my boy," he said. "Pick up our host in the hall, don't you know."

The three men did not talk as they strode through the dark garden, but when they crossed the bridge Mercer halted and demanded to be shown the scene of the accident. Campion glanced at him curiously. He made an odd figure in the half-light, his top-heavy shoulders straining the seams of Sutane's overcoat; while his attitude towards the affair, which was that of a disinterested but privileged spectator, was disconcerting.

"It must have been suicide," he pronounced judicially when Campion had given him the bare facts. "I shan't say so, of course, if they don't want it known, but any fool can see it must have been intentional. An extraordinary thing for a woman to do. Fancy going to a stranger's house for the week-end and calmly breaking her neck there, making trouble and inconvenience for everyone. Still, I'm not surprised. I thought she was definitely queer in the living room this morning."

He moved on and they followed him willingly. It was chilly in the early dawn and Uncle William's teeth were chattering, while Mr. Campion, for private reasons, had no desire to talk about Chloe Pye's death.

Mercer drawled on. His articulation was maddeningly bad and he appeared to be thinking aloud.

"The woman wasn't even a dancer," he said. "I saw her once. No talent at all. Poyser told me she was thundering awful on Saturday night. Why did Jimmy put her in the show? Do you know?"

He did not seem to expect an answer but went mumbling on until they came through an immense kitchen garden to his house on the edge of the estate.

Campion was aware of a long narrow brick front silhouetted against the sky, and then Mercer kicked open the door and they passed through a stone-flagged, oak-beamed hall into a vast studio or music room which took up at least half of the entire building.

Campion's first impression of that extraordinary room was of incongruity; his second, of extravagance. A remarkable wireless set took up the whole of one wall. It was an extraordinary contraption which looked as if it might have been designed by Heath Robinson in the first place and afterwards allowed to grow, in Virginia-creeper fashion, over everything which happened to lie in its path.

A huge concert Steinway took up the centre of the floor and there was one superb armchair.

The rest of the room was pure chaos. Piles of dusty papers lurked in every corner, books lay about in wild disorder, and the exquisite Cantonese shawl which covered the wall above the fireplace was dirty and had been badly scorched.

Mercer moved a heap of papers and wireless parts from a side table and produced a tray with a tantalus and glasses from beneath them.

"Help yourselves. I don't drink at night," he said and threw himself into the armchair, only to get out of it again at once. "This damned coat is tight," he said, peeling it off and throwing it on the floor as if he had a grievance against it. "I hate tight clothes."

Uncle William helped himself to a stiff drink and insisted on mixing one for Mr. Campion. They stood leaning on the mantelshelf while Mercer lounged in the chair and regarded them, his light eyes sombre.

"It happens very soon—death, I mean," he said solemnly. "There was a woman we didn't know and didn't particularly want to know. She was crude and noisy and blasted ugly, and now she's dead. Where's she gone?"

Uncle William coughed into his glass and his plump pink face was embarrassed.

"Mustn't be morbid, my boy," he said. "Very sad and all that. Shockin'. Got to face it."

Mercer looked surprised.

"Good God, you don't believe all that, do you?" he said with a superiority which was somehow adolescent but none the less irritating because of that. "Sad... shocking... they're just words. I was thinking as we came along tonight how extraordinary it was that she should have gone so quickly. You'd think some of her would remain. That awful teetering laugh, for instance. I mean, you'd think the things that made her the highly coloured piece she was would disappear one at a time at least, not all go out bang, like turning out a switch. It's a curious thing, that. I never noticed it before."

Uncle William stared at him as if he suspected his sanity.

"My dear feller, get to bed," he said. "You're shaken up. We all are."

"Shaken up?" Mercer was indignant. "I'm onto an idea. I'm not shaken up. Why should I be? I didn't even know the woman and if I had I probably shouldn't have liked her. Her death doesn't affect me at all. It's nothing to do with me. It's nothing to do with any of us. I think Jimmy's making too much fuss about it. After all, she only fell under his car. He couldn't help hitting her. Good heavens, there's nothing morbid about me! I was only thinking of the facts of the case. This morning she was a howling nuisance about the house, so I couldn't help noticing her peculiarities. Now all that has just gone. Where to? There's an idea in it. See what I mean? It's a concrete idea. You could work it into a number, even. 'Out in the dark where my arms cannot hold you.' See the sort of thing. That's how these songs get written. Something occurs to one and starts a train of thought."

"I should like to go to bed," said Uncle William heavily.

Mercer frowned. "I think you're right," he said regretfully. "One must sleep. It's a frightful waste of time. A stupidly arranged business. Why not let us live half the time and keep it light always instead of this mucking about, going to bed and getting up again and shaving. It's waste."

Campion eyed him narrowly, but there was no trace of affectation in his heavy dark face. He was obviously perfectly sincere. The belief in an omnipotent intelligence which his argument implied was so unexpected and out of character that Campion was at a loss to account for it until the simple truth dawned upon him. Mercer did not think at all in the accepted sense of the word. Ideas occurred to him and engendered other ideas. But the process which linked any two of them was a dark procession taking place in some subconscious part of the brain.

That his efforts at constructive thought were childish was made apparent by his next remark.

"There's no really good rhyme to 'hold you' except 'enfold you,' is there?" he said. "It's a rotten language. I must get Peter Dill onto the lyric. I think I may do that song. It's got possibilities, all that 'where are you' business, 'so near and yet so far away.'"

"That fellow's insane," said Uncle William as the door of

69

the large bedroom which they were to share closed behind them some minutes later. "Hope the sheets are aired."

There were three beds in the large old-fashioned room, and he opened them all solemnly before giving a considered opinion on the two best. Mercer had indicated the door of their room casually as they came upstairs and it was Uncle William who had demanded and finally obtained pyjamas for them both.

He sat up in the bed he had chosen, his white curls brushed upward and his face as pink and shining as a newly bathed cherub's, and sniffed.

"Money," he said as though he detected its odour. "Lots of money but no decent spendin'. Feller probably never considers his bank book one way or another. Your bed comfortable?"

"Very," said Campion absently. "It's a patent of some sort."

"Most likely." Uncle William did not sound approving. "These wealthy, careless fellers get all kinds of things wished on 'em. Salesmen come round to the door."

"Not with beds, surely?"

"With anythin'." The old man spoke with the unanswerable conviction of one who knows. "They get at the servants if they can't find anyone better. There are servants here, I suppose?"

"Sure to be." Campion spoke mechanically, his mind occupied by the delicate problem of Chloe Pye's death and his own attitude concerning it. He had never withheld vital information before and his sudden decision to depart from his usual impartiality bothered him considerably. After all, a woman had been killed, and presumably by one of the people with whom he had spent the day. It was a situation commanding thought.

Uncle William was in talkative mood, however.

"There may not be any servants. You never know with a feller like Mercer," he remarked. "D'you know what I think about him, Campion? He's the kind of feller who ought to be hangin' round sleepin' on people's floors, pickin' up scraps of comfort, lookin' after himself like a London pigeon, but, by means of a trick, don't you know, by means of a trick he's made a fortune out of those footlin' songs of his and it's put the feller out of gear. I've met men like him before, but never one with money."

Mr. Campion, whose attention had been captured only midway through this harangue, looked up.

"I think you're right," he agreed. "He hasn't got much to spend his money on except himself."

"Exactly." Uncle William was becoming excited. "And he's a chap who doesn't want much. He's always thinkin' about gettin' his own way and of course he gets it. He's not a feller who wants diamonds."

"Diamonds?"

"Well, elephants, then. Figure of speech."

"Oh, I see." Mr. Campion remained thoughtful. "His songs are very successful," he said.

"Sensuous twaddle," declared Uncle William with forthright disgust. "I'm not musical but I know rubbish when I hear it. Still, it seems to go down. Anythin' too silly to be said can be sung. A German feller pointed that out."

Campion shook his head.

"All Mercer's stuff has something," he said. "They're not merely rot for rot's sake. There's genuine feeling there, however horribly expressed. That's what makes some of those songs so unbearably embarrassing."

Uncle William brightened.

"Like a common feller tellin' you his troubles and shockin' you because they remind you of your own sacred thoughts about some magnificent little woman?" he said unexpectedly. "I've noticed that, you know, but never brought myself to mention it. Oh, well, we're all snobs at heart."

The discovery seemed to please him. He chuckled.

"The extraordinary thing is that the feller knows nothin' about women," he went on. "It's a joke in the theatre, you know. Sutane's known him since he first started writin'. Never been in love in his life. Never even bought a woman a meal. Treats 'em gently but isn't interested in 'em, as though they were pet rabbits or something. Must get it all out of his own head. I remember my cousin Andrew—the one who made all the trouble—telling me a long rigmarole all about that one evening. 'Wish fulfilment,' he called it; never forgotten the word. It sounded unhealthy to me and I told him so. But since I've come out into the world, as it were, I've noticed there's something in it. Mercer's a thoughtless chap. Quite extraordinarily selfish. There must be several bed-

71

rooms in this house, but he lumps us in here together because he's too lazy to point out another."

Campion did not reply. Uncle William turned off the light over his bed and settled himself. But he was still not inclined to sleep.

"Suicide or accident," he murmured, adhering to his philosophical vein, which was new to Campion. "What does it matter? Don't want to be hard but I feel she's better dead. Age wouldn't suit her book at all, would it?"

Campion remained silent but his companion was not to be quelled.

"Campion . . ." His voice sounded insistent in the greyness. "Yes?"

"We've landed ourselves among a funny crowd, my boy, haven't we? A damned curious bandarloggy lot. Nothin' like Cambridge."

Campion relinquished his own thoughts regretfully.

"Bandarloggy?" he enquired.

"Indian," explained Uncle William. "Means the 'monkey people.' Got it out of the Jungle Books," he added modestly. "Got all my India for my memoirs out of the Jungle Books and *Around the World in Eighty Days*. Tried *Kim* but couldn't get along with it. Funny thing about those memoirs, Campion. If I'd done the decent thing and stuck to the truth no one would have read 'em. As it was, they laughed at me and I made a small fortune. I'm not a chump, you know. I can see how that happened. Better be a clown than a pompous old fool. Mother wouldn't have realised that, though, and she was a clever woman, God rest her soul. I stumbled on it and it made me. I say, shall I have to go to the inquest on Miss Pye? Haven't attended an inquest since that silly affair of Andrew's. Don't know if I want to."

Campion stirred. "Where were you all the evening?"

"Me?" Uncle William laughed. "I was all right. No use sounding like a policeman. I didn't see the woman after dinner. I'm no witness. I was in the little music room behind the dining room, listening to Mercer. I don't mind his strumming when there's no words. It's these fellers bleating out their vulgar private thoughts who make me uncomfortable."

Campion raised himself on one elbow.

"You were listening to Mercer play all the evening, from after dinner till when?"

"Until Linda came in looking like a ghost and told us all about the accident."

"I see. Where was Konrad?"

"That little runt?" The old man was contemptuous. "He says he left Miss Pye by the lake and came upstairs to his bedroom, which is over the room we were using. He lay there with the window open, listenin'—or so he says."

He turned over and hunched the clothes round him.

"Don't wish to be unkind," he said over his shoulder, "but if I was a woman one look at that feller would make me want to cut my throat."

7

Sutane lay on his stomach on a felt-covered table basking in the ultra-violet rays of the lamp which Miss Finbrough tended as though it had been a sacred fire.

He was leaning on his elbows, and his face, which was turned towards the assembled gathering, wore a gloomy and introspective expression.

The room was large and very light, and the pink Empire chintz curtains swayed lazily in the summer air. Outside, the treetops were green and gold, and small puffs of white cloud sailed by in an infinite sky.

Uncle William, a trifle embarrassed by the unconventional aspects of this morning audience, sat on the window ledge with Campion lounging at his side. Sock Petrie leant back in a big basket chair. His eyes were hollow with lack of sleep but he watched Sutane unswervingly.

Mercer sat in an armchair also, his hands folded in his lap. He looked profoundly bored.

Benny Konrad was the only other person in the room. Clad in shorts and a sweater, he was lying on his back upon the floor, raising one leg after the other with monotonous regularity. The silence had lasted some minutes and now the only

73

sound was his deep breathing—one, two, three, in; one, two, three, out; one two three, in—and so on, it seemed, forever. His petulant young face was red from his exertions and one strand of his soft yellow hair lay damply on a forehead as clear and modelled as a girl's.

"Too hot," said Sutane suddenly, and Miss Finbrough laid a scarlet hand upon his skin.

"Nearly over now," she murmured soothingly. "I'll go on to your legs. Two more minutes."

"Inquest this afternoon at the pub, then," Sock remarked. "That cuts out the *Swing Over* rehearsal for you, James, but I don't see how it can be helped. They'll keep to the chorus, I suppose. What was Maisie like yesterday?"

Sutane frowned. Miss Finbrough had discarded her lamp and was exploring the small of his back with fingers like little steel hammers.

"Oh, all right, you know, all right." He spoke without enthusiasm.

"I thought she was frightful," said Konrad brightly. "Up—down, up—down, up—down . . ."

Sock gave him a long speculative glance.

"Comfort Konrad," he said gravely. "It suits you. You ought to adopt it. You've got a distinct streak of the Puritan, haven't you, Konnie?"

"I don't know, I'm sure." Konrad spoke carelessly but there was a dissatisfied expression on his face, and he looked like a girl who is not quite certain if she has been complimented or attacked. He went on with his exercises.

"The Press is friendly, then?" Sutane was clearly unaware that he had asked the question three times already.

"They're just as they always are, bless 'em." Sock spread out his long, unexpectedly fine hands. "More interested than usual, of course. It's a funny thing," he added with conscious naïveté, "that I should have spent the best part of my life getting you into the news and the last few months keeping you out of it."

Sutane allowed a brief grin to twist his mouth.

"Yes, it's a two-edged sword," he said and put his head down on his arms because Miss Finbrough had decided to ministrate to his neck muscles.

Suddenly, however, he looked up, shrugging away from her vigorous fingers.

74

"Oh, I got an invitation card," he said, "last night. I forgot all about it. It's in the inside pocket of my jacket, Sock, old boy. In the bedroom next door, if you don't mind."

Sock grimaced as he got up.

"You shouldn't have gone," he said. "It doesn't seem so frightfully important now, though. Who did you get it from?"

"Councillor Baynes of Merton Road." Sutane mimicked the arch refinement of his erstwhile guest. "He was just delighted to oblige. Oh, dear me, yes indeed. Just delighted. He kept everything, every scrap of paper that ever came into the house, and if I'd just wait a moment he was sure he could produce the ticket. Yes, there it was, just as it came to him, envelope and all. Oh, dear, dear, dear, wasn't that lucky? Such a pleasant afternoon. Such a distinguished house. Could he ask me to wait and see Mrs. B.? She was just changing her dress."

It was a flawless caricature, as broad as it was cruel. The councillor was re-created before their eyes. Almost they saw his moustache quiver.

Everyone laughed except Konrad, who protested primly that unconscious vulgarity was too depressing.

When Sock returned with the invitation card Sutane left his couch to join the group round the publicity man, and Campion caught a glimpse of Miss Finbrough's face over his shoulder. She was furious. Her bright blue eyes were hard and her lips compressed. Sutane ignored her.

"Look, Campion," he insisted. "Does it tell you anything at all?"

The young man in the horn-rimmed spectacles eyed the proffered papers dubiously. Neither the card nor the envelope was in any way remarkable. They were both of the type somewhat mysteriously called "cream laid," and either could have been purchased from any stationer's in the kingdom. The blanks on the printed "At Home" card had been filled in by hand in green ink and the calligraphy was a fair specimen of the standard hand taught in the schools of some years ago. It was round, flowing and astonishingly devoid of character. The printed R.S.V.P. had been cancelled with a single stroke and the postmark on the envelope was the familiar but unhelpful Central London stamp.

"I'm afraid there's only the handwriting," he said at last.

"The odd thing is it doesn't seem to be disguised at all. No one recognises it, of course?"

"No one I know," said Sock decisively. "I know several people who write rather like it but none exact."

Konrad giggled. "It's a woman's," he said. "One of your pretty ladies is turning nasty, Sutane."

Jimmy turned and regarded him coldly for a moment, and presently Konrad got down to his exercises again, his face hot and his eyes sulky.

Sock continued to study the card.

"The green ink does make me think of a woman. I don't know why," he admitted. "Although the whole silly trick was a bit feminine, wasn't it? Know anyone who writes like this, James?"

Although Sutane was nude, save for a face towel, his dignity was unshaken.

"If I did I should be talking to the girl," he said stiffly.

"If she was alive," murmured Konrad from the floor.

The words shot glibly from his tongue, almost, it seemed, by accident. He became pale with alarm as soon as he had spoken and went on with his training at redoubled speed.

"What the hell do you mean by that?" Sock swung round upon him, outraged. "Chloe's handwriting was like Chinese algebra—you know that as well as I do. What are you getting at?"

Konrad did not answer. The colour had returned to his face. He appeared to be deaf as he swung backwards and forwards.

"Have you seen Chloe's hand writing or not?" Sock persisted.

"Perhaps I wasn't talking about Chloe Pye," Benny Konrad muttered without looking at his persecutor.

"Who else then?" Sock was inclined to shout. "Sit up and stop dithering. Sit up, damn you!"

The slender figure on the floor came slowly and gracefully upright, his bare legs spread out in front of him. He looked meek and a trifle hurt and had adopted a sort of maidenly dignity which was infuriating.

"Well?"

"What were you hinting at?"

"I wasn't hinting at anything." Konrad wriggled. "I'm not that kind of person. I wish you'd let me get on with my work, Petrie. I've got to keep right, you know."

"Keep right!" Sock gurled over the words. "Look here, Konnie, what did you imply just now when you suggested that the woman who wrote these invitations might be dead?"

Konrad bridled. "I'm not going to sit here and be shouted at," he said. "I didn't imply anything. A remark came into my head and I let it out."

"Through the blowhole!" The untidy young man was beside himself. "You ought to have your head tied up inside a little blue silk rubber bag. Can't you control your tongue at all?"

Konrad closed his eyes.

"I know you don't mean it," he said, "but you're doing me a lot of harm. I've got a serious responsibility tonight. I must keep my nerves cool. It's not so easy to step into a big part at a moment's notice when one's been thoroughly upset already, even if one has been understudying for months, ruining one's reputation in obscurity. You wouldn't understand it, but there's an emotional strain."

Sock opened his mouth but he was forestalled by Sutane, who had paused in the act of climbing onto the massage table again. He turned and they had a momentary impression of his intense irritation. His face was not expressive but the muscles of his lean torso flexed and a flood of colour spread over his chest and up his neck to the cheeks.

"No need to excite yourself, my dear chap," he said. "I'm not deserting you tonight."

"What?" Konrad forgot his dignity. His face puckered and he sat up in an unconsciously theatrical pose, his knees drawn up under him. "You're not going on tonight, Sutane?" he said, his voice unsteady in his helpless disappointment. "You can't! Poyser said . . ."

Sock picked him up by the back of his neck and landed him neatly on his feet. Sutane had become very white but he climbed onto the bench and signalled to Miss Finbrough to begin work again. Konrad was trembling violently under Sock's hand.

"Poyser said . . ." he began again.

Sock glowered at him.

"Think of something else," he advised in a dangerously level tone. "James has told you he's made up his mind to go on with the show and it's very decent of him."

77

There were tears in Konrad's eyes, and his mouth grew red and ugly as he struggled to control it.

"But I'd understood that I was to rehearse this afternoon," he stammered.

"This afternoon you'll stand up in the coroner's court and explain why you left Chloe at the lake. You were the last person to see her alive. You know that, I suppose?"

"Yes, I do. I've told the superintendent all about it once this morning. I put on a couple of records for her and I began to dance myself, but she was sarcastic, frightfully offensive and jealous, and so naturally I left her and came in. I lay on my bed and listened to Mercer playing downstairs. I knew I should have to stay for the inquest. That's what was worrying me."

Sock showed his teeth in an amused smile.

"Now you needn't worry any more," he said. "You've told the superintendent, have you? Did he believe you?"

Konrad blinked. "Of course he did. Why ever shouldn't he? I told him I wasn't going to stay putting on records for a woman who was rude when I wanted to dance myself and he quite understood."

"What records did you play?" put in Mr. Campion from his corner.

"Delius' 'Summer Night on the River,'" said Konrad promptly. "It wasn't at all suitable for dancing and I told her so. It was then that she was so rude to me. So I told her that if she wanted to stand about looking like a sentimental crane she could jolly well wind up her own gramophone. As I came away she put on something else—a piece of Falla, I think."

"I see. You went straight into the house then and up to your room?"

"Yes."

"Anyone see you?"

"I passed Hughes in the hall."

"How long did you stay in your room?"

"Until I heard all the rumpus downstairs. It was about an hour and a half, I suppose. I came along to find Mrs. Sutane phoning for the police."

Campion nodded. "All this time you were listening to Mr. Mercer playing in the small music room beneath you?"

"Yes, of course I was. I've told the police this once."

Campion would have soothed his irritation but Mercer

forestalled him. He turned in his chair and eyed Mr. Konrad thoughtfully, as if an idea had occurred to him.

"What did I play?"

Konrad stiffened and his manner became wary.

"Your new tune," he said promptly.

"Yes, I did in the beginning. What else?"

Konrad hesitated "Odds and ends of stuff, mostly. Old tunes of your own and a lot of beginnings of melodies. Nothing outstanding. The kitchen wireless set was bleating away as well."

Mercer laughed. It was an explosive, uncharacteristic sound which made Campion realise with surprise that he had never heard him laugh before.

"Good enough," he said. "Bear him out, Uncle William?"

"Eh?" Mr. Faraday looked thoughtful. "Yes, I do. Not musical myself, of course, but it sounded very nice, don't you know. Couldn't actually identify the tunes by name. Never could. But very melodious, attractive-sounding stuff. Can't be more explicit. Wish I could."

Sock looked down at Konrad. There was a puzzled expression on his weary face.

"In fact, Mercer played just what you'd expect him to," he said. "One of his typical recitals. Thinking out loud on the piano."

"Well, I can't help that, can I?" Konrad's golden head was thrown back defiantly. "I don't know what it matters. I didn't see the accident, if that's what you mean. I only know what everybody knows and what Sutane will find out if he insists on going on in *The Buffer* this evening. He killed Chloe Pye, he ran over her, and he murdered her."

Sock hit him. The blow caught him just under the jawbone, lifted him an inch or so off the ground, and sent him flat on his back on the carpet. Campion and Uncle William reached Petrie at the same moment and Mercer edged his chair a little farther away from the fracas. Konrad tottered to his feet. He was livid and quite speechless with rage and pain. But his histrionic gift had not deserted him. With his eyes closed and his face tragic he took three staggering steps forward and would have fallen into a more graceful position, his golden head pillowed on his arm, had not interference come from a most unexpected quarter.

Miss Finbrough left her position behind the massage table

79

and swooped down upon him like a Valkyrie. Her plump plain face was a glistening crimson into which her light brows and lashes had entirely disappeared. She took Konrad by the soft part of the arm and her metal-hard fingers touched his bone.

"You dirty venomous little beast!" she said and shook him.

Surprise and pain startled the young man out of his histrionics. He opened his eyes and stared at her.

"Don't you dare..." he said, and the ridiculous words were embarrassing in his mouth. "You're trying to protect him too, are you? You're all trying to protect him and make him think he can go roaring round the roads killing people without getting into trouble for it, just because he's got his name in lights outside a theatre. You'll soon find you're wrong. He murdered that woman. Her blood is on his head. Thousands of helpless cyclists are killed every year by people like him who drive cars as though they're on a railway track."

His final pronouncement came by way of an anticlimax. Mercer emitted a shrill crow of delight and even Sock smiled. Miss Finbrough gripped her captive afresh.

"Be quiet!" she said. "You've done enough harm as it is. Think what he's gone through already. He's overworked, tired, exhausted—"

"Finny, shut up." Sutane bounded to his feet. He stood draped in his towel, cold, irritable and infinitely more intelligent than either of them. "Oh, dear God, what a pack of apes!" he said. "What is this?—a nightmare in rehearsal? Pull yourselves together, for heaven's sake. Konrad, I don't know what you're doing in my dressing room at all. Get out. And as for you, Finny, my dear good girl, stick to your damned job, do."

Miss Finbrough released her quivering victim. She stood for a moment looking at Sutane, a plain middle-aged woman, very red and hot with unaccustomed emotion.

"I'm sorry, Mr. Sutane," she said meekly and turned away. As she stumbled towards the door a sob, which embarrassed them all because it was so genuine and at the same time so hideous, escaped her.

Konrad glanced after her and shook himself. He was still quivering.

"I'm sorry if I've been rude, Sutane," he said with a touch

80

of bravado, "but I feel these things. Other people do too," he added.

"Exit line," said Sock.

Konrad picked up his sweater and walked over to the door. On the threshold he paused.

"You can end my engagement whenever you like," he said. "But I still maintain that from a humane point of view Chloe Pye was murdered."

There was a moment's silence after the door had closed. Mercer moved at last.

"Suppose she was?" he said.

They all stared at him but he was looking at Sutane, and his eyes were questioning and amused.

The spell was broken by the arrival of Hughes, who announced somewhat surprisingly that Dr. Bouverie was below and would be glad if he might have a word with Mr. Campion.

8

When Mr. Campion followed Hughes downstairs he descended into a small world of chaos.

White Walls normally contained an excitable household whose everyday balance was only maintained by the nicest of adjustments, so that this morning, when the proverbial monkey wrench had landed squarely in the heart of the brittle machinery, the very building seemed in danger of disruption and all its people to suffer in some degree from mild confusional insanity.

On reaching the hall the butler looked about him helplessly. At the front door a flustered parlourmaid was coping inadequately with a persistent young man who carried a camera, while in the alcove beneath the stairs Linda Sutane was talking to someone on the telephone, her soft deep voice sounding strained and pathetic.

Of Dr. Bouverie there was no trace.

"He wanted to see you most particularly, sir." Hughes seemed put out. "He was here a moment ago." Even while he spoke his glance wandered anxiously to the front door, where the maid was weakening.

At that moment the whole house heard the doctor's voice on the floor above. The old man was bellowing and apparently with rage.

"Ah, of course," said Hughes with relief. "It slipped my mind, sir. He'll be up with Miss Sarah. I forgot." He glanced down the hall again and quivered. The unwelcome caller was almost in the house. "Would you mind going up to him, sir? I think I really ought..."

The finish of the sentence was lost as the impulse proved too strong for him, and he bore down upon the intruder like a bulldog who has burst his collar.

Mr. Campion went upstairs again and guided by the doctor's voice, which had now sunk to a menacing rumble, turned a corner in the upper hall and came upon the fiery old gentleman. He was absorbed in conversation with the nurse Campion had seen on the evening before.

"Bring the maid to me," shouted the doctor. "Don't stand there like an imbecile. Bring the maid to me—and the dog, don't you know."

The woman hesitated. She was elderly and in figure what is somewhat obscurely called "comfortable." Her face was plain and sensible but there was a particularly obstinate gleam in her brown eyes which reminded Mr. Campion vividly of certain important personalities of his own early youth.

"The child is afraid," she began for what was all too evidently the third or fourth time.

Dr. Bouverie's jowls quivered and swelled.

"Do as you're told, woman."

She gave him a single defiant glare and strode off, her starched apron crackling.

The old man turned and peered at Campion.

"Morning. I'd like to see you in a moment," he said and glanced over his shoulder into the room upon whose threshold he stood. He made a vast imposing figure in his loose clothes. His wide collar was cut to lie almost flat, so that his many chins should not be discommoded, and there was a cluster of Little Dorrit rosebuds in his buttonhole.

"Where's the mother? D'you know?" he demanded. "Telephoning? Ridiculous. Perhaps you can help me. Come in here, will you?"

Campion followed him into a large white room furnished as a nursery. Superimposed upon the original modern décor, with its gaily painted screens and educational pictures, were evidences of an older school of thought: a chair in hideous brown wicker, an ancient fireguard and an extraordinary quantity of airing laundry.

Dr. Bouverie pointed to a low bedstead beneath the window on the far side of the room.

"The child's under that," he said. "Don't want to drag her out, don't you know, and if I pull the bed I may hurt her. Raise it gently. Take the foot, will you?"

Campion did as he was told and together they lifted the cot onto the middle of the linoleum. Sarah Sutane crouched in the angle of the wall. She was kneeling, her plump arms over her head and the soles of her little round feet completely visible beneath the arc of her many petticoats. Dr. Bouverie walked over to her.

"Where did the brute bite you?" he enquired conversationally.

Sarah quivered but did not stir, and when he stooped down and picked her up she remained rigid, so that he carried her, still in her original kneeling position, to the bed.

"There's nothing to be frightened of now." The old man was not unkind but not unduly sympathetic. "We must see the abrasion, don't you know. It simply wants a little lukewarm water on it. Dog bite is not dangerous. You won't go mad or any rubbish of that sort. Where did he catch you?"

Mr. Campion suddenly felt very young himself. That half-contemptuous tone which yet carried such absolute conviction reminded him of a time long ago when he had first heard it, and the thought "That's how God talks" had come to him with the awful certainty of truth.

Sarah relaxed cautiously and peered at them through a tangled mass of tear-wet hair. She was very white and her jaws were set rigidly. There was a scratch on the inside of her upper arm and the doctor looked at it with professional interest.

"That all he gave you?" he enquired.

A commotion behind them silenced any reply the child might have made. The nurse reappeared, angry and sullen, and with her came a bright-faced country girl in an untidy uniform. The maid's round eyes were shining with excitement as she carried a little black-and-white mongrel terrier by the scruff of its thin neck. Her manner suggested both triumph and daring. Dr. Bouverie surveyed the trio.

"Put the dog down, don't you know."

"It might fly at her, sir." The maid spoke brightly, almost, it seemed, hopefully.

"Put it down."

Sarah gulped and the nurse could restrain herself no longer.

"She's frightened, poor lamb," she said. "Hark at her. Put the dangerous thing outside the door. You're frightening her to death, sir. She'll have a convulsion."

There seemed to be a certain amount of truth in her prophecy. Sarah was sitting upright on the bed, her eyes fixed on the dog and her face working horribly. Dr. Bouverie took her wrist in his hand and his eyebrows rose, yet, as the maid turned to the door, he shouted at her with irritable obstinacy: "Put the dog down."

Unwillingly and with considerable dramatic effect the girl set the dog on the floor and darted backwards. The terrier remained crouching, his eyes bright and frightened. Dr. Bouverie picked him up and ran his hands over the trembling body.

"Not a very fierce little dog," he said. "Now, you, little girl"—he looked at Sarah—"why did he bite you?"

The maid stepped forward, eager to talk.

"They were running in the field, sir, and he leapt at her," she said breathlessly. "The dog's shut up when Miss Bellew's Dane is here and he's always very fierce when he's first let out. Miss Sarah began to scream so I ran up to hold him off." She swelled at the recollection of her own bravery. "Then I saw he'd bitten her so I shouted for Nurse."

Mr. Campion cleared his throat and ventured a question at the risk of annoying the doctor.

"Did you tell her they'd have the dog destroyed?" he enquired.

The girl started and stared at him as though he had exhibited supernatural powers.

"Well, yes, sir, I did," she said after a pause. "I wanted to comfort her," she added hastily. "I told her that Mr. Spooner, the groom, would shoot him."

Dr. Bouverie looked at Campion and laughed abruptly.

"That's the end of that mystery," he said. "Here, little girl, here's your dog." He threw the animal onto the bed, despite the nurse's scream, and the child seized it, hugging it with a passionate affection which only a dog could possibly appreciate. The colour surged into her face and her eyes grew heavy. The terrier licked her eagerly.

Dr. Bouverie brushed the palms of his plump hands together.

"Put her to bed," he said. "Give her a hot-water bottle and a cup of milk cocoa. I'll send her a sedative. Somebody had better call down at my house for it. Keep the dog where it is."

"But the bite, Doctor..." The nurse was irritable.

"Paint it with iodine, my good woman. It's only a scratch. They were playing and he caught her. She's suffering from shock. This very silly little girl here told her that she was going to lose her pet and that it was going to be shot, so naturally she was frightened. She is very fond of him."

Sarah and the dog remained clasped in each other's arms. It was not a sentimental picture but rather a terrible one. The child's agony of affection was piteous.

The little maidservant hovered, indignant to discover her heroism and forethought so cruelly repaid. Dr. Bouverie regarded her.

"Are you a Mudd?" he enquired.

"Yes, sir. From Rose Green."

"Thought I recognised the shape of your skull." The old man seemed pleased. "You be off about your work and don't get hysterical. All your family are fools. You noticed there was a bit of excitement in the house and you thought you'd stir up a little more. Isn't that it?"

"No, sir." Miss Mudd was scarlet.

"Don't lie." Dr. Bouverie had adopted his God voice again. "Be off. Never interfere."

The nurse followed them out of the room, protesting.

"Sarah can't sleep with the dog, sir."

"Why not?"

"He may have fleas."

The old man looked down at her. "Then wash him," he said. "There are worse things than fleas. Listen to me. That's a very lonely, overimaginative little girl in there, and if you take her dog away she'll lie awake and see him standing waiting to be shot. She'll hear the bang and she'll see him bleed and she'll see his little dead body as clearly as if you'd killed him in front of her eyes. Cruelty, my good woman, is a very relative thing. That child is suffering from shock and it may interest you to know that more people die of shock than from any other disease. Go and cover them up. Keep them warm."

"If you say so, Doctor." The woman was still indignant but impressed in spite of herself.

The old man grunted at her in an Olympian fashion and would have passed on had not a thought occurred to him.

"Give the dog some warm milk," he said. "It's a nice little dog."

As they went down the stairs he glanced at Campion.

"Lucky guess of yours," he said and made the word sound a compliment.

Linda was still at the telephone as they passed through the hall. She sounded almost hysterical, Campion thought, and checked an impulse to go uninvited to her assistance.

"But of course," he heard her say. "Of course. You must come here. Anything we can do we will. Oh, it *has* been a shock for you. I know. I do realise that, of course."

Dr. Bouverie touched Campion's sleeve and led him out into the sunlight. On the step he paused, drawing in deep breaths of summer air through his small nose. He looked like some great animal, Campion thought; a bison, perhaps.

"I don't like nerves," he said. "Rolling pasture, beautiful trees, pretty flowers, birds—all respectable things, don't you know. Decent. Solid. I sometimes feel we should all be better off if we didn't think. All this intensive cultivation of the mind is bad. We're not constructed for it. Human machine won't stand up to it. Walk with me on that grass over there. I want to talk to you. Now about that poor woman who died last night; do you know if she was in the hands of a medical man?"

Campion considered.

"I'm not sure," he said, "but I should hardly think so. She's only just back from a two-year colonial tour, you know. I'll find out. Sutane's the man to ask."

"Wait a moment." The old man spoke hastily. "I don't think I'll make any definite enquiries, don't you know. That's the business of the coroner. I only wondered if you'd noticed anything about her yourself or if you had heard she'd suffered at all—coughs, choking attacks, spasms of holding the breath."

Mr. Campion's pale eyes became shrewd behind his spectacles.

"No," he said cautiously. "I should hardly think so. She was a professional dancer, don't you see. Still, one of the great men discovered these clinical disturbances are not always present in every case. Who was it? Morgan?"

Dr. Bouverie paused in his stride.

"You're a very extraordinary young man. Studied medicine?"

"Purely from the forensic point of view," Mr. Campion explained modestly. "When you mentioned those symptoms I naturally thought of *status lymphaticus*. You found that at the P.M., I suppose?"

"I did. I don't know if there's any harm in telling you. Most interesting case."

Dr. Bouverie paused after he had spoken. Campion remained encouragingly silent and the old doctor eyed him.

"Consider myself a good judge of character," he remarked unexpectedly. "You've been very civil to me and I'm inclined to trust you, don't you know. Rely on your discretion?"

"Yes, I think you may, sir." Campion did not smile.

"Good." Dr. Bouverie looked every inch the eminent Victorian he was. "As a matter of fact, I'd like to talk it over with an intelligent man who knew the poor woman. The mischief is we don't know much about *status lymphaticus*. I'm afraid that must be faced. We know that if the thymus persists after a certain age—five, isn't it?—a certain state results. The trouble is that this state seems to vary with each patient. Now this woman, don't you see, had adenoids and tonsils removed at some time, probably in childhood, so there's nothing to help us there. I opened her up, don't you know, and I found the thymus considerably enlarged—considerably. The heart was not actually constricted but the aorta was narrower than is usual and the heart itself was a little undeveloped, so you see this makes a different problem of it."

Mr. Campion felt his steps growing heavier and was exasperated with himself. It came to him suddenly that he did not want the truth to come out. He did not want this pompous but likeable old personage to put his blunt finger on the point that was sticking out a mile. He did not want the Sutane ménage to become disorganised by the tremendous emotional and physical upheaval of a murder enquiry, not because of Uncle William and his success, not because of Sutane and his career, but because of Linda, who in thirty hours had become a personality of altogether unreasonable importance in his own life.

Having faced this, he felt better.

Dr. Bouverie was talking again.

"I refreshed my memory on the subject this morning," he said. "The experts seem to be still quarrelling about it. No one knows what the weight of the thymus in a normal healthy body ought to be. But the fact remains that when one gets a sudden death from insufficient causes it very often is this overdevelopment. I've had several cases in my time. One poor fellow died under chloroform having his teeth out, I remember, and a child up at Birley stuck its head through its crib rails and died apparently by act of God. Then down on the Lower Green a man got his brother by the throat in a quarrel and the fellow died in his hands, but not from strangulation. We were all very puzzled at the time. In all these cases the thymus was very much enlarged."

He cleared his throat and it occurred to Campion that he was enjoying his own lecture.

"To go back to this poor wretched woman," said Dr. Bouverie. "Looking at her last night we both noticed the skull fracture caused by the fall. There was a Pond fracture of the vault with an extended fissure to the base, by the way. The head injuries would have killed her in an hour or so had she not been dead already."

Campion took a deep breath. It was coming, then.

"She was not killed by the car?" he said dully.

"I don't think so." Dr. Bouverie was pleased with himself. "She died from fright, you know. Fright acting on the *status lymphaticus*. As she stood waving to Mr. Sutane she felt faint, overbalanced, and the shock killed her. When she reached the ground she was dead."

Campion stared at the old man and controlled an insane desire to laugh with relief. It took him some seconds to realise what had happened, but gradually it dawned upon him. Dr. Bouverie was a man of simple and direct thought. From the beginning he had been confronted by a problem of accident or suicide. At first he had accepted the actual injuries made by the car as the cause of death, so that he was not concerned with that aspect of the case. The question which had bothered him to the exclusion of all others was why Chloe Pye had ever left the bridge. Now his discovery of the enlarged thymus had provided him with an explanation and he had accepted it. The simple fact that Chloe Pye's heart must, in this hypothesis, have ceased to pump less than five seconds before her head and rib cage were crushed and that bleeding would in that case have been copious had still miraculously escaped his attention. Campion felt like the child at the party who tries not to watch the conspicuously placed thimble in the old nursery game. He tried to remember Chloe Pye as she had appeared on the night before; he saw again her torn bathing suit and her lacerated chest where the tire had crushed and ripped it. There should have been blood there, quantities of blood, not merely the superficial bleeding of the smaller veins.

The doctor's discovery, however, explained the real cause of death. Campion wondered who it was who had so frightened Chloe Pye that she had died. No great strength would have been needed to kill her, perhaps even no strength at all. The thought of the man in the doctor's story who had taken his brother by the throat only to feel him die in his hands returned to his mind. He wanted to leave the old man before the question which rose to his lips escaped him. Were there any slight bruises on her neck, on her shoulders?

He was saved from the indiscretion by the appearance of Sutane, who came striding across the lawn towards them, a loose silk dressing gown flapping round his angular form. He was eager and inquisitive and the force of his personality swept over them in a wave of which they were physically and uncomfortably aware. In his intensity of need he reminded Campion of the luckless Sarah, and it was evident that he had the same effect upon the doctor, for the old man spoke of the child at once.

"Purely shock, Mr. Sutane. The incident was quite sufficient to account for it."

The younger man stared at him as if he were demented.

"Shock?" he said. "Good heavens, the car passed over her!"

Dr. Bouverie stiffened and his old eyes were severe.

"I'm talking of your daughter, sir," he said.

Sutane blinked and they were aware of his mental effort as he tore his mind away from the one subject to the other. It was the most striking thing about the man—this extraordinary vividness of the unspoken expression of his thoughts.

"Sarah?" he said, not without interest. "What's the matter with her?"

Dr. Bouverie froze. Campion felt his contempt and he regarded the two of them helplessly. He knew that the doctor could never conceive a situation in which a man might love his child and yet have literally no time in which to think of her, while Sutane would never realise that a world existed in which time for thought was not only unrationed but as free and bountiful as to have no value at all.

"Your little daughter is being well looked after. A maid frightened her. She thought she was going to lose her dog." The doctor spoke coldly and with active dislike for the monument of human selfishness which he thought he saw before him.

Sutane listened to him, his head on one side, and quite evidently thought him a little mad.

"Has she found the dog now?"

"Yes. They're both being looked after, I'm happy to say."

Sutane passed a weary hand over his forehead.

"My God," he said.

Glancing at Dr. Bouverie's expression, Campion was reminded of an old gentleman of his acquaintance who used to recount how he walked round the house of a despised contemporary and "mentally spat." Dr. Bouverie was mentally spitting now. Campion changed the conversation.

"Sutane," he said, "do you know if Chloe Pye suffered from semi-choking or fainting fits at any time?"

The doctor coughed warningly, but his eyes were interested. So was Sutane. He looked at them both sharply.

"I never heard of it," he said. "I didn't know her at all, you see."

Dr. Bouverie glowered. "But she was staying in your house..."

The faint colour came into Sutane's face.

"I did not know her," he said quickly. "Until she joined the cast of *The Buffer* I had never met her, except casually at parties." In his anxiety to sound convincing he adopted an intensity which defeated his object. "She was a virtual stranger to me."

90

The doctor was put out by the underlying antagonism in the voice.

"You'll tell that to the coroner," he said.

Sutane paused in his stride. "Naturally," he said and, turning on his heel, he walked swiftly and angrily away.

As he conducted the doctor to his car Campion remembered Chloe Pye sitting on Sock's knee in the morning room and heard afresh her squeaky protest: "Jimmy and I are old friends."

9

"There are times, my dear feller," said Uncle William, "when the whole world gets out of gear and tumbles helter-skelter about one's ears, makin' one feel damnably uncomfortable and at a loose end. At those times there's only one thing to do about it, and that's to light a good cigar, take a glass in one's hand, and wait until one sees a ray of light shinin' at one through the gloom. That's been my rule all through my life and it's never failed me yet. Sit down, my boy, and I'll get the drinks."

Looking more bearlike than ever in his old gentleman's suit of brown-and-beige-striped flannel, he waved Mr. Campion to a chair by the fireplace in the small music room and went to a cupboard in the bottom of the bookcase.

"Dear people," he observed as he surveyed a half decanter of scotch whisky which he found there. "Fancy rememberin' me at a time like this. This is my own supply. When I first came down here last year Jimmy pointed the cupboard out to me and told me he'd given orders that a decanter and glasses should always be kept there so that I could get a drink whenever I liked without havin' to fidget round for it. That's what I mean about these people, Campion. They're dear good souls, kind, thoughtful and intelligent, who make a feller feel he's livin' at home. A better home than some I've known," he added thoughtfully. "Poor Mother! No sense of comfort as we know it today. Still, a very grand old woman, Campion. Here's to her. God bless her."

Campion drank a silent toast to Great-aunt Caroline and wished she were still alive without actually desiring her awe-inspiring presence in the moment's dilemma. Uncle William continued.

"Sutane, Konrad and Sock at the inquest, Linda up with the child, Eve driving Mercer to Birley, and that Finbrough woman safely out of the way," he said with satisfaction. "We're alone in peace to think a bit."

"What happened to Slippers Bellew?" Campion enquired.

"Oh, she left. Sensible girl." Uncle William's bright blue eyes applauded her intelligence. "As soon as the news came last night Sock bundled her into her little car and she drove off down the lane, going the other way to avoid the trouble. Not as callous as it sounds. As Sock pointed out, she's not a woman; she's a performing animal with a reputation. He told her that she couldn't do anything to help and might have to carry the show if Sutane dropped out for a night or so. She's not quite what you'd expect from an actress. Lives entirely by schedule. So much sleep, so much exercise, so much work. Gives an entirely different impression from the stage."

He shook his head with mild regret and settled himself opposite Campion.

"Hate carrying tales," he remarked, cocking an eye at the younger man. "Don't like it. Never did. That's the mischief of a rumpus of this sort. People takin' other people in corners and chatterin'. Can't get away from it. Bound to occur. Very funny scene in here just before lunch while you were talkin' to the doctor in the garden."

"Oh?" Campion was encouraging and Uncle William nodded.

"Very funny scene," he repeated. "Made me think. May be nothin' in it. Still, I thought I'd repeat it as I'm not sure I wasn't meant to. I came down here after you left the bedroom— saw no point in watchin' Sutane dress—and had just settled myself when Konrad came sidlin' in lookin' for me. Didn't encourage him. Can't stand the feller. It was he who insisted on talkin'. Said didn't I think it funny Chloe Pye, of all people, dyin'. I answered him. I said I didn't see it was any more peculiar that she should die than anybody else. In fact, I made it pretty plain to him that I could spare the woman.

Never have believed in false sentiment, Campion. She was devilish awful alive, and the place is quieter without her playin' the hussy in every room one went into. No point in refusin' to admit that. Well, we beat about the bush for a bit and then he came out with the tale he was determined to tell me. I pooh-poohed it at the time, of course, but it had its points of interest."

He paused and tucked his small fat feet round the legs of his chair.

"There was a bit of mystery about the way the woman got into the show. You know that?" he began slowly. "Sutane just announced it one day and in she came. Well, there's nothin' in that. He may have liked her dancin', although you know my views. However, this little runt Konrad says he was sittin' in the theatre at the rehearsal of a new scene and Sutane was a couple of rows in front of him, watchin' the show, not knowin' Konrad was there. The feller was eaves-droppin'; got to face it. The woman, Chloe Pye, came along in the dark and sat down next to Sutane. Konrad said he didn't like to move and so had to sit and listen."

Uncle William snorted by way of comment.

"Well, apparently Miss Pye started talkin' about some telephone messages she'd had from Sutane, and Konrad repeated her words. May not be accurate, of course. Still, tell you for what it's worth. The little twip says she said, 'Darlin'' —she used to talk like that, it means nothin'—'darlin', don't be a fool. Your wife has asked me down and I'm comin'.' The next thing Konrad heard—and he must have sat there with his ears flappin'—was Sutane sayin', 'I don't want you down there, Chloe. I've done all I'm goin' to do and I won't have you in my house.'"

Uncle William paused, drank deeply, and blew his nose.

"Monstrous thing, this listenin' and repeatin', bandyin' words to and fro, probably all wrong," he rumbled unhappily. "But this next bit is interestin' if true. Konrad says that Chloe Pye—and what a hussy, Campion, forcin' herself on a feller when told point-blank she wasn't wanted! No hintin', mind you; told point-blank—Konrad says that Chloe Pye said, 'How are you goin' to stop me, my lamb?' and Sutane replied straight from the shoulder, like the dear feller he is, 'I don't know. But if you try to break up my home I'll stop you, if I have to strangle you.'"

He sat back in his chair and surveyed Campion with unblinking eyes.

"The cat's out of the bag," he said. "I've repeated the story. Felt I ought to. Mind you, may be all a pack of lies. Still, it's a funny tale to invent and Jimmy told me himself that he didn't want the woman here, but she froze onto Linda one day behind the scenes and the unsuspectin' girl parted up with an invitation. What I feel is, Campion, it's not the sort of gossip for Konrad to go round repeatin', is it? That's why I couldn't find it in my heart to blame Eve."

"Eve?" enquired Mr. Campion, temporarily out of his depth.

Uncle William's pink face darkened.

"Was comin' to her," he mumbled. "She was just outside that window over there sittin' in a deck chair. Overheard Konrad talkin' to me. More listenin'."

"Did she say anything?"

"The scene I referred to took place," said Uncle William briefly. "I left 'em. Seemed best. When people are hurlin' abuse there's always the chance of one of 'em confusin' the issue and thinkin' you've said somethin' yourself. I came away."

They sat in silence for some minutes. It was cool and dark in the small north room. Outside, the garden was sparkling in the afternoon sun.

Mr. Campion considered Benny Konrad.

"I've heard several references to a 'rally,'" he said. "What's that?"

"Konrad's Speedo Club." Uncle William spoke contemptuously. "One of these publicity notions these fellers have to get up to. You ought to have heard of it, Campion. The feller's the high priest of the bicycle. Ludicrous sort of idea."

Dim recollections of Press paragraphs floated into Mr. Campion's mind. Uncle William prompted him.

"Konrad had a very successful dance act some years ago with a bicycle and lent his name to some sort of advertising stunt which was illustrated. Pictures of him everywhere with a certain firm's machine. One thing led to another, as these things do, and a club was formed with Konrad as president. He presents prizes and attends races in France. That sort of thing. There was quite a large membership once, I believe, composed of a lot of enthusiastic young fellers who used to come and see him act and applaud. The trouble is, he's not good. Can't carry a show alone. After his failure in *Wheels within Wheels* he was lookin' for a shop, as we call it, and was devilish glad to take Sutane's understudy with a couple of unimportant numbers in my show, *The Buffer*. However, he still works hard at his publicity. This rally is the important day in the club's year. It's a small body now but very enthusiastic. They see him as the hero of their hobby, a sort of prince—poor misguided souls."

He leant forward and placed a stubby forefinger on Campion's knee.

"Konrad's the sort of chap who's got all the paraphernalia for success except the essential talent," he said earnestly. "He's like a feller in a fine tail coat without the chest to fill it out."

"What do they do at this rally?" Campion was still interested.

"Ride from a pub in London to a pub in Essex, and finish at a pub somewhere else for a meal and speeches. Takes place next Sunday week."

Uncle William poured himself another drink.

"I'm goin' to have a brief nap. These are stirrin' times. Think about what I've told you, Campion. Jimmy's a good feller. Can't have him covered with contumely, especially from the mouth of a little tick. Think it over, my boy."

Campion rose to his feet.

"I will," he promised and his lean face was thoughtful.

He had a very clear recollection of Sutane's appearance at the window on the evening before and his subsequent behaviour at the scene of the accident, and an uncomfortable doubt assailed him.

Leaving Uncle William reposing in an armchair, his short legs crossed at the ankles and his face composed for philosophical contemplation, Campion went out into the vast hall, on whose stone squares the sunlight laid long shimmering fingers from the front door. The house was placid and quiet in the drowsy afternoon.

He remained looking out into the garden for some minutes and did not hear Linda come down until her foot touched the stone behind him. She looked white and tired, and the angle of her jaw seemed sharper and smaller than he had noticed it before.

"She's asleep," she said. "Poor darlings! They look like a

95

coloured plate in a Christmas supplement. Rufe is a good little chap. He woke when I moved but he didn't stir. He's very fond of her."

"And how's Nurse?" enquired Mr. Campion.

She laughed and her eyes met his. Campion looked away from her and across the lawn to the trees beyond.

"We'd better use both rooms for tea," she said. "There'll be a lot of us."

He followed her into the drawing room unwillingly and helped her to roll back the folding doors which separated it from the breakfast room.

"They're bringing Mrs. Pole back with them, and her son." Linda sounded weary. "She's Chloe Pye's sister-in-law. Her husband is abroad and she's the nearest relative available. She seems very much upset." She sighed and he glanced at her.

"Difficult?"

"I'm rather afraid she may be. She kept me on the phone for nearly three quarters of an hour this morning. It's ghastly, isn't it? I can't feel it's a death somehow. It's a filthy thing to say, but it's more like a new production."

She accepted the cigarette he offered her and sat down in the window, while he remained standing before her.

"If you had some sleep now it would be a good thing," he said, feeling slightly silly. "I mean, you've had a tremendous strain in the last twenty-four hours—this business and the child."

She looked up and surprised him by her expression.

"I did care about the child," she said. "I do love her. I'm not careless. I do do all I can. I'd let her go, even, if I thought she'd be all right. But she's so young, so terribly young. Poor, poor baby."

She glanced out of the window. She was not crying but her mouth was not perfectly controlled. In her need she was disarming and he forgot the suffocating and novel selfconsciousness which she had begun to engender in him.

"That's quite obvious, you know," he said gently.

"Is it?"

"I think so."

She smiled at him in a grateful, watery fashion which unaccountably turned his heart over, reminding him inconsequentially and, therefore, irritatingly of its exact position in his body.

"I couldn t get to see the doctor because of Mrs. Pole," she explained earnestly. "There's such a lot of that sort of thing. I haven't got any definite work but I never seem to be able to be on hand at the right moment. It seems absurd to talk about the house, with an army of servants, but in a place like this, with crowds of people rushing in and out perpetually, all of them without warning, there's a lot of managing to be done. Servants don't expect to have to think, you know. If you can give them a curriculum they can carry it out, but when you can't you've got to think for each of them whenever thought is required. And, anyway, they're alternatively overworked and bored stiff. Then there are little odd things like arrangements, trains to be met, and people to entertain when the others aren't actually needing them. I don't neglect Sarah, honestly I don't. I'm with her every spare second I have. I'm not much good, though. It's so difficult to get your mind to work like a child's, and if it doesn't the child's either bored or puzzled. She's so lonely."

She paused for breath and, catching sight of his face, seemed to remember for the first time that he was a comparative stranger.

"I'm sorry," she said with a certain youthful stiffness. "I've been so exasperated all day because I couldn't see Doctor Bouverie about Sarah. It was all so ridiculously unjust that it's been rankling and you were about so I threw it all at your head. I'm so sorry."

Campion sought in his mind for some suitable rejoinder at once graceful and pacifying. It did not present itself to him, however, and instead he made the observation uppermost in his mind, stating it baldly and without art. "You're lonely yourself, aren't you?" he said.

The girl shot him a single comprehending glance.

"You're clever," she said. "Much cleverer than I thought. That sounds rude. I don't mean it to be. . . . Eve and Mercer should be back soon. It's awfully good of her to drive him about."

He accepted her clumsy change in the conversation politely and watched her profile against the window. She went on, talking a trifle hurriedly.

"They went in to Birley to get some music-manuscript

97

paper. No one in the world but Mercer would insist that he wanted manuscript paper at a time like this. Nothing ruffles him. His man was out, so I'm afraid Eve was forced into offering to drive him. He doesn't touch the car himself. They'll all be back soon. It will be an accident verdict, won't it? Sock said you'd fixed everything."

"I did nothing," said Campion, rather too truthfully, he thought. "But yes, I think it'll be accident."

Linda nodded. "Why should she take her life?" she said. "Poor girl! I thought she seemed so pleased with herself. And she was very much *en grande tenue*. It seems so extraordinary."

"*En grande tenue?*"

She looked a little embarrassed.

"In full regalia, sexually speaking," she said. "Sort of energy people put on, or put out rather, when they're hunting. You know what I mean. Some people do it subconsciously the whole time and some just adopt it when they have someone particularly in mind. It's one of those things you notice instinctively."

Mr. Campion raised his eyebrows.

"Chloe Pye was in full regalia, was she?"

"Yes, I think so." Her quiet voice was thoughtful. "I wondered who she was interested in. Sock, I imagined. Lots of women like Sock very much. He looks as if he could do with cherishing. Not exactly dirty; unbrushed, if you see what I mean."

Campion grinned.

"That would hardly do for Chloe Pye, would it?" he suggested.

"I don't know." Linda eyed him gravely. "I only met her once before she came down here. I was alone in Jimmy's dressing room one day last week and Sock brought her in to see me. She said she'd like a week-end in the country and I offered her a tentative invitation which she seized. Jimmy was rather upset when he heard of it and wanted me to put her off, but I didn't like to because it would have been so rude. I wish to God I had."

She paused. "Perhaps it was an accident," she said at last, but her voice carried no conviction. "It's all very horrible and frightening."

"Frightening?"

She looked up at him and he caught a fleeting expression in her eyes which jolted him.

"I talk too much to you," she said. "It's a gift of yours, making people talk, because you understand what they say, you know."

Campion sat down.

"I'm quite trustworthy," he said briefly. "Why are you afraid?"

She hesitated and suddenly turned to him.

"Have you ever had rats in the house?" she demanded unexpectedly. "If you get mice they're just a nuisance, like flies or too many old magazines, but once you get rats you're aware of an evil, unseen intelligence which is working against you in your own house. It's an inexplicable feeling if you haven't experienced it, but if you have you'll know what I mean. Its the 'enemies about' sensation. That's what I've got now. There was something wrong about that woman's death, and it came on top of a lot of wrong things."

She remained looking at him, curled up on the window seat. Her gold skin was warm against the dark satin of her dress and her small face was alive and intelligent. She was chic, compact, very much a definite person, and it dawned upon Campion that he was in love with her and that he would never again be completely comfortable in her presence.

She was quite right about the situation at White Walls. There were enemies about, and if he deserted her now it would be a desertion indeed. He did not take his eyes from her face but he ceased to see her. The discovery he had just made was not an overwhelmingly astonishing one, for it had been knocking at the door of his mind ever since he had first seen her. He found it shocking, however, not because she was Sutane's wife and Sarah's mother, and therefore not for his pursuing, but because a phenomenon which he had hitherto believed to be more than half an old wives' tale had been at last revealed to him as a fact instead of a fashion. He knew that he had come down to White Walls in a normal state of mind, and yet within an hour an outside force had conquered and possessed him.

"You're looking at me as though I'd done something blasphemous," said Linda Sutane.

Campion stiffened as though she had boxed his ears. Presently he grinned at her. His eyes were dancing and the long creases down his cheeks had deepened. He looked suddenly very much younger and very much alive.

"Fair comment," he said lightly and added, "the cruelest observation you could possibly have made."

She stared at him curiously for a moment and he saw a certain timidity creep into her expression which delighted and invigorated him even while it appalled him.

Linda shook her head, an involuntary childish gesture to shake away a thought.

"Perhaps it's all imagination," she said.

"Perhaps it is," he agreed. "Whatever it is, I'll see it through."

She put out her hand.

"I don't think it is," she said. "Do you?"

He got up and walked aimlessly down the room.

"No," he said, looking down at the empty fireplace. "I know damn well it isn't."

Hughes startled them both and looked a little bewildered himself when he came in an instant afterwards.

"Mrs. Paul Geodrake, madam," he murmured. "I told her you were out, but she caught sight of you through the window. She told me to tell you she was sure you would spare her a moment. She's in the dining room. I had no other place to take her." He glanced reproachfully at the open double doors.

"Who is she? Do we know her?" Linda seemed surprised.

Hughes sank his voice confidentially.

"She lives in the Old House on the lower road, madam. You were out when she called originally and so was she when you returned cards."

Linda drew back.

"I can't see her now, because the others will be here at any moment."

"Her husband's father, old Mr. Geodrake, was friendly with your late uncle, ma'am." Hughes seemed hurt. "She said only for a moment. She's a rather determined lady."

Linda capitulated and he went off satisfied.

Mrs. Paul Geodrake came into the room as if it were a fortress she had stormed. She was a fresh-faced, red-haired woman in the mid-thirties, smartly if not tastefully dressed, and possessed of a voice of power and unpleasantness unequalled by anything else Campion had ever heard. It occurred to him at once that the fashion for well-dressed stridence was out of date. Also he wished that she were less determinedly vivacious.

She swooped upon Linda, her hand outstretched.

"I had to come," she said, her bright intelligent eyes fixed searchingly on the other woman's face. "I've been sitting at home thinking of you and I suddenly made up my mind to run up and tell you you're not to worry. After all, we're next-door neighbours, aren't we?"

Linda looked at her blankly. A lesser soul would have been silenced by that expression of frank bewilderment, but Mrs. Geodrake was of stern stuff. She looked at her small hostess with a compassion that was not altogether untinged with satisfaction.

"You poor child," she said. "It's been frightful for you, of course. The village is full of it. They get things so exaggerated, don't they? And they will talk."

Linda said nothing. She had not spoken since her visitor's arrival, and Mrs. Geodrake, taking pity on her gaucherie, helped her out.

"Aren't you going to introduce me?" she said, dropping her voice a tone or so and eyeing Campion with a frankly appraising air which he found disconcerting.

Linda performed the ceremony politely and Mrs. Geodrake repeated the name, doubtless committing it carefully to memory.

"Not your husband?" she said and shot an arch twinkle at the other woman.

"No," said Linda.

"He's at the inquest, of course," said Mrs. Geodrake, aware of but not in the least disconcerted by the absence of conversational support. "My dear, do you know old Pleyell, the coroner? A perfect sweetie. Awfully stiff, of course, but quite a darling. You'll love him. He'll see you through and do the decent thing. Frightfully unfortunate for you—only your second year here. Who did you have? Doctor Bouverie, wasn't it? Such a charming old character, isn't he? How is your little girl? I heard in the village a dog bit her. Children never ought to have dogs. They're so frightfully cruel to them, don't you think? I'm dying to have a borzoi, but my husband doesn't like them. Do you have to obey your husband, Mrs. Sutane? I cut the word out of our marriage service, but it hasn't made any difference."

She laughed and they joined her politely if rather breathlessly. Campion had the uncomfortable feeling that he ought to do something to stop her and wished it were his own house.

Mrs. Geodrake opened her bag and produced a cigarette case.

"I'll smoke my own, if you don't mind. I sing," she said with a brief artificial smile as Linda produced the box somewhat belatedly from the mantelshelf. "Tell me, was she a great friend of yours, this girl who was killed?"

The concern in her voice was so superficial that it reached the cipher point.

"No," said Linda helplessly. "I'd never met her before."

"Oh, I see. A friend of your husband's. How interesting!"

The bright eyes suddenly reminded Mr. Campion of those of his old friend, Superintendent Stanislaus Oates.

"No, no." Linda was forced on to the defensive now. "She was simply appearing in his show, so I asked her down, don't you see?"

"Oh, a business friend?" Mrs. Geodrake filed the hard-won fact for future reference. "How terribly awkward for you. Still, it's so much better than someone you knew well and rather liked. Do tell me, how did she come to be nude? The village is too intrigued. The policeman's blushing all over, my dear. Were you having a nudist party?"

They both stared at her blankly, but before their honest astonishment could turn to irritation they saw something wistful behind her shrewd, hard eyes. Campion found himself thinking of the original Miss Hoyden of the play, not the tempestuous vulgarian which generations of exuberant actresses have made of her, but the author's own overhealthy and tragically unentertained piece whose energetic imagination fashioned from the half-heard gossip from the gay world a life of idyllic licence and excitement which only the freshest spirit and the strongest constitution could possibly survive for a couple of days. The stage, Bohemia, parties, romance; Mrs. Geodrake evidently saw them all as synonyms.

He stole a glance at Linda. She still looked a little bewildered.

"Oh, no," she said. "She'd been rehearsing down by the lake. She wasn't nude. She was in a bathing dress for dancing, you see."

102

"Alone?"

Mrs. Geodrake seemed disappointed.

"Yes, quite alone."

The sound of voices floated in from the hall and Linda got up with determination.

"It was very kind of you to come," she said and held out her hand.

"Not at all. I felt I had to." Mrs. Geodrake ignored the hand and turned towards the door with expectant interest. "Is this your husband coming?" she said. "He'll know about the verdict, won't he? I'm dying to hear it, aren't you?"

She smiled at them disarmingly as she spoke, and it occurred to the indignant Mr. Campion that the "superb self-possession" ideal extolled by the novelists of the last generation had been a serious mistake. Linda's hand dropped to her side and the door opened and Mercer looked in.

He caught sight of Mrs. Geodrake, did not recognise her, stared at her, and went out again promptly without a word, passing Sutane in the doorway.

10

"Death by misadventure." Sutane glanced across the room and spoke without relief. He looked pale and preoccupied and appeared to be imparting the information without considering it. Even Mrs. Geodrake, who had risen, her eyes eager and ingratiating, made no attempt to speak to him.

He came into the room, glanced at the visitor casually, as at a stranger in a hotel lounge, and, planting his back to the fireplace, waited, with his heavy-lidded eyes on the open door.

Hughes and the parlourmaid, who had entered through the breakfast room, were busy with tea trays and occasional tables. Apart from the gentle clatter they made there was no other sound in the room.

Mrs. Geodrake sat down again.

Outside in the hall someone giggled nervously. It was a particularly inane sound, not at all unusual in itself; rather, startlingly familiar; but in the precincts of White Walls it was an anachronism.

"This way, Mrs. Pole." Konrad's voice came in to them, gentle and insincere. They entered together, the man consciously graceful, bending slightly from the waist, his feet carefully placed at each step, his golden head bent, and the woman self-conscious, triumphant, enjoying herself with all the energy of an amateur actress in the leading tragic role of a play for charity.

She was small and plump and not so much clothed as looped and festooned in black. Black chiffon hung from her hat, from her shoulders, and from her black-gloved hand. From her flat pointed shoes to the crown of her toque she dripped mourning in its most prosaic form.

Beside such a determined display of funeral Konrad's curling yellow hair looked flippant and in bad taste.

Behind them walked a large sulky youth in a black suit a trifle too small for his puppy-fat body. He was painfully ill at ease and with the earnest idiocy of adolescence was covering it with baleful fury. His face, neck and hands were all very red and prominent. Sock wandered beside him, looking both exhausted and alarmed. Eve and Mercer came last, the man unwillingly.

Konrad glanced at Linda more to ascertain her exact position than to convey any message.

"Mrs. Pole," he said softly. "This is Mrs. Sutane."

Chloe Pye's sister-in-law raised her veil and her nervous laugh echoed through the room unhappily.

"Pleased to meet you," she said. "Isn't it awful?" She giggled again with unfortunate effect.

The two women shook hands and Linda conducted her visitor to a seat near the tea tray.

Mrs. Pole gave up the unsatisfactory notion of hitching her veil over her ears like an inverted yashmak, an expedient which both blinded and embarrassed her, and pushed it up over her hat, revealing a round determined face and red-rimmed blue eyes.

She was a great talker, a little out of her depth at the moment but clinging bravely to her unusual prominence and

104

displaying from time to time glimpses of that obstinacy of purpose which was her chief characteristic.

Mrs. Geodrake was temporarily forgotten. She sat gracefully on a small settee in the middle of the room, her intelligent eyes alight with interest and an amusement which was only too clearly unsympathetic. She was a member of the audience who had got in to the play and was frankly and unselfconsciously enjoying it.

Mrs. Pole looked about her.

"Where's Bobby?" she said sharply.

"Here, Mother." Robert Pole shouldered his way towards her through what he obviously took to be a hostile crowd. He was introduced to Linda and shook hands with her, scowling.

Mrs. Pole accepted tea and sandwiches and her son took up a protective position behind her chair. Konrad rose to the occasion gallantly. He ran about with cups and plates and cream jugs, posturing and gesturing as if he were actually on the stage.

Chloe Pye's sister-in-law had a loud voice with an accent which would not have been noticeable if she had not made capricious attempts to counteract it at unexpected moments.

"I'm thankful for a cup of tea," she said. "Poor clever Chloe..." She gulped and used her handkerchief. "It's been such a shock. We all went to see her on Saturday night, you know. Dad—that's my husband—was away on business, so we took my neighbour and I'm sure I talked about Chloe all the way home. I never thought I'd find her like this. Have you seen her, Mrs. Sutane? My dear..." She lowered her voice and imparted some gruesome details. "She was so pretty, too, wasn't she, for her age? You'd have thought sometimes, from the stage, she was nothing but a young girl. It was a terrible strain on her, though. You could see it if you looked into her face. Now she's gone. I'm going to take her home. Dad would wish it. I've seen the undertaker."

Mrs. Geodrake moved a little closer. "It must have been a terrible blow to you," she began invitingly.

The other woman looked at her gratefully and set down her cup.

"Oh, terrible!" she agreed. "Did you know her? She was so talented, even from a girl. We used to think she was a genius." She gave her little high-pitched giggle again.

Mrs. Geodrake's intrusion into the conversation focussed

general attention upon her. Sutane looked at her as though he had never seen her before that particular moment, as perhaps he had not. He turned an enquiring glance upon his wife.

However, Mrs. Geodrake, who seemed to be able to see all round her, glanced up before Linda could speak.

"I wondered when you were going to notice me, Mr. Sutane," she said, smiling at him archly. "I'm Jean Geodrake. I live next door to you. I came in this afternoon to sympathise with your wife."

There was silence while she spoke and Sutane, who was no more proof against a direct and smiling glance than any other man, looked puzzled without being put out.

"About the accident," amplified the lady. "Frightful for you all. In your house, I mean."

Mrs. Pole sniffed reproachfully and burst into embarrassing tears. Mrs. Geodrake rose to the situation.

"Oh, of course, you're a relative, aren't you?" she said, turning round upon the other woman. "An aunt?"

"Sister-in-law," snapped Mrs. Pole, a dangerous light in her blue eyes. "More like a sister," she added defiantly.

"She didn't come to see us much." The words were blurted out a full tone more loudly than their utterer had intended and Robert Pole's face became a violent crimson. He stood lowering defensively.

Mrs. Pole turned on her son.

"She did, you wicked boy," she exploded. "Didn't we all go up to her new flat? Didn't I put up her curtains? What are you talking about? She was very fond of us. I'm sure Dad, her brother, worshipped her. Why, we were all so pleased when she got on."

Mrs. Geodrake's smile was sweetly diabolical.

"I'm sure you were," she murmured. "She wasn't born to the stage then?"

Linda intervened with quiet determination.

"You must have had a dreadful day, Mrs. Pole," she said. "Would you care to come upstairs and take off your things?"

"No, thank you." The visitor was roused. The glance she bestowed on Mrs. Geodrake intimated clearly that she was standing no nonsense from any condescending bit of a country woman, however many airs she gave herself. She thanked Mrs. Sutane, who no doubt meant well, but she could easily take care of herself—her with her great grief.

"Chloe's father was quite a wealthy man," she said with dignity, her red eyes on Mrs. Geodrake's eager face. "He had her taught dancing from when she was a baby. I've heard Dad, my husband, say that she used to look a little queen in her white dresses. When she was old enough she joined a troupe of properly looked-after children and danced in pantomime. Later on she struck out for herself. None of us ever thought we'd sit in a coroner's court and hear a jury foreman say they'd brought the verdict in of death by misadventure because of insufficient evidence."

Both Linda and Mr. Campion looked at Sock abruptly. He nodded and turned his head away with a weary gesture.

Mrs. Pole was still talking. Her manner was a curious mixture of dignity and defiance, and the essential strength of character of the woman was apparent.

"None of us ever thought we'd learn when it was too late that she was seriously ill, poor girl, that her glands had overgrown and almost any little shock might kill her. If we had we might have been more charitable and understood a lot of her funny little ways."

Linda sat down beside her.

"I didn't know she was ill," she said.

"Oh, yes! When they operated on her after she was dead, poor girl, they found all this out. It's been a terrible shock to me to hear it all for the first time in an open court. It seems her glands..." Mrs. Pole's voice died away into a modest murmuring as she embarked on a subject which she considered her particular province.

Sutane turned away from her with relief and looked again at Mrs. Geodrake, who was still smiling with ill-suppressed mischief in her eyes.

"Why haven't we seen you before?" he enquired politely. "We're not often here, of course—or at least I'm not—but how extraordinary we should have missed you altogether."

He had turned on the full force of his charm and the woman opened before it, became human, if still a trifle girlish.

"Oh, but I've seen *you*," she said. "All of you. One notices people in the country. There are so few people who are faintly interesting. I've seen you all—you and Mrs. Sutane and your sister and your little girl. I've seen you too," she added, flashing her teeth at Konrad. "I nearly spoke to you last night. You didn't notice me."

She spoke archly and evidently without intentional dramatic effect, but everyone in the room, with the exception of Mrs. Pole and her son, paused abruptly, as though a stone had been thrown amongst them. Mrs. Pole's lowered voice whispered on.

". . . she was large as a child, inclined to put on weight. It worried her very much. She took things . . ."

No one was listening to her. Although no one looked at him directly, general attention was concentrated upon Konrad. He was standing before Mrs. Geodrake, a cup of tea in his hand. One knee was a little bent and his head was slightly on one side. It was one of his most elegantly careless poses.

"I don't think you did," he said.

The woman was blissfully unaware of the sensation she was making. Her loud voice ran happily on.

"Oh, but I did," she said. "In the lane about—when was it?—ten o'clock."

Konrad laughed. He sounded rattled.

"Not guilty, dear lady. It wasn't me."

"Oh, but it was," she insisted, glad to be in the limelight. "I passed the end of the lane. Our house is on the lower road and I was going down to the pillar box. I glanced down the lane, desperately curious to see some of you, and I caught sight of you at once. What am I doing? Dropping bricks? Don't tell me you were going *courting*, as the village says. Now look here, just to prove to you that I'm right I'll tell you what you had on. A yellow pullover and nice clean white flannels. Am I right?"

She glanced round at the rest of the room enquiringly. Her instinct had selected Konrad as an unpopular figure and she was teasing him in an innocent if misguided effort to ingratiate herself with the other men.

Konrad drew back from her as if she had stung him, and his expression became sullen. When he did not speak at all Sutane stepped in to save the silence.

"Quite right, Mrs. Geodrake. He's indicted. Tell me, what do you do with yourself down here all day?"

His quiet affable question relieved the situation, but as the visitor plunged into a tedious recital of her daily round, with an accent on its undeniable dullness, his dark eyes rested upon Konrad speculatively.

108

Eve and Sock watched him, also, and Campion was interested.

The hero of the Speedo Club retired to the hearth and took up a languid position against it. He looked profoundly uncomfortable.

Halfway through Mrs. Geodrake's recital Mrs. Pole suddenly became aware that she had lost her audience. She put down her cup, wiped her fingers on her wet handkerchief and began drawing on her skinny black kid gloves.

"We shall have the funeral from our house," she said to Linda, but in a tone clearly intended to bring the whole room to order. "I've given your husband the address and the flowers had better be sent there. It will save a lot of trouble in the long run. I quite realise there'll be a lot of publicity, but I'm prepared to put up with that. She was a very popular girl and it's only natural her friends on both sides of the footlights should want to come and pay their respects. You can trust me to see that it's all done nicely. I must be off now because I've got to call at the stationer's before seven and buy the cards. They ought to be put in the post at once. Oh, dear, oh, dear, it is a shock!"

Her feelings overcame her again and she rubbed her red eyes.

"I can't help it," she said to Linda, her voice breaking. "She was all alone in the world, you see, in spite of—well—of everything."

The thought which had only just escaped expression seemed to embarrass her and, as was evidently the habit in her family, she combatted it with a burst of vigorous self-justification.

"After all, she was an actress in her way," she said angrily. "Everyone knows actresses are different to other people. They have more temptation, for one thing. Men flatter them and give them presents and they have to be nice because it's part of their work. She was a good girl, I'm sure—at least her family always thought so, and now's the time to be charitable if ever, when the poor soul's lying dead."

This perfunctory dismissal of what had been both Chloe Pye's lifework and chief publicity plank had the ruthlessness of a pronouncement of time itself and the more sensitive of them shivered a little. Arch, inviting Chloe Pye was dead indeed. It was like the drawer closing on a last year's hat.

"I've chosen Friday because of the matinees on Saturday,"

said Mrs. Pole, rising. "I'll see her solicitor tomorrow. And Bobby, you go up and get her cases. We may as well take them along. I expect they'll give me the key of her two rooms. She was always short, poor girl. There's her jewellery, of course. You'll hear about that from the lawyer."

She laid a moist hand on Linda's arm.

"You mustn't mind me being practical, Mrs. Sutane," she said. "It's a time for practical people. That's why I'm glad, in a way, I'm here and not Dad. He'd just sit still and suffer. So would we all if we could, but those of us who've always had to do the dirty work know that's no use when there's things to be seen to. Go along, Bobby. Don't stand there gaping."

Sock took the young man out of the room and Mrs. Pole wiped her eyes again, preparatory to retiring from human ken behind her monstrous veil.

"You've all been very kind, I'll say that," she said in the tone of one conveying an unexpected compliment. "There's no hard feeling, Mr. Sutane. You couldn't have pulled up in time and if you had it wouldn't have been any use. She was dead already. The old doctor made that clear. He's a friend of yours, I suppose?"

"No, not at all. We hadn't met him before. His partner attends the servants and we have our own man in town." Linda refuted the implied accusation guiltily.

Mrs. Pole, who now looked like some monstrous black toadstool, nodded.

"He seemed a nice honest old chap," she said. "Is that Bobby down with the bags? How are we going to get to the station from here?"

"My man's waiting with the car." Sutane came forward resolutely.

She shook hands all round, very nearly speechless with an emotion which appeared to be quite genuine.

"You'll all get cards," she said from the doorway. "Give me any names and addresses you can think of. Good night and God bless you all."

Sock and her son escorted her to the waiting car. When the purr of the engine had died away down the drive Mrs. Geodrake rose to go, albeit somewhat reluctantly.

"I'm so glad to have made friends with you all at last," she said with an honesty which was unanswerable. "I hope you'll

110

all come and see us as soon as you've got over all this. So trying for you! Good-bye, Mrs. Sutane, good-bye."

She glanced brightly at Konrad, who avoided her.

"I'm sure there's a mystery about you," she said happily. "I'm sure you had some secret reason for not wanting to be seen in the lane. Say we're friends."

She held out her hand and he took it grudgingly.

Sutane laughed. To the woman who did not know him it was a natural and delightful sound, but to the others, who were familiar with his moods, it was a danger signal.

"Let's get this straight," he said. "It was pretty dark, wasn't it?"

"No, not very. He's a distinctive person, you know." Mrs. Geodrake was only too delighted to continue the discussion. "I saw him quite distinctly as I came back from the post. I was on the lower road and he was in the mouth of the lane."

Konrad stared at her, violent colour replacing his pallor.

"It wasn't me," he said thickly. "That's all I can say. You're mistaken. Some other evening perhaps."

"No, it was last night." Mrs. Geodrake was laughingly insistent. "I won't be bullied. I'm a good witness. What were you up to, you naughty person?"

Konrad began to shake a little and seemed to be about to speak. Sutane took the visitor gently by the elbow.

"Charming of you to have called on us at last," he murmured and directed her gracefully out into the hall.

With their going the room remained in silence for a moment and Konrad, with his head down, strode for the doorway. Eve stepped in front of him. She looked very young with her dark hair standing out round her face and her eyes vivid.

"What were you doing?" she demanded. "Were you creeping about watching?"

Konrad paused. The direct attack seemed to give him just the resistance necessary for him to compose himself. He laughed easily and Campion remembered suddenly that he was an actor.

"The good woman is potty, my dear," he said. "I was not in the lane last night. She saw me some other time and is trying to make herself interesting. There's no point in you getting so excited about nothing. I've got to go and change now. Don't be childish."

111

He was very convincing and she stepped aside, allowing him to pass her.

Looking back on the scene afterwards, Campion wondered whether, if she had been less precipitate then, the other deaths would have occurred.

11

Mercer's attack upon Mrs. Pole was all the more startling because of its singular unfairness and because it came from such an unexpected source.

"What a woman!" he said. "What an unmitigated, incredible, utterly loathsome piece of vulgar female muck! Didn't you want to vomit every moment she was in the room? Don't you hope the car'll crash while she's wallowing in unaccustomed luxury and she'll break her revolting and scaly neck?"

The rest of the gathering regarded him with mild astonishment, a reaction which he appeared to resent intensely. His dark-skinned face became suffused with blood and his light eyes were honest in their hatred.

"You think what you like," he said, planting his slightly unwieldy body on the arm of a chair. "But—I mean to say, did you listen to her? Did you see her?—that awful mourning! That filthy unctuous weeping, with one predatory eye on anything her blasted relation might conceivably have left! Can't you see her going over old clothes, turning out linen baskets, opening up old portmanteaus, trying on dirty half-worn rags that wouldn't fit her, grovelling under beds, searching down the sides of upholstered chairs?"

"My dear!" Linda sounded shocked. "She was all right. A bit ordinary, perhaps."

"Ordinary! My God, if I thought that I'd cut my throat." He laughed derisively and appeared for the moment to have transferred his sudden dislike to his hostess. Linda coloured.

"You're so intolerant," she complained. "She means well and, anyway, she's got to be herself."

"That's what disgusts me," said Mercer in the tone of one settling an argument finally. "I wonder if she's told the undertaker to preserve the bathing dress. Well-darned, it might suit little Evelyn—one never knows."

"Don't, please, dear! You're disgusting." Linda turned her head away. "It was very kind of her to take Chloe's things. It saves me from sending them on afterwards."

"I wonder if she's got everything. There was a handbag somewhere about."

"Yes. I saw that." Eve spoke languidly. So far she had taken no part in the discussion but had watched the scene with scornful amusement. "It was on the piano in the breakfast room."

"Was it? I'll get it." Mercer heaved himself to his feet. "There's probably the return half of her rail ticket in there. We don't want to lose that." He flung the words at them contemptuously and went into the other room, leaving everyone with the sense of personal insult all the deeper because it was so utterly undeserved.

There was an ominous silence for some little time and presently he came back with the red kerchief and Chloe's book.

"No bag," he said. "Sure she had one?"

"Of course she had one. Besides, I saw it." Eve spoke briskly. "It must be there. It's one of those fold-over things, white with a gilt snap."

They all drifted into the other room and the search began in that curious desultory fashion typical of a mass activity of which the majority does not quite approve.

Mercer alone was eager. His sudden and violent dislike of Mrs. Pole seemed to have given him an unwonted energy. He searched as a child might, looking in the most unlikely places and leaving chaos in his wake. Eve and Linda came behind him, tidying.

"It's not here." He made the announcement as if he were stating a highly suspicious and significant circumstance. "Where is it? If she had a bag it hasn't vanished into space. It hasn't burst. Where is it? Call the servants."

"It doesn't matter. It'll turn up." Linda spoke hastily. "It may even have been packed with her other things."

Mercer thrust his hands into his pockets.

113

"I think it ought to be found," he said obstinately. "That woman would suggest anything. It may even have a bob or two in it. That'd worry her. That'd give her something to squawk about. I'll ring the bell."

"Oh, please don't." Linda put out a hand involuntarily and as Sutane came swinging in, with Sock behind him, she looked at him with appeal.

"Chloe's handbag?" Sutane stood glancing about him, a certain caution in his manner suddenly becoming apparent. "Yes, that's right, Mercer, we ought to find it. Eve, look in the other room and when you've got it bring it to me."

The search began again, with Mercer leaning on the piano, irritable and impatient.

"We've been all over this room," he said bitterly. "It's been moved. Call the servants."

Sutane pressed a bell at once and when Hughes arrived questioned him brusquely. The nervous vigour of the man was astonishingly evident and Mr. Campion watched the performance with growing interest. Hughes bridled at his employer's tone and went off to find the parlourmaid responsible for the room.

The girl who came was startled but informative. The bag had been on the piano that morning and she thought she had seen it there when she had come to tidy up the newspapers during lunch. It was a white bag. She had not moved it.

With his pale face pink with indignation, Hughes reaffirmed that he had not moved it either, and condescended to make enquiries in the kitchen, although he was certain that no other servant had been into the room all day. He went off, his feathers ruffled.

"It's because it's a handbag, dear," explained Linda in response to Sutane's raised eyebrows. "It suggests money, you see. He's insulted."

"Damn fool," said Sock unhelpfully. "Well, it's gone anyway. You hang on to it when you find it, Linda. I shouldn't— shouldn't open it."

"That's all very well." Mercer was querulous. "It was on there and now it's gone. Who moved it? Has the nurse been in here, or the kid? Where is it?"

Linda gaped at them.

"You're all very excited," she said. "What does it matter? This is absurd."

114

"What's absurd, my dear lady?" Konrad came bustling in, resplendent in a dinner jacket. His cleanliness and general air of satisfaction seemed to add to Sutane's growing savagery.

"Someone's taken a handbag," he said without preamble. "A white handbag with a gilt clasp. It belonged to Chloe Pye. Have you seen it?"

Konrad smiled.

"Yes, I think so," he said. "A little suède pochette, was it? I'll get it."

He went out of the room, Mercer at his heels.

They were back almost immediately, Konrad passing the composer on the stairs as he came down again.

"This is it, isn't it?" he said brightly, turning the small scented bag over in his hands. "Has the sorrowing sister-in-law phoned for it?"

Sutane took it from him and hesitated, his fingers on the flap. Campion intercepted the glance he shot at Sock and was further enlightened.

"Where was it, Konnie?"

"Oh the table in the upper hall. I noticed it as I came down just now." The young man was nonchalant and clearly very pleased with himself.

"That's a lie. I saw him coming out of his room with it—or at least I heard him shut his door, which is the same thing." Mercer's eyes were snapping with excitement.

Konrad looked him up and down.

"You're mistaken," he said coolly. "I picked it up off the table outside my door. Why the anxiety?"

Mercer shrugged his shoulders.

"Why did you take it upstairs to your room?" he said. "I've been pretty bored with all this business so far, but now I'm beginning to be interested. I've never liked you, Konrad. You've always seemed to me to be a fishy little person. And now it's dawning on me that you're damned fishy. You were the last man to see Chloe alive. You were creeping about in the lane just before she died, and now you're hiding her handbag."

"I say, old boy"—Sock laid a hand on his arm—"you're a bit forthright, aren't you? Forget it, Konrad. The general excitement's getting the lad down."

Mercer wrenched himself away and went over to the piano, on whose polished top Sutane had shaken the contents of the

115

bag. He stood looking at the small roll of notes, the lipstick, the compendium and the black moiré cardcase. There was also a small amount of loose change and a tube of aspirin tablets.

Sutane showed him the bag was empty.

With Squire Mercer the stimulating effect of Mrs. Pole still persisted. He stood by the piano, presenting a back view to the rest of the room. His hands remained in his trouser pockets so that his jacket was runkled over his heavy buttocks and his short legs looked springy and alert. His shoulders were enormous and his untidy head on its short neck was bent a little. He seemed to be enjoying his unusual burst of energy.

Presently he opened the cardcase, which, however, yielded nothing but its legitimate contents. He turned on Konrad.

"What did you take out of here?" he demanded. "It's no good bleating at me like a tenth-rate stage parson. You've pinched something. What was it?"

Mr. Campion, who had attended many family quarrels in his time, was puzzled. Mercer was behaving in a typically irresponsible fashion, but neither Sock nor Sutane showed the least inclination to curb him. Both of them stood looking at Konrad fixedly, and Eve, too, kept her angry eyes on the young man.

Konrad was very pale and Campion, glancing at his petulant face, was suddenly aware that his eyes were venomous.

"I told you I didn't open the thing," he said, his voice squeaky with passion. "If I had it wouldn't be any affair of yours, Mercer, so keep out of this. I know how you all feel about me and I don't care, I tell you, I don't care. But I'll make you all pay for it in the end. This is a warning. I may hold my tongue for a day or two until my rally's over, but after that you can look out, all of you—and I mean that."

He remained glaring at them, a weak, spiteful, but, in the circumstances, extremely comic figure. Yet no one, Mr. Campion was interested to note, seemed in the least amused by him.

Konrad hesitated. He was beside himself with fury and, although aware that his exit line had been spoken, yet could not tear himself away from the stage.

"You've always hated me," he repeated feebly and added

with inspirational triteness, "now you're darned well going to be sorry."

He turned and went out, slamming the door behind him. Sock listened.

"Uncle Vanya has fallen downstairs," he remarked pleasantly if inaccurately. But there was no smile on his lips and his eyes were solemn.

Mercer turned back to the piano.

"Now all this muck can go to that ghastly woman," he said, laughing as he shovelled the odds and ends back in the bag again.

Sutane glanced at him and then at Sock and finally eyed Campion speculatively. The hall door slammed, a phenomenon in itself since in summer it was always kept open. Linda flushed.

"We can't let him go like this," she said. "He's a visitor here. Besides, it's so incredibly silly."

She hurried out of the room and Sutane stood looking down at the toes of his shoes and whistling idly. Presently he took two or three little dancing steps, keeping his feet within an inch or two of their original position. The occupation appeared to absorb him. Mercer watched and Sock put his arm round Eve, who did not appear to notice or resent the familiarity. Nobody spoke.

Hughes came in, still pink and very much on his dignity.

"Mr. Konrad has just gone off in his car, sir, but he appears to have left his bicycle, the silver-plated one. It's in the cloakroom."

"Who the hell cares?" said Sock briefly, while Sutane turned on the servant the full force of his personality behind the outburst.

"It doesn't matter," he said. "Don't stand there goggling. It doesn't matter. It doesn't matter in the least. Go away."

Hughes looked aghast. He opened his mouth to speak, changed his mind, and went out, closing the door softly but firmly behind him. Sutane began to whistle again. The atmosphere of the room had become oppressive. Eve threw off Sock's arm and, leaning across the piano top, began to play with the bag. With her sombre eyes and vivid, unhappy face she looked like an incarnation of the brooding spirit of the gathering.

117

"He's done that so that he can come down again and pick it up," she said thoughtfully. "Gutless little tick, isn't he?"

No one answered her, but her voice broke the spell of silence.

"I shall take Finny up to town tonight," Sutane remarked, looking up. "Henry needs guidance. Tell her to get her hat on, will you, Sock? Then I must go. What's the matter, Linda?"

The girl had come in quietly but her expression had betrayed her.

"Hughes is going," she said blankly. "He waylaid me in the hall. He seems to think that things are too difficult, and he's going tonight. He says he's ill. What did you say to him?"

"Nothing, absolutely nothing." Sutane was exasperated. "My God, these people ought to be on the stage! Still, it doesn't matter, does it? The maids can carry on."

She stood watching him helplessly and he turned to the door.

"I must go. Dinner when we come back, then. Finny's coming up with me. I may bring Dick Poyser back tonight and I want Campion and Uncle William to stay here if they will. I don't think there's anything else. I'm rather glad Hughes is going. He doesn't really suit us."

His last words were delivered over his shoulder as he went out. Linda turned away and Campion, who had developed a keen understanding where she was concerned, realised some of the sense of despair which descends upon a housewife when the mainstay of her staff deserts her in a time of upheaval. An idea occurred to him.

"I've got a man," he said. "Not a very polished soul, I'm afraid, but he'd do anything you told him and he'd tide you over the next day or so until you can get someone suitable. Shall I get him down?"

Her relief was so heartfelt that he was seized by momentary misgivings. Magersfontein Lugg was not everybody's idea of the perfect butler, and in his impulse to be of service to her Campion had not stopped to visualise that lush personality in the Sutane household. However, it was done. Linda had seized the suggestion.

"I'll go and fetch him," he said gallantly.

"Oh, no, don't you go. Jimmy said you weren't to. Can't

118

you phone him?" Her anxiety made her appeal unexpectedly vehement and he smiled at her.

"I don't think so. Lugg's a good chap, but it's a major operation to shift him. Rather like transporting an elephant. We'll be back tonight."

He hurried out of the room before she could speak again and dropped in on Uncle William, who was still napping, the empty decanter at his side.

"Keep an eye on the ladies? Certainly, my boy," he said, blinking rosily. "Must have overslept. I'm gettin' old. Terrible thought. You seem pleased with yourself." He stretched out his plump toes like a cat and hiccuped discreetly. "What d'you want me to do? Only got to command."

Campion considered. "If you have a chance, talk to Eve," he said. "Find out where she's been all her life, what she's interested in and what her ambitions are. If she cares to talk about her childhood encourage it."

"Eve, eh?" Uncle William's bright blue eyes were interested. "A sulky little miss if ever I saw one. Don't understand these new young women. Too much below the surface for my taste."

He got up.

"Don't like women who sit about brooding," he said. "Never did. Still, I'll do what I can. Anything in particular you'd like to know?"

"No. But 1920 is the crucial year."

"The child was hardly born!" Uncle William objected.

"I know. But she may be able to tell you about the family," said Mr. Campion, and as he went out to find the Lagonda he thought it very significant that the only thing that Benny Konrad should have taken from Chloe Pye's handbag, since he himself had examined it early that morning, should have been a cheap silver wrist watch with a broken strap. The watch had interested him when he had looked at it because of the inscription on the inside of the case:

C. FROM J.
ALWAYS

1920

119

12

Ex-Inspector Blest set his glass on Mr. Campion's desk and reached for a cigarette from the silver box beside it. The study in the Bottle Street flat was warm and quiet. Outside, the blue dusk was beginning to fall over the city and from Piccadilly the quiet snoring of the traffic came soothingly up to them.

The ex-inspector was a large sandy man with raw red ears and boundless good nature lurking shyly behind a defensive bluster. At the moment his pride was in the process of slow recovery.

"I don't mind working with you or even for you," he said. "I didn't care for him going over my head. That's all. He's a queer sort of chap, isn't he? I don't really like him. Too 'I'm-so-busy-get-out-of-my-light.' If he's overworked why doesn't he take a job his own size? I've got no time for blokes who are too busy to live. I was going round to see him when you phoned me. What's he done now? Run over one of his own actresses? Reading between the lines, it sounded like suicide to me. What was her trouble? Love again? Why these women keep killing themselves for love I don't know. Have you ever noticed the only men who ever kill themselves for love are farm labourers? It's a fact. You watch the newspapers. It's having such a long time to brood, I suppose. Well, here's to you."

He took up his glass again and Mr. Campion, venturing to assume their reconciliation complete, came gently to the matter in hand.

"So it was a charwoman," he began. "What variety? Pail, brush, flat cap and curlpapers, or just somebody's nice old aunt in her shopping second best?"

"The last, I'm afraid." Blest was despondent. "The kids at the messenger office remember that the flowers were brought in by an old woman. When I pressed them they said she might have been a char, but whether she had on a brown raincoat or a black artificial fur they do not know. One kid says he remembers a large safety pin showing but more he can't say. The chap at the desk can't remember anything at all. Not very helpful, is it? That's about all I've done and there's been more work in it than you'd think. I had to find the right office first."

He surveyed his feet without affection.

"Mr. Campion," he said suddenly, "I don't want you to be offended, but I've had an idea. Do you think there's a chance this fellow Sutane is having us on a string? I mean, it's not going to turn into a publicity stunt on us, is it? You're sure there is something up?"

Campion sat looking in front of him, his lean face unusually grave. In his mind's eye he saw Chloe Pye lying by the side of the lane, the dreadful irregularity of the line of her head and the tear across her breast, and he remembered her sitting on Sock's knee, her haggard face alight with a vivacity which must in youth have been so very charming.

"Oh, Lord, yes, there's something up," he said. "Don't worry about that."

"Something serious?" Blest cocked a curious eye at him and he pulled himself up guiltily.

"Sutane *is* being persecuted," he said. "There *is* a campaign going on against him. I've told you about the uninvited party. That was genuine. There are other things too. Some I don't follow at all. But from a first look round I think the cause of the trouble is fairly evident. There's a small-part man in the show called Benny Konrad. He's the fellow you want."

"Konrad? I've seen him. Really! Well, now, I shouldn't be surprised." Blest wagged his head and looked worldly. "Very likely. He's a dancer, too, of sorts, isn't he? Now you come to mention it, this is the type of thing they get up to, those little chaps. Petty. Got a mean streak in 'em. Anything to go on?"

"Not much. What I have I'll give you." Mr. Campion was speaking cautiously. "I know he's insanely jealous of Sutane. He was going to take the leading part tonight, and when he was disappointed he practically wept. Then yesterday evening he was seen down the end of the lane that leads from the house. He swore he hadn't been there with quite unnecessary vehemence. That was just after the party, you see, and

I happened to notice that just after dinner he went upstairs and came down wearing a key chain. This evening I drove out onto the lower road on my trip up here and I found what I thought I should. There's an A.A. phone box on the road about a hundred yards from the mouth of the lane. He must have sneaked out to phone, not wishing to use the one in the house. It's not much, I know, but it's a little lead. He's got an accomplice."

The ex-inspector frowned. "It could be," he agreed. "It's a foothold anyway. What's his idea? Just spite or has he got any plan?"

Mr. Campion studied his fingernails.

"I've got an unpleasant mind," he said, "but it occurs to me that if Sutane has a nervous breakdown Konrad is his under-study. If a man's overworked there's nothing like a spot of persecution to send him over the edge. This fellow may feel he's being kept under by Sutane."

"Huh!" Blest sounded pleased. "That's a help, I won't deny it," he said. "I'll get hold of the brightest kid from the bureau and take him round to have a look at this fellow's char—or not?"

"Yes, do, only be careful. Don't start the hare running. I don't think you'll find it as simple as that, either. Konrad lives in a service flat at Marble Arch."

Mr. Campion was in his most diffident mood. He had no wish to teach his grandmother to suck eggs and all but said so in as many words.

"I fancy he has a friend, you know," he went on at last. "Some earnest soul about his own age, or a little older, who burns to see the lad succeed. This is probably his handwriting."

Blest took the invitation card that Councillor Baynes had so thoughtfully preserved and his red face brightened.

"Full of ideas, aren't you?" he said appreciatively. "Got his address?"

Campion shook his head.

"No. I don't even know if he exists. But if Konrad is responsible for these little attacks on Sutane—and I think he must be, you know—then he obviously has an accomplice, if only to write these invitations."

He paused and went on consideringly.

"The man I have in mind is youngish, overinterested in Konrad's career, and a silly hysterical type generally. The city's full of them. It may take you a bit of time to find the man you want, but Konrad is a man who goes in for fans. I should look up the secretary of this Speedo Club he sponsors."

The ex-inspector rose. His enthusiasm had revived.

"That's about it," he said, tucking the card into his wallet. "I'm grateful to you, I admit it. This accomplice is taking shape before my eyes. We'll get him, although the chances are Sutane won't prosecute. These private clients never do."

He sighed for the great days of his professional career and looked about for his hat.

"If I can get a tie-up between the accomplice and the char, then between Konrad and the accomplice, we're sitting pretty," he remarked.

Campion leant across the desk. His eyes were narrowed and he seemed absorbed in the blotting paper beneath his hand. Looking at him, the ex-inspector considered privately that he looked less of an ass than he had ever seen him. There was an unusual purposefulness in his bent shoulders and in the poise of his lowered head.

"I say, Blest"—he spoke with studied casualness—"I don't know if all this stuff is sound. It's just my honest opinion at the moment and you're very welcome to it. In return I want every scrap of information you can collect about these people, however irrelevant it may seem. And as a favour to me, don't let anyone suspect you're working on them."

"Oh?" Blest's interest was revived again and he paused encouragingly. "Anything you say," he added after a moment or so. "Anything you say."

Still Campion did not confide and the detective applied a gentle pressure.

"Spotted anything big?" he enquired wistfully, something of an elderly Golden Labrador in his expression.

Campion looked up and laughed.

"Rats in the house," he said. "There's something going on there. Quite a lot I don't understand at all."

Somewhat to his surprise the ex-policeman understood him instantly.

"That's a way of putting it," he said appreciatively. "Rats in the house. Lumme, you don't half know when you've got 'em, do you? We had a flat in the city once. Lock the doors, bung up every hole with glass, and yet you couldn't even turn round without feeling something dirty that didn't like you was

123

watching the back of your neck. Rats in the house! You'll be going down again then?"

"Yes, I think so." Campion spoke soberly and Blest laid an unexpectedly fatherly hand on his shoulder.

"Take a tip from an old pro and don't feel it personally," he said. "That's always the trouble with us. We come up against nice people, people we can understand and enjoy a drink with, and then out comes the dirty linen and it gets us down if we aren't careful. Once we start thinking about right and wrong and extenuating circumstances we're sunk. Take it from me."

He drew back, a little embarrassed by his own homily.

"Hullo?" he said.

"Front-door latch. Lugg coming in."

Campion glanced across the room.

"He was out gallivanting when I arrived. He didn't expect me before the morning."

Blest chuckled. "You'll get the sack from that chap one of these days," he said. "Quite the aged family retainer now, isn't he? What does he weigh?"

"Seventeen stones and eight pounds, and proud of it. I'd recognise your little pipe anywhere, Inspector Smart," observed a sad, thick voice from the hallway. "Don't go before I hang me coat up. I'd like a look at your face again. Just to look at it."

The last words were followed by a minor disturbance which shook the walls a little, and Mr. Lugg billowed grandly into the room, his large white face wearing an unusually friendly expression.

"'Ullo," he said, eyeing his employer with truculent nonchalance. "I thought you was stayin' till Tuesday. Got yourself mixed up in a suicide now, I see. People lay theirselves open to somethink when they ask you down for a week-end, don't they? 'E's a 'arbinger of catastrophe," he added, smiling at Blest. "Take 'im to the pictures and someone's took ill behind yer."

Campion eyed him bitterly.

"He's a conscious clown," he said. "The life and soul of his pub in the mews. Well, I can rely on you then, Blest, can I?"

"You can. And thank you." The ex-inspector shook hands. "So long, Dirigible," he added, prodding the newcomer. "Don't ask me. Look it up."

He went over to the door, but Lugg was before him, his short arms stiff at the sides of his black coat.

"This way, sir, if you please," he said with dignity. "Mind the rug or you'll break your neck. Good day, sir . . . and next time you come 'ere 'ave some gloves so I can give 'em to you like a Christian. So long."

He closed the hall door and it was some little time before he returned, coatless and undoing his winged collar.

"That's better," he remarked, regarding the strip of starched linen. "That won't do again. I use one every time I go out nowadays. I was askin' my friends about laundries. Ours doesn't seem any worse than most, if that's any comfort to you."

He opened a drawer in the bureau and looked thoughtfully at its contents.

"We'll 'ave to buy some new collars," he said. "What do you feel like for supper? I'm 'aving me old tinned 'errings. Per'aps you'd better run out to your club."

Campion got up. "You pack," he said. "I've lent you."

The ponderous form in the vast black trousers and the tight white shirt remained bent over the open drawer. There was a moment of uncomprehending silence.

"Wot?" said Mr. Lugg at last.

"I've lent you. You're to be Mrs. Sutane's butler—God help her—for a day or so, until she can get another man."

Mr. Lugg straightened his back and surveyed his employer with steady dignity. His small black eyes were cold and unfriendly.

"You're barmy," he said. "I'm no butler. I'm a gent's 'elp."

"Well, then, learn a new trade." Campion took out his wallet and studied the card he had taken from it. "I'm going out now and when I come back I want my things packed for a week and yours too. Not in the same bag. Have them at the foot of the stairs and be waiting yourself. We're going down to the country tonight."

"Country?" echoed Lugg in a voice of mutiny. "Butler in the country? You're snuffing round another crime, I suppose? I wish you'd drop this private narking of yours. You're getting old for it, for one thing. It's not smart any more. It's old-fashioned and, in most people's opinion, rather low. I'm sorry to 'ave to tell yer like this but that's 'ow I see it. My friends think you're very vulgar to allow ourselves to get mixed up

125

with crime. Crime's gorn back to its proper place—the gutter—and I for one am glad of it."

He was silent for a moment or so and evidently decided on the other tack.

"I was goin' to suggest we travel, you and me," he said.

"Travel?" Campion was temporarily detracted from his own hasty preparations.

"Mr. Watson's gent is goin' on a sea trip on 'is yacht," murmured Mr. Lugg with crafty casualness. "A very refined type of person one meets, he says, and the motion of the boat is not disturbin' after the first day or so."

His employer regarded him with distaste.

"You make my flesh crawl," he said earnestly. "When you were a ticket-of-leave man——"

"'Ere—'old 'ard!" Mr. Lugg became both human and re-proachful. "Be a gent! Some things we don't bring up if we're decent. I'll do anything you ask me in reason, you know that, but I don't 'ave to be blackmailed into it. I'm glad to see you do look a bit ashamed. You had ought to."

"I was going to say that in those days I found you infinitely more attractive," said Campion, gathering up the shreds of his dignity.

"More shame on you, then." Lugg was not suppressed. "I've bettered myself, my lad, and don't you forget it. What's this noo silly idea of yours now? I'm to take a job as a butler and keep me eyes peeled, I suppose? That's not very nice in itself, is it?—getting into people's houses and nosin' about. It's a low, mean sort of trick *and* an old one. Still, I'll do it for you. I'll be obligin'. I'm to be a detective."

"You're to be a butler," said Campion coldly. "An ordinary butler. You're to do your work and to give satisfaction. And, believe me, you won't have time for anything else. Now, for heaven's sake, shut up and get on with the packing."

He moved towards the door. Mr. Lugg sat down heavily.

"It's madness," he said. "You've never seen a real butler: I 'ave. You're lakes! Where am I goin'?"

"White Walls, where I've been staying. It's a big house with a lot of people in it. The Sutanes own it. Jimmy Sutane, the dancer."

"Oh, the Sutanes..." said Mr. Lugg, and his small black eyes became crafty. "There's something chick about the stage," he added unexpectedly. "Per'aps I'll come after all. I don't

126

mind what I do so long as it's not common. Right you are, I'll pack. It'll mean wearin' a coat all day, I suppose?"

"It will. And it'll mean keeping your mouth shut." Campion's tone was final. Lugg sighed.

"All right, Cocky," he said. "I'll do you credit. Where are you orf to now?"

Campion glanced at the card in his hand.

"To call upon a lady."

"Reely?" Lugg was sarcastic. "Give 'er my love."

"I can't," said Mr. Campion. "She's dead."

Lugg guffawed. "Take 'er some flahs then, smarty," he said. "And stay out fer a bit. I've got to 'avé my meal before I pack."

13

The warm air, foetid with the vapours from the canal, came gustily down the wide road, bringing with it a cloud of stinging dust and the rustle of paper and prematurely fallen leaves on the pavement.

Through the vase-shaped pillars of the balustrade the gleam of grey-and-gold water was visible, and below, on the towpath, a horse plodded, its feet heavy on the clay.

The tall houses, their stained sides and chipped stucco hidden in the lamplit half-light, rose up with all their original Georgian symmetry, and only the brightly lighted scenes within their many uncurtained windows betrayed their descent in the social scale of an unfaithful city. It was all very quiet and homely and forgotten.

Campion found the number he sought and pressed open the elegant but unpainted gate. The hall door under the square porch with the pillars stood open and a single dusty bulb within cast a grudging light upon worn dark oilcloth and patched, buff-painted walls.

The lower windows were in darkness, but from somewhere

far above a wireless set whimpered, its programme maddeningly just out of earshot.

Campion pulled the bell and at the far end of the hall, at the foot of a short flight of stairs, a square of bright light appeared, only to vanish again immediately. He waited, and after a time the door opened once more and crisp footsteps came hurrying towards him.

The woman was not entirely unexpected, in type at any rate. She was small and brisk, her hair elaborately dressed in an old-fashioned style and her silk dress enlivened at neck and elbows with little bits of white lace. Mr. Campion took his courage in his hands and threw away his discretion.

"It's about Miss Pye," he said. "Could I have a word or two with you?"

He was lucky. He knew it the moment he had spoken. She came out to look up at him, and the light from the street lamp opposite the gate fell upon her face, showing it to be small and shrewd, with bright eyes and a turned-up nose which had been much admired in the nineties.

"Why, yes," she said, glancing behind her with a gesture of a conspirator. "Come along to my kitchen. We shan't be disturbed there."

She took his sleeve and pulled him after her, her skirts rustling as she hurried.

"There," she said as they came into a neat little room, bright in spite of its utilitarianism. "Sit down and make yourself comfortable. It's not very swanky but it's cosy and clean."

She had a pretty laugh with a catch of real gaiety in it, and her friendliness contained the whole art of the hostess.

"I don't know who you are," she said, smiling at him, "but you seem a nice boy. Did you know Chloe? Poor girl, what a finish! And she thought she was on velvet. . . . Have a drop of stout? It's all I've got in the house at the moment. . . . Nonsense! You will. Of course you will."

She bustled over to the dresser and, looking at her in the uncompromising light, he judged her to be about sixty, but alert and very pleased with herself and not, at heart, much older than she had ever been.

The panel over the shelf above the range was papered with stage photographs, and as she turned with the glasses she caught him looking at them.

"There I am, on the left," she said. "The one with the saucy little bow. Don't pretend you've heard of me, because you haven't. You were in crawlers when I was kicking my heels about. Renee Roper, that's the name. Don't worry—I never came to the West End. I did my dirty work on tour. Now what's all this about Chloe, poor girl? You were a boy friend, I suppose?"

Mr. Campion hesitated.

"Well, not exactly. I knew her very slightly, as a matter of fact. But I was interested in her and I wanted to know more about her."

"She doesn't owe you money?"

Her intelligent eyes became suddenly hard and he hastened to reassure her.

"Oh, no," he said. "Nothing like that. Frankly, I've got no business to come to you at all. But the fact is she had something I wanted to know about and——"

"Don't tell me any more." The woman leaned across the table to pat his arm. "I understand. All her things are going to those terrible relations. And you've got a wife. So if there was a letter or two from you lying around it might be very awkward. Don't go into it, my boy. You're not the first good-looking youngster who's come to me in the same sort of trouble, I can tell you. I'll take you up to her room in a moment and you can have a look round. I can't do it for a minute or two, so finish your drink. Don't you say a word to anybody, mind, because if that woman Pole got to hear of it I'd never have a moment's peace."

Mr. Campion looked embarrassed. It was hardly the story he would have thought of himself, but in view of all the circumstances it seemed cavalier to refute it.

Renee Roper mistook his silence.

"They'll be there if they're not destroyed," she said and added, a practical touch overlaying her good humour, "if I know Chloe they will be there. I won't say a word against her now she's gone, poor thing, but we weren't exactly old pals. She rented my little box room at the top of the house when she was away and usually when she was in London she took my first-floor duo. Very nice it is. Practically a bathroom as well."

"Have you known her long, Mrs.——?"

"Miss," she corrected him and sat smiling, her eyes bright.

129

"They never married me, duck," she said, and her laugh was gurgling and happy as a child's. "Oh, dear me, those were the days. Let's see, I've known Chloe on and off for ten or eleven years and I haven't known her well. She wasn't my type. She was all right, though, and you probably knew the best side of her."

Mr. Campion looked interested but unintelligent, and she surveyed him quizzically.

"Men tired of her very quickly," she said and there was a question in her tone to which he did not respond so that she went on hastily. "She had plenty of boys, I'll say that, but they saw through her after a week or two. I am a cat! I don't really mean that. Yes, I do, though. Be honest, Renee. She was spiteful and mean and a sight too possessive for my taste. I'll say it even if she is dead, poor, poor thing. Mind you," she added, refilling her glass after a sharp glance to see that her visitor was still well supplied, "while they were in love with her they'd give her the top brick off the chimney. While it lasted she was the ace all right."

Mr. Campion was leading up to a few delicate questions concerning the identity of his supposed rivals, but he was forestalled. Miss Roper was safely embarked on a flood of gossip.

Chloe Pye had favoured wealthy men friends, it seemed, especially in her latter years. Since she had mainly appeared in vaudeville she had not been thrown in close contact with her own profession and had acquired most of her admirers from what was, in Miss Roper's frank opinion, the wrong side of the footlights.

"She was proud when she was up and frantic when she was down," she summed up. "There's plenty like her and they're not all on the stage. When she had a place in the West End, and she did from time to time, she'd be as starchy as you please when she called round to fetch something from the box room, but she was very different when she first came home from abroad, broke to the wide. Before she got a shop at the Argosy she was very nervy."

She nodded to emphasise her point, and her small face, which was still cheeky in spite of her age, wore a serious confidential expression.

"That's a fact," she said.

Cautious footsteps on the linoleum-covered stairs outside caught her attention and she sprang up.

"There's that woman down at last," she announced. "Wait a moment."

She trotted out, her elaborately dressed head held high and her dress rustling consequentially.

There was much whispering outside in the hall, and presently she came back alone. She was smiling.

"They're having a time at the theatre," she said. "They've been nervy there for some time and now this looks like a real bit of bad luck. Actors are a superstitious lot. That woman was from the Argosy. She brought back a lot of Chloe Pye's things from her dressing room. Between you and me, I think the management's had a taste or two of Chloe's relations and doesn't want 'em nosing around backstage. This girl said she'd take the stuff up so I gave her the keys. That's why you had to wait."

Mr. Campion's eyes grew blank.

"From the theatre?" he enquired, relapsing for a moment into the protective inanity of his early youth. "An actress?"

Miss Roper chuckled.

"No, ducky," she said. "Not every woman employed round a theatre is an actress, by a long chalk. I don't know what this girl's job is but you can take it from me she's not an actress. A little boiled cart horse, that's what she looks like. A secretary or something, on the theatre-management side, perhaps. She told me her name—Finlay, or Finborough, or something. Well now, are you coming up to find those little billets-doux of yours?"

He followed her quick light footsteps up the stairs to the big square room which, with the little bedroom behind it, took up the whole of the first floor. It was much the kind of room he would have expected; bright with chintz and dusty hangings. It had a three-piece suite arranged round the fireplace, and over the mantel was an ill-drawn sketch of Chloe in costume, carefully framed and signed with a flourish.

The other pictures varied between the sentimentally lewd and the illustrated Scotch joke variety wherein Glengarried dogs take the place of figures. There were no books and a small writing table with drawers was the only sign of mental activity.

The landlady sniffed.

"Soon gets musty, doesn't it?" she said cheerfully. "Like to open a window for me?"

While he did so she went over to the desk.

"Hullo!" she said. "You're not the first, my boy. The girl from the theatre had done a bit of looking round, too. See, the drawers aren't quite closed and someone's been through them pretty quickly."

She displayed the tousled contents of the top drawer with growing amusement.

"They were all tidy when I brought her laundry up this afternoon," she said, "and I happen to know because I took a peep. I don't mind telling you I was looking to see if there was any loose cash about. She owed me a week or so and I thought I'd like to be sure it was there before me and that sister-in-law of hers came to high words. There wasn't a halfpenny, of course. Not that I'd have taken it. At least I don't think I would. Certainly not more than I was owed. Although God knows I've given her plenty in her time. Here, I wonder if she's been up in the box room, too? I gave her the key. Come on."

The visitor had been in the box room. After careful consideration of the two tin trunks of old letters, programmes and picture postcards which were up there, Miss Roper pronounced her opinion that the woman had gone through them with a "quick tooth comb."

"What d'you know about that?" she said, her eyes widening and a mischievous smile hovering at the corners of her lips. "Some people have got a nerve, haven't they? I wonder what she was after, the cat.... Doing a kindness for one of the fellows in the company, I'll bet!"

She chuckled hugely.

"You're not the only one, ducky. There's dozens of you! Well, now, what about these letters of yours? That Pole woman will go all through this lot. It'll broaden her mind for her perhaps."

The notion seemed to delight her, and Campion, who realised that his work had already been done for him by Miss Finbrough, sought about for some plausible way out of the situation.

"I don't think I need bother," he said. "My—er—what I was looking for evidently isn't here."

132

Her quick eyes took in his expression and once more she gave her own explanation to his words.

"Oh, you were a *real* writer, were you?" she said. "I know . . . great piles of stuff all on the same sort of writing pad. Reams and reams of it! I know. That's the kind that gets destroyed, my boy. No girl wants to take round a pantechnicon. You needn't have worried. It's the little dangerous half sheets that get kept. Who's going to wade through a life story every time they want cheering up? Well, now that your mind's at rest, come on. Let's go down."

As they descended through the great shadowy house, whose elegance was departed forever, she went on to talk about the accident.

"One of the Brock brothers, on my second floor, said it sounded like suicide to him from the papers," she remarked. "The jury didn't have enough to go on, or something. But if there's one thing I am sure of, it wasn't that. Chloe never killed herself. She was far too conceited, if you know what I mean. Besides, I ask you! There she was safe in a nice long run, starred and everything. She had never done so well for herself——never! If you ask me, she had a nice fat pull with that management, because she was going off. That's got to be faced. She wasn't the nice little girl you knew, you know. She was forty-two to my certain knowledge. It didn't sound to you like suicide, did it?"

"It wasn't," he assured her absently. "I was down there at the time."

"Really?" She pounced on the admission. "You saw the accident? Well, that is a mercy. You're just the boy I want. I wonder if I could ask you to have a few words with one of my lodgers? It'd be a Christian act and help me a lot. I'm worried out of my mind about him. A word from someone who actually *saw* it might make all the difference."

Mr. Campion hesitated, but to refuse her would have been more than churlish. She dragged him into the kitchen again.

"You sit down and have a drink and I'll fetch him," she said, forcing him into a chair. "He's only a boy, just down from college. Oxford or Cambridge—I forget which. And of course he's writing a play and renting my attic. I think he's got a little money but he says he gets the right atmosphere here, and so I do what I can for him. It's probably a dreadful play. You can tell it's old-fashioned by the mere fact that he

133

wants to write it in an attic. I tell him that, but you know what these college kids are—I don't know what they teach 'em at those places; they just seem to keep 'em a steady thirty years behind the times, as far as I can see—but I want you to talk to him because Chloe got at him. I won't say what I think of her for doing it. She was old enough to be his auntie. He thinks she was I don't know what, and this has bowled him clean over, poor kid. He won't eat and he can't sleep. He's half enjoying it, mind you, but it's not good for him. He's got it into his head that she committed suicide and he's to blame."

She laughed but her face softened.

"Aren't they wonderful at that age? If you told him he was too sure of himself by half he'd either not believe you or cut his throat. Just see him and tell him it was an ordinary accident. Be a dear—to please me."

She went out before he could protest, even had he wished to do so, but put her head round the door again to whisper an admonition.

"Don't laugh at him. He's very unhappy. He's only been in love once before and she was a girl in a shop who reminded him of the Dame sans Mercy. From what he's told me, she was more like Ophelia. Anaemic, anyway."

She disappeared again and was gone for some considerable time. Campion stood by the kitchen table and thought about Miss Finbrough and the one person in the world for whom she would have come on so questionable an errand. He wondered what she had found in her brief search.

Miss Roper's returning footsteps recalled him to the matter in hand. The door opened and she came hurrying in, her face pink and motherly.

"Here's Mr. Peter Brome to see you," she said briskly. "I know you'll like to have a chat."

Campion glanced over her head at the young man who came so unwillingly into the brightly lit room. He was very young and very handsome in the downy, small-boy fashion of his kind. At the moment his face was unnaturally grave and he conveyed the impression that he was holding himself with particular care, as if his grief was some great overfull pitcher which he was carrying and which any jolt must spill. It gave him a curious clumsy and unsteady air, embarrassing both to himself and to those about him. He wore an old tweed sports

134

jacket which hung limply on wide flat shoulders, and the highly polished pipe which he gripped, as though it were both his mainstay and his passport, was unfilled.

He towered over Miss Roper, who was clearly delighted with him, and addressed Mr. Campion in a naturally deep voice which an effort towards maturity had rendered positively sepulchral.

"How do you do?" he said. "I don't know your name." The baldness of the statement seemed to worry him and he added, "Not that it matters," and blushed violently at the ungraciousness of his own words.

In view of the delicacy of his mission Mr. Campion gave his second-best name and they shook hands solemnly. There fraternisation came to an abrupt stop. Peter Brome moved stiffly and purposefully across the kitchen until he came to the wall, where he turned round and took up a position too nonchalant to be real and barely safely balanced.

Miss Roper looked at Campion appealingly.

"Tell him about the accident," she commanded. "He wants to know."

"No. No, please!" Peter Brome's gesture was unwieldy but emphatic, and his deep voice was quite expressionless. He looked desperately uncomfortable and Mr. Campion felt very old.

"Come out and have a drink," he suggested.

Mr. Brome's embarrassment increased beyond dignity's endurance point.

"You ought to have a drink with me," he said and his grave and unhappy eyes met Campion's own.

"My dear fellow, let's have several drinks," persisted Mr. Campion, resenting the one-foot-in-the-grave sensation which was stealing over him.

"You'd better not hang about or they'll be shut," put in Miss Roper with practical cheerfulness. "Off you go. If I don't see you again then, my boy, good-bye and good luck. I'm pleased to have met you. Not a word to Mrs. You-Know-Who and you can trust little Renee. Good-bye, my dears. Don't fall in the canal coming home."

She bundled them out into the soft warm night and waved to them as they reached the gate.

Mr. Campion and his hatless companion walked down the paper-strewn pavement, the wind behind them.

135

Peter Brome shook back his locks, which were more untidy than strictly Byronic, and looked up at the sky, tattered by the dark irregularities of the housetops. Campion wondered uncharitably if he knew the lamplight was shining on his magnificent profile and decided in all honesty that probably he did not.

"Quite a dear old thing," remarked the young man abruptly, "but frightfully embarrassing. Some sort of frustrated mother complex."

Campion, who thought for a moment that he was talking about Chloe Pye, was saved from an impossible *gaffe* by his companion's next remark.

"She insisted that I come down to see you. I feel I'm imposing on you frightfully, but when—when a thing happens that's utterly senseless and ghastly one's natural morbid inquisitiveness wants to know how, even if—if the reason why is simply incomprehensible, don't you think?"

The long speech had unsettled him and the pitcher was rocking dangerously. Mr. Campion spoke hastily.

"It really was an accident," he said.

"I wish I could believe that." Peter Brome implied his polite rejection of the theory. "I don't know why I'm talking to you about it. I don't mean to be rude, of course. But if you'd known her as I did. God, the dreadful unreasonableness of it! The appalling unbearable *waste*! She was a wonderful person."

His voice wavered and was silent, and the face he lifted to the London stars was angry and, in its extraordinary beauty, rather terrible.

With the weight of his thirty-six years heavy on his shoulders, Mr. Campion reflected that high tragedy was a right thing and man could justly exult in it, but low tragedy, with its horrible undercurrent of derisive laughter, was deadly stuff indeed.

His desire to kick his companion was tempered by the suspicion that the impulse had its root in envy.

They reached the Spiked Lion, a rather regrettable little hostelry of the refined back-street variety, in silence.

As Peter Brome struggled with the etiquette of drink-buying for a perfect stranger to whom one is in imminent danger of unburdening one's soul, his solemnity returned and he stuck rigidly to his somewhat bigoted idea of small talk, firing abrupt and disconnected questions at his acquaintance and being careful not to betray from his expression that he had understood any word of the replies.

The other drinkers at the bar were known to each other and were inclined to resent the intrusion of strangers, so Campion's visit was not prolonged. They drank their two modest half pints each and, honour and hospitality both being satisfied, came out into the night again.

Feeling that he might now decently return to his own troubles, Mr. Campion was about to take his leave when he was disarmed.

"I'd like to talk to you about her," said Peter Brome. "Half my life has suddenly gone, you see. I didn't know her people and I shall never see or hear of her again. It really is like a door shutting."

It dawned upon Mr. Campion just in time that a clear and vivid word picture of Chloe Pye as she had really been would not help Mr. Brome in his present loneliness. Campion suppressed it, therefore.

"I'd like to walk down to the canal, if you don't mind. There's a bridge there. We can look over it."

Peter Brome stated his desire meekly but with a childlike confidence that it would be gratified, and they walked on over the dry, deserted pavements to the shining and mildly odorous water.

"I suppose if I told you that I'd like to chuck myself in there you'd think I was a fool?" said Mr. Brome, not altogether unexpectedly as they took up their positions against the greasy stucco balustrade and looked down at the froth and leaves in the sluggish stream.

"My dear chap, you'd die of diphtheria, not drowning," said Campion involuntarily, and his companion broke out into sudden happy laughter.

"I am a fool," he said despondently, his amusement vanishing as soon as it had come. "God, I ought to be shot!—clowning and posturing about when she's gone. 'Chloe's a Nymph in flowery groves, A Nereid in the streams.' That's D'Urfey. But the Cartwright one is the best. She was a year or two older than me, you know.

> "'Chloe, why wish you that your years
> Would backward run, till they meet mine?

137

That perfect likeness, which endears
Things unto things, might us combine? . . .
So, by this, I as well may be
Too old for you as you for me.'

I was tremendously pleased when I found it. I thought it was
a sort of omen. And now . . ."

He braced himself against the stucco and stretched, as if
the vigorous physical effort relieved him of some of his
intolerable burden of sorrow.

"Was—was she frightfully cut about?" he demanded gruffly
and settled himself with a grim stoicism, all the more difficult
because it was conscious and he disliked himself for it, to
hear the worst.

Mr. Campion felt out of his depth. He was shocked to
discover that he could not remember if a horror was better
balm than an anticlimax. He compromised, as many have
done before him, by giving a faithful but not highly coloured
account of the whole tragedy.

Peter Brome listened in silence, his face very white and
young in the lamplight.

"Thank you," he said at last. "Thank you. You've practically
convinced me. I was so afraid it was suicide, you see."

"Why? She was very happy at the theatre."

"Oh, yes, at the theatre." Peter Brome's tone expressed his
contempt for those material matters which are such an anxiety and yet such a comfort to those who grow wearied of their
own emotions. "It was her life that was so difficult. We were
in love." He met the other man's eyes squarely, as though
defying him to show any amusement.

Mr. Campion was grave, however. He was not too old to
know that love in any of its tricksy forms was not negligible.

"I wanted her to marry me," Peter Brome continued with
dignity, "but she always said no, putting up all kinds of
ridiculous suggestions—the little difference in age and that
sort of thing."

"How old are you?" enquired Campion helplessly.

"Twenty-two. Quite old enough to know my own mind,
God knows. Well, when these objections of hers went on I
began to realise that there was something else she hadn't told
me, because she did love me. Otherwise she wouldn't— oh,
well, I know she did. We were going on the river last Sunday.

138

We'd fixed it up and were both looking forward to it rather seriously. So when she told me she'd got to go away for the week-end I was pretty fed up and we had our first serious quarrel."

He paused and his eyes were anguished as the enormity of his tragedy overcame him. He pulled himself up and went on.

"Well, it seemed to upset her as much as it did me. We made friends again and it all came out. She was married, you see, and the fellow had found her again after they'd parted for some years and naturally he'd found out his mistake and wanted her back. She was going down to see him to try to make him give her a divorce. She wouldn't tell me his name. I swore I'd never mention it to a soul but it doesn't matter now. She was brokenhearted and so was I. The next thing I heard this had happened."

Campion did not speak.

He stood with his hands on the balustrade, his shoulders a little bent.

Seen through sophisticated eyes, Chloe's story took on a very different flavour from the straight tale of young love in difficulties which he had just heard. As he stood looking at the water a company of little circumstances ranged themselves in his mind and slipped quietly into a neat pattern.

Sutane making a place for Chloe in the show in spite of all opposition; Sutane sitting in the dark stalls, ordering Chloe not to accept his wife's invitation; Sutane insisting to the doctor that Chloe was a stranger to him; Chloe sitting on Sock's knee, referring to Sutane as an old friend; the little watch with its inscription; and finally, providing the key to the whole, Miss Finbrough searching through the dead Chloe's papers with reckless haste.

His pale eyes grew hard behind his spectacles, and he was barely aware of Peter Brome's deep young voice sounding earnestly at his side.

"You probably disapprove of divorce. Forgive me, but you've forgotten what love's like. It's tremendous. It's the only thing that matters. You're helpless. It's quite unreasonable. There's so absolutely nothing you can do. It suffocates you."

Mr. Campion, who had been growing rapidly more human in the past few days, experienced a desire to fly screaming from this awful ghost of dead summers who murmured such emotional truth and intellectual fallacy so unjustly in his ear. One cry of protest alone escaped him.

"You haven't a monopoly on tragedy, you know," he said, but unconsciously he made his tone light and friendly, "not you twenty-two-year-olds."

Peter Brome was misled by the gentleness, which he mistook for toleration.

"No, but we're new to it," he said. "It can't be worse. If it were, people would be dying from it every day. Nothing can be worse than this. It's inconceivable. Why, it's so frightful it almost goes the whole circle. It's a horrible thing to say, but it's nearly—nearly rather *fine*, it's so exquisitely hurtful."

Mr. Campion thought of Linda, of Sarah, of Chloe as the daylight saw her, of Sutane, and lastly of himself. He took Mr. Brome's hand and shook it warmly.

"Good-bye," he said abruptly. "She died very quickly and without any pain at all. It *is* rather fine when you think of it. Good-bye."

He hurried away, his long thin shadow jolting and flapping down the lamplit road.

Mr. Brome remained on his bridge with his tragedy, which was as sad and lovely and remote as the stars above his tousled head.

14

On the following morning Mr. Campion sat long over his breakfast, his thin body practically submerged in the plush billows of a crimson settle. At that hour the club dining room was hushed with that particular variety of breathy peace sacred to the sober business of facing the world again.

The heavy curtains, corded and swathed with Victorian generosity round the vast windows, seemed to resent the strong sunlight which burnished their fringes and strove to disclose the intimacies of their weave, so that the great room was made misty by the little war between light and shadow.

The warmth, the comfort and the general air of friendly privacy soothed Campion and made him feel sensible and secure in mind. From his present sanctuary the events and emotions of the previous evening seemed to have had a dreamlike quality, but without the happy illogicality which makes most dreams so pleasant in retrospect.

Peter Brome had led him into Pirandello's world and today only the common facts remained, and these were as important and as unpleasant from one angle as another.

On reflection he was glad that he had telephoned to Linda excusing himself and had sent the protesting Lugg to White Walls alone. "Young George," the garage mechanic who sometimes obliged him by driving the car, had superintended the transportation and had delivered his report upon it, recording that the lady herself had come to the front door to receive her temporary butler and that Mr. Lugg had been the perfect gent throughout. Young George was of the opinion that Lugg would be okay if he kept it up. Campion devoutly hoped he might. As he sat looking over his paper at the dust particles in the beam of light from the nearest window he went over every detail of his conversation with Linda. He remembered it with surprising clarity. He heard again her quick, disappointed protest and his own apology and hasty insistence that there was work on the case to do in town. He remembered the pause which had followed it and afterwards her polite but unconvinced acceptance and her genuine gratitude for Lugg.

He had rehearsed the whole incident from the first sound of her voice to his own final good-bye before he checked himself and stared blankly and unhappily before him. He had no doubt that his bittersweet preoccupation with her would wear off in a little while, but now the unreasonableness, the thundering idiocy, of the whole phenomenon still exasperated him.

For the first time the pity of it occurred to him; the sudden realisation left him startled and angry. In common with most other unembittered mortals, he cherished a secret belief that the mental, emotional and physical female equivalent of himself did somewhere exist, so that to discover it and find it unattainable was an elementary form of tragedy none the less

141

painful because it was a hackneyed tale. Moreover, he was also faced by the disturbing reflection that the chance of any such miracle occurring twice in the lifetime of a man of his own peculiar and lonely temperament was remote.

The situation shocked him, and he found himself resenting it bitterly. Since he was not of an age to enjoy it, the prospect of becoming involved in a bona fide tragedy revolted him and he took temporary refuge behind a time-honoured shield and denied the existence of the attraction.

He looked down at the newspaper and read the report on the inquest of Chloe Pye, which was recorded in full. Since no publicity given to the dead woman could now conceivably be considered advantageous to her, the journalistic conscience had found itself soothed, and this and a dearth of other news had combined to make a double column of the story in the cheaper press. Optimism had made Sutane careless. It had been an open verdict, not "misadventure" as he had said. The jury had returned "death from shock, accelerated by a state of *status lymphaticus*" but had also recorded that there was no evidence to show if the dead woman had fallen from the bridge by accident or design. Sutane's part in the car accident immediately after Miss Pye's death had been very fully reported by the newspapers and there were several references to his recent ill luck in the gossip columns. It was not a satisfactory story and one which left an unpleasant impression on the mind. The fact that Chloe had been in a bathing dress at the time of her death was mentioned every-where, but without explanation, and the whole history of fast cars, house parties and hinted suicide suggested wild doings which money and prestige had hushed up. The whole thing was most unfortunate. The public, who hero-worshipped Sutane, had no objection to him enjoying himself but could only be expected to resent any hint that he was relying on their hero-worship to get away with something which would spell disaster to any private member of that public itself.

Campion set down the paper and forced himself to look at his own problem coldly and to consider the miserable discovery which had led to his decision to disappear unobtrusively from the affair and from the society of the Sutanes.

Regarded dispassionately, it resolved itself to a simple enough question. If you are violently and unreasonably attracted to a married woman, to discover immediately afterwards that to the best of your belief her husband has killed, either by accident or design, a previous wife, in order, presumably, to retain his present ménage intact, do you involve yourself further in the situation, denouncing him for his crime and walking off with the lady?

"No, you don't," said Campion aloud, and with such a wealth of feeling that the club servant who had approached him on silent feet stepped back in astonishment.

The message proved to be a summons from Ex-Inspector Blest, who had called at the flat in the hope of catching Campion before he started for the country and had been redirected by a caretaker to the Junior Greys. Campion went to the telephone unwillingly, but Blest was in a tenacious mood and would have none of his excuses.

"What on earth are you playing at?" he demanded, his tone aggrieved and suspicious. "Why the high and mighty all of a sudden? Stubbed your toe on your own dignity? I want you, Mr. Campion. I want you to take sights. I'd like your opinion, I would really. It was your idea in a way. Listen . . . I've found him."

"The accomplice?" Campion betrayed an unwilling interest.

"I don't know yet. One thing at a time." Blest was irritated. "I've found the secretary of the bike club. His name is Howard, and he works in a wholesale chemist's in the Hampstead Road. I met him last night. He'll be at the Three Eagles in the Euston Road about twelve. I'll get him going and you drop in casually about half past. I want you to look at him. What's the matter with you? On to something else?"

Campion, who was finding himself unduly jumpy, disliked the quick curiosity in the last question and capitulated.

"Half after noon, then," Blest repeated. "Don't put on your best clothes, you know. It's not exactly a palace. So long. I'm relying on you."

He rang off, and at twelve twenty-five Campion descended from a bus in the Tottenham Court Road and walked down towards Euston.

The young man deep in conversation with Blest in a corner of the Three Eagles was disappointing. Considered as an accomplice of the elegant Konrad, he was unlikely to the point of being absurd. He was a large, carelessly dressed person with a very clean neck and collar and very dirty fingernails. His face was raw from exposure to the wind and

143

conveyed somehow that it was cast from an inferior design on which no time or thought had been expended, while the fact that his head was almost shaved to the crown, where a limp, greasy layer of thick hair lay like a roof, did not improve his appearance.

He had a loud, aggressive voice with considerable force of character behind it, and at the moment he was riding his hobbyhorse hard.

"It's the game, that's what matters to me," he was saying, conscious of the virtue in the statement but none the less sincere for all that. "It's all honorary with me, you know. I don't take a penny of the club funds, and wouldn't, not if they asked me. It's the road I like. You see things awheel. Get to know the country you was born in. You come into your rightful heritage, that's what I say. Besides, it's so cheap! A chap like me can afford it."

"I agree with you," said Blest heartily and, catching sight of Campion, introduced him as a Mr. Jenkyn. "Haven't seen you about lately," he added mendaciously. "Mr. Howard here is secretary of the Speedo Club—cycling. Heard of it?"

Mr. Howard paused to remark on his pleasure at meeting Mr. Jenkyn and hurried on with his confidences to Blest.

"Even the name's amateurish," he went on, taking up his harangue at the point where he had left it. "See what I mean? Speedo. . . . It's a slang word, isn't it? To my mind that strikes the note of the whole outfit—not quite the article. If we was a proper club we could affiliate ourselves to one of the big outfits, and there's benefits in that. Records and championships and that sort of thing, with decent prizes to compensate you for your trouble. As I was saying to some of the chaps last Saturday, what are we now? What *are* we? A blasted publicity organisation for a chap who isn't a real enthusiast. If he was a real wheel lover it would be different. If he was keen on the game any one of us would be pleased and proud to do him a bit of good. But when he comes down by train and gets tired out by a thirty-five-mile spin, then you're apt to ask yourself, aren't you?"

"You certainly are," agreed the ex-inspector. "You'd like to change things a bit, I daresay?"

Mr. Howard drank deeply from his tankard and his small green eyes narrowed.

"I could resign, myself, and join one of the big clubs," he

144

said, "but then I shouldn't be a secretary—not for years, anyway—and I like organising. It satisfies you if you've got it in you. Besides, if you can see the way to work really difficult things like runs and club dinners and sight-seeing tours and you haven't got the authority, it gets on your nerves to see someone else doing it badly."

He spoke feelingly, and Blest nodded his complete agreement. Stimulated by a second pint Mr. Howard spoke again.

"If we called ourselves by a proper name—the Merton Road C.C. or something like that—and got rid of our stage associations we could be one of the finest, smartest little clubs in London," he said with sad conviction. "As it is, what happens? Where are we going? Our real tiptop liners are leaving us for clubs with more scope, while a handful of older members who like to get round the stage door run this bloke's publicity stunts for him. They get free passes for the show—we all do, I admit that—but I'm not a cyclist. I like fresh air and the road under me."

He paused and refused the cigarette Campion offered him, explaining that smoking was bad for his wind.

"They've given him a presentation machine," he said in a burst of confidence which he obviously considered indiscreet but was unable to control. "Silver-plated and all slap up. I did the collecting because I was asked to and I'm good at collecting. I've got a gift. I like it. But I don't approve of it. I think a silver-plated bike is silly. I think if the other clubs get to hear of it they'll laugh at us—and rightly so. That's the kind of thing that irks you. If you're a first-class man awheel, well up to any amateur standard, you don't want to feel that every other user of the road privately feels that your club is nothing but a pack of pansies on bicycles. It's degrading— degradating. I'll get my own way in the end but it's taking time. There's a lot of snobbery to fight. There's a posh flavour about anything connected with the stage, and some of the silly beggars fall for it. I'm very nice to Konrad when I see him though I don't like him personally. In the finish he'll drop out of sight and we'll get on with making a first-class job of the club."

At this point Mr. Campion bought another round and the conversation became general. Mr. Howard was consumed by his enthusiasm for his chosen sport, however, and returned to it almost at once.

"He's useful in a way, of course," he admitted. "He's got influence. An article like this, now, needed writing, you know. It was time it was said."

He pulled a folded evening paper from his coat pocket. It was the first of the fuller editions and contained a short topical article on the magazine page with the heading: "Murder on the Roads. A Cyclist's View. By Benny Konrad, President of the Speedo Cycle Club."

Blest skimmed through it, with Campion reading over his shoulder. It was a bright little essay written with deliberate intolerance and printed to provoke correspondence. Cyclists were briefly mentioned, but the danger of the speeding motorist was the main argument.

"It's come at a good moment," said Mr. Howard, replacing the paper in his pocket. "There's thousands of us chaps on the road, every one of us with our lives in our hands. These motorists just kill us. They can't see us half the time. This article could have been much stronger, but I don't suppose the editor would stand for it. He's got to think of his advertisers. Still, it's come after that business in the paper yesterday where Jimmy Sutane ran down some poor girl and killed her. Did you see the bit? Konrad is in the same show as Sutane and their names are linked together. I expect that's why he wrote this and the paper, noticing the connection, printed it. That's how they work these things. Anything topical. That's the motto of the newspapers."

They finished their beer and went out into the sunlight, where they parted from Mr. Howard. Blest glanced after his jaunty figure and sniffed.

"Well, that's not *him*," he said, "is it?"

Mr. Campion agreed. "No," he said thoughtfully. "No, that's not the accomplice. A trying lad in his own way, no doubt, but not a dirty little tick. There's nothing underhand about our Mr. Howard. Konrad doesn't seem to be too popular with him, does he?"

The ex-inspector grunted.

"If you ask me, young Mr. Konrad won't be too popular in other quarters this afternoon," he said. "He's employed by Mr. Sutane, isn't he? What the hell does he think he's playing at, coming out with an article like that? He couldn't have written it in the time, of course. That's something they've had by them. But he must have authorised the use of his

146

name. They probably read it to him over the telephone."

Campion frowned. "I don't think there's much in that," he said with more hope than conviction. "After all, there's very little actual connection . . ."

"Don't you believe it!" Blest interrupted him. "That's an example of the association of ideas. There's whole campaigns of advertising run on that principle. You know and I know that Sutane has done nothing reprehensible and there's no mention of his name in that article. But who reads a newspaper accurately?—one in a hundred. The average half-interested person sees one day that Sutane has been in an accident in which a woman has been killed, and the next day he sees 'Murder on the Road' by Benny Konrad. The name 'Konrad' makes him think of the name 'Sutane' and the last thing he heard in connection with it. The two ideas are put together in his own mind. It's child's play. I had it all explained to me once."

"He'd hardly dare do it deliberately," said Campion slowly.

"Maybe not." Blest was vigorous. "But whatever it was, it wasn't tactful. If you ask me, Master Konrad is shouting for trouble and I shouldn't be at all surprised if he got it."

Campion looked at him aghast, a certain little chain of incidents returning to his mind.

"Oh, no," he said vehemently. "No."

Blest cocked an eye at him.

"You've got something up your sleeve," he said. "I've noticed it all the morning. But don't trouble to tell me. I shall know sooner or later. This is only the beginning of this business. I can feel it in my bones."

Mr. Campion sighed and his lean face looked suddenly drawn.

"You're wrong," he said but added heavily after a pause, "or at least I hope to God you are."

My dear Campion——[Uncle William's cramped hand fluttered crazily over the page.]

Since your rather extraordinary desertion I have stuck to my post, gathering up such odd scraps of information as have come my way. I have no doubt that you know what you are up to and have some very good reason for going off in this remarkable manner. I shall be glad to hear it when we meet in the near future. Let me say now that I have absolute faith in you, as I have always had, and I am perfectly sure that you are well equipped to bring to a satisfactory solution all the little difficulties with which we now find ourselves beset.

This house is not a very happy harbour at the moment, I am afraid. Konrad's bicycle is still in the cloakroom, I noticed this morning, so I suppose we still have a visit from him hanging over our heads. This depresses Linda, I fancy, for she seems a little less her usual laughing self.

Eve is a curious girl. I used at one time to have a light sure hand with a woman, but I confess I can make but little of her. She has some secret; I am sure of it. Such long hours alone, brooding, are not natural in a girl of her age. In 1920 (you will remember you asked me to enquire particularly into that date) she was one year old and lived with her dear mother in Poole, while Jimmy was away on the Continent. Afterwards she was sent to a convent school in the West Country, her mother dying when she was eight. From that time the good nuns looked after her until two years ago, when her brother conceded to her request that she might attend an art school in London. She has finished there and now there is some talk of her continuing her studies in Paris. From what I remember of that city it seems hardly the place to send a young girl to alone, but I have no doubt it is greatly changed. The war

148

saddened but purified. A pity if true in the case of Paris, but there you are.

To return to the girl. Her lassitude puzzles me. At seventeen one should be up and doing, straining at the leash, the blood boiling in the veins, but she is not really anxious to continue her art work and speaks of it without great enthusiasm. I shall hammer away at her, gently of course, but at the moment she remains an enigma.

Jimmy returns here each day and is growing rapidly more and more distraught before my eyes. Sometimes I feel it is only his work and his indomitable courage which keep him going at all. Young Petrie flits in and out in a newer car, his own having gone to perdition long past its time, and Richard Poyser, a type I cannot bring myself wholly to trust, has visited us once. He was here to lunch and seemed very excited over a foolish article which some wretched newspaper fellow persuaded young Konrad to set his name to. I read it and confess I saw nothing to it, but both Poyser and Jimmy seemed to think it unfortunate. Of course, one is apt to forget that Art is a hard taskmaster and when a man like Jimmy is suffering from overstrain "how easy is a bush supposed a bear," as my immortal namesake says.

Squire Mercer, with typical callousness and what I think I may allow myself to call damned selfishness, has flown to Paris to attend some function but is expected to return before the end of the week, if not in time for the funeral.

The only happy people here are the child and your man Lugg. He is shaping as well as can be expected and appears to have become devoted to little Sarah, whom he insists upon calling "the young mistress," an appellation which seems to afford them both great pleasure. I fancy I detect a note of derision in it at times, but she seems to have grown very fond of him in this short time, which speaks well for the kindness of his heart, a virtue which, in my opinion, must much more than outweigh any other shortcomings.

In spite of the noise they make between them as they practise opening doors to visitors, answering bells and so on, I think that Linda is very glad of him. He certainly provides a touch of gaiety in an otherwise sad, unhappy house.

I hope to see you at the funeral of Chloe Pye. (What a trial to others that woman must have been in her life, and now in death she retains the same character. De mortuis!)

I shall come to Town with Jimmy. The relative, who seems a very ordinary sort of person (I think you met her), has shown an almost morbid anxiety to have everyone connected with the woman's death and her work represented at her funeral. Jimmy is naturally anxious to give no offence and I understand that he and all the male principals in My Show, as well as those of us present at the house party, will follow the coffin to its last resting place. I am particularly anxious that you should do your duty and appear. The arrangement is that we shall follow the hearse to the cemetery and afterwards return to the house for a few minutes. I did protest at the latter suggestion, which seems unnecessary, for it is not, thank God, as though we were near relatives, but the good Mrs. Pole seems adamant and Jimmy is bent on humouring her, a very wise move taken by and large. I hope to see you, therefore, at 101 Portalington Road, tomorrow, Friday, at five minutes to two o'clock. Do not disappoint us. I have sung your praises so loudly to Jimmy that I feel I have a personal responsibility.

With kind regards, my dear boy,

Believe me, ever yours,
WILLIAM R. FARADAY.

P.S. Have just opened this letter again after a turn round the garden, during which I made a somewhat strange discovery. I fear it may lead to nothing more interesting than some pretty yokel idyll, but I report it for what it is worth. Deviating from my usual route round the flower beds and the lake I took a path through the plantation. There are some very fine trees here and the sight of them reminded me of my boyhood's bird's-nesting days. Although a little late in the season, I determined to try my luck and see if my eye had lost its cunning. Rather foolish you will think, no doubt, but it was lucky in a way that the notion came to me, for I soon discovered a this-year's mavis nest just within reach of my hand in the crutch of a young elm. I put my fingers in and drew out a screw of paper, of all things! It was a sheet of plain white note and the words upon it were scrawled in pencil in a hand so hurried I could not hope to recognise it instantly even had it been known to me, which I do not think it was. I copied out the message in my notebook and I now send you the page for what it is worth. I left the note where it

150

was, not liking to take it, but I have the calligraphy pretty well photographed in my mind and you can rely on me to look out for it.

W.F

The enclosure consisted of the memorandum leaf from a pocket diary, and the message, written in Uncle William's flurried pencil, was brief but quite remarkably to the point. On the back of the page he had scribbled an explanatory note: *Found Thursday, mid-afternoon, in bird's nest in crutch of tree, quarter of a mile inside the White Walls boundary (rough estimate).*

The message consisted of a single line, poignant even in that shaking stylised hand.

I love you. I love you. Oh, I love you.

16

The small room with the bay window and the clean hard stuffed furniture was heavy with the smell of flowers. The sweet cloying scent hung over the whole house, half hiding those other smells—cooking from the kitchen, camphor, floor stain, and the miserable, mean odour of damp handkerchiefs. Petals lay on the imitation parquet in the dining room, on the imitation Chinese carpet in the parlour, and on the imitation Persian runner in the hall. They lay, too, on the narrow staircase down whose sleek red steps the elaborate casket with the silver-plated handles had come swaying dangerously less than an hour before.

It was over. Chloe Pye had gone. The hideous yellow earth in the cemetery had opened and taken her in. The crowd, attracted by her name, her profession, the manner of her dying and the eminence of her mourners, had gone shuffling off again, stumbling over unnamed graves or pausing idly to read the inscriptions on the more ostentatious headstones.

Campion stood in a corner of the parlour fireplace, bending his head a little to one side to avoid the shaded tassel of a hanging candleholder. The room was packed to bursting point, as were the other two downstairs rooms, but there was no murmur of conversation to alleviate the sense of physical discomfort, and the sombre, dark-suited throng stood miserably in a dreadful intimacy, shoulders to breasts and stomachs to backs, their voices hushed and husky and self-conscious.

Outside, in the sunlit suburban street, a few people still waited. They were curious; but silent and well-mannered because of the nature of the occasion. The great moment when the procession, with black horses, silver trimmings and a glass-sided hearse topped with flowers and old-fashioned black plumes like folded sweeps' brushes, had set out at a snail's pace, was a thing of the past. Mrs. Pole's first essay at pageantry was over, but there still remained a few well-known mourners to be seen again.

The houses over the road had blinds drawn as a mark of respect in all the rooms below stairs, but behind the net half curtains of the bedroom windows bright inquisitive eyes peeped out eagerly, and from the house on the left came sudden flashes as the afternoon sun caught the lenses of a pair of opera glasses.

A scrawny maid with a black armlet on a black dress, assisted by a perspiring waiter hired from the nearest restaurant, struggled through the crowd with trays on which there were goblets of bright crimson port and dull yellow sherry. As they approached one they would mutter an imperfectly comprehended formula concerning whisky and soda on the dining-room sideboard "if any gentleman would care for it."

Sutane stood on the hearth rug, outwardly at ease. The bones of his head were unusually apparent, but his blank dark eyes regarded the crush in front of him steadily, if sombrely. There was no way of telling if he was thinking at all.

Uncle William was held in the crush on the other side of the room. Campion caught a glimpse between two black hats of his indecorous pink face and gaily blue eyes. He was not attempting to move because to do so he would have to pass through the small open circle surrounding Mrs. Pole, her son and a solid daughter, fat and self-conscious in a hideous black suit but sticking to her mother's side gallantly with the stoic heroism of adolescence.

Mrs. Pole was triumphant and deeply happy but she played her part still, never allowing the satisfaction which filled her so exquisitely to show sufficiently to mar the perfection of her presentation of patient and dignified grief.

It was at the moment when physical discomfort and mental unease seemed to have reached their ultimate pitch that the woman with the glass in her hand came burrowing through the crowd towards Sutane. She stood just in front of him and looked up with a little sly, secretive movement of her head which brought her face just below his own. It was an indescribable gesture, arch and yet ashamed, and it was not at all pleasant.

Campion glanced down at her and experienced that little sense of shock that is part disgust and part irritation at oneself for being disgusted.

She was white and bloated in the face and poor and bent in the body. Her loose black coat was not very clean, and yet the small eye veil on her hat was arranged by fingers which had known deftness. Her eyes were greasy and shiftless, and there was an ominous twitch at one side of her mouth.

"Well, Jimmy," she said, "don't you know me?"

Sutane stared at her, and at his side Campion caught some of his horrified surprise.

"Eva," he said.

The woman laughed and raised her glass to him. She would be drunk again in a very little while.

"Little Eva herself," she said. "Come to see the last of the poor old girl for old times' sake. Things had changed, hadn't they, for her and me—and you too, old boy. You're doing very well for yourself, aren't you? West End manager and everything . . ."

She had not raised her voice, but because she was the only person in the room who seemed to have something definite to say to anyone everybody listened automatically. She became aware of the silence and turned on them with a swing that was just a little too sudden. Those immediately behind her looked uncomfortable and began to talk hurriedly to each other. The woman returned to Sutane.

A little later in the day she would be grotesque and disgusting, with exaggerated movements and blurred, drivel-

153

ling speech, but now there was only the promise of these things. She came a little closer.

"I suppose you couldn't use a bright little soubrette who knows the ropes?" she murmured and smiled with sudden bitterness when she saw his involuntary expression. "That's all right, Jimmy boy, I'm only kidding. I couldn't walk across a stage these days. I've gone to hell. You can see that, can't you?"

She laughed again and seemed on the brink of further confidence. Sutane interrupted her. He was as nearly flurried as Campion had ever seen him.

"Where are you living now?"

"With my old mama—old Emma, you remember her." She was easily diverted and ran on in the same confidential way, as though she were telling secrets. "We're in a slum in Kensington. You've forgotten that kind of life. D'you remember you and Chloe and me and Charles on the boat going over? That was a good time—years ago."

She paused and Campion kept his eyes studiously on the wall opposite him because he knew that Sutane was looking at his face. The woman continued.

"Poor old Chloe! I never thought she'd beat me to it. I'm the one who ought to be in my grave. I'm not safe out alone nowadays. I shouldn't be here if someone hadn't brought me along. He's a nice boy to look up her old pal and bring me along. to see the last of her. He's going to take me back too. He's got to or I shan't get back. There he is, over there. Little Benny Konrad. I'd never seen him before. Nice of him, wasn't it?"

Her weak, indeterminate voice trailed away and she laid a flabby hand in a tight discoloured kid glove on Sutane's wrist.

"So long, old boy," she said and gave him once again her odd, bleary smile with the nauseating dash of coquetry in it. "We'll have a drink to the old days sometime perhaps?"

The remark was barely a question, but amid the bitterness and defeat in her voice a little flame of hope quivered and died and she smiled to herself. She went away, the crowd parting for her as she blundered towards Konrad.

Sutane rattled the money in his pockets, glanced sharply at Campion, who did not look at him, and prepared to make the initial effort towards escape.

"Campion, we'd better go," he said softly: "Come on."

154

Mr. Campion followed him with a curious unwillingness. As they approached Mrs. Pole there was a momentary diversion. The maid reappeared in the doorway holding a florist's envelope above the heads of the visitors. It was a sensible enough precaution, since the crowd was very thick, but it gave her entry an air of triumph which was incongruous. She reached her mistress as Sutane and Campion came up and they overheard her breathless message.

"Boy just brought these, ma'am. Said order bid delayed. Would you please excuse?"

Mrs. Pole took the frail package and tore it open in a ponderous irrevocable fashion which she seemed to find compatible with her tragic role. A large bunch of purple violets fell out on to the floor and the daughter stooped to retrieve them, blushing painfully. Mrs. Pole discovered a card in the debris of the envelope and read from it aloud.

"Chloe from Peter—'That perfect likeness.'"

The quotation puzzled her and she repeated it, turning the card over as if she expected to find a clue to its meaning upon the other side. Frustrated, she shrugged her plump black shoulders and dismissed the mystery.

"Somebody who knew her, no doubt," she said. "She had a lot of friends. What a pity these came so late, or they might have gone with the others. Put them in water for me, Joannie. If I have time I'll take them down to the grave tomorrow. What a lot of flowers she's had! Wherever she is, I'm sure she's pleased. Must you go, Mr. Sutane? It was very kind of you to come. I know she would have liked to have seen you all here. Poor, poor girl!"

Sutane shook hands with her and murmured a few eminently suitable words. Campion, who was not without grace himself, admired his elegant and comforting ease.

As they struggled out of the door the daughter of the house panted behind them, clutching Peter Brome's bouquet.

They had passed the straggling group of sight-seers outside the iron gate, had seen them nudge each other and stare at Sutane with studiously blank faces, and they were halfway down the broad hot road to the taxi rank before Uncle William caught them up. He was blowing gently and still flourished a crisp white handkerchief as he appeared between them.

"Don't blame you for forgettin' me," he said. "Distressin'

155

experience. Glad to get out myself. Terrible situation if grief was genuine, but more bearable than this. Not so embarrassin'. Haven't felt so damnably indecent since I was a child at the same sort of function—better class, of course."

The final observation was in the nature of an aside, a placatory offering to some past relative, no doubt.

Sutane did not speak at once. He was striding along, his head thrust forward and his hands in his pockets. His face was sombre and Campion was very much aware of his thoughts.

"Ghastly," he said suddenly. "Ghastly. It didn't even make you wish you were dead. We'll take that cab over there. Campion, I want you. Don't clear off."

He spoke with his old nervous authority which it was only possible to disobey and not to ignore. Mr. Campion climbed into the cab after Uncle William, feeling that he was making a great mistake.

As they settled down Uncle William produced an old-fashioned cigar case and solemnly presented them each with a half corona.

"This is the time for a risky story," he remarked unexpectedly. "Must get back to normal. Pity I can't keep the things in my head. Still, we can wash our hands of that affair now. That's over. Done our part. Done it well. Goin' to take you both to my club. Won't take a refusal. Don't often make use of it but it's still there. The one place you can get a drink at this hour."

It was a difficult journey back to the city. Campion was anxious to escape and yet strangely loath to make a definite move towards that end. Sutane was silent and moody, and Uncle William alone appeared to have a practical aim in view.

They went to his club finally, which was in Northumberland Avenue—an extraordinary institution which seemed at first glimpse to be a cross between a cathedral and the old Café Royal. In a dark corner of the lounge they sat sipping whisky and soda, conversing only very occasionally and then in whispers.

Sutane left to telephone to the theatre where *Swing Over* was in production, and before he went he looked at his host meaningly.

"He's got it into his head you're goin' to run away," murmured Uncle William. "Bundle of nerves, poor feller. Glad you turned up. Never doubted you would, after my letter. Pathetic business. Had to square up and face it. The silly woman brought us a lot of trouble. Thought she would the first time I saw her. What did you think of my enclosure?"

"From the bird's nest?"

Uncle William nodded, his pink face serious.

"Yes. Rum go. Startled me, don't mind admittin' it. May be nothin' but it struck me. Voice in one's ear, as it were. Out there alone in the woods... nothin' about but greenery and sunny air. Touch of the romantic in my nature, you know. Always has been."

In response to this final confidence Mr. Campion kept silent. There seemed to be nothing he could say. The old man put down his glass.

"Been thinkin' about it," he said. "Prepared myself to find it was a servant-girl romance. Thought I'd thrash it out just the same in case it wasn't. It's still there. Had another look at it this mornin', but the writin' is nothin' to go by. Badly formed, scribbled in pencil, might be woman's, might be man's. It's not Linda's."

Mr. Campion sat up with a start.

"Of course not."

Uncle William's bright blue eyes grew wide and he shot the younger man an unexpectedly shrewd glance.

"Nothin's impossible," he said. "Got to be prepared for everythin' in this world; that's my experience. I examined her hand very carefully and it's a peculiar sort of calligraphy. You'd know it anywhere. Squarish stuff. Well, not bein' able to take the note away, thus raisin' the alarm, I put my brains to it, Campion. These are my deductions. First of all from the matter. You remember the phrase?—good. Well, from the matter, it's either a very young man or a woman. Women in love will write anythin'. Known it to my cost. Great argument against teachin' women to hold a pen at all. Men are more cautious. Inherent in 'em. Boys are different again. When love seizes a boy it makes a silly young jackass of him. Follow my argument, Campion?"

"Perfectly. The tree was right in the grounds, you say?"

Uncle William sighed.

"See I'm too long-winded for you," he said regretfully. "Had it all worked out. Long and the short of it is, think it's Eve. She's the age."

"Eve? Who to?"

"That's the point." Uncle William wagged his head. "Shall have to keep my eye on the tree."

He paused and his bright eyes were contemplative and kindly.

"Poor little girl," he said. "May have nothin' to do with the business we're investigatin' at all, except that it accounts for noises in the garden at night and footprints in the mornin'. Still, we'll respect her secret."

Mr. Campion considered Eve Sutane.

"Sock," he said aloud. "Even Konrad."

"Girl's demented if she's writin' love notes to Konrad. Loses my sympathy." Uncle William's whisper was hearty. "May be anyone. Secret love affair is very attractive at that age. Maybe there's a feller among the neighbours. Can't rule out anyone—grooms, gardeners, anyone.... I remember my sister Julia, the stout one—you met her over that dreadful affair of Andrew's—yes, well, she, you know ... oh, dear me, yes! There was a great row about it at the time. Cried herself ill, poor girl. I was packed off back to school; never got the full story. Mothers were more like mothers in those days."

His voice rumbled and died.

"Leave this to me," he whispered as a nearby old gentleman glowered at him. "If it's important I'll ferret it out. If it isn't, I can keep my mouth shut, I hope. Delicate affair, best in my hands."

He looked down at his plump bear's paws and folded them. Campion smiled.

"You and Blest can manage this thing between you," he said. "I've got to go now. Sorry I haven't been of any more use."

Uncle William took him by the sleeve.

"No, my boy," he said solemnly. "Believe I've got a glimmer of your difficulty, but a soldier can't desert his post, a lawyer can't desert his client, a gentleman's got to meet his engagements. Speakin' like man to man now, you understand. Old stuff, I know. Made a lot of fun of these days but still holds good. Jimmy here is a decent feller in trouble. Don't know what it is but feel it just the same. More trouble than I thought. Think of him. Decent feller. Bein' worried. Frightened. Driven perhaps to doin' things he wouldn't normally think of doin'. Your commission is to get him out of it. Put things straight for everyone. Speakin' personally, there's my

158

show to think of. If anythin' happens to Jimmy I go back to Cambridge and retirement... a damned dull life for a man who's tasted a bit of the real thing for the first time at sixty. But I'm not harpin' on that. I'm thinkin' of everyone and I'm thinkin' most of you. Dear decent feller. Remind me amazin'ly of myself as a young man. Don't let yourself down, my boy. Ah! There's Sutane..."

17

At nine o'clock at night Campion and Sutane were still together and still acutely embarrassed by each other's presence. It had been an uncomfortable evening. Uncle William had watched over Campion and what he considered was Campion's duty with all the faithful obstinacy of a bobtail sheep dog and had only consented to go when the departure of the last train for Birley became imminent.

He left them in the Savoy grill and padded off, pausing in the doorway to cast an admonishing glance at his old friend. Sutane's eyes, which were dark without being bright, narrowed and a faint smile passed over his crooked mouth.

"Lovable old boy," he observed. "The ass *par excellence*."

Campion nodded absently. The moment which he had seen approaching all day with relentless, unhurried pace had now arrived. He wished he had not been so abominably weak but had made his escape immediately after the funeral.

He did not want to hear Sutane's confession. He did not want to pledge his word to a secrecy upon which he had already decided. It was all over as far as he was concerned. Chloe Pye was safely buried and he did not want to know definitely how she had died.

Sutane glanced at his wrist.

"I want to go down to the theatre if you don't mind," he said. "I didn't play on the day of the funeral. It seemed to be the sort of gesture that was expected of me. It gives me an opportunity to see what Konrad makes of the show. He won't have the wheel turning, of course. We didn't want him to make a fool of himself or break an ankle."

The final remark, a very human touch of weakness which had escaped him in spite of himself, embarrassed him as soon as he had made it. He laughed and his unhappy, intelligent eyes were apologetic. Campion experienced a warm wave of liking for him, which he resented, feeling it exasperatingly unfair.

They went to the theatre, postponing the evil moment for yet another twenty minutes. Konrad was on the stage when they stepped into the back of a box. He and Slippers were in the midst of the "Leave it to Me" number in the first act. The house was friendly and well fed, but disappointed to miss Sutane, and so much mass regret made a cool, heavy atmosphere in the great auditorium.

Campion watched Konrad with interest. He was technically sound, skilful and eminently satisfactory to look at, but his exhibition was not inspired. No personality came out over the footlights to grip the attention of the silent watching throng and force its sympathy. There was no ecstasy. The irresistible and final appeal was not there. The magic had departed. There was no light in the lantern.

Slippers was her flaming self, but her small light was not fed and strengthened by her partner. Rather he took from her, revealing the frail quality of her little gift.

The man at Campion's elbow sighed. It was an expressive sound, mainly of regret but containing a definite underlying hint of satisfaction.

"It's not there," he said softly. "I knew it. He knows it, poor beast."

The roar as the curtain descended drowned his voice. It did not come from the stalls or the circle, both of which gave a kindly if not enthusiastic hand, but from the pit and gallery, which seemed to be at least partially inhabited by a deliriously excited throng. The noise was prodigious and it went on too long. Slippers and Konrad took two calls. Konrad was shy and boyish before the curtain. His smile of gratified surprise was modest and ingenuous. The stalls gave him an extra hand because of it.

As Sutane glanced up at the dark gallery a glimmer from the stage caught his face. He looked worried but not annoyed.

"That damned claque again," he said. "How very silly of him. He can't afford it, you know."

They stayed to watch the curtain rise again on the Alexandra Palace scene, with the chorus in high boots and roller skates assisting Rosamund Bream and Dennis Fuller to enact a travestied version of the now famous "Leg-o'-Mutton Escapade" from Uncle William's memoirs.

During the garter business, that piece of inverted humour amusing to the audience only because it was funny to them that their fathers should have considered it funny, Sutane touched Campion's sleeve and they went backstage.

There were a few surprised nods of recognition as they passed down the corridor, but no one stopped the great man, and when he closed his dressing-room door behind them his mood had not altered.

"Look here," he said, motioning his visitor to a chair and glancing round for a cigarette box to offer him, "I owe you a sort of explanation."

"No," said Campion with a firmness which surprised himself. "No, I don't think so. I've been afraid you were going to come out with something, but frankly I don't think it's necessary."

He paused abruptly.

The other man was staring at him. Since meeting Sutane in private life Campion had almost forgotten his better-known stage personality, but now he was forcefully reminded of it.

Here in the theatre Sutane was his remarkable, magical self again. Once more he seemed a little larger than life, with all his many physical peculiarities exaggerated and his restless, powerful spirit pressed down into the dangerous confinement of packed explosive.

"My dear chap," he said, "you've *got* to listen to me."

He swept aside some of the miscellany on the dressing table and perched himself on the cleared space. One foot rested on the seat of the chair and he kept his long, expressive hands free to emphasise his words.

"When I said I'd never met Chloe Pye before she came into *The Buffer* I was lying," he said abruptly.

It occurred to Campion irrelevantly that the dramatic intensity of the words was not lessened by his histrionic skill.

"I lied to the doctor. I lied on oath in the coroner's court. I knew her very well sixteen or seventeen years ago."

161

"Yes." Campion could not bring himself to express surprise. His apathy seemed to irritate the other man, but in some curious professional capacity, and Sutane hurried on, his words clipped and his tone sharp and impersonal.

"You guessed that, of course. You heard that wretched woman talking to me this afternoon. Konrad dug her up to satisfy some dreadful complex of his own. She was appalling, I know it—horrible! She made me crawl. I hadn't seen her for fifteen years. When I knew her she was a jolly little creature, very full of pep, shrewd and able to take care of herself. Today—did you see her? She was like a disintegrating corpse. I met Chloe in Paris in 1920, or '21, I forget which."

Campion stirred and with an effort threw off the oppressive spell of the stronger personality.

"It doesn't matter," he said, glancing up into the other man's face. "I don't want to know. I'm not interested."

Sutane sat very still. He was snubbed and hurt. His pained astonishment had a childlike quality which was endearing.

"I lived with the woman," he shouted suddenly. "I lived with her for two years. I was her partner in a vaudeville act. We toured Canada and the States."

Campion relaxed. Into his pale eyes behind the big spectacles there crept a new and cautious expression. It was not happening as he had foreseen. The miracle had occurred. Sutane was not confessing. Sutane was not trusting him. The discovery came in a blessed wave of relief. The man was, mercifully, still not his friend.

"Yes?" he enquired gently.

Sutane settled down. "I knew you'd listen. I wanted to tell you. Well, we broke up finally—you know how these things happen. Chloe ceased to be the brilliant star I was bobbing along behind. I grew tired of being 'and partner' on the bills. We split. She went off to the eastern States alone and I came back and built up a career. When she came home again we did not meet. I saw her name about and doubtless she saw mine. But vaudeville doesn't mix much with revue, and we never ran into each other. She had no need of my help, even if I could have given her any. She had her own methods of getting along. There were several affairs from what one hears. She had a few in my time."

Now that he had captured his audience and was safely embarked upon his story he seemed to derive a certain

162

amount of enjoyment from the telling. He regarded the other man quizzically. Perched upon the table, he looked like some thin, attractive monkey, his eyes sad and clever and disillusioned like an ape's.

"Four weeks ago she turned up here and wanted a shop," he went on slowly. "You saw the sort of woman she was. She was vain and crazy to appease her vanity. All her life she had relied on her sex to get her by and now she was beginning to find it hadn't anything like its old power. That's the devil of it, Campion! It goes so quickly. One day it's there and the next day it's gone. The wretched women can't bring themselves to realise it. When Chloe came to me what she really wanted was reassuring. To herself she blamed a change in the times, manners, type of man—anything but the obvious truth. She chose me to come to because I had once loved her and because I was in a position to give her a job."

"Why did you give it to her?"

Sutane looked down at his feet.

"God knows," he said and sounded as though he meant it.

There was a pause, but he went on again after a little while, his voice resonant and youthful in his eagerness to get the story out.

"I told her I was happily married, and I thought she was convinced and that any damned silly attempt upon me was ruled out. She seemed very sensible. I hadn't realised her full trouble than and thought she was merely hard up. Anyway, I took her on. There was a sort of excuse for it. We were justified in having an added attraction for the three-hundredth performance and the receipts could stand it easily. She jumped at it, of course, and almost at once I regretted the decision. I remembered all the things I'd forgotten about her—her energy, her constant nattering at one, and her incredible vanity."

He broke off and looked at Campion shyly.

"If you're nervy already that sort of relentless pursuit gets under your skin, doesn't it? Besides, she was so appallingly general, if you see what I mean. She had become impossible. I didn't want her at White Walls, for instance, and I told her so. Yet she came just the same. You suddenly find you're at the mercy of a woman like that. There's nothing you can do, short of hitting her. After she was dead I thought I'd risk keeping quiet about our old association. We'd never appeared together in England and no one knew about us, as far as I know, save for a few old-timers like Eva who had dropped out of sight. If there had been any serious public enquiry into her suicide I should have to have spoken. As it was, there seemed no point in it. I used a different name in the early days—La Verne or something equally footling—and I have never used the story of that tour in my publicity because I was not very proud of it. Chloe wasn't a big enough name, and, of course, there was the private side of it."

He spread out his hands in a gesture of finality and looked at Campion inquisitively.

"Why were you so anxious for her not to come to White Walls?"

The other man put the question hesitantly, disliking himself for disguising it.

Unexpectedly, Sutane was ashamed. He sat looking at his feet again, wriggling them inside his shoes.

"Linda thinks I'm the most remarkable and magnificent person in the world," he said simply. "I was afraid Chloe might come out with some tasteless revelation in front of her. She might have done that easily, you know. She had just that kind of insanity. Linda terrified her, fortunately."

Since Campion did not speak but sat with a perfectly expressionless face, he continued hastily.

"Linda is not an ignorant, foolish little nincompoop. Don't think that. I was considering myself, not her. God! Would you like to introduce some of your old loves to your new ones?"

Campion pulled himself together. He got up and spoke carelessly.

"Look here, Sutane," he said, "I understand. It's all quite clear to me and it's over. I shall respect your confidence, of course. In my opinion you took an appalling risk in denying any past acquaintance with Chloe, but, as you say, it didn't matter, as it turned out. Now, I've finished. Blest is looking after your other trouble and he'll solve it for you in a day or so. Quite by chance I think I was able to put him onto the right line, but that's really no credit to me. He'll get you proof and between you you'll be able to clear it up for all time. It's a job for a professional and he's doing it very well."

He smiled. "I think I'll fade away," he said.

Sutane did not speak. Now that he had finished his performance and was off stage again, as it were, his moroseness had returned and he sat limply, his joints relaxed, looking like a resting marionette.

Campion had collected his hat before his host glanced up. Sutane did not smile.

"You don't understand, old boy," he said. "I'm an important person—so damned important I'm terrified whenever I think of it. Three hundred people in this theatre are dependent on me. With Konrad dancing, the show wouldn't last a week. There's not another star in London who could carry it. It depends on me. Then there's White Walls. Gardeners, Campion. Maids—Linda—Sarah—Eve—Sock—Poyser—old Finny—the nurse—they're all dependent on me. On my *feet*. Every time I look at my feet I feel sick with apprehension. Every time I look at this damned great theatre I go cold with terror. White Walls turns my stomach over. I'm frightened of it. They're all directly or indirectly supported and held up by me, and I'm an ordinary poor little bloke who has nothing— God help him—but his feet and his reputation. Nothing must go wrong with me, Campion. I've got nothing to fall back on. A businessman has his organisation and his firm, but I've got nothing. I'm doing it alone. Now do you understand?"

There was no art in this appeal. It came out unadorned with all the poignancy of truth.

"I've got no money. The whole ridiculous organisation takes every ha'penny I make, and I make something fabulous. I go bobbing along with my coattails flapping, like Eliza on the ice. If I was run over by a bus I shouldn't care—it would be over. I shouldn't see the crash. But if I get driven into a breakdown, if I once lose my nerve...I'm terrified, I tell you. Terrified!"

He got off the dressing table and solemnly executed an intricate little dancing step. His lean body in the dark mourning clothes, which he had not changed since the funeral, trembled in the air. The ecstatic movement, so indescribable and so satisfying, was there. The sight of him was amusing, stimulating and aesthetically comforting.

"That's all," he said, his long face puckered. "That's all I've got, and it depends on my mind, which is being attacked. That's all it is and it supports a mountain. It's a dizzy cathedral balancing on a joke. If there's anything in your

165

power that you can do to help me you've got to do it. Can't you see that? You've got to be on my side."

It was an extraordinary appeal, utterly unanswerable. Campion kept his hat in his hand, but he did not go.

After a while they went down the corridor and into Konrad's dressing room, where an anaemic young man was helping the understudy into a suit of white tails. Konrad was delighted with himself. Made up for the lights, his face was indecently pretty.

"Hello, Jimmy," he said, "how am I doing? Going down all right?"

"Sounds so. Haven't seen you yet." The unnecessary lie tripped out so naturally that even Campion believed it for a moment. Sutane went on.

"It was charitable of you to dig out Eva this afternoon."

Konrad bent closer to the mirror, before which he had seated himself.

"Oh, did you know her?" he said casually. "One likes to do what one can at such a time. Chloe's dresser told me they had been great friends, so I looked her up. Frightful case. Positively puts one off gin, my dears. Oh, by the way, I wanted to see you, Jimmy. I'm calling in at White Walls for my precious bicycle on Sunday morning. The club is meeting at Boarbridge, just down your line, for lunch. I simply couldn't face a thirty-mile run before eating, I mean, it's inhuman. So I thought I'd come down to Birley in the morning, take a cab up to your place, change, collect my machine and ride down to the station, taking the local train for the odd fifteen miles. The boys will think I've come from London and be on the station to meet me. Sock can bring my case back to town, can't he? It's all arranged."

"It sounds like it." Sutane was annoyed and Campion reflected that it was queer that few things should be more irritating than the elaborate arrangements of others which involve, however slightly, one's own house. Konrad flushed.

"Well, it was all arranged when I was down there last week-end," he said.

"Was it? Who with?"

"You, I think. I told someone. It must have been you." Konrad turned a face towards them which was scarlet under the grease. "If you're going to be childish, throw the bicycle

166

out of the gate and I'll change behind a hedge," he said and giggled.

Sutane flushed.

"You made no arrangement with me," he persisted obstinately. "But it doesn't matter in the least. There'll be a room at your disposal on Sunday morning."

Konrad rose. He made no attempt at thanks.

"I have nowhere to keep the bicycle in town," he said petulantly. "I live in a service flat, as you very well know, and the fools won't let me bring it into the theatre. If I leave it down at the garage it may get tarnished. It's silver-plated."

The callboy interrupted Sutane's comment, which was rude, and Konrad resumed his mood of excited triumph.

"I must fly," he said quite unnecessarily. "Sweet of you both to have dropped in to wish me luck."

The door closed behind him and Sutane glanced round the room with distaste.

"Blast the bicycle," he said briefly. "Little ass. Did you hear him getting at me? It's an unwritten law in the theatre that one never watches one's understudy work, you know. He forgets I'm the producer as well."

He did not leave but wandered round the small apartment, conveying contemptuous dislike for all that it contained. The dresser kept out of his way as far as possible in the confined space and watched him with an oblique and respectful eye.

Konrad's personality as displayed in dressing-room adornment tended towards the sentimental and old-maidish. His many mascots included a small model of the Discus Thrower and a child's stuffed white dog with a blue bow round its neck. A number of photographs, many of himself, adorned the walls, and there was also a poster of the ill-fated show in which he had starred. A small hanging bookcase below the grating of a window contained an incense burner and half a dozen volumes as well as a box of very expensive Cyprian cigarettes.

Sutane took down one of the dusty books and opened it. From where he stood Campion could see that it was verse. The dancer glanced at the flyleaf and his face changed. He was suddenly deeply and quietly angry, and the bone at the angle of his jaw showed white through the skin. He handed the volume to Campion, who read the inscription.

167

In friendship. B. 1934.

The words were written in green ink and the handwriting was uncomfortably familiar.

"Where's that invitation card?" Sutane's tone was ominously casual.

"Blest has it," said Campion.

Sutane put the book under his arm. Outside the door he glanced at the other man.

"I'll see Blest tomorrow. We'll go, shall we?"

He made no comment on the discovery, which was curious since there was so much that might have been said. Campion was surprised until he saw his deep, weary eyes in the gleam of a wall light. Then he saw that he was consumed with anger and was holding it down only with extreme difficulty.

They parted at the stage door. Sutane smiled and shook hands.

"If Blest fails I shall still rely on you, my dear fellow," he said.

As Mr. Campion walked away down the dark side street to the avenue vivid with lights and roofed with summer stars he was appalled to find that he did not care if Sutane's suspicion concerning the inscription and the invitation card was well founded.

Hitherto he had been an observer only in the many dramas which he had investigated, and that circumstance had given him an unfounded sense of superiority. Tonight he felt cold and disillusioned; no longer shocked but frankly despairing to find himself both so human and so miserably unhappy.

18

The rumour appeared in London somewhere about teatime on what afterwards proved to be the closest Sunday of the year.

It ran through the lazy crowds in the park, sped along the broad dusty streets, dived underground with the tube trains, was carried to the suburbs on a thousand plump red buses, growing and changing as it travelled, trickled into clubs, houses and teashops, mounted a million stairs to flats and rooftops, and waved its coloured tongues in every idle ear.

It was not a definite story at any one time; rather, a series of unsubstantiated statements ranging the whole way from the frankly electrifying to the merely sad. Its effect was gently unsettling, producing in the public mind a vague sensation of excitement only faintly tinged with alarm, as though it had been an unexplained bump in the night or the just incomprehensible shouts of newsboys in far-off streets.

It came from one of the great railway termini where trains were thought to have been delayed for anything between one and twenty hours. Because it was a Sunday the usual channels of news were stopped, but the bus conductors, who can generally be relied upon to know most things, had a wild story about unidentified enemy aircraft reducing the garrison town of Colchester to smouldering ruin.

In the Corner House in Coventry Street the waitresses had a theory that it was not enemy aircraft at all but two Air Force bombers who had come to grief in a built-up area while carrying out secret practice on the South Coast, and an enterprising newspaper vendor in Oxford Circus chalked "Pit Explosion: Many Dead" on an empty board and actually sold a quantity of leftover morning papers before his fraud was discovered.

As the evening wore on the scattered theories became less diverse and the scene of the disaster, whatever it was, became fixed as a railway station on an eastern line. The words "air raid" persisted, however, even after the more general term "explosion" had become frequent, and it was not until the running news bulletins in lights above the rooftops in Trafalgar Square and in Oxford Street came out with the gist of the story that the town settled down to take in the piquant and rather horribly risible truth.

Mr. Campion had gone away on Saturday to Kepesake in Suffolk and had spent a soothing week-end in that remote village, where London and European news is not heard at all until it becomes stale, or discussed until it becomes history. He heard nothing of the sensation, therefore, until he sank down into the corner of a compartment in the London train at Ipswich station on Monday morning and opened the paper which he had caught up in his flight past the bookstall. Then it was presented to him baldly and with as much detail as could be gathered in the mysterious circumstances.

Above and beside a quarter-page photograph of what appeared to be, at first sight, the snow-covered relics of a serious fire, the headlines were briefly informative.

HOME COUNTY STATION OUTRAGE.
FIFTEEN DEAD AND INJURED.

MYSTERY EXPLOSION.
WELL-KNOWN DANCER AMONG KILLED.

Mr. Campion's startled glance travelled hastily down the column, where, as usual, the portentous young voice of the *Morning Telegram* did its best to disguise its natural feather-brained exuberance with heavy dramatics.

Three people met their death yesterday morning in what may well prove to be one of the most extraordinary and perhaps far-reaching accidents of modern times. Twelve others lie in the Boarbridge cottage hospital injured, some of them gravely so. At the moment the cause of the accident is unknown, but Scotland Yard officials (called in by Lieutenant Colonel Percy Beller, chief constable for the district) are understood to believe that high explosives were instrumental in causing the disaster.

Among the three persons who lost their lives was thirty-two-year-old Benny Konrad, the London revue star, who had travelled to Boarbridge to meet members of a cycling club of which he was the president. Richard Duke, who was also killed, was a member of the cycling party. The third person to die was a porter.

Having given what it felt was the main story, the *Telegram*, in accordance with its custom, began again in fuller style.

Late yesterday morning, when the twelve-three from Birley had just pulled out and the slow up train from Yarmouth, laden with summer travellers, was in the station, the quiet

170

little country junction of Boarbridge was visited by an explosion so sudden and terrible that Mr. Harold Phipps, the stationmaster, tells me that he has seen nothing like it since the War.

At the time, unfortunately, the down platform was crowded with visitors. Some forty members of a cycling club had foregathered there to welcome their president, Mr. Benny Konrad, the revue star, who had come from London to take part in an annual celebration outing.

Mr. Konrad, who was in cycling kit, wheeling his machine, a new gift from the club, was laughing and chatting with his friends when there was a sudden deafening explosion and the quiet station was reduced to a shambles of groaning men and women.

The glass in the roof with which the platforms are sheltered was shattered, as were many of the windows of the stationary train, and a number of the injuries were caused by splintered glass.

Two hand trucks of milk cans were being drawn by a porter at the time of the accident, and in the panic after the explosion these became strewn upon the line, adding considerably to the general confusion.

Doctors were rushed to the scene and the two small waiting rooms were turned into temporary casualty stations. Trains on the line were held up for nearly an hour.

Tonight the cause of the disaster is still a complete mystery. The theory held by some that an infernal machine had been dropped by a passing aircraft has now been generally abandoned, although the stationmaster still stoutly adheres to that view. No one in the thriving little market town of Boarbridge noticed any aeroplane in the vicinity during the morning.

Railway officials are silent. The regulations regarding the conveyance of dangerous goods are very strict, but it is just possible that a parcel containing explosive matter may have escaped the vigilance of the authorities.

The mystery is deepened by the fact that Mr. Phipps insists that both platforms were clear of goods parcels at the time of the accident, and the senior porter, Mr. Edward Smith, who is prostrate from severe shock and superficial burns, assured me when I visited him in his cottage in Station Lane that he took nothing from the goods van of the down train save Mr.

171

Konrad's bicycle, which was collected by its owner immediately on arrival.

In the circumstances the County Police made an instant decision to ask the official help of Scotland Yard experts, and last night Inspector Yeo of the Central Branch of the C.I.D. travelled to Boarbridge, bringing with him Major Owen Bloom and Mr. T. P. Culvert, both of the War Office research department.

Last night it was understood that the accident is not thought to have been political in inspiration, but that possibility is not yet wholly ruled out.

The dead are: Benjamin Evelyn Konrad, thirty-two, dancer and revue star, Flat 17, Burnup House, W. 1; Richard Edwin Duke, nineteen, 2, Bellows Court Road, S.E. 21; Frederick Stiff, forty-three (porter), Queen's Cottages, Layer Road, Boarbridge.

The list of the injured followed and made appalling reading. Five women, three children and seven men had received wounds of varying gravity, most of which could be accounted for by flying glass from the roof or carriage windows.

Mr. Campion put down the paper and stared blankly at the grey upholstery in front of him.

The whole story seemed so utterly incredible that he read it through again carefully before he could attempt to assimilate it. He glanced at the other paper, which the fat man in the corner was holding between himself and the world, and there also he caught a glimpse of the same story, so that his first wild notion that the *Telegram* had gone mad and invented the tale in a fit of wanton idiocy was brushed aside as it deserved.

Gradually he accustomed himself to the facts. Konrad was dead, startlingly dead, blown to hell with his ridiculous bicycle and two other unfortunate mortals. Konrad, who until this moment had figured in his mind as a busy little self-seeker blithely scattering trouble broadcast in an attempt to achieve his own dubious ends, had been wiped out by an accident. Of all the forty million to whom the disaster might have occurred it had overtaken only three, and one of those had been Konrad. As a piece of irony he felt it surpassed itself. He did not take his eyes from the paper all the way to London.

172

A small paragraph tucked away at the foot of the news story recorded that Konrad's was the second violent death to occur in the Cast of *The Buffer* within a fortnight, and mentioned as a coincidence that he had been present among the guests at Sutane's house when Chloe Pye had met her tragic end.

Campion was still startled and shocked when he arrived at Liverpool Street. He took a cab to the Junior Greys and was hesitating in the lounge, trying to decide if his strong impulse to phone Sutane was a wise one or the reverse, when he received a message from Scotland Yard.

The note said briefly that Superintendent Stanislaus Oates would be glad if Mr. Campion would make it convenient to call upon him at three o'clock that afternoon.

In the ordinary way Campion was not a wavering or unduly apprehensive spirit, but he spent the half hour before lunch and the hour after it in a restless, nervy mood which all but demoralised him.

At five minutes to three he was walking down a long bare corridor which smelt vaguely of disinfectant behind a helmetless constable and a moment or so later had stepped forward to shake hands with the dour figure who had risen to greet him.

His recent promotion had no more altered Superintendent Stanislaus Oates than had any of the previous steps in his career. He remained at heart the eager, solemn young countryman whose concentration and tenacity had first earned the commendation of a rural inspector nearly thirty-four years before.

He was not an unfriendly man, but even Campion, who probably knew him better than anyone outside the force itself, was never in danger of permitting familiarity to grow into amicable contempt.

The superintendent stood for a moment, his shoulders stooping and his pepper-and-salt head bent over the blotter on his desk.

"Ah, Campion," he said. "Sit down, will you, mate?"

The form of address was a relic of his Dorset days. All through his thirty-four years' slow ascent through the service he had carefully suppressed it, but now that he had attained the peak and promise of his career he brought it out occasionally, a minor laxity permissible in one of his eminence.

"Been away?"

"Yes. To Kepesake. I spent the week-end with Guffy Randall and his wife. Do you mind?"

"No. When did you go?"

"Saturday morning."

"You're staying at your club?"

"Yes."

"Lugg's away?"

"Yes."

"Where?"

"White Walls, near Birley. Jimmy Sutane's house. Why?"

Campion leant back in the visitor's chair. He knew that his forehead was damp and wondered at himself. Presently he took out a handkerchief and sat looking at it.

The superintendent seated himself and rested his elbows on the desk. He had a sad, bony face and very interested grey eyes.

"What do you know about Benny Konrad?"

Suddenly Mr. Campion felt more at ease.

"Very little," he said cheerfully. "I've been acting as honorary adviser to Blest on a private investigation which seemed to be leading towards him. That's all. You've seen Blest, I suppose?"

The policeman's country eyes flickered with a brief smile.

"Yes. We've seen Blest. Saw him last night. He looked us up."

Mr. Campion thought he had begun to understand, and the sneaking, unnameable fear which had been nibbling at the back of his mind all the morning was allayed.

"You're consulting me, I take it?" he said brightly. "It's a great honour. I appreciate it."

Oates laughed, a dry little explosive sound expressing friendliness and good humour but no amusement. He was singularly seldom amused.

"I'm questioning you in pursuance of my duties," he explained laboriously. "What was Konrad up to? Do you know?"

"Up to?" Campion echoed him blankly. "My dear man, why are we playing detectives? Come down to earth. You've seen Blest and so you know all Blest knows. I can't tell you any more, old boy. That's all there is to it. Konrad had been playing the fool around the theatre and he was on the verge of being found out. That's the lot."

174

"Ah!" The superintendent seemed partially satisfied. "You've heard about the way he was killed?"

"I've seen the papers. It seems to have been a nasty accident."

"Oh, it was." Oates was genuinely moved. "I went down myself last night and took a look at the place. Then I went on to the hospital and the mortuary. It was fearful. The mess was terrible. Women cut about with glass, you know, doctors digging splinters as long as my fingers out of them. The men who were killed were in a frightful condition. Konrad had a piece of metal blown clean through his head. It had dug a furrow you could put your wrist into clean through the top of his scalp. And the poor porter chap! I won't make you uncomfortable with a description. They got a steel nut out of his stomach."

His pleasant dry voice ceased but he kept his eyes on Campion's own.

"It was fearful," he repeated. "I'm not a squeamish man myself but the sight of that milk and blood and glass everywhere upset me; it made me feel sick. A very extraordinary and dreadful thing altogether," he finished with a touch of prim severity.

Campion had remained silent throughout the harangue, his face growing more and more grave as his earlier apprehension returned.

"I don't quite see where all this is leading," he began cautiously. "I'm completely in the dark. I mean, the cause of the explosion had nothing to do with Konrad, surely?"

"I'm not so sure." The superintendent wagged his distinguished head. "I'm not so sure at all. I don't know if I ought to tell you, but the opinion here at the moment is that someone threw a bomb at the little blighter."

For the second time that day Mr. Campion experienced that rarest of the emotions—genuine astonishment.

"No . . ." he said at last. "I don't believe it. It's incredible."

"Ah, you think so?" Oates seemed disappointed. He looked down at his desk. "Major Bloom is coming along in fifteen minutes or so. He's been at work on the evidence all day. I'm hoping he'll have some definite information for us. So far we've been working on the few hints he could give us last night. From the first look round he told Yeo that in his opinion there was no doubt that the explosion originated roughly on the spot where Konrad was standing. They can tell you that, you know, these fellows, from the general direction of the damage. It's very ingenious how they work it all out. There's no guessing. It's all very scientific. Yeo was particularly impressed."

"But..." began Mr. Campion and was silent. "A bomb?" he said at last. "What sort of a bomb?"

"That's what I'm waiting to find out," explained the superintendent severely. "Something very efficacious. I'd like you to have seen that station, my lad. I wouldn't have gone down there myself in the ordinary way, but Yeo and I are friends and the county police sounded so excited on the phone that I couldn't resist taking a peep. Yeo's coming up at four for a conference. He's been interviewing people down there all day."

In spite of his seriousness there was still a touch of the schoolboy about Oates, a certain naïve excitement which betrayed him every now and again. His work still fascinated him.

"Now look here, Campion," he said, "you knew Konrad. Would you say he might have any secret political activities? We don't get many bomb outrages over here, you know, and when we do they're nearly always political or the efforts of lunatics—usually an unhealthy combination of the two. What would you say, now? Let's have your frank opinion."

He spoke coaxingly and Mr. Campion was frankly sorry not to be able to oblige him.

"I'd say 'no,'" he said. "I can't help it, but I would, definitely. He wasn't a friend of mine, of course—I didn't know him well—but no, no, I really couldn't see him mixed up with politics of any sort. What an absolutely unbelievable thing to happen!"

Oates leant back in his chair.

"Mr. Campion," he began with unusual formality, "I've known you for a long time and we've done a bit of work together. If you're going to be in this affair I'd like you to work for us. I'm not saying that I don't trust you, now. Don't think that. But I want all the facts from you, and if you're working for me then I know you won't be working for anyone else behind my back. Consider yourself an expert called in on the case, just as the major is."

Having known the superintendent for fifteen years, Campion was able to appreciate the effort such a decision had cost that logical and conventional policeman. He was properly impressed.

"My dear chap, anything you like," he said lightly. "You know all I know at the moment. I was called in by Jimmy Sutane to help Blest in uncovering a sort of persecution campaign. I thought I saw Konrad was at the bottom of it and I tipped Blest on to him. Then I rather lost interest and faded away. From what I saw of Konrad he certainly did not strike me as a likely candidate for public assassination. The only feasible explanation that occurs to me offhand is that your bomb thrower was demented and mistook him for somebody else."

"Who else did he look like in a vest and cycling shorts?" demanded Oates with practical curiosity.

Campion shrugged his shoulders. Words were beyond him.

"Mr. Sutane was at his own house surrounded by his family twenty miles away when the explosion occurred," observed the superintendent sadly. "We can be fairly sure who was on the down side of the station where Konrad stood, but some of the travellers on the up line may have escaped us."

Mr. Campion blinked.

"Didn't anyone see someone throw the thing?"

"No. No one's come forward. Yeo's working on that now." Oates leant across the desk and his unexpectedly youthful eyes were indignant. "Can you imagine any living person doing it, Campion?" he demanded. "Scattering death or disfiguration among a crowd of innocent, helpless bodies on a country railway station? The man's either hopelessly insane or a—a bad, dangerous fellow. We'll have to lay our hands on him. There's no two ways about it."

Campion smiled faintly at the "bad, dangerous fellow." The superintendent's maidenly restraint was typical of him and bore no relation to the depths of his feelings. Stanislaus Oates had spent much of his life in the pursuit of murderers and had invariably delivered them into the hands of the public hangman with serene satisfaction whenever he had the opportunity. There were very few greys, in his view; only varying depths of black. He had once expressed a certain sympathy for Crippen, but only because the little doctor had permitted himself to succumb to temptation. Once Belle Elmore was dead, Crippen was already half hanged, and very

177

properly so too in the gentle Oates's opinion. Yet Crippen, Campion remembered, had been "a poor weak scoundrel." The "bad, dangerous fellow" was evidently in a different class altogether.

Oates was not without softness, however, although he reserved his sympathy always for the right side.

"There's a young woman maybe going to lose a leg and a lad of eighteen with his face cut to ribbons in the hospital. If it had been a train accident I'd have been simply very sorry, but when it's wanton, deliberate wickedness it makes me spiteful. It's a fact, now. We'll have to get this fellow."

Campion glanced up.

"The authorities are clamouring, too, I suppose?" he ventured.

Oates smiled. "Yes, they're nattering," he said cheerfully. "But they'll have to wait for us. We can't go worrying our heads about them when there's work to be done."

His bland superiority was superb. Campion felt curiously comforted. In a world of conflicting loyalties it was a relief to find someone who could really put his finger, if only to his own satisfaction, on the exact spot where right ends and wrong begins.

The superintendent took a large flat watch from his waistcoat pocket and considered it.

"Time for the major," he said. "Now I'm trusting you, mate. I don't have to ask anyone's permission. I'm the superintendent of the Central Department of the C.I.D. and I can have what help I think fit. I want you to sit in that corner over there. You've been working on Konrad and you can work some more."

Mr. Campion went over to the small hard chair obediently. There had never been any ceremony between them, and Oates's sublime conviction that an invitation to work for the police was the highest honour man could hope to receive was unanswerable. He sat down.

Major Bloom was ushered in almost immediately and Mr. Culvert, his assistant, came with him. The major was tall and heavy, with lumbering movements and eyes which peered shortsightedly from behind truly terrible steel-rimmed glasses. He shook hands with nervous affability and betrayed a pleasant Midland voice.

Mr. Culvert, his assistant, hovered round him deferentially. He was a small, neat young man, precise to the point of primness. His quiet, cultured voice contrasted with his chief's burr, as did his ease and self-assurance. Yet no one could have confused the master with the apprentice. Mr. Culvert only too evidently considered that he was out in charge of his god, a fragile, breakable deity who was to be protected and placated in every way. They made an odd, knowledgeable pair.

The major sat down in the visitor's chair, smiled nervously at Oates, and fumbled in the leather brief case which Mr. Culvert held open for him. He found the notebook for which he was searching at last and looked up with a sigh.

"We've hardly begun yet, of course," he said with a nervous giggle. "This is going to take some time. You do realise that, don't you? I know you people are always in such a hurry. I haven't prepared any sort of statement and I haven't had time to go into the analysis of the metal at all, but there are just one or two points that may be of interest to you at the moment."

Oates thanked him gravely.

"Make it simple," he said.

The major blinked. "I don't think I follow you..."

"Make it simple, sir. I'm not very up in chemistry. Let's just have the straight tale first."

"Oh, yes, I see. I see. Of course." The expert seemed alarmed, and he glanced at his assistant helplessly. Mr. Culvert coughed.

"First of all, the superintendent should know that you're satisfied it was a grenade, sir," he murmured.

Oates nodded. "Oh, ah, it was, was it? Well, we feared so. An amateur grenade would you say, sir?"

"Well, no, you know. It's a funny thing but I don't think it was." The major got up and walked down the room; his shyness dropped from him and his voice rose with sudden authority. "I can't be certain, but as far as I can see the explosive was either amatol or tetrol. That's as near as we shall ever get. Tetrol. Tetramethylaniline, you know. I think it was that. That's by the damage and the action on the cast-iron casing. One of the doctors gave me a most valuable specimen of the casing, taken from the porter's chest. We can say that for certain, can't we, Culvert?"

"I think so, sir."

"Amatol..." The superintendent was making notes. "Where would that come from, now? Could an amateur obtain it?"

"I don't know. I suppose he could. It's very usual stuff. The wholesalers have it." The expert appeared to resent the interruption. "However, what I'm trying to tell you is that it didn't look like amateur work to me. The casing was grooved inside, you see. It wasn't one of your petrol cans, or the dreadful tea-caddy things that we get sometimes. As far as we can tell at the moment from the evidence we've received, it was a very decent, well-constructed grenade, not at all unlike a Mills bomb but rather more powerful."

"How much more powerful?" Oates sat up with frank interest.

"My dear good man, how can I possibly tell you? A Mills bomb, now, holds about three ounces of explosive. I think in this case you might multiply that by anything up to four. That's on the damage. Don't run away with the idea that the grenade used was four times as large as a Mills bomb. That's not what I'm saying at all. It might have been any size. It depends on the casing and on the filling. And don't ask me how big it was or what shape it was because I can't possibly tell you and no one on earth except the men who made it and placed it can."

He paused and eyed them with frank, weak blue eyes.

"I'm working now on the scraps of metal which we've been able to collect, you understand, and, while I think of it, there are some pieces embedded in the platform. I'd like those. Every tiny piece is of value to me. You never know... I may, with luck, be able to tell where the iron came from. The country of origin, I mean."

He stopped, seemed suddenly to become aware of the unfamiliar surroundings, and sat down abruptly.

Oates remained quiet for a moment, digesting his astonishing information.

"How do these things go off?" he enquired at last. "Can you tell me that, sir?"

The major permitted himself one of his unhappy little giggles.

"There are nine-and-sixty ways," he murmured, "but in this particular case I think there really must have been the usual cap and detonator. This isn't evidence, you understand.

180

This is simply my present opinion. It was something very like a Mills bomb; I really can say that."

Oates sat looking at him, his head a little on one side.

"You mean someone must have pulled a pin out before throwing it?"

The major seemed to hesitate on the brink of a confidence but thought better of it and remained cautious.

"Something like that. A pin, or a switch, or a screw."

"I see." Oates seemed only fairly satisfied, and after an enquiring glance at his chief Mr. Culvert broke in to remind the superintendent in his prim, deferential way that the investigations were at a very elementary stage.

The major rose again and heaved himself over to the desk, where he made a rough sketch on the superintendent's clean blotting paper.

"You take an iron casing filled with explosives and projectiles," he said, breathing gustily on Oates's bent head. "Into that you introduce a tube of thin perforated metal, which is roughly hourglass in shape, narrow in the middle. Inside the tube you put a striker, which is held in place by a rod, with an arm on the end of it. The rod is connected with the switch or screw on the outside of the casing. Now above the striker you put a little spring, so that when the rod is turned the arm slips aside and the striker plunges down, being guided by the construction in the hourglass, onto a small anvil. The anvil is formed by the base of the hourglass. On the anvil is the cap and detonator, probably fulminate of mercury. Understand what I'm telling you?"

"Yes, I think so." Oates was blinking. "And this is what was used?"

The major shrugged his shoulders.

"That's what I can't tell you. I'll never be able to tell you. But I think so. Something very simple, but professional work. I may have something more to say later on. It's a rather interesting point, but I don't like to commit myself at the moment. All I'll admit now is that it was a grenade and it was professionally made."

"Ah!" said the superintendent and was silent.

A young constable knocked and put a polished face inside the door.

"Chief Inspector Yeo, sir."

The superintendent looked up with a grin.

181

"Hallo, Freddie," he said. "Glad to see you. Come in. We've got some nice bad news for you here, my lad."

19

Chief Detective Inspector Yeo came in briskly. He was square and efficient, with a solid bullethead and an insignificant, almost comical face. His snub nose and round eyes had been a serious disadvantage to him all his life, undermining his dignity and earning him friends rather than admirers. Even Oates, who had the utmost respect for his quite extraordinary ability, was inclined to sympathise with him whenever he saw him.

At the moment he was very tired and his plump face was drawn.

The superintendent performed the introduction briefly. He ignored Yeo's sharp glance of enquiry and offered no explanation for Mr. Campion's presence.

"You wouldn't have had time to prepare any sort of report, of course?" Oates was inclined to put the question mischievously. "You're just off the train, aren't you? Anything new?"

Yeo shook his head.

"Nothing," he said gloomily. "Plenty of negative evidence. However, my men are still slogging away at it and the local people are very helpful but they've got their hands full. One rather wretched thing happened. The porter's wife chucked herself into the local millpool this morning. She was left with two little kids. Couldn't face life without her husband and all that. She was a bit crazy, of course; demented by the shock, probably. They got her out, but it was no good. Makes you feel a bit sick, don't it? It's a nasty, callous business. No sense in it."

He wiped his forehead and his thick short neck with a vast handkerchief and looked glum.

The superintendent made no comment on the extraneous

tragedy so briefly recorded but his face grew very hard, and Mr. Campion, who was sitting quietly in his corner, was reminded that Oates was a countryman who had come from just such another village with just such another millpool, and more than probably with just such another porter.

The superintendent plunged into business.

"Major Bloom holds the view that the grenade was professional work. Does that help at all?"

"Professional?" Yeo looked at the major blankly. "That's a funny thing. It must have been in a parcel lying around. Someone's hiding some little technical offence against the railway. Must be."

He spoke hopefully but without great conviction.

"We've made fifty-four interviews and taken thirty-nine statements," he went on slowly, "and at the moment if I heard you gentlemen had decided it was a thunderbolt I should be convinced and thankful. It's an extraordinary thing, but no one admits to having seen anyone throw anything at any time, and they're nearly all strangers to each other, so it can't be conspiracy."

The major, who had been listening with interest, leant across the arm of his chair.

"Could you give me a good eyewitness report of the two or three minutes before the explosion?" he enquired.

Yeo grimaced.

"I can, sir, but I'm afraid you'll find it very ordinary. There doesn't seem to have been much to see. There's one young chap who gives the down platform view very clearly."

He opened a battered attaché case and took out a sheaf of typewritten sheets.

"I'll read it to you. Here he is. Joseph Harold Biggins, 17 years of age, 32, Christchurch Road, N.E. 38. He was one of the cyclists and he's in the cottage hospital with half the skin flayed off his chest, poor chap. I won't bother you with all the preliminary stuff, about how he got to Boarbridge and so on. This is what he says about the actual thing."

He cleared his throat and began to read in expressionless police-court tones.

"'When the train pulled out of the station Mr. Konrad, our president, who we had come to meet, was standing about halfway down the platform holding his bicycle. We advanced to meet him and, as our secretary had been detained outside

183

the booking hall, I and Duke went forward in front of the others. Mr. Konrad was in cycling costume and seemed very pleased to see us. He smiled as we came up and said, "Hallo, boys, here I am," or something like that. I cannot swear to the exact words.

"'There was a bit of a pause because of shyness on the part of the members, and to make everybody comfortable Mr. Konrad indicated the bicycle he was holding, which was a present from the club, and said: "Is she not a beauty? She runs like a bird." He then turned the bike sideways, showed off the drop handlebars with the special grips, pretended to switch the lamp on and off, etcetera. That is the last I remember.

"'There was a sort of roar and I remember falling. When I came to I was in great pain and Duke was lying over me. I did not realise he was dead until I saw his face.'"

The inspector ceased abruptly.

"A terrible business," he said. "All the statements are like that. Just horror coming out of the blue, you might say. One woman in the up train said she saw Konrad and the bicycle shoot into the air, but the porter with the milk cans was between her and him and he staggered forward, you know, pulling the whole thing on top of him. The sight of all the churns toppling over onto the line in a shower of glass from the roof seems to have sent everything else out of her mind. The thing couldn't have been *in* a milk can, could it? I don't know much about these things, but it seems to me..."

He broke off questioningly. The two experts, who had been exchanging glances, were on the verge of speech. Mr. Culvert appeared to be urging his chief to make some sort of confidence and the major suddenly capitulated.

"I wanted to be more sure, d'you see," he began in his soft homely accent, "because, frankly, the idea is so—so *peculiar*. But in view of that first statement made by the young boy I think we really might consider the evidence of the fragments of glass and the bicycle, even at this dangerously early stage."

Both policemen and Mr. Campion regarded him with polite bewilderment.

"What glass?" demanded the superintendent.

Yeo was interested.

"You're referring to the little chunks of thick glass taken

184

from Duke's body?" he said. "I wondered about that myself. What's on your mind, sir?"

Although he had decided to confide, the major was still very guarded.

"You must understand that I'm not giving you evidence," he said. "There's still an enormous amount of work to be done before I could consider the case for the bicycle lamp to be absolutely watertight. There are certain comparisons we'll have to make, or a clever counsel could make us look like a pack of idiots. These legal fellows, you know, are very difficult."

"We haven't got that far," murmured the superintendent dryly. "We don't know if we're going to have to make an arrest at all. You people may have to go to war or something. It may be a political business, clean out of our province."

The inspector, however, had heard remarkable words.

"The bicycle lamp?" he said.

"Yes. Yes. As far as we can see, though I really don't like to commit myself." The major was excited. "The grenade was inside the bicycle lamp—where the dry battery should have been. Some of these lamps turn on with a screw, you know, and my own personal theory—which isn't evidence—is that the man with the bicycle exploded the grenade when he turned on, or attempted to turn on, the lamp. That explains all the facts, you see: the state of the bicycle, which was injured in a most significant fashion; the tiny pieces of thick lens glass in the one man's body; the general direction of the damage; the fact that nothing appears to have been thrown; the . . ."

He broke off. No one but Mr. Culvert was making any pretence of listening to him. The two policemen were staring at each other, speculation in their eyes, while Campion had frozen and sat staring rigidly in front of him, his mind leaping from one appalling conjecture to the next.

"He brought it with him!" said Yeo. "God Almighty, he brought it with him!"

"You'll have to trace the original lamp and find me a similar one for comparison with my fragments," put in the major, who appeared to be completely blind to the sensation he was creating. "That's most important if it comes into court. That woman in the train too. You spoke of her just now. She must have seen the explosion itself. If one of us was to question her she might remember a great many little details which seemed

185

to her unimportant at the time, and we may get a lot of stuff to help us to establish absolute proof. You see, I'm thinking that there was probably a very short time fuse—say two or three seconds—fitted to the thing. That would have made it considerably safer to handle, and he could have moved the bicycle, or spoken even, actually after he'd ignited the fuse by turning on the lamp. As far as we know, he made no attempt to save himself.

"I haven't gathered all the circumstances yet. What was he doing. Making a protest of some sort?"

His final words percolated through the superintendent's preoccupation. Oates looked up slowly.

"He had no idea what he was doing," he said. "That's certain. He was ignorant. He didn't know it was there."

Yeo rose to his feet.

"But all those people?" he began, his round eyes wide and shocked.

As the obvious truth dawned upon him the colour rushed into his face.

"It was a mistake!" he ejaculated. "It was a mistake. It ought not to have happened there. It ought to have happened on a lonely road somewhere. It's a mistake. It's a murder gone wrong!"

He remained for a moment bewildered by his own discovery and then, as another thought occurred to him, he swooped down upon his brief case.

"Oates," he said unsteadily, "it's all here. That bicycle was given to Konrad by the cycle club. The collection was taken and delivery made by the secretary. His name is Howard. I've got his statement somewhere. He didn't like Konrad. That has emerged in several statements. It struck me at the time. He wasn't present on the station at the time of the explosion and—this is the point—he works in a wholesale chemist's. I've just remembered it."

Mr. Campion rose from his chair in the corner and came quietly forward. His voice was heavy and impersonal and he stood limply, as though the weight of his own body had suddenly become oppressive to him.

"I'm afraid that's no good," he said, unaware of the chief inspector's startled glance. "Konrad was given that bicycle weeks ago. You'll have plenty of proof that he's been all over it with the excitement of a woman examining a new handbag.

186

But he had not seen it for five days before he collected it on Sunday morning and hurried down to Birley station on it to catch the slow down train for Boarbridge. During that five days it had been standing in the cloakroom at White Walls."

"Where's that?" The inspector put the question sharply.

Oates answered for Campion.

"Jimmy Sutane's country house. He's the actor chap Blest was telling you about. Remember?"

20

"Mr. Campion . . ."

The chief inspector set down his modest glass of Bass and leant confidentially across the coarse linen tablecloth.

"When Mr. Sutane phoned you last night and you spoke to him, what did you say?"

It was late in the day for lunch and Bonini's stuffy upper room was practically deserted. They had that corner by the window which gives into Old Compton Street to themselves and Yeo's gentle murmur carried no farther than the ear for which it was intended.

Campion, who was looking a little leaner and, in the inspector's opinion, a good deal more intelligent than his usual, casually elegant self, blinked thoughtfully as the explanation of the hasty and pressing invitation was revealed to him. He glanced at Yeo, sitting square and absurd before him, and was inclined to like him very much.

Their acquaintance was of long standing and each man knew the other well by repute, but this was the first occasion on which they had had actual dealings.

"He wanted me to go down there," said Campion truthfully.

"Why didn't you go? You don't mind a few questions, do you?" Yeo was smiling affably but his manner betrayed caution, for, as a valued expert and the C.I.D. "super's" personal friend, Mr. Campion merited careful handling.

"I thought I'd keep out of it."

"Quite. Quite. I can understand that."

The inspector was satisfied only in part. He tried another line.

"It's an A case," he observed. "We're out to get him. I saw our chief constable and the assistant commissioner this morning. I've got the whole force behind me and I can have anyone I like to call on. The case is to get real preference. The man we're after is *dangerous*, you see, Mr. Campion. I mean, you could call him antisocial, couldn't you? If he's a private person with facilities for tapping stuff which is nothing more or less than war material, and doesn't mind who he does in, well, I mean to say, he *must* be stopped!"

His earnestness widened his eyes and shortened his nose until he looked like a comedian in the midst of his act.

"He must," he repeated. "We've got to get him. That woman with the injured leg is in danger. If she dies there'll be four persons killed, eleven injured, and no one knows how much damage."

Campion smiled crookedly.

"My dear chap," he said, "don't think for a moment that I don't agree with you. I do. The whole nature of the thing is so preposterous that I don't think any sane man could argue with you about it. Whatever the circumstances turn out to be, nothing could ever excuse or extenuate such an incredible piece of stupid wickedness. When you get your man you'll have to hang him. I do see that."

Yeo shot him a relieved but still puzzled glance.

"Both Oates and I knew you were sound," he said naïvely, "but frankly we were wondering if you weren't holding something back—something that might put us on to a *motive,* for instance."

Campion did not respond, and the detective continued after a brief pause.

"You've had time to get to know all that lot down there, and they're a funny crowd. I can't help thinking that if there had been anything a bit fishy going on beforehand you'd have noticed it. Something that might have led up to this, I mean. We're at a great disadvantage coming in only after the event, with the newspapers printing all they can find the instant after they find it. There was that actress woman who died down there... did she fall or did she jump? No one knows and it doesn't really matter. Still, it was a funny thing to happen, all the same. I don't like coincidences. It's silly to pretend they don't occur, but I don't like them.'

Mr. Campion raised his eyes from his plate.

"You're concentrating on White Walls?"

"Well, yes, in the main." Yeo lowered his tone and scowled at the plump Bonini, who was bearing down upon them with hostly affability. The restaurateur altered his course, affronted, and the inspector, having satisfied himself that he was not overheard, went on with his story.

"It's four days now and we've been working steadily, with a certain amount of results, of course. As soon as you came out with your piece of information about the bicycle—which saved us quite a bit of time, by the way—I checked up on it and found you were right. Konrad had received the bicycle on the second, nearly a fortnight before the rally, and I found quite a number of people at the theatre, and in other places, who had actually seen the lamp alight. Bit by bit we narrowed it down to the time when he took it to Mr. Sutane's house. There's a chauffeur there—a decent, sensible chap... I don't know if you know him? He's one of these gadgety lads who was very taken by the bicycle. He swears that on the first Sunday Mr. Konrad had it down there he, the chauffeur, made a complete examination of it and was particularly impressed by the lamp, which he described to me as 'super.' He was able to give me complete specifications and these tallied exactly with those I got from the firm which supplied the machine."

He paused and Campion nodded his comprehension and approval. The inspector lit a cigarette.

"Well," he said, "we've covered the lamp all right until the time Konrad left the bicycle in the cloakroom at the house. He went up to town on the Monday by car. On the following Sunday he came back in a cab with very little time to spare. The evidence is that he rushed up to the room which had been prepared for him, hurried into cycling kit, leaving his other clothes strewn about for someone else to pack—your man, Mr. Lugg, was very chatty on that question, by the way—and tore down to the cloakroom, where he snatched his

189

bicycle and rushed off on it, catching the train at Birley by the skin of his teeth. No one noticed the lamp at the time.

"Mr. Lugg says he saw the bicycle standing in the cloak-room all the week, but he never thought to examine it. If you ask me, he was lucky. It's a natural thing to do, isn't it? —switch on a lamp."

"But the grenade couldn't have been there long." Campion was aghast. "Think of the danger. There's a child in the house. Anything might have happened."

Yeo shook his head knowingly.

"It all depends who put it there," he said. "If you ask me, the man who did this job wasn't the imaginative type. He's straightforward and ingenious; that's how I see him. Single-track mind. He argued that Konrad would ride that bicycle until it grew dark, and then he'd switch on his light and sit there with his head over the lamp until it blew up and killed him. Looked at like that, it seems foolproof, doesn't it?"

Campion considered the problem unwillingly.

"It must have been put there on the last morning. Probably the whole lamp was changed and a similar one substituted. Now I think of it, it must have happened like that."

"You're right." Yeo was pleased and he beamed upon his guest as at a promising pupil. "Major Bloom has had a bit more to say. He's now prepared to swear that the explosive was in the lamp all right, but the minute fragments of lamp which remain are not consistent with them being part of the actual one supplied with the bicycle, the specifications of which we have from the chauffeur and from the firm which sold it.

"So you see, as far as we know for certain, someone changed the lamp after Mr. Konrad left on Monday and before he took the bike away on the following Sunday. I agree with you the substitution probably took place towards the end of the time, but we can't prove it, can we? That leaves us with everybody who came and went in that house for the best part of six days—and believe me there's a crowd of them."

Campion hesitated.

"What about *after* he left the house?" he suggested dubiously.

"Impossible. I've checked the time he left the door with the time he came flying into Birley station. He could only just have done it. The bicycle was thrown into the guard's van and the guard remembers sitting near it the whole journey.

190

He nearly fainted when I told him about the grenade. I had to laugh—couldn't help myself."

Yeo grinned at the recollection but frowned again and sighed as the problem presented itself once more.

"If we could get on to the motive we'd have a definite lead," he said, eyeing Campion meaningly. "As far as I can gather from the people down there, no one liked Konrad but his sudden death is the last thing any of them wanted."

Still Mr. Campion refused to be drawn. He sat back in his chair, his face grave and friendly, but he made no suggestion.

Yeo, who was a man of infinite patience, continued the attack.

"You know the family and the immediate circle, so I needn't reintroduce them," he said. "There's an old man called William Faraday staying there. He was mixed up in that Cambridge case some years ago, wasn't he? You met him then. He's a friend of yours. He admits he had no time for Konrad, but he was the author of the show Konrad was appearing in and he's drawing big money for the first time in his life. Even if he were the type to go to the length of procuring the grenade and fixing it up, I can't see what he could possibly gain by Konrad's death, and the scandal might be definitely detrimental to his pocket. The same goes for Mr. Sutane, the composer Mr. Mercer, and the manager Mr. Poyser, who was in the house over the Saturday. Then there's Mr. Petrie, the secretary and publicity fellow; his job depends on Sutane's success, and he's not too flush for cash. The servants are out of it, as far as I can see, and the women don't appeal to me as suspects. Either the wife or the sister could conceivably have done it, but I'm hanged if I see why they should. Konrad doesn't seem to have gone in for love affairs and, apart from that consideration, the same main deterrents apply equally to them as to the men."

He shook his head.

"People don't go murdering for nothing unless they're homicidal maniacs. This is the work of a reasonable but callous mentality with a blind spot. Someone who wanted the chap to die and wanted him to go away and die, and didn't much care where. That's how I see him. But why he should do it at all I do not know."

There was silence between them for some time. Mr. Campion found he was doing his best not to think at all.

The chief inspector leant across and prodded his arm with a blunt forefinger.

"Faraday's a friend of yours but the others aren't," he said. "You went to White Walls for the first time less than a fortnight ago?"

Campion grinned.

"It seems longer."

"I'll lay it does. They've had a packet down there." Yeo's eyes were bright and still friendly. "Blest has done well. I've had everything out with him, of course. Oates and I have gone over that persecution story from A to Z. That's how you got into the business in the first place. We know all about that and we've taken it into consideration. But however irritated Mr. Sutane was, he'd hardly go killing Konrad when he could sack him, would he? Or he might have lost his temper and socked the fellow, but he wouldn't go messing about with explosives and delayed-action methods. Besides, there wasn't the time. Blest told Mr. Sutane his suspicions on the Saturday after he had located the accomplice, and Konrad met his death on the Sunday. That grenade had to be obtained."

Campion roused himself with an effort.

"Where did it come from?"

"We don't know yet. Major Bloom's still working on it."

For the first time throughout the interview Yeo showed signs of his normal reticence.

"I seem to be doing all the talking," he remarked. "What about you saying a few words?"

"I've been agreeing with you." Campion spoke carefully. "Everything you've said I've thought myself. I'm in the dark. The crime has astonished me. It's not the kind of thing I could ever imagine emanating from that house. But if it has, then I'm sorry but I don't want to be near it."

Yeo shrugged his shoulders.

"That's where you have the advantage over us professionals," he said acidly. "I can't choose myself. I've never known you like this, Mr. Campion. You're usually so keen. If I was asked, do you know what I'd say? If I didn't know you were a comparative stranger to these people I'd say personal feelings were involved. Yet Faraday's the only friend you've got in the bunch and, frankly, I can't for the life of me see how he can be in it."

"Look here, Inspector, if I thought I could help you put

your hands on the man you want I'd do it." Campion's voice was unexpectedly strained. "You must believe that. But I can't. I do not know. I cannot think of anyone with any motive who could conceivably have done such an appalling, such a stupid, thing. You say Blest found the accomplice? Who was he? May I know? It's a point of professional interest to me."

"You can see him if you like." Yeo was the soul of affability. His reputation for tenacity had not been lightly won. "I'm going to look him up after this. Who do you think it was? Beaut Siegfried, of all people."

"No, really?" It seemed to Campion that he had not heard that florid name since his childhood. "The dancing master?"

"The old haybag himself," agreed Yeo disrespectfully. "He's ballet master now, by the way. Regular old pressed rose. Blest got him to admit he wrote those invitations. Don't ask me how. I don't want to know. I'd get kicked out of the force if I used some of the methods these private chaps employ. Blest was never more than a divisional inspector, you know. He was a bit too hot for anything. Anyway, he managed old Beaut. Mr. Siegfried wrote to Mr. Sutane a nice little letter of apology for 'what was, perhaps, an only too unfortunate practical joke.' Sutane has accepted the apology, Blest says. It was about all he could do in the circumstances. It was a silly trick, enough to make anybody wild.

"But not *murdering* wild," he added after a pause and cocked his head at Campion like a terrier at a mousehole.

In the end Mr. Campion accompanied the inspector to the studio in Cavendish Square, accepting the honour in the spirit of good fellowship which he was no less anxious than the police to maintain. After years of the closest and most friendly co-operation with the authorities he felt his present position on the fence very keenly, and his resentment at the combination of circumstances which had forced him to take it up grew deep.

As they came across the fine square in the warm odoriferous London afternoon Yeo coughed.

"This is just a little friendly chat. You're my unofficial sergeant for the time being. There's been so many infringements of the regulations already where this chap is concerned that I don't think another matters very much. You'll have to lie out of it if you ever see him again. He knows me. We've had one or two little chats in our time."

As they climbed the shallow steps to the graceful Georgian doorway another thought occurred to him.

"He's a bit of a sketch," he said. "Thinks he's the School of Scandal, or something."

Beaut Siegfried interviewed them in his beautiful studio. He was a thin, elderly man on whom old affectations hung like faded garlands. His court breeches and silk stockings betrayed ageing, sharp-boned legs, and the shoulders beneath his long-skirted velvet coat were bent and weak. He had fine white hands and was childishly proud of them, letting them drop into careless, graceful poses whenever he remembered. His face beneath his fluffy hair, which was still brown and still curly, was the face of the traditional withered spinster, prim, lined and spiteful, the eyes slightly prominent and disconcertingly blank.

When they were shown in he was posing with a fiddle, a shaft of sunlight from a high window falling on his bent head. He laid the instrument down with a little sigh as they appeared and advanced across the polished floor to meet them.

"My dear Chief Inspector," he said, "this is a pleasure. I am free, too. None of my dear boys and girls will be here till six. They still come to me, you see, and I teach them to move their beautiful bodies with the true grace. But they won't be here till six o'clock and so I was able to have you shown in at once. A glass of amontillado? Just a little one? In my crystal glasses."

Yeo refused and sat down uninvited, motioning Mr. Campion to do likewise.

Siegfried remained posed in front of them, the light playing on his hair and on the soft folds of his coat. There was an irregular board in the floor, Mr. Campion noticed, to show him just where to stand if this effect was to be satisfactorily attained.

Yeo regarded his host blandly and with a certain satisfaction, as at a peculiar pet.

"I came to talk to you about Konrad," he said. "I thought you might be able to help me."

"Konrad?" Siegfried threw a white hand over his eyes. "I can't think of it," he said. "I sent some roses but I can't think

194

of it. Don't ask me to. He had such a gift, such a spirit! To die so young!"

He had a curious soft voice with a crack in it and a refinement of accent which was oddly not at all unpleasant. Campion found himself wondering what on earth he had been like at school.

Yeo's round eyes were amused.

"Do you know of anyone who didn't like him?" he enquired baldly.

"Oh." The dancing master dropped his hand and his sharp, withered face became startlingly inquisitive. "Oh. Why do you ask me that?"

"Because I thought you might know," explained Yeo stolidly. "He was a star pupil of yours or something, wasn't he?"

"Well"—Siegfried was flattered—"I taught him all *I* knew. His poise, his grace, his divine spirit, was all mine. But his modern technique... No, I don't think I can lay claim to that. I used to scold him sometimes for leaving the classical school of sheer beauty for the intricacies of the terrible new rhythm."

"Anyway, you knew him," Yeo persisted. "Had he any enemies?"

Siegfried hesitated, his mouth narrowed and pursed and his eyes growing spiteful.

"There were people who were jealous of him," he said primly.

Yeo waited patiently until with a shrug of his bent shoulders, which proclaimed as clearly as if he had spoken that he was throwing off restraint, Siegfried took the plunge.

"It may be slander," he said. "I don't know, I'm sure; the law's so ridiculous. But I do think someone ought to be told. I'll let you know in confidence, Inspector, but I'm not going to be badgered afterwards. The poor boy was *persecuted*."

It seemed extraordinary that one wizened old creature could hold so much living forceful venom.

"Sutane," he said. "That man Sutane. He's not a dancer. He's an acrobat and the mob have made a god of him. He's got no soul, no poetry, no spirit at all, and when he saw Benny he was jealous of him. He's dogged the boy. He's forced him into his shows and kept him out of sight all because he simply *daren't* let him appear."

He forgot the shaft of sunlight and came a little closer,

195

thrusting his face into the inspector's own and bubbling a little at the lips in his excitement.

"Benny's been here and *cried* to me," he insisted. "If Benny had a good entrance Sutane took it away. If there was an opportunity for costume Sutane disallowed it. If Benny got an ovation Sutane sneered at him. The boy was simply a mass of nerves after a month or two of Sutane. I don't know what happened at the end. I can't read the newspapers. They're disgusting. But whatever it was, Sutane was morally responsible. There, now I've told you. My conscience is clear. But do understand I *won't be worried*. I won't make a statement and I certainly won't go into court. I've got my boys and girls to think of. I teach them to be artists in the true sense of the word and I won't be hindered."

"Konrad never complained to you of anyone except Sutane?" Yeo was stolidly impervious to the gibbering face so near his own.

"No. No one but Sutane." The old man stood biting his thin lips, his prominent eyes staring and vindictive. "Sutane was killing him in spirit, stifling him and devitalising him. But I don't want to hear anything more about it. It upsets me. The tragedy has happened and the poor boy is dead."

He walked back to the great Italian chest in the corner and picked up his violin. Yeo took his leave.

They were shown to the door by a respectable elderly char-woman who fitted the messenger boy's description of the woman who had despatched the garlic bouquet.

As they came away they heard the quavering strains of a little air of Puccini's rendered atrociously.

Yeo walked along in silence for some minutes.

"There's nothing there," he said at last. "I saw it at once. You can see how that monkey business round the theatre came to happen, can't you? Konrad was eaten alive with jealousy, transposed it in his mind, as they all do, and he and Siegfried egged each other on until they had to break out into action or burst."

Campion nodded. The action had been typical, he reflected; little sporadic eruptions of weakness, petty, absurd and infuriating.

Yeo laughed.

"The old devil wasn't mentioning his brush with Blest, was he?" he said. "You'd think an experience like that would teach him to keep his mouth shut, but I thought it wouldn't. He is an old woman and no mistake! Oates can't stay in the room with him, but he makes me laugh. There's nothing vicious about him. He's just a bundle of old fancy dress and always has been. Why don't you accept Mr. Sutane's invitation and go down to White Walls, Mr. Campion?"

The suddenness of the question had its desired effect and took Campion off his guard.

"Because I don't want to," he said.

Yeo sighed.

"Think it over," he advised. "You could be very useful to us on the inside like that. See here, these are my last words. You don't think Mr. Sutane is the man we want and I can't see why on earth he should be, any more than anyone else. It's to his interest to have the thing cleared up quickly, because we're going to keep at it if it takes us from now until eternity, and we'll ruin him before we've finished, We can't help ourselves. So whose hospitality will you be abusing? Think it over . . ."

Mr. Campion walked about London for nearly four hours. The complete privacy of a sojourn among four million total strangers was comforting and the exercise soothed him.

As he came up the quiet, dignified street to the Junior Greys the evening sun picked out the colours at the windows of the solid grey-white buildings and the air was pleasant and full of the quiet laughter of a London after work. He began to feel free again. The gnawing, shameful preoccupation with Linda which had been at first amusing and then shocking and finally downright terrifying was now battened down, banished, part to some far-off corner of his mind and part to a spot somewhere at the base of his diaphragm.

He felt responsible again and his own mind's master.

There was a message waiting for him with the club porter. It was brief and mysterious, without being particularly disturbing. The caretaker at Bottle Street had phoned to ask if he would call in at the flat the moment he returned. Because it was so near, barely three streets away, he went round at once and hurried up the familiar staircase, fumbling in his pocket for his key.

As he came to the foot of the final flight he paused abruptly, his new-found peace scattered as the battens were burst upward and all the mental and emotional confusion of the past ten days took possession of him once again.

Linda Sutane, who had been seated on the topmost stair just outside his door, rose wearily to her feet and came down to meet him.

21

As Campion stood balancing his lean body, his heels on the curb and his shoulders braced against the high mantelshelf, he looked at the girl seated in his wing chair and made the disturbing discovery that the progress of an affair of the heart does not cease at the point where the two parties are separated, resuming its course when they meet again, but rather continues its relentless progress slowly and inexorably all the time, whether the participants are together or apart.

Linda Sutane looked smaller than he had remembered her. Her black suit with the pleated white collar was a Lelong, and the hat perched on her sleek hair gave her a new air of sophistication which he liked and found somehow comforting.

She had followed him into the flat without speaking and had seated herself without glancing about her. Her silence had demoralised him and he stood looking at her, his hands in his pockets, wishing that she would speak and put the ridiculously disturbing meeting on some concrete basis of reality at least. At the moment he felt he was suffering from an hallucination with the added disadvantage of knowing very well that it was not one.

She glanced up at him and he saw that her small face was white and stiff and her honey-coloured eyes dark with worry.

His heart contracted suddenly and painfully, and this, the final emotional straw, turned the wheel right over and he felt gloriously and freely angry with her. The whole monstrous imposition of love confronted him and he boiled at it.

"Well," he said spitefully, "this is very nice of you."

198

She drew back into the chair and tucked her feet up under her so that it contained her entirely.

"Uncle William thought you would come to help us if I asked you myself, so I came to find you."

She spoke with an unusual ingenuousness, and he saw that she was ill at ease and received an unworthy satisfaction from the discovery.

"But, my dear lady," he said, "if there was anything I could do, believe me, I should be wandering round your delightful garden, badgering your servants, leaping about from flower bed to flower bed with a reading glass, and generally behaving like the complete house-trained private tec. But as it is, I really don't see how I can impose myself upon you. What can I do?"

She stared at him.

"You've changed," she said.

The suddenness of the direct attack defeated, or rather deflated, him. He fumbled for a cigarette case and offered it to her. She shook her head in refusal but did not take her glance from his face. She looked hurt and puzzled and reminded him irritatingly of Sarah.

"We're in dreadful trouble," she said. "The police come every day. Do you know about it? What they think about Konrad?"

"Roughly, yes."

"Yet you won't do anything?"

For what was probably the first time in his life Campion ceased to think during an interview. There are occasions when the intellect retires gracefully from a situation entirely beyond its decorous control and leaves all the other complicated machinery of the mind to muddle through on its own.

Since he was a highly bred product of a highly civilised strain, his natural instincts were offset by other man-implanted cultures and taboos, and the result of the war between them was to make him, if inwardly wretched, outwardly a trifle insane.

"My dear," he said, "I'll hold the whole blithering universe up for you. I'll stop the whole dizzy juggernaut of British police procedure for you if you want me to. I'm all-powerful. I'll wave a little wand and we'll find it all isn't true."

For a moment she wavered maddeningly between anger

199

and tears and finally crept further into the depths of the chair, to sit looking out at him like a wren in a nest.

"How is Lugg?" said Campion. "And Uncle William? And the helpful Mercer? Sock, too, and Poyser and Miss Finbrough? You all have my most sincere sympathy and if I were a first-class magician I'd put the clock back a month or so, say to the beginning of May, with the greatest of pleasure for you. As it is, however, I'm not the man you thought me. God bless my soul, I'm not the fairy queen after all."

He was concentrating on making her angry. It seemed to have become the only important thing in life.

"I'm a cad at heart," he said cheerfully. "I can't work the oracle and miracles are beyond me. You see, there are quite a number of other powerful spells at work—the porter's wife, for instance."

He was very much alive now and laughing. The vacuity had vanished from his face, leaving it lean and pleasant. He had taken off his spectacles and his pale long-sighted eyes were darker and sharper than before.

Linda nodded to him gravely as if he had imparted a secret to her which she had already known.

"Come down with me now," she said and held out her hand to him.

He looked at the hand, shooting it a sharp quick glance which took in everything there was to notice about it: its shape, its texture, and the very faint blue veins under the golden skin. A colt in the field looks in the same way at the skip of feed held out to entice it.

He turned abruptly and went over to the cocktail cabinet.

"Let us drink and discuss this," he said. "A White Lady?"

He was a long time over his preparations and she watched his thin, muscular back and the short fine hairs at the base of his skull.

"The rats are right in the house now," she said in a small quiet voice behind him. "We shall have to see them soon. It's like being besieged by ghosts. Jimmy's insane with worry and everybody's different. I thought it was only in the house but now I'm beginning to find the whole world's like it. I thought you'd like to help."

"I would," he assured her lightly. "If I could, I'd come beetling down like a homing chipmunk. You see, it's the size of the thing which discourages me so. Have you noticed that

200

about murder? It goes by compound interest. Two are twice as bad as one and three are three times as bad as two. I may run round and muck about with the insides of motorcars in a little case of dubious suicide, but when I see such a quantity of carnage I know when I'm beaten. I knew a mongrel whippet once called Addlepate. He'd take on any bull pup single-handed but he gave one look at the bull-pup ring at a country show and raised his eyebrows and walked away. I sympathised with him. I'm like that myself. Your cocktail, lady."

She took the glass and set it down untasted. He found her bewildered expression unbearable and so he did not look at her.

"If you found out the truth and told, I wouldn't blame you," she said.

"I don't know. It might be a howling cad's trick to tell. Things like that sometimes happen," he said and laughed.

She turned her face into the upholstery of the chair and he paused abruptly and stared at her, his eyes wretched. There was a long silence and in it he was acutely aware that he was in his own familiar room and that she was in it, too, and no right thing there.

He took the handkerchief from his breast pocket and dropped it lightly onto her hand.

The movement roused her and she took it up and looked at it.

"You're very hard," she said. "I didn't realise that. Incredibly hard."

"Solid rock," he agreed. "Granite. Beneath the superstratum of mud you come to stone. The ghastly monotony is relieved here and there by occasional fossilised fish."

"Oh, well, it's been very—very interesting," she said and climbed out of the chair.

She smiled at him, her brown eyes shining.

He did not echo it. His face was pinched and grey.

"Did you come by car, or may I take you to the station?"

She moved close to him and looked up at him, her face working.

"I'm frightened," she said. "That's really why I came. I don't know what's going to happen next. I'm alone down there with them all and I'm physically frightened. Don't you see?"

201

Mr. Campion stood staring down at her with his arms hanging limply at his sides. Presently he lifted his chin and looked over her head. His expression was blank and introspective.

"All right," he said with sudden brisk decision. "We'll go now. This is my full responsibility, remember. It's nothing to do with you at all. Both your husband and the police have asked me to make an investigation and I'll try to do it. That's all. But I'm afraid . . ."

He broke off and she prompted him.

"What?"

"Afraid the time may come when you will think I'm a pretty low-down sort of tick, Linda my sweet," said Mr. Campion gravely.

22

"Ease it," said Mr. Lugg through the door. "Put yer back into it. Ee-ease it. Don't git excited and don't be frightened. I'm here. I'll let you out if you can't do it, but come on—try. Don't be a little wet."

The long corridor which ran from east to west throughout the whole top floor of White Walls was silent save for his earnest injunctions, and Mr. Campion, who had been looking for him ever since his own arrival, was confronted by a monstrous back view of that vast familiar form.

"Steady—steady now! I can 'ear it goin'."

The white arc of a bald head appeared over a much greater arc of broadcloth tail coat, like an up-ended crescent moon, as its owner applied a great ear to the panels of a door. There was a grunt of regret.

"Lorst it. . . . Never mind. Try again. You'll never do it if you don't try. Take the pin out. 'As it lost its shape? Wot? Well, *square*, you snufflin' little chump! I showed you. Got it? Now then, in she goes. Quietly!—quietly! You don't want to

202

rouse the 'ouse. 'Ere she goes—'ere she goes.... That's it. Now then..."

The ominous scratching at the door lock ceased as with a triumphant click the bolt shot back and the door slid quietly open, to reveal a flushed and excited Sarah with a bent hairpin in her hand.

"Done it!" she screamed, dancing round the old man like a demented puppy. "Done it! Done it! Done it!"

"Shut up." Lugg let out a friendly blow at the side of her head which would have felled an ox and mercifully missed its half-hearted objective. "Don't bawl the place down. You'll get us ticked orf again. No need to go orf like a gin palace on a Saturday, even if you can pick a lock with anyone twice yer size. Now, there's something useful I've learnt yer, only don't advertise it. That's the kind of trick you want to keep under yer 'at—see? 'Ullo..."

The final utterance was in the nature of a warning. They both stiffened and Mr. Lugg's beady bright eyes rested coldly upon the thin form at the far end of the corridor.

Campion came forward.

"Lugg, what are you doing?"

"Amusin' the child." Lugg was truculent and casual. "I'm a nursemaid now. Didn't they tell you?" He looked down at his pupil and winked. "Run along now, Miss Sarah," he said with travestied formality. "Nuss will no doubt be a-searchin' of for you. You do not want to cause her any anxiety? I thought not. We will continue our 'obby later on. Go on, get out. Beat it, there's a good kid."

Sarah squeezed his hand and slipped the hairpin into his coat pocket.

"Thank you, Mr. Lugg," she said with rehearsed dignity. "That was most int'resting."

She walked off sedately, only breaking into uncontrollable giggles when the newcomer had been safely passed. Campion waited until she was out of earshot and spent the time surveying his only real responsibility with a chilly interest guaranteed to inspire shame.

"You think you're a damn fine sort of a fellow, I suppose?" he said at last. "A sort of ministering Boy Scout, bringing a little dusty sunshine to a misunderstood child?"

Lugg sniffed to convey that he was not impressed.

"I'm very fond of my fellow creatures," he said. "Besides,

you never know when a simple little wrinkle like that might come in useful. Every kid ought to learn 'ow to pick a lock. She's a helpless noisy little bit. She's bound to come up against it sometime in 'er life. I'm preparin' of 'er for it. I'm doin' 'er a bit of good. You lay orf. I like 'er. She's all right."

"She reminds you of yourself when you were a child, no doubt?" enquired Mr. Campion affably.

Lugg looked down over a highly coloured career to some distant hotbed in the slums of Canning Town.

"No," he said seriously. "Not reely. She's simple to what I was. It's the bringin' up what does it. Well, you've turned up at last, 'ave you? About time too. I've 'ad a room ready for you for a week. Come on. I'll show it to you now you are 'ere."

He waddled down the corridor with Campion behind him.

"There you are," he said, flinging open the door of the chamber immediately above the small music room. "Mr. Benjamin Konrad's late apartment. The last gentleman 'oo slept in 'ere was blown to Beunos Aires. 'Ope you'll be comfortable."

Campion walked through the chintz-hung room and stood looking out over the wide garden, misty in the twilight.

"Well?" he enquired over his shoulder. "Noticed anything of value about this business?"

"No. I'm keepin' right out of it." Lugg heaved a leather suitcase onto the bedspread and began to pitch out its contents. "You didn't think to bring me a shirt or two, I don't suppose?" he said. "I'm right away from civilisation down 'ere, you know."

"No, I didn't. Leave those things alone. Pull yourself together. You can't have been going about in a trance. You must have noticed something. What have you been doing?"

"What I was asked—bein' a butler." Lugg sounded smugly satisfied. "You lent me to the lady as a butler and a butler I've bin. It's not my line but I've made a job of it and in a way I've quite enjoyed it. The servants are well under my thumb and in my spare time I do my best to amuse the kid, 'oo I like. Give me a year or two with that kid and I'll make somethink of 'er. She's got the makin's of a first-class little tough. I'm very strict, you know. No swearin'. Nothin' unladylike. She's give me a few tips too. If there's somethink I don't know and don't like to lower meself by askin' the servants, I mention it

204

to 'er and, if she don't know either, she gits it out the nurse. It's mutual.

"Oh, we've *'ad* the police here—I can see by yer face that's all your interested in. There's a sergeant stayin' at the pub down the road now, as far as I know, but I've not let a pack of flatties bother me."

He seemed to regard the final statement as a sign of virtue.

"That was what you told me, wasn't it?"

Campion sighed. "Quite," he said. "Oh, by the way, perhaps I ought to have mentioned it; if there is a fire while you are here you will act—temporarily, of course—as a fireman. And if the river at the bottom of the garden overflows and floods the lower story you should become for a brief hour or so a boatman, conveying members of the household to safety as best you can."

Lugg was silent for a moment.

"You're not quite yourself, are you?" he said at last. "Anythin' up? Fun's fun, but no need to be spiteful. This is a mad-'ouse, you know. If I was the inspector I'd arrest the lot, give 'em good food and attention for a month, and 'ang the one 'oo was still crackers at the end of the time."

Having delivered himself of this dictum, he returned to the suitcase.

"Serve the boss right for allowin' the bike in the 'ouse," he remarked over his shoulder. "I see by the papers they suspect the lamp now. I thought there must be somethink like that by the way they was carrying on about the machine. I ban newspapers in the kitchen. I tell 'em I've got the inside stuff and everythin' they want to know they must take from me. I 'ad to do somethin' like that or they'd all be leavin', and I don't want the blarsted 'ousework of a place this size on me 'ands."

He paused and glanced sharply towards the door just before someone knocked.

"Come in, Mr. Faraday," he called out and added as he opened the door with all the dignity of a better-trained man, "I knoo it was you, sir. 'Eard you breathin'. 'Ere is Mr. Campion—at last."

A subdued and almost pallid Uncle William came padding softly into the room.

"My dear boy," he said with genuine emotion. "My dear boy."

Lugg bristled and his small and bright black eyes contained a gleam of jealousy.

"Wot 'o, the fatted calf," he murmured derisively.

Uncle William, who was slow of perception, did not see the allusion instantly and appeared to think some personal insult was intended. He swung round with parade-ground severity.

"I'll trouble you to control your tongue, my man. Get out. I want to speak to your master."

The fat man by the bedside dropped the sponge bag he had taken from the case and stood staring, his huge face dark with indignation.

"Be off with you," insisted Uncle William with more vigour than impressiveness.

Lugg looked at Campion and, receiving no hint of encouragement, moved ponderously towards the door.

When it was actually closing behind him and he had not been recalled, he paused and put his head in again.

"If you 'ave not dined, sir, there are a few cold bits on the sideboard in the dinin' room," he said with tremendous dignity, and, having recovered his self-esteem and achieved the last word, he surged off to his own domain below stairs.

In the bedroom Uncle William frowned and cast a worried glance behind him.

"I don't want to hurt the fellow's feelings," he said, "but this is no time to stand on ceremony. What a business, Campion! What a terrible business! You probably know more about it than I do, if the truth were told, but I've watched some of the effects down here. We're livin' in a nightmare, my boy. I've woken up from a nap more than once with my heart in my mouth. One can't forget it even for a moment. It hangs over one's head day and night. Day and night!"

He gobbled a little and wiped his face with one of his stiff white handkerchiefs.

"Just when we thought the worst was over, bar the shoutin', and were quietly gettin' back to normal again, that silly little whippersnapper calls in for his bicycle and rides off on it to meet his death. When I first heard of it on the Sunday night I own I wasn't brokenhearted—except for the other poor souls, of course. Konrad always struck me as a weed and it didn't upset me to hear that he'd gone to the Great Incinerator. But yesterday, when the London police arrived with the local man and started puttin' us through it about the bicycle, it came to me in an overwhelming flash that we were back in the mire again, and well over the ankles this time."

He sat down in a chintz-covered armchair, which was too small to contain his plump sides with comfort, and remained hunched up, looking down at his red leather house slippers.

"The police are confused, shouldn't wonder," he remarked presently. "Last Friday was the funeral of that silly woman who began this run of bad luck, and on the Saturday Jimmy gave up his matinee to put in the best part of a long day on the new show. All the principals came down here on Saturday mornin' and most of 'em stayed the night to go on with the work over Sunday. It's goin' to be a terrible performance, I'm afraid. Didn't like what I saw of it. Still, that's neither here nor there. When Inspector Yeo started askin' me who was in the house at the end of last week I was hard put to it to give him a full answer. I told him he'd never arrive at the truth by the elimination of possible suspects.

"There was a prince here for a night—Friday or Saturday. A Russian feller. Very civil. Seemed to be an old friend of Jimmy's. Knew him in Paris years ago. Kept me awake half the night with tales of wolf shootin'.

"The place has been full of people. I said to the police sergeant it's like lookin' for a tiger in South America. If he's there he's in disguise. And if you accept that, he may be any one of the peculiar-lookin' fellers about."

He paused, blew, and raised a worried plump old face to his friend's.

"We're in the devil of a hole, Campion," he said. "Which of us is it? D'you know?"

He received no answer and bowed his head, so that his misty tonsure, frilled with yellow-white curls, made a sudden and pathetic appearance.

"I can't believe it," he said. "And I'll tell you something, Campion. I'm not an obstinate feller by any means, but there is one possibility—only a faint one, mind; but I'm not a fool, I see it—there's one possibility that I'm shuttin' my eyes to. Come what may, I'm not goin' to believe it. Understand?"

Mr. Campion glanced over the garden again.

"I rather thought you might feel like that," he said.

Uncle William looked up sharply. His bright blue eyes were hunted and shifty.

"Why should..." he began but thought better of it. "No

point in fruitless discussion," he said. "Feel like a rat in a treadmill once you start thinkin'. Tell you what I've done. I've consulted my heart and made up my mind and I'm stickin' to my decision. It may not be the right way, but battles have been won on it, my boy. If you don't mind we won't mention it again. . . .

"I don't like the girl goin' off like this, do you? What's she up to?"

Campion swung round from the window.

"What girl?"

"Eve. Didn't Linda tell you?" Uncle William seemed put out. "What's Linda holdin' that back for? Thought she'd get you down here safely first, I suppose. Can't tell with a woman. Yes, well, Eve's gone, you know. Went off yesterday afternoon. Got the chauffeur to take her to the station with a small suitcase. The feller said she'd been cryin'. I've been sittin' by the telephone all day, waitin' for her to ring up. Nothin' yet."

Campion stared at him in fascinated silence. Uncle William dropped his eyes.

"Queer, isn't it?" he murmured.

"Very." Campion's tone was sharp. "Do the police know about it?"

"No. No, I don't think they do, as a matter of fact. That is, they don't realise we don't know where she is."

Campion leant back against the window ledge.

"You'll have to explain, you know."

Uncle William shrugged his shoulders and stirred uncomfortably.

"Feel I may be makin' a mountain out of a molehill, don't you know," he observed in a particularly unsuccessful attempt to hide his concern. "I'm gettin' on myself and, realisin' the girl's so young, I'm apt to be a bit of an old woman. Very likely Linda feels much the same and doesn't think it was worth mentionin'."

Mr. Campion thought of that long silent drive through the country lanes and wrenched his mind away from the contemplation of it.

"What happened exactly?" he demanded. "When the chauffeur came home he was questioned, I suppose?"

"Yes, well, we saw him comin' in, don't you know, and asked him where he'd been."

Uncle William managed to sound reluctant without being actually evasive.

"The long and the short of it was that there was a certain amount of general surprise when we heard the girl had gone off without a word. Someone ran up to her room to see if she'd left a note and when we found she hadn't we were all standin' about, worried, and then Jimmy, who was down here after waitin' to see the police, suddenly seemed to remember that he knew about it. He said she'd be back today. The sergeant didn't ask for her this mornin' when he came round, and no one mentioned her bein' away. There's so many people comin' and goin', the police can't keep track of it all unless they come out into the open and keep the house under general arrest."

He drew a deep breath and blinked uneasily.

"I asked Jimmy straight out where she was and he said he thought she was stayin' with a woman friend in Bayswater. Linda knew the name and after Jimmy had gone to town she rang the woman up. But Eve wasn't with her and hadn't been."

His voice trailed away.

Campion digested the somewhat disturbing story.

"Was she in the habit of going off up to town at a moment's notice and staying the night with friends?"

"Not without a word to anyone, my dear fellow." Uncle William sounded shocked. "That's a funny thing for anyone to do. Monstrous in a girl of seventeen or so. I'm worried about her, Campion. She wrote that note I found in the bird's nest all right."

"Oh, she did? Who to?"

"I never found out." He reported the failure regretfully. "Couldn't keep my eyes on the tree all day. It was still there on Saturday. On the Sunday mornin' too. But on Monday I was prowlin' round early, tryin' to get my mind accustomed to the new catastrophe, when I caught a glimpse of someone in the woods ahead of me. I knew it was Eve by her pink dress. Presently she came past with her face screwed up and tears in her eyes and when I said 'Good mornin'' or somethin' equally footlin' she didn't look at me. When I got to the nest it was empty, but there were small fragments of the note scattered over the grass. Shouldn't have noticed them if I hadn't been lookin' for them. They were quite dry and it had

209

showered heavily in the night, so I took it that she'd only just torn the paper up."

For an instant a shy twinkle appeared in his eyes.

"Rather neat work," he murmured. "Don't you think?"

"Very." Campion was properly impressed. "Has Sock been down here?"

"Several times. Run off his feet, poor lad. Don't know when he sleeps. Extraordinary thing! Have you noticed it, Campion? If a feller's under twenty-seven no one ever thinks he needs rest of any kind. Jimmy's not a hard man but he looks on Sock as a sort of messenger boy on wings. You don't think the girl would run off to Sock, do you? I mean, two young people on their own. No restraint. No curbin'. Monstrous."

Campion passed his hand over his hair.

"Who's in the house now, besides ourselves and Lugg?"

"Only Linda and Miss Finbrough. Jimmy will be down in an hour or two and heaven knows who he'll bring with him. Mercer's at his own cottage, in bed. Poisoned, silly feller."

"Poisoned?"

Uncle William chuckled.

"Caught a cold comin' home on Friday night," he said with malicious amusement. "Serve him right. Ought to have gone to the funeral. Terrible feller to have anythin' the matter with him. There were we, worried, nervous, distraught, and there was he fidgetin' about a cold comin' on. On Sunday I lost my temper with him. I told him to go to bed early and take somethin' hot and keep himself to himself instead of whinin' about the place, doin' nothin' except scatterin' infection. What did the silly feller do then but wait until the last moment, when we were all thunderin' upset, havin' heard of the news of the rumpus on the wireless at nine o'clock, and then go down to the kitchen here to borrow a bottle of ammoniated quinine from the cook. He took it home, wearin' my ulster without a by-your-leave, and sent his man for a spoon. Naturally the feller, not knowin' what was wanted, brought the first one he saw, and Mercer took a tablespoonful in half a tumbler of water. The sensible dose is half to a whole teaspoonful.

"Well, he went to bed, woke up half deaf and blind, and let out a howl for a doctor. I saw the medical man." He smiled at the recollection of the meeting. "He called it cinchonism, and

Mercer's still laid up. Better now, though. Saw him today. Told me the cracklin' in his ears was dyin' off a bit. Still, he's very sorry for himself, stupid feller."

Linda did not appear when they went downstairs and Campion was grateful to her for her forbearance. A still-reproachful Lugg brought Uncle William his half decanter and set it down before him without a word. The old man sat looking at the golden-brown liquid in the cut glass for a long time. Campion thought his mind had wandered from it, when he suddenly bounced to his feet.

"Don't think I will," he announced. "Got to keep the mind clear. Don't drink as I used to—nothin' like. Still, can't sit lookin' at it. Put it away in the music room in my cupboard. Come for a turn in the air."

He stowed the whisky away, his plump hands infinitely gentle, and they went out into the warm scented garden. They were still strolling on the lawn when the Bentley's headlights drew great fingers across the dark grass.

Sutane was alone. They saw his slender, rackety figure silhouetted against the beam as he sprang out and came towards them.

"Campion!" he said. "Good man. Knew you wouldn't desert me. Eve back, Uncle William?"

"No." The old man's tone was unwontedly brusque. "Understood you were goin' to find her and tell her to come home at once."

Sutane did not answer immediately, and they had difficulty in keeping up with him. As they ascended the steps to the brightly lit hall Campion glanced at his face and was startled by what he saw there. Every superfluous gramme of flesh had gone, leaving it an oddly vivacious death's-head with the powerful, vigorous nerves almost apparent.

"Oh, yes." Sutane spoke lightly. "That's right. So I was. But the theatre's in such a hysterical state. Two deaths in the cast, you see, and they're a superstitious lot. I forgot all about it."

He glanced at Campion obliquely and his dull, intelligent eyes were smiling and confiding.

"She'll turn up tomorrow, won't she?" he said.

23

The sleeping house was bright and a little stuffy in the early morning when Mr. Campion came quietly downstairs at half past six. The brilliant sunshine which even in the country seems so much cleaner at that hour than at any other in the day burst in through the curtains, making little patches of vivid colour on stone floor and carpet, while outside the gilded tops of the trees were dancing in the morning wind.

Campion had surveyed the cloakroom and the hot, sun-bathed lounge with some care before he became conscious of a quiet scuffling in the drawing room and put his head in to find Mr. Lugg and his assistant already at their housework.

Clad in a singlet and a pair of ancient grey-black trousers, a luggage strap about his middle and disreputable carpet slippers upon his bare feet, the temporary butler was dusting the china in the Georgian wall cupboard, while a galvanic little bundle in pyjamas and a red dressing gown scrubbed away with a rubber at the polished parquet floor. They were both engrossed in their work. Sarah's tight pigtails were screwed up on her small round head and her grunts and squeaks betrayed both concentration and considerable effort.

"Go on, git right in the corners. I don't want to 'ave to go over it after you." Lugg spoke over his shoulder as he rubbed a great thumb over the delicate face of a Dresden milkmaid. "Pretty stuff, this," he observed. "Not of great value, you know, and it makes a lot of work. But I like it. Little dolls, that's what these are. Toys reely."

Campion waited with commendable caution until the fragile group was back in its place again before he spoke.

"Good morning," he ventured.

Lugg swung round. "Gawd! You give me a turn," he said reproachfully. "What on earth are you up to now? I 'ave to git up in the dawn to git the work done in comfort and peace, but you needn't. The drawin' room I always see to meself. I don't let a maid touch it. That means gitting up early so that I'm not seen about in me slacks. It lowers yer dignity if you're seen comfortable.

"Go on, git on with it!" he added to his aide, who was listening to the conversation with apprehensive eyes. "'E ain't yer nurse. She 'elps me do the floors because I ain't so nippy on me knees," he explained, returning to Campion. "What's the good of 'er sittin' up in bed waitin' for the 'ouse to wake? Much better make 'erself useful. You ain't tired, are you, chum?"

Sarah shook her head contemptuously, and Campion, realising that his presence was constraining a conversation between two persons whose minds were singularly of an age, left them and went back to his quiet investigations.

He did not find what he was looking for in any of the downstairs rooms, although his search was thorough, but the failure did not seem to depress or even to surprise him, and, as signs of life began to appear in the house, he drifted out into the bright garden.

There his progress was equally slow. He pottered round the terrace and the shrubbery between the kitchen and music-room window, paying special attention to the water butts and the ornamental pool in the rosary. To his left the kitchen garden lay prim and tidy. Its rectangular beds were divided by moss-grown gravel paths and were bordered by fine box hedges nearly two feet high. The mid-season clipping was in progress, and the plump round tops of half the bushes were already replaced by neat square angles.

The gardener whom he met nodded at the half-finished work and regretted that he had not been able to get back to it.

"Friday and half day Sat'day I done that piece," he remarked. "I couldn't get to it Monday and Tuesday, and on Wednesday and Thursday I was down at the lake with the rest of 'em, helping the police."

He cocked an inquisitive eye at Campion, who did not rise to the bait but continued his walk after murmuring a few idle uninformative pleasantries.

He came on Linda as he approached Uncle William's bird's-nest copse. She came down towards him in a yellow

213

linen frock. Her head was bent and her eyes were dark and preoccupied.

He hailed her hastily, and she looked up at him with a faint air of guilt which delighted him unreasonably.

"I've been for a walk," she said. "I didn't feel like sleeping. It's breakfast time, you know. Come on."

He dropped into step beside her and they walked along between the fine, flamboyant flowers, his tall lean figure towering over her.

"When the police came the other day did they do anything besides ask questions?" he said suddenly.

"Oh, they looked about a bit, you know. I don't know what for." Her voice had a brittle quality and was determinedly light. "They were very secretive. Rather heavily tiptoe, in fact. They borrowed the gardeners to look for something in the lake. When I offered to let them see over the house they jumped at it."

"Why did you do that?" he said curiously. "It was very wise, of course."

She was silent, but as they came across the lawn to the terrace she shivered suddenly.

"I want it to end," she said. "Whatever is coming, I want it to come and be over. D'you know?"

He nodded, reflecting that her complete comprehensibility constituted half her charm for him.

"Did they find anything?"

"No, I don't think so. They'll come back today."

They mounted the terrace and came in through the open windows, to find Uncle William seated at a small oval table which had been set up for the meal. Miss Finbrough was beside him, eating steadily, obviously without thinking what she was doing.

She was directly in front of Campion as he came in and he was startled by the change in her. Her vivid colour, which was perhaps her most salient feature, was still there, but it was no longer the plump and shining redness of rawness and health. Now she was turgid-looking and dry-skinned, red with the redness of sandstone. Her strength seemed to have been drawn into herself, as if the muscles of her body had become knotted and hard.

She blinked at Campion dully and gave him a brief, mechanical smile.

214

Uncle William put down the *Times*. He had been looking at the small advertisements, which, in common with a great many of that eminent paper's subscribers, he found the most interesting reading of the day.

"Friday," he said. "So it comes round again. Good mornin'. Couldn't sleep. No reflection on your excellent beds, Linda my dear. Can't read the paper. Doesn't seem to have any interest. No sense of humour either; an occasional pun in Greek, nothin' more. It's worry with me; just worry."

He started violently as the door behind him opened and he turned to cast a belligerent glance at the newcomer, who proved to be Mercer in a fine newish suit.

The composer came in noisily, making the door shudder as he threw it to behind him. He still looked pale from his recent misadventure and his eyes were hollow.

"Hello," he said. "Hello, you down again, Campion? God! I feel ill. I'm going to town to see a specialist about this damned cinchonism, Linda. I'll be back tonight. My man's calling for me here, taking me to the station and meeting me off the last train. It's the ten-two, isn't it? I think I'll have some tea."

His complete self-preoccupation came as a relief to them all, if only as a counter-irritant. He threw himself into an armchair and held out a still-quavering hand for the cup Miss Finbrough passed to him.

"I've been deaf!" he shouted to Campion. "My ears have been popping like machine-gun fire. I've been blind and cross-eyed."

"Still, it hasn't killed you," muttered Uncle William, goaded into gentlemanly sarcasm. "Merciful thing."

"It is. Damned lucky." Mercer held the cup to his grey lips. "I had a wretched policeman sitting on my bed all Wednesday, asking me idiotic questions about things he could quite easily have found out from somebody else. I was so ill that I told him what I thought of him, his force, and his stupid great notebook. He didn't come again. It's a poison, you know, cinchona bark. I could have died from it."

Uncle William's forget-me-not eyes looked dangerous and Linda cut in.

"You'll be back tonight then, Squire?"

215

"Yes, probably. I've got some work I want to finish. This damned business has wasted days."

Miss Finbrough seemed to be on the verge of collapse.

"Business?" she said faintly.

"Well, poisoning then." Mercer was happily oblivious of the contretemps. "That little dance thing I was mucking about with turned out very well. I've got something good there. Dill doesn't like my title, 'Pavane for a Dead Dancer.' He wants to try some other idea. These lyric writers think they're little tin gods. He feels it's highbrow or something."

"He probably feels it's in very bad taste, sir," snapped Uncle William, getting the rebuke in adroitly before he could be stopped.

"Bad taste?" The other man was genuinely surprised at first, but afterwards, when he suddenly saw the objection, he defended himself irritably. "Don't be a *perishing* fool," he said with quite unnecessary violence. "All this other affair will be forgotten long before we can get a song out. If you're going to talk poppycock like that it shows you don't understand the public mind any more than the average dirty-nosed child. You, for instance, do you remember what was in the papers six months ago? Of course you don't!"

Uncle William began to simmer. He shared the practically universal belief that the word "public" is opprobrious when applied to almost any other noun and more particularly so when it is allied to the word "mind." He felt himself insulted and was about to say so when a fortunate diversion was caused by the arrival of a soberly clad Lugg, who announced that Mr. Mercer's car was at the door.

The composer got up hastily.

"Is it?" he said. "Good. I don't want to miss that train. Did I leave my coat in here? Are you sitting on it, Linda? No, it must be outside. Find it, Lugg, will you? Good-bye, Linda. I may drop round on you tonight if I'm not too tired when I get in."

He went out with rather more clumsiness than usual, and the girl looked after him.

"He's made himself very ill," she remarked. "Jimmy's terribly worried about him. Quinine is filthy stuff. It makes one feel beastly. Fancy getting all that down him—a whole tablespoonful!"

"Miracle to me he didn't take the whole bottle, the fuss he

216

was makin' over a little cold," said Uncle William unsympathetically. "Wonderful to be so interested in one s ailments. Jimmy ought to snub that feller. Think I'll go up and see Jimmy, by the way. He'll be awake by now. I'd like a word with him."

Miss Finbrough made a sound that was midway between a sob and a hiccup.

"You can't," she said flatly.

"Oh?" The old man turned slowly in his chair to look at her, and as the silence grew the others imitated him until she was in a circle of startled and enquiring eyes.

"Why not, Finny?" There was a hint of sharpness in Linda's tone as she put the question.

"He's not there. He's gone. He went out early in the car. If the police ask for him I was to tell them he'd be at the theatre after eleven o'clock."

Miss Finbrough spoke with a dullness which gave her voice a spurious complacency.

Linda flushed.

"But I haven't seen him," she said. "I didn't even see him last night. Hasn't he left any message for me?"

"He's very worried, Mrs. Sutane." The other woman was reproachful. "He knocked at my door at five this morning and told me to go down and make him some breakfast. I got everything ready and then he wouldn't eat it. He just rushed into the kitchen, swallowed a cup of tea, and then went off in the car."

She began to tremble violently and took out a crumpled handkerchief.

"You'll have to excuse me," she said. "I don't feel well. That's the only message he left."

Even in her agitation the ghost of her dominating personality remained. Somehow it enhanced her weakness. She went out and presently Linda followed her.

Uncle William looked up.

"Remarkable thing," he said. "Convey anythin' to your mind, Campion?"

Campion did not reply. He pottered round the room for a minute or two and then, having convinced himself that the women were safely upstairs and Uncle William lost in his own unhappy thoughts, he went out to the kitchen and borrowed two iron weights from the cook's scales.

217

In the privacy of the small music room he fitted the four-ounce disc into the eight-ounce one and tied them both in a handkerchief. Then, opening the window wide at the bottom, he stepped back and pitched the white bundle as far as he could into the most thickly shrubbed portion of the garden before him.

It went over the wall into the kitchen garden and he hurried after it, sliding over the low window sill onto the iron-hard turf below. It was not hard to find. The white heap lay between two rows of lettuces. He picked it up and with his eye measured a wide arc with himself at a point on the circumference and the window as the centre.

His line lay through some currant bushes, over a couple of paths and an onion bed, and ended at the wall on one side and a marrow patch at the other.

He made his search carefully, making a width allowance of four yards either way.

The marrow bed yielded nothing save a fine collection of surprising gourds, but at the farther box hedge along the second path he stopped abruptly. It was here that the clipping had ceased and the gardener had paused and laid down his shears at noon on the Saturday before. His barrow and garnering boards were still there by the side of the path.

Campion walked on slowly until his eyes rested upon a dark irregularity in the smooth sharp outlines of the newly clipped shrubs.

When at last he found it he plunged his hand down among the dense springy branches and a sigh escaped him. He slipped his handkerchief off the weights in his pocket and used the cambric to protect his find from his own fingerprints.

The birds sang, and the scent of flowers from the other garden came over the low wall on a breath of sparkling sunlit air as he stood looking down at his discovery.

It was a silver-plated bicycle lamp.

24

The clubroom of the Hare and Hounds was overfilled with furniture in spite of its size. The vast table, at which sat Chief Inspector Yeo, Detective Sergeant Inchcape, both of the C.I.D. Central Branch, Chief Inspector Cooling of the county constabulary, and Mr. Albert Campion, private and unwilling investigator, supported, as well as the paraphernalia belonging to these gentlemen, thirty-seven ash trays, each inscribed with varying advertising matter, a polyanthus rosetree in a remarkable pot, a cracked bottle of solidified ink, and a Bible with a red marker.

The rest of the room was in keeping with this centrepiece and contained some very fine connoisseurs' specimens of early camera portraiture.

"He wiped the lamp and simply pitched it out of sight, thinking that no one would remark on it even if it were found. He's been reckoning entirely without the major. We weren't expected to find out how that explosion originated."

Yeo made the pronouncement with a gravity befitting his position as the most authoritative person present, and the local inspector, who was a fine solid man of military smartness, nodded his grave agreement.

Yeo glanced down at the typewritten sheets of notes before him.

"As soon as you turned the lamp in yesterday, Mr. Campion, we saw at once that it was clean-wiped," he said, "and of course we recognised it from the manufacturer's specifications. They are prepared to swear that it is the actual lamp they delivered with the bicycle. Inchcape here reported your evidence about the hedge clipping and I'm inclined to agree with you. The gardener must have found it if it had been there when he cut the box. That fixes the time it entered the hedge as somewhere between twelve noon on the Saturday,

219

and, I think we may presume, ten-fifty on the Sunday morning when Konrad took the bike away. Who was in the house during that time?"

Inspector Cooling sighed.

"Thirty-seven persons off and on," he said sadly. "We've interviewed about half of 'em so far. Well, we'll carry on. It's spadework that does it."

Yeo grimaced.

"There's only the family and Mr. Faraday, not counting Mr. Campion, at the house now, I take it?" he said. "I shall go down there again this afternoon. Sutane has a matinee, of course. He didn't come home at all last night, did he?"

"He stayed at his flat in Great Russell Street, sir. He often does before a matinee." Sergeant Inchcape supplied the information gladly from his meagre store. "They're all at the house with the exception of the young lady, Miss Eve Sutane. She went to town on Wednesday and has not yet returned. Her absence escaped my notice on Thursday, but I learnt of her visit to friends from a maid yesterday, Friday. The explanation given to the household is that her brother thought she needed a little change. Miss Finbrough gave that out."

He paused and sucked his teeth, an appalling habit which he allowed to punctuate his every second remark. It gave him a consequential, self-satisfied manner which was either irritating or amusing, according to the temperament of his hearer.

"Have you got the address?" Yeo enquired. "No. Well, it doesn't matter. I'll pick it up when I go down this afternoon. It's of no importance, but we may as well keep on the careful side."

He glanced at Campion.

"We're still up against the same old snag. There's still no motive," he observed. "We're grateful for the lamp—very grateful—don't think we're not, but that only proves what we knew already, you know. The crime emanated from that house. The lamps were changed there. But who amongst the whole outfit should want to do such a thing is still a mystery. Isn't that so?"

His final question was addressed to his police colleagues, who murmured their agreement and followed his glance to the tall thin man who sat amongst them.

Campion was lounging in his chair, his hands in his pockets

and his eyes half closed. He might have forgotten the conference.

"I was saying, Mr. Campion, as you were on the inside you were the one to spot the motive," prompted Yeo. "What are you thinking?"

Campion glanced at him out of the corner of his eye.

"'There are forty policemen sitting in this room, but I would rather have you, my darling,'" he said.

"Beg your pardon?" Yeo sounded startled.

Campion got up. He was laughing, but without deep amusement.

"It's out of a play," he said. "Sir James Barrie wrote it. It's a sort of fairy story. You wouldn't know it. I'll wander along now, if I may. Should I find any more spare parts I'll ring you. See you this afternoon. I'm doing all I can."

As the door closed behind him the county inspector smiled with unexpected sympathy.

"He feels his position, don't he?" he remarked. "He's a friend down at the house. It's not very nice."

Yeo raised his eyebrows.

"A man can't have friends in our profession," he said with dignity. "Right's right and wrong's wrong. He knows that. He's been to school."

Cooling nodded, not wishing to disagree in any way with the distinguished visitor and most especially so on such an incontrovertible point.

Mr. Campion walked back down the dusty lower road. He passed the Old House and avoided Mrs. Geodrake, who eyed him wistfully from the front garden, where she was weeding with ostentatious assiduity. He observed the A.A. phone box where Konrad had rung up Beaut Siegfried on the night Chloe Pye had died, and came up through the woods where Uncle William's bird's nest still perched, empty and forgotten.

He made a solitary and somewhat forlorn figure. Even the sight of Lugg, vast and impressive in a cutaway coat and posed ridiculously in a flower bed as he indicated suitable blooms for Sarah to cut for the drawing-room bowl, did not move him to comment.

He felt he was chained to a very slow avalanche. Sooner or later, today or tomorrow, it must gain impetus and roar down in all its inevitable horror, breaking and crushing, defeating and destroying. He could do nothing to impede it. With an effort he might possibly accelerate its present pace, but he did not want to. White Walls lay quiet in the shimmering sunlight. In the beds the blue butterflies flirted brightly with the flowers. The light wind was warm and caressing.

Surely the night, tomorrow night, the next rainy day, surely, surely one of these would be time enough?

But at that moment, of course, he knew nothing of the shabby little coupé drawn up on the verge by the side of the Birley road.

Sock phoned at three o'clock, before Yeo had put in his promised appearance. Lugg brought Campion to the telephone and he took the message and made his inevitable offer.

"I'm at Birley station." Sock's young voice sounded thin over the wire. "I can't get a cab anywhere. Someone pinched my car yesterday. What? Oh, in the usual place at the end of the alley. I was a fool to leave it there, but it's cheaper than a garage. Some ass simply walked off with it. Yes, rather, the new one, blast him!"

"I'll run down for you." Campion sounded friendly. "No, I won't worry the chauffeur. My dear chap, I've got nothing to do. In fifteen minutes, then."

He passed the coupé on his way to the station. White Walls was some way off the beaten track and the nearest way to the railway lay across a belt of meadow land between two main roads. The lanes were in good repair, if not much frequented, and Campion drove fast.

The blue coupé had been parked on the wide grass verge and sat there shabby and forlorn, with its windows closed; it might have been there for ten minutes or ten years, and Campion barely noticed it as he sped past.

Sock came clattering down the station steps as the Lagonda climbed the hill. He was a little more presentable than usual in costume, but his dark youthful face was worn and strained and there was an irritating air of suppressed excitement about him, as though he were conscious of taking a part in strange and important events.

"This is extremely good of you," he said as he sank into the comfort of the front seat. "I'm lost without a bus of some sort. I had to come down. I must see Jimmy and the only time to get hold of him these days is at the week-end. I hope we don't have to take the show off. We'll know on Monday."

"Oh, is that in the wind?" Campion spoke dully, reflecting

that there is nothing so uninteresting as something which has been all-important for a long time and is suddenly outclassed. "The publicity's ruined it, I suppose?"

"It's not the publicity, curiously." Sock seemed surprised himself. "The bookings haven't fallen off as you'd think. In some parts of the house they've even improved. It's the cast. The whole place is a mass of hysteria. I've never seen anything like it. It's the drama in the blood, I suppose. Three quarters of the chorus passed out after the show last night. We've all had the hell of a time. The new show is nearly as bad. None of them have got a hap'orth of ballast. It's only Jimmy who holds 'em all together, and he looks as if he was going to drop dead at any moment. Have you seen him lately? He's amazing! Takes such *risks*, Campion... I go cold for him sometimes. But he gets away with 'em by sheer personality."

He sighed and slid further down into the deep upholstery.

"My car going was the last straw," he remarked.

Mr. Campion made sympathetic noises and his passenger chattered on.

"I used to leave the old one in the cul-de-sac near the flat. I've got a hovel just off Baker Street, you know, and in this fine weather it saves a garage bill. People are amazingly honest in London, and, as I never left anything in it, it seemed as safe as houses. Where I made my mistake was that I forgot the state of the old bus. I did the same thing with my new secondhand one, and it was all right for a week, but yesterday, just about four o'clock, I went home to write a bit of copy. It took me a certain amount of time and I didn't come out until seven. Then I found the car had gone. The chap who sells papers on the corner saw a man take it. He just walked over to it, got in and drove off. I told the paper man what I thought of him, naturally, but he said he didn't like to interfere in case I'd lent it to a friend. I couldn't really blame him. Still, he gave the police a description and they're having a look for it. Meanwhile it's just annoying."

He was silent for some moments as they negotiated the right-angle turn at the bottom of the hill.

"Jimmy told me you were down here," he said at last. "I saw him yesterday for a moment or two. He's a queer bloke. I don't know anyone I admire more, but you've got to know how to take him."

He paused. There was clearly something on his mind and Campion listened to him beating round the subject with a deepening of that new sense of apprehension which had become habitual with him.

Sock cleared his throat.

"I used to be rather keen on Eve at one time," he remarked a little too casually. "But she went off me and I rather thought our James frowned on the idea, too, so I let it go. She's a sweet kid when you get to know her, and I felt rather sore about it in a vague sort of way. But Jimmy has been damn marvellous to me and I didn't want to muscle in where he didn't want me. After all, I'm not a startling proposition; I know that. I'm only telling you this, by the way, to get over my point about Jimmy.

"A day or two ago he sent for me and gave me a dressing down about the girl. He practically asked me point-blank what I thought I was doing to let her escape my manly clutches and who the hell I thought I was to pass up something pretty good. I practically fainted on the spot. He is a funny chap, isn't he?"

Mr. Campion's face became even more expressionless.

"He probably feels that she may need a spot of supervision," he suggested cautiously. "Elder brothers go all paternal at times. She's not here now, by the way."

"No, I—I thought not." Sock sounded confused. "Besides, she's lost all interest in me, if ever she had any. As a matter of fact, I thought I caught the nasty whiff of 'metal more attractive.' She's been pretty hard hit the last week or two. It's y'uth—y'uth and the balmy summer air—that does it with these 'ere young girls."

"Who's your rival?" Campion's question was hesitant.

"I don't know for certain." Sock shook a wise young head. "I've had a dirty suspicion for some time, but I won't slander the girl, bless her. After all, she ought to draw the line somewhere. I say, Campion! Campion, hold on a minute!"

The last remark was jerked out of him as he swung round in the car and sat staring over his shoulder. Mr. Campion pulled up obligingly.

"What's the matter?"

"Look!" Sock was kneeling up in his seat, his face ludicrous in its astonishment. "Look, I say! That's my bus!"

Campion turned his head and stared at the shabby blue

coupé which he had passed on his outward journey. He dropped the car into reverse and ran backward, with Sock hopping on the running board.

"The shape caught my eye and then I saw the number plate," he babbled excitedly. "This is fantastic—incredible! I don't believe it! I bet the ticks have run her dry of oil and seized her up."

He sprang to the ground as they came to a standstill and ran over to the stranded car. For a moment he stood peering in through the window and then without a word wrenched open the door. Campion saw him bending down, his head and shoulders hidden from view in the dark interior.

The next moment a rug came hurtling out and a cry that was not a scream or a shout, but somewhere midway between the two, escaped its owner.

Sock drew back slowly. His face was livid and his young eyes were horror-stricken. He put his hand over his stomach.

Campion sprang from the Lagonda and, pushing past the younger man, peered down into the coupé.

The body lay doubled up on the floor with its legs forced round the controls and its head jammed against the front of the passenger seat. That it was a dead body was painfully apparent. The skull had been battered unmercifully and there was blood on the mat and on the rug.

Mr. Campion, who was hardened to such unpleasant sights, peered down into the small dark face.

"Who is it?" he demanded.

Sock forced himself to look again.

"I don't know," he said at last, his lips shaking. "I don't know. I've never seen the chap before in my life."

25

Mr. Campion dozed. The night had gone on, it seemed, for ever. The wooden armchair in which he lay had been designed by a man with definite but erroneous ideas concerning the human form, and he was peculiarly uncomfortable.

It was four o'clock in a scented country dawn, with a world astir in the fields and a light, exciting wind shivering through the leaves.

In the room in which he sat, on the iron mantelshelf below the fly-blown tariff of licenses obtainable from His Majesty's revenue officers, a round tin clock ticked with a shudder a second.

From the local superintendent's office next door came sounds that had gone on all through the night: voices and footsteps, slow country intonations and the brisk, clipped abbreviations of the town, chair legs scraping on wood and solid boot heels clattering on uncarpeted boards.

The phone bell alone was silent, and everyone in the police station, including Mr. Campion, who listened even in his sleep, was waiting for that shrill, familiar alarm.

Dr. Bouverie s old Fiat drew up in the quiet street outside with a roar and a grunt and the tempestuous old gentleman heaved himself out of it, bellowed at his sleep-dazed chauffeur, and plunged into the building, the plaid-lined skirts of his mighty overcoat swinging about him like sails in a storm.

His authoritative voice had a penetrating quality and Campion sat up with a jerk. The new, straightforward, bona fide murder had evidently caught the old man's imagination, and the full force of his astonishing energy had been loosed upon its elucidation with a generous disregard for the hour and his own and everybody else's personal convenience.

"Got down to it at once, don't you know."

The familiar roar percolated through the door panels of the superintendent's room.

"We must get it cleared up. I can't have this sort of thing in my district. I've been working all night. Stopped for a meal at eight o'clock and went back to it. Sweat's been pouring off me. I had to change and bathe before I came over or I'd have been here an hour ago. Young Dean wanted to give up at one o'clock, but I kept him at it and I think we've got it clear now, between us. Superintendent, lend me a man for a moment."

Alone in the small front office on the first floor, Campion stretched his cramped limbs and brought his mind round to face the situation once again. When at last he put his head inside the superintendent's door he was confronted by a spectacle which might have been very funny in any other circumstance.

A group of interested police, with Yeo and Inchcape prominent among them, were watching a remarkable performance which was taking place in the centre of the room. A chair had been placed in the foreground and against it sprawled a youthful constable whose head and shoulders were completely covered by the doctor's greatcoat, while the old man loomed above him, spanner in hand, and demonstrated the method of murder with great dramatic effect.

"The first blow caught him on the vault, Superintendent, just about here."

Dr. Bouverie brought the spanner down none too gently.

"That cracked his skull for him, don't you know. After that the man seems to have gone mad. He beat the poor creature wildly. Lost his own head, I should say. Call it blood lust if you like, but I should be inclined to say terror. Like a trapped horse, don't you know. Kicks itself free, whatever the damage. I'll prepare a full report for you. No time yet. The organs are perfectly healthy—very good indeed. Decent heart, lungs sound, age between forty and fifty, well-nourished, stained hands . . . get up, my man!"

The final remark was addressed to the constable, who was breathing somewhat stertorously beneath the suffocating coat.

The constable scrambled to his feet and emerged grinning; he was very proud of himself.

The doctor dropped the spanner into his side pocket. His pugnacious old face was stern and alive, and his invincible dignity permeated the room. Viewed dispassionately, there was a great deal that was comic about him, but the essence of the man was far from ridiculous. It passed through Mr. Campion's mind that this serio-comic element was the very stuff of tragedy. It was the dreadful reality of disaster which took the fun out of funny things, reminding the brain perpetually that something truly frightful had honestly occurred.

Dr. Bouverie turned his head and caught sight of him. He got up at once and held out his hand.

"Hallo, Campion," he said. "You mixed up in this too? Two corpses within a fortnight and you about each time, yet no possible connection between the two affairs . . . that's an extraordinary coincidence."

The local superintendent, a friendly lump of a man with an

old-fashioned police moustache and service boots, caught Campion's eye and winked. He cut in hastily before the younger man could speak to the doctor.

"How long had he been dead, sir?"

Dr. Bouverie returned to the subject with alacrity.

"I've been puzzling over that," he said, his grey eyes as bright as if he had been in the thirties, "and I'm inclined to put it at twenty-four hours as a maximum and twelve as a minimum from the time I first saw the body at four o'clock this afternoon. That is to say, somewhere between four on Friday afternoon and four on Saturday morning. Can't you find a witness who noticed how long the car stood there?"

Inchcape glanced at the superintendent and, receiving his nod of assent, plunged into the question.

"We've been working on that," he said. "We've found a man who is prepared to swear that it was not where we found it when he went down to the Queen's Head at eight-fifteen on Friday night, but he noticed it standing just where it is now when he returned about half past ten. He suspected a courting couple and did not look inside. There's no way of telling if the car was driven after the man was dead, is there?"

"Why not? The man was not moved after he died. I can say that for certain, don't you know."

The old man was fascinated by the puzzle element in the case.

"Oh, yes," he went on. "I can give you clear proof of that. From the way he was lying with his feet round the controls I doubt whether anyone could have driven the machine an inch once he was dead."

Yeo coughed and the local superintendent turned to him deferentially. Campion noticed that the distinguished visitor from Scotland Yard was being received with proper country hospitality. Yeo addressed the doctor.

"You're *sure* he was not moved after death, sir?"

"Perfectly." The old man's magnificent authority was comforting. "As I see it, he was driving the car. His passenger suddenly clapped the rug over his head and set about him. The position of the wounds, all on the left side, and the way the body fell, show that quite clearly."

"I see." Yeo was silent and his comedian's face was thoughtful. "I don't know this part of the country," he began, "but it

228

seems to me that the road to the town from the spot where we found the body is fairly lonely?"

"So it is now," agreed the superintendent. "There's not a house on it until you pass the station turning." He paused. "Suppose the murderer took the last train to Boarbridge?" he said suddenly. "He could walk down to the station without being seen and there is just that one train after nine o clock. The station opens at six. I'll send a man down to find out if there was a stranger about then. There's an idea there—a good idea."

Dr. Bouverie was quite prepared to take an even more active part in the investigations than he had done already, and they had some difficulty in getting rid of him gracefully. It was only when he proposed routing out his old friend Lieutenant Colonel Beller, the chief constable, who had only just been persuaded to go home to bed, that the alarmed superintendent put his foot down.

"Ah, well, ye see, we're on to something, sir," he said, "and we don't want to hurry it. That all depends on a telephone message from Scotland Yard. Sergeant Cooling, of the Central London Branch, has nipped up to town with the dead man's fingerprints. There's a great likelihood that the dead man is the same fellow who was seen to steal the car up in London. We've just heard the sergeant was able to get hold of the department before it closed and he's keeping them at work on it now. We're all sittin' here waitin' to hear what he's got to tell us."

The vigorous old man was partially satisfied. The assurance that a great many people were losing their sleep in a decent public endeavour to clear up the mystery which had smirched his beloved district comforted him considerably.

"All right, Larkin," he said a little wistfully. "I'll leave it to you, if you prefer it. I'll get back now. What is it? A quarter to five? Yes, well, I shall have a couple of hours' sleep and invite myself to Beller's table for breakfast. We shall be down here about half past eight. Good night. Good night, Campion. Don't forget to come and see my roses when you're passing. Very fine show. Very fine indeed."

He went at last and the tension in the office relaxed considerably. The young constable who had taken part in the demonstration was despatched by the superintendent to make "farmer's tea" and went off to do so amid grunts of approval from the local members of the conference.

The party spirit, which is never far absent when country-men get together to observe a Londoner, became very apparent when he returned and they sat round sipping the somewhat remarkable beverage, half thick sweet strong tea and half whisky, from immense coarse white cups. Yeo, who had been not unnaturally suspicious of the concoction, expressed sincere gratification at its taste, which reminded Campion of the cheap "flavoured caramels" of his youth, and the excitement which had been growing all the night bubbled up to boiling point.

"I doubt not the superintendent's right he took the down train," remarked Inchcape, the local inspector, giving up all attempts to conceal his pleasant country accent. "Where else would he go? He wouldn't be hanging about the fields, surely?"

The superintendent glanced at Yeo.

"That all depends who it was, don't it?" he said slyly, his own country intonation increasing now that the doctor had gone.

Yeo nodded and his round eyes turned towards Mr. Campion, who avoided his glance.

It was just before five when a sergeant came up from below stairs.

"The young gentleman would like to speak to you, sir," he said. "He's been thinkin', seemingly."

The superintendent gave the word, and he and Yeo exchanged significant glances.

Sock came in looking haggard and exhausted. The pains to which the whole police station had been put to get it into his head that he was not under any sort of arrest, but had merely been invited to stay in the charge room until he remembered why he had not come down by train that afternoon and had merely waited in the booking hall until Campion had come to fetch him, had not been successful.

The evidence of the station officials had been disconcertingly full. A porter had seen Sock walking up the hill that afternoon. A booking-office clerk had seen him phone from the box in the hall and the ticket collector had watched him kicking his heels on the steps until Campion and the Lagonda had arrived.

Sock caught sight of Campion as he came in and appealed to him direct.

"It's a damn silly story. So I have to tell everybody?"

The superintendent intervened tactfully. He had a vast experience of that other half of the world which he so delightfully called "the gentry."

"We're all officers, sir," he began in a fatherly, not to say motherly, fashion, "and we're all working hard to get to the bottom of the mystery. There's not one of us here who can't keep his mouth shut if it be that we're not called upon to know something in the way of duty. Sit down, sir, and tell us how you come to get into the town."

Sock dropped into the chair so lately vacated by the doctor.

"I'm a fool," he said. "I ought to have told you this right away. I would have done only I felt it had nothing whatever to do with the murder and—"

"Ah, you must let us be the judges of that, sir." The superintendent was still parental but firm. "Your car's been stolen in London and you come down to a country place the next day, and the first thing you see on your way from the station is your car with a murdered body in it—well, that's a big coincidence now. We had to check up on your story as a matter of form and we found out you didn't come by train like you said you did. Well, that sets us thinking. We feel we'd like to have a talk to you. You don't want to talk to us and so we say we're very sorry but we'd like you to sit downstairs until you do decide to tell us something. That's fair now. You can't say that isn't fair."

Sock laughed and looked remarkably young again.

"You're perfectly right, Superintendent," he said. "I'm an idiot. I was driven down here by car this afternoon—that is to say, Saturday afternoon; it's Sunday now, isn't it? I left London by train Saturday morning and went to Watford. From there I was driven down here to Birley in a Hillman Minx. I got out at the station because the driver of the car didn't want to go to White Walls. The rest of my original story is perfectly true."

"I see, sir." The superintendent paused long enough for the constable in the corner to complete his shorthand notes. "Now, who was the driver of the Minx? You'll have to tell us that."

Sock sighed helplessly.

"Eve Sutane," he said.

Yeo beamed and Inchcape sat forward.

"The address in Watford where the young lady met you?"

231

murmured the superintendent with the delicacy of a good
maître d'hôtel.

Sock hesitated.

"Is this really necessary? I'm betraying a confidence."

"I'm afraid so, sir. What address?"

"St. Andrews. 9, Cordover Road."

"And the name of the occupier?"

"Major and Mrs. Polthurst-Drew. For God's sake, don't
drag them into it. Eve's been staying there with the daughter.
Her name's Dorothy. Is that enough?"

Yeo leant forward and touched the superintendent's arm
and a nod of mutual understanding passed between them.
Yeo cleared his throat, and the side of Mr. Campion's mind
that was not sick with apprehension noticed with amusement
that the country superintendent's velvet-glove technique had
impressed the Yard man and he was inclined to pay it the
sincerest form of compliment.

"There are just one or two little points I should like to clear
up, Mr. Petrie," he began affably. "Why did Miss Sutane
hesitate to drive you right up to her own home?"

Sock fidgeted and suddenly capitulated.

"She's very young," he began awkwardly. "She ran away on
Wednesday and Jimmy—I mean Mr. Sutane—and I have had
the devil of a job looking for her ever since."

His audience took some seconds to digest this information,
and when he spoke again Yeo had resumed his familiar
sharpness.

"The young lady was missing for three days and no one
mentioned it . . . why was that?"

Sock smiled disarmingly. He was at home with brusquerie.

"We'd had a spot of bother already, Inspector," he murmured.
"As you know, she's ridiculously young and her brother
wanted to keep her out of the newspapers if possible. That
was quite natural. I think he said she was staying with
friends, and, after all, that did prove to be true. She went to
town on Wednesday afternoon and called at the Drury Lane
studio of some art-school friends whose name is Scott. They're
sisters. While she was there she met the Polthurst-Drew girl,
whom she knew, and who asked her down to Watford for a
day or so. Mr. Sutane saw the Scotts at once. It was the first
place he thought of looking. But they had some barmy idea of
shielding their dear little pal from cruel guardians and what

232

not, and like little lunatics they swore they hadn't seen her. It was only Friday night, when we'd tried everywhere else, that I got the idea of going back to the Scotts with a romantic yarn of deserted but undying affection and they coughed up the right address. I went down there this morning and she drove me as far as Birley in Dorothy's car. I was trying to get her to come home, but she wouldn't listen to me. No one knew that there'd been a spot of difference—no one at White Walls, I mean; except Jimmy, of course—so I thought I'd pretend I'd come down from town by train. There you are. I've told you the full strength."

He sighed and lay back in his chair.

"It's a great weight off my mind," he said frankly. "I didn't bash any unknown car thief over the head and you can go through every moment of my time in the last twenty-four hours and prove it."

Yeo nodded gravely. There was a preoccupied expression on his round face.

"You spoke of a difference between Miss Sutane and her brother," he said. "What was that?"

Sock's hesitation was barely noticeable and his reply was glib and convincing.

"I don't know. I don't think it was important. Eve is inclined to be—well—young, you know, and Jimmy is naturally nervy. It was probably something very trivial. It usually is when they have a row. Perhaps he told her she was spending too much or using too much lipstick. . . . I don't know."

"She didn't tell you?"

"She drove me here in silence. I was nearly frozen out of the bus."

The local superintendent smiled indulgently.

"Wouldn't it have been better to tell us all this before?" he murmured. "We had to hold . . ." he coughed, ". . . ask you to wait, because of your car turning up so strangely."

"I know. That's fantastic! Why should it happen here? It's an incredible coincidence." Sock looked about him earnestly. "It's crazy," he said. "Was there anything in the man's pockets to show who he was?"

No one answered this unprofessional question, but the superintendent, who seemed to have taken an incomprehensible liking to the young man, made a little concession.

233

"I'll tell you one thing," he said. "It wasn't robbery. He had quite a quantity of money on him. That's not for publication, mind."

"Not robbery?" Sock repeated dully. He shook his head. "I'm all in," he confessed. "My mind doesn't work any more. Can I go now? Coming, Campion?"

The lank figure in the corner roused himself.

"No," he said. "I'm waiting for something. You take the car. Someone will run me down in the morning. Make my apologies, won't you?"

The superintendent glanced up.

"Stay in the district, won't you, sir?" he murmured pleasantly. "Just till we get the address verified. It won't take long. Tomorrow teatime, perhaps. We'll let you know. Meanwhile, we'll have to hold the car."

"Lord, yes! I don't want it. This has put me clean off it." Sock's smile was sickly. "Good night, everybody. I'll do the polite for you, Campion. I'll tell 'em you're not exactly on the tiles. So long."

When he had gone Yeo frowned.

"It seems a straight story," he said. "Why make such a mouthful of it? He knows more about the row than he cares to admit. I'll have to get that out of the girl."

The telephone bell silenced them all. The instrument stood trilling on the superintendent's desk for what seemed a full minute before Yeo leapt upon it and clapped the receiver to his ear. Campion saw his face light up.

"Good man!" Yeo said enthusiastically to the weary Cooling in London. "Oh, good man! Wait a minute." He pulled a pad towards him and wrote from dictation.

As the minutes went by his spirits soared and his comical face became jubilant.

"Beautiful," he said at last. "Just what I wanted. Stay where you are and do the necessary. Oh, he's still there, is he? Give him my compliments and tell him this is my show. Don't put him off. I want the old ferret right on the trail. Yes, righto. I'll ring you later. Don't say I called him a ferret. That's a breach of discipline and you never know. Yes, fine. Goodbye."

He hung up the receiver and sat grinning at them.

"Listen to this. Just listen to this," he said at last without

234

attempting to disguise his delight. "They've got the prints on the files and here's the dope we want."

He began to read from his notes in a steady, monotonous drone.

"'Georg Kummer, alias Kroeger, alias Koetz, thought to be a Pole. About forty-four or forty-five years old. First attracted police notice in this country in January 1928 when he appeared before the Bow Street magistrates on a charge of failure to register as an alien. Papers found to be unsatisfactory. Deported. Reappeared June 1929. Charged with felonious conspiracy in Glasgow and sentenced to six months in the second division in company with four others. Deported. Next heard of in France, following year, in connection with arson charge. No sentence but deported from France. Became mysteriously wealthy during and just after Repudiation of Arms agreement by Severino government. Reappeared in England, 1932, and was apprehended by police after he had been working in a firework factory for three months. Once more deported. Last heard of 1934, when he was acquitted by a Viennese court on a charge of concealing arms and war material. (Foreign information by courtesy of Austrian police, who applied to us for English details concerning him.) Note: This man is known to have been employed by several governments in his capacity as a chemist. He is believed to hold valuable degrees in his subject but has always come to grief through a crooked streak. He is subject to sudden and great changes in his financial condition. During the last two years his headquarters have been in Vienna. Last permanent address: 49, Wien-Strasse 7.'"

Yeo paused and cleared his throat. His eyes were dancing.

"I didn't read the physical description because they've checked it up that end. He's the chap who pinched the car all right. The paper seller described him to a T. Well, there you are. It's what I've had in the back of my mind ever since I saw the stains on his hands. See who he is? He's the man who made that ruddy bomb."

26

At six o'clock breakfast arrived from the Red Lion over the way and the superintendent entertained his own inspector and the two distinguished visitors to the meal in his office. Yeo had become a new man since the message from the Records Department. The hunt was up and he was getting into his stride. His good humour had developed a certain vigorousness which might have been almost horrific in a less attractive personality. He sat eating a great plateful of bacon, fried egg, sausage and steak, his round eyes sharp and eager and his stubby fingers crumbling his bread as if he felt it represented an enemy.

"It must have been blackmail," he said. "I knew it as soon as I saw the body and heard the story of Petrie's stolen car. There had to be a connection between the two cases. I'm not prepared to accept a miracle. We're not out of the wood yet, but if this should turn out to be another stroke of chance then I'll resign and go in for conjury."

"When shall we know?" enquired Inchcape, who had been startled into meekness by this sudden turn of events.

"I can't say." Yeo was ready and happy to talk. "Cooling will have gone ahead under our super's direction. The Austrian police may take their time, but I don't think so. Foreigners often seem to be a bit quicker than us," he added naïvely. "We'll find out how long he's been over here and we'll find his lodgings. Once we can take a look at them I think we'll be sitting pretty. My guess is that he's been over here about ten days and when he came he brought that grenade with him."

The local superintendent looked uneasy.

"About the gentleman we're after..." he murmured. "Since there were no fingerprints on the car, other than the deceased's and Mr. Petrie's, it shows he wore gloves, don't it? Probably they were ordinary gloves which he didn't trouble to take off. He'd never have wiped the whole car clean, even if he'd thought of it, would he now?"

"The lamp was wiped," said Inchcape with his mouth full. "Still, every kid knows about fingerprints these days."

Yeo looked at Campion.

"We're going to catch this fellow, you know," he observed. "I don't see how we can help ourselves. Did you ever hear of a chap who behaved so silly? There's no subtlety about him at all. He's behaving as if he's a god or something."

"Ah, they're often like that," said the superintendent. "Not insane. Just sort of exalted."

Yeo went on with his harangue, addressing Campion in particular.

"I see a chap who is a sort of great white chief in his own little world," he said meaningly. "A bloke who's used to getting his own way in everything. The people who work for him think he's something a bit bigger than life, and, because they stand for him doing the most amazing things, he thinks he can do the same elsewhere. He wanted to get rid of Konrad, and he must have had a good reason, mind you, or he wouldn't have bothered himself, so what did he do? He thought out a scheme which sounded all right and did what he was in the habit of doing in his business. He called in an expert. The expert delivered the goods and was paid for his trouble. Our man put his stunt into action and it went wrong. Instead of simply killing Konrad he raised little hell and got the police on him hot and strong. He kept his head—or more probably didn't quite realise what he *had* done—and went on with his own work in his own admiring circle. However, the expert who had delivered the grenade wasn't barmy. He could read the papers and he knew a good thing when he saw it. Our man was blackmailed by him. That settled it. Having found a simple way of getting rid of tiresome people, the man we have in mind proceeded to get going once again. He borrowed a car, choosing the one that he knew would be in a certain spot at a certain time. He seems to have got Kummer to do the pinching and I think how he did it was this. I think he stood at the end of the street, making the excuse that he was buying a packet of fags or something, and asked the chemist to bring the bus down for him. He probably just pointed it out and said: 'Bring it along, will you, old boy?' or something like that. Then he got in and they drove out to the

237

most convenient lonely spot he knew, a spot from which he could either walk home or pick up his own car. Then he made the other chap pull up for something, threw the rug over his head, and beat him up with a spanner."

"But why so near home?" protested Inchcape.

"Why chuck the bicycle lamp out into the garden?" retorted Yeo. "Because it never dawned on him that we might be able to prove anything against him. I've known plenty of men like that. Forty-five per cent of the criminal classes have that bee in their bonnet. Be careful of your fingerprints and you're okay; that's their motto."

Campion stretched his long legs under the table. He looked haggard and weary.

"If the murder took place about nine or nine-thirty..." he began and paused.

Yeo was regarding him with a slow, not unsympathetic smile.

"Mr. Sutane wasn't at the theatre after four o'clock on Friday," he said. "He didn't appear that night. Phil Flannery, his new understudy, went on. I didn't know that until after you left us yesterday or I'd have told you. We were going to interview him yesterday evening and then this broke. I thought it would be best to wait to identify the body."

Campion sat still and Yeo eyed him.

"My case is mainly theory, I know that," said the Yard inspector. "Several points have got to be cleared up before we can make an arrest. That's why I particularly don't want anyone scared. We want that motive."

Campion hardly heard him. His pale eyes were hard and introspective. As he sat staring down at the uneaten food congealing horridly on the coarse plate it dawned upon him painfully that the moment had arrived. The inevitable hour when he must pay for his return to White Walls was now at hand.

He got up.

"I'm going back now," he said. "If you'd care to run me down in the police car, Inspector, I'd like to have a word with you."

Yeo rose with alacrity.

"I'd like to. This last business makes all the difference, don't it?" he remarked as they moved towards the door. "I must say it wasn't in my book at all. I never thought he'd do it again so soon. The quicker we can pull him in the better. We don't want him taking a dislike to someone else."

He coughed. His heavy jocularity had struck the wrong note, even to his own ears.

The telephone delayed them. It was the local sergeant phoning from the station to say that no one at all had joined the late down train on Friday night. The ticket collector remembered the occasion perfectly.

Yeo shrugged his shoulders.

"It was only an idea," he said. "He must have fixed it with a second car somehow. Perhaps they came down in separate buses, as Kummer appeared to be driving the coupé. We'll have to work on that. There's a lot of routine enquiries to be made. We're going to have a busy day. There's the weapon to find yet. That's in a ditch or a furze patch, I'll bet my last dollar. It *would* be. We must find it, of course. The doctor thought it might have been a spanner. Fancy looking over twenty-five square miles of rough country for a spanner . . ."

Campion blinked.

"He may have got rid of it in the same way as he got rid of the bicycle lamp—chucked it away as soon as he had finished with it," he suggested meekly.

Yeo stared at him.

"He might," he said. "Lord! He's a fool, isn't he? I don't think he knows we're on the earth. The boys have been looking all round the car, of course, but I'll make them go over that area with a tooth comb. I'm beginning to hate this chap. He's so insulting."

Inspector Inchcape, who had been listening to the conversation, came to life.

"I'll see to it right away," he said quickly. "You'll be back, won't you, Inspector? Our chief constable, he do like to be in on everything. He's a wonderful particular gentleman. He and the doctor'll be down just after eight, I'll lay a pound."

"I'll be back," Yeo promised. "Are you ready, Mr. Campion?"

They drove out of the quiet little town into the lanes. The sun was climbing swiftly and the light mist over the low-lying meadows promised great heat in the middle day.

When they came to a convenient straight stretch just before the White Walls approach Yeo pulled up.

"Now, Mr. Campion," he said, "I've been waiting to hear from you. I've let you see my position pretty clearly, haven't

239

I? I'm going to get that man. Sooner or later evidence must come in which will get me a warrant. At the moment I can't stir because the P.P. doesn't like the idea of us holding him on suspicion, and although I can build up a first-rate case I can't substantiate every point until Cooling gets his stuff. What I need is the basic plank, the thing that pins it on to *him* and him only. I want the motive. I shall get him in a day or two, but in the meantime what else is he going to get up to? He's not particular who he makes trouble for, is he? Look at Boarbridge."

Campion shivered a little. He felt cold and strangely dispassionate.

"Yes," he said abruptly and with an authority Yeo had never heard in his voice before. "Yes, you're quite right. Now look here, there's a masseuse at White Walls, a Miss Edna Finbrough. Get her to go down to the station with you. Don't rouse her out of bed now. If you do you'll start the alarm and you must avoid that if you're going to get your man without trouble. When you get this woman down to Birley on some suitable pretext put her through it. She's tough but she's cracking. I've seen that for days."

"What do we want out of her?" Yeo was beginning.

But the thin man who seemed suddenly to have become so dry and impersonal went on without hearing him.

"Tell her you know that she went to a theatrical lodging-house on the Monday evening after Chloe Pye died. I'll give you the address. She made an excuse to go through Miss Pye's rooms alone and while she was there she ransacked the place for papers. I think she found what she was looking for and took it back to the person who had sent her. That paper was almost certainly destroyed that same night, but she can tell you what was on it, and for her information you will be able to get concrete evidence of the motive you need."

"Do you know what the paper was?"

Campion regarded the policeman coldly. He was very controlled and seemed almost callous about the whole subject.

"I don't, but I can guess. It was a marriage certificate."

Yeo whistled and his face looked like a comic mask.

"A-ah!" he said. "Now you're talking. That's something like."

His companion ignored him.

"I think Konrad got to know about this marriage and was

240

prepared to use his information. That is why he was killed. You may have some difficulty in getting it out of Miss Finbrough, but she knows."

"Like to see her yourself?"

"No." Campion's tone was sharp. "That's a job for the professional police. That's all I can give you. I shall be at the house all day. When you've found out what you can, perhaps you'll let me know? I'll stay on the spot until you make the arrest. I should keep Miss Finbrough out of the way until then. Don't let her communicate with the house."

"Good Lord, no!" Yeo spoke fervently and the glance he shot at Campion was almost affectionate. "This is just what I wanted. If you're right you'll have put him just where he ought to be. I told you you had to come down here."

Campion did not speak and Yeo, whose energy was mounting rather than diminishing after his long night, let in the clutch and roared on down the road.

"I'll be along for the woman about eleven," he said as he set his passenger down at the drive gates. "Don't worry. I'll be discretion itself. If this comes off I'll hand it to you. Did he kill the first woman too?"

Campion shrugged his shoulders.

"I see. It's like that, is it? We'll never prove it anyway." Yeo was grave and he made a little depreciatory grimace. "Nasty business. Hard on the family. Well, we've got enough to go on with, God knows. Once he's inside he may talk. Sometimes they like to—that conceited type. The newspapers are going to have a treat, aren't they? Well, so long, and thank you."

Campion came slowly up the drive and saw the white house, like a lovely ship in full sail, in the blazing morning. As he crossed the lawn a bundle in a gaily striped dressing gown detached itself from a deck chair and came padding towards him. It was Uncle William.

He looked pink and sleepy and pathetic, the wind ruffling his thin curls and his face puckered with weariness and anxiety.

"Been waitin' since the dawn," he mumbled. "Had to. Been prayin', practically. Everythin' all right, my boy? Relyin' utterly on you."

Campion turned away and went into the house.

241

27

At noon, when the garden was sweltering luxuriously in the full heat of the day and the house was peaceful in that odd Sunday quiet which is mysteriously different from the peace of other days, Uncle William let himself into Campion's room and advanced to the end of the bed.

He stood there for some little time, his hands in the pockets of his white trousers and his shoulders bent dejectedly. He looked more bearlike than ever.

"Awake, Campion?"

The man on the bed regarded his old friend steadily. His appearance gave no indication that he had slept at all. His eyes were cold and wakeful and the skin was drawn tightly over the bones of his face.

"Feller came and took Miss Finbrough off to help the police," observed Uncle William presently. "Didn't hear the rights of it. Somethin' about needin' her assistance. As a masseuse, I suppose. Couldn't understand it. So many confusin' things happenin' all round one."

His worried old voice trailed away into silence and he padded over to the window and looked out.

"What's in the wind?" he asked at last.

Mr. Campion sat up in bed. His impersonal, authoritative mood which Yeo had first noticed earlier in the morning still persisted.

To Uncle William, who was a little bewildered by it, he seemed to have suddenly become a stranger.

"Where is everybody?" he demanded.

"Linda's out there." The old man nodded towards the garden. "Sock's gone off in the Bentley, and Jimmy and Slippers are practisin' in the drawin' room with Mercer playin' for them, and in a damned condescendin' fashion, I don't mind tellin' you. Jimmy seems to have to keep up his practisin' all the time. He's workin' himself to death, poor feller. When's this infernal cloud goin' to lift, Campion? Upon my soul, it's a sin to have to think about some things on a day like this. Did the police succeed in findin' out who the ruffian in Sock's car was?"

Once again Mr. Campion ignored his question and asked another.

"Where has Sock gone?"

"To see Eve." Uncle William wandered back from the window. "We all waited up for the boy last night," he explained, his small blue eyes rounding childishly as he made the confidence. "He came in dead-beat, had a word or two with Jimmy, and then they both told us the full story in the drawin' room. He seemed ashamed he'd told the police so much, but, as I said to him, there are times when a man must choose between makin' serious trouble all round and givin' a friend away. Then the conscience is the only guide. I told him I was glad to see he had one, and I flatter myself I spoke to him like a father."

He paused.

"It wasn't as if the girl had done anythin' really wrong, you see," he added, neatly destroying his argument at a stroke. "Sock's attracted to her. He didn't actually say so, but I could see it with half an eye. So that's that. What a time for a lovers' quarrel, Campion! One can't expect women to be considerate, I know, but fancy runnin' off like that without a word when we were all so worried about somethin' else! If the girl wasn't so young I'd call her a hussy. Even so, I didn't see quite why she chose that particular moment to clear out, did you? Sock wasn't quite up to the mark last night and I didn't care to press him. She'd had words with Jimmy, I understood. Don't know what about; do you?"

"Some other man, I think." Campion spoke absently.

"So I gathered. But I didn't see who if it wasn't Sock."

Campion dragged his mind away from the all-engulfing disaster which was so quickly approaching and tried to remember his conversation with Sock Petrie in the Lagonda before they had passed the shabby blue coupé.

"She went off Sock and had a soulful affair with someone unlikely," he said. "Either Sutane found out about it and put his foot down, or, since that note of hers was left uncollected for so long, perhaps the man faded away on his own account."

"And the poor little girl felt the world had come to an end," cut in Uncle William happily. "That sounds more like the truth to me. It would account for her refusin' to come home. That's it, Campion; depend upon it. A blow at the pride. Known it drive a young girl off her head before now. Poor creature! Who is the whippersnapper? Far too big for his boots. I'm an old man but——"

"No," said Campion and added firmly: "I shouldn't."

The belligerent light died out of Uncle William's eyes, albeit a trifle reluctantly.

"Perhaps not," he said. "I was forgettin'. Make matters worse, of course. Still, it's a pity we don't know who he is," he added wistfully, looking at his plump fists. "Feel I'd like to do somethin' useful, you know. Suspense is gettin' us all under the weather. It's like a storm blowin' up. These dear people are bein' heroic. They're forcin' themselves to carry on. Jimmy looks like a skeleton and Linda's walkin' about like one of those dead workers in Haiti—what-d'ye-call-'em?—zombies."

Campion took hold of himself.

"Oh, yes," he said quietly, "I want to talk to you about Linda. Before she married, where did she live?"

"With her mother, naturally." Uncle William seemed to consider the question superfluous. "The old lady was the sister of the feller who owned this house. She has her little estate down in Devon. Very pretty place, I believe. There's money in that family, you know. Linda goes to stay with her sometimes and takes the child. What d'you want to know for?"

Campion shrugged his shoulders.

"Idle curiosity," he said. "I wondered what her background was, that was all."

The old man was silent for a long time.

"If you're worryin' about all this publicity breakin' Jimmy financially, she's got a home to go to," he said at last, and his eyes, meeting Campion's own, dropped furtively. "I've made up my own mind and I'm stickin' to it," he added with apparent irrelevance. "I told you that in this very room days ago. Linda's taken a fancy to you."

Mr. Campion stiffened.

"I don't think so."

Uncle William became the Man of the World, *circa* 1910.

It was his third happiest role, but one which he particularly enjoyed. His blue eyes became shrewd and tolerant.

"When a woman's lonely—nice woman, trustworthy, sensible, capable of controllin' the team she's drivin'—then these harmless little affairs do her good, cheer her up, keep her young," he said surprisingly. "They mean nothin'. She thinks of them as she thinks of the ornaments in her hair. The same with a man. It flatters him and keeps him a boy at heart. As long as they mind their manners and steer clear of sentimentality, it's a good thing. After many years of experience I can honestly say I approve of it. Spice of life, you know. I don't like the dish drenched, but a modicum here and there improves the meal."

Campion sat looking at him and once again Uncle William was conscious of him as a stranger.

"I don't know if that's your view, my boy," he added with hasty capitulation. "Bachelor's view."

Campion laughed.

"'If you haven't got the temperament, philandering isn't pleasure,' Guv'nor," he said. "That's a quotation from Don Marquis, probably the one philosophic poet of the generation. As far as I remember, he said it apropos of Lancelot and Guinevere, which makes it a very enlightening remark."

Uncle William looked mystified and uncomfortable.

"Spanish feller?" he observed, feeling no doubt that the operative word, which he particularly disliked, had a continental origin. "Sorry I interfered, my boy. One stumbles across things and makes the mistake of rememberin' 'em. Fact is, I keep leapin' on any subject which will take my mind off the trouble. Daresay you do too. Don't care what happens to my show—I'm past that. I'm simply holdin' my breath and prayin' for a bit of peace for myself and my friends. When's it goin' to end? That's what I want to know, Campion. When's it goin' to end? Well, I know you'd tell me if you could. Since you can't I'll go down and potter until lunchtime."

He padded off on plump crimson-shod feet and Campion got up and dressed slowly. He had ceased to consider his own personal part in the heartbreaking and irrevocable business. That problem had been faced and settled in his own flat when Linda had made her final appeal to him.

Since then he had found it possible to consider the miserable programme which circumstance and the unalterable part of his character had laid down for him by going through it steadily with one half of his conscious mind shut down. That there were flaws in this arrangement he discovered only too soon. He found himself doing unexpected things, making unreasonable detours, avoiding meetings, all to save himself the emotional reactions which he would ordinarily have experienced had he not taken his original precaution of mental semianaesthesia.

This morning, for instance, he found that he was dressing himself with extraordinary deliberation and not out of any particular desire for sartorial elegance. When the explanation did occur to him it shocked him. It was not pleasant to find that he was aiming to be late for lunch, so late that he might unobtrusively avoid eating Sutane's food at Sutane's table.

The discovery of this primitive taboo, with its physical reaction which decreed that he should not be hungry in spite of his neglected breakfast, left him both startled and irritated. It was like finding one half of himself suddenly under new management.

He pulled himself together impatiently. Yet when Lugg came surging in half an hour later he was still in his shirt sleeves.

The temporary butler was aggressively cheerful.

"Another corpse yisterday, I 'ear," he remarked, sitting down to rest his feet. "Quite an outin' for you, ain't it? Enjoyin' yerself? There's a bunch o' narks at either end of the lane, by the way. Does that mean anythink or is it just you showin' orf?"

His employer did not turn his head and, receiving no encouragement, Mr. Lugg was silent for a moment or so. When the hush became oppressive to him, however, he made a further attempt at small talk.

"This is life, ain't it?" he observed with relish. "A certain amount o' class but still free and easy. I'm like a duck in water 'ere, you know."

Campion knotted his tie with careful neatness.

"We shall probably both be leaving tonight," he said without looking round. "Don't mention it to anyone. Simply get everything ready."

The fat man did not blink. His small eyes rested on the tall figure silhouetted against the light.

It was a moment of great sadness.

Finally Lugg sighed.

"I knew it," he said heavily. "I felt it comin' on. As soon as I saw you in the passage last week I thought to myself, 'Ullo, I thought. It's a funny thing, ain't it, 'ow you take to a place?" he went on, philosophic resignation in his thick voice. "I'd git sick of it in time, but up till now I've took a pride in the drawin' room and I've bin interested in trainin' my young mate. She's on the three-card trick now. Comin' along a treat. We'll go after she's gone to bed, eh? We don't want a bloomin' cryin' setout. You've made up yer mind to go today? It's a lovely day."

His wistfulness was pathetic and Campion felt sudden sympathy for him.

"I'm afraid so," he murmured. "The party's over. Sorry."

Lugg heaved his mountainous shoulders.

"I'll take me tail coat," he remarked. "I 'ad it sent from the stores on your account. Largest they 'ad. Ten bob extra. It wouldn't fit anybody else. Make them look funny. You might ask all these people to dinner one night and I could wear it then, eh?"

Campion glanced out of the open window at the dancing garden.

"I shouldn't hope for that, Lugg," he said. "Take the coat by all means, if you want it. And now clear out, old boy, will you? I'm not in a chatty mood."

The large man got up obediently and lumbered towards the door.

"Per'aps I'll git 'er perfect this afternoon," he remarked optimistically. "She can't quite git the flip of the card in time with the moody. Oh, well, even the spadgers go back to London when the 'op pickin's over. Git on with yer dressin'. Gong's goin' any minute now."

He went off sadly and ten minutes afterwards Mr. Campion followed him, late for lunch.

28

Mr. Campion sat near the house because he wanted to hear the telephone bell when it rang. Tea had been served on the terrace and now the company had split up into little groups. Linda, Sock Petrie and Eve were walking among the flower beds. The young man had brought the sulky, smouldering-eyed girl home just before the meal and Campion had marvelled at her self-possession as she had come swinging in to take her seat amongst them all. She had given no explanation and there had been no hint of apology in her manner; only an impenetrable, youthful defiance, both cool and rigidly polite.

Sock had managed her very well. He had adopted a cheerful superiority, whipping her over dangerous places in the conversation and devoting his whole attention to her.

Sutane and Slippers had rushed out for a cup of tea and rushed back again to the drawing room. They had both slept during the afternoon after their arduous morning's work and had decided to put in another hour to the gramophone, since Mercer had grown tired of accompanying them.

That wearied genius had returned to the grand piano in the morning room and now sat there, strumming his endless improvisations with the double doors closed to shut out the dance music.

Uncle William sat in a corner under the window. The Sunday papers were on his stomach and the decanter was at his side. He invariably refused to drink tea, insisting that it was effeminate or poison to his system, according to the company in which he found himself.

Campion looked out across the flower beds, where the rainbow gladiolas and the second delphinium crop were blazing in the last of the full sunlight, and wondered if the day would ever end. The atmosphere of oppression had grown slowly until it was now unbearable.

They were all aware of it, even Mercer, whose habitual self-absorption had turned him into a silent, inanimate dummy at tea.

Campion had not looked directly at Sutane all day, although he had been acutely conscious of him all the time. The extraordinary nervous force of the dancer's personality had pervaded every room which he entered until the whole house seemed to tingle with him. He had rehearsed with a cold, passionate energy which had called forth comment even from the gentle Slippers Bellew.

Campion was sitting on the low wall of the terrace, his long arms resting on his knees and his head bent, when Linda appeared before him. He had not seen her leave the others and her sandalled feet had made no sound upon the grass.

He looked up at her and preferred not to see the shadows in her eyes.

"How long?" she said.

"Soon." The word escaped him involuntarily. It was the last thing he would have chosen to say, and he rose, angry with himself and a little frightened.

To his relief she did not seem to see its significance.

"I hope so," she said.

As they walked over the turf together it occurred to him that it was for the last time, ever.

They were both silent for a while and when she spoke it was with a directness which startled him.

"Everyone knows except me. Jimmy knows. You know. So, I think, does Eve. You'll stay with me until I know?"

"Yes, I'll stay."

"I shall be sorry when you go," she said.

He did not reply and was grateful to her when he realised that she did not expect him to.

Her next words appalled him.

"When it's all over we shall go to America—Jimmy and Sarah and I and perhaps Uncle William. They like Jimmy over there, you know, and it's a wonderful country, especially for children. American children really have a childhood. Sarah will be wildly happy—nearly as happy as she is now with old Lugg. They're going to write to each other when he goes away, she says. It ought to be a grand correspondence. You were very kind to lend him to me. He's been appreciated."

Campion glanced sharply towards the house, but he was wrong. The phone bell had not rung. He glanced down at the girl and she caught sight of his expression. To his amazement she took hold of his hand and walked along looking down at it.

"It's going to be difficult to say this," she said, "and I probably shouldn't dream of doing it if things were remotely normal. But I like you better than anyone I've ever met. You're not a boy, so you won't go away with your head swelling and your virtue outraged because you think I'm telling you I've fallen in love with you—which I haven't, yet. But I don't think I shall see you again. We shall rush off to the States, for one thing. Anyway, it's in my mind to say this now. I like you because you're the only person I've ever *suddenly* liked who hasn't turned out to be a dreadful error of judgment. I made a fool of myself to you and you understood it. You didn't make love to me when the idea occurred to you and I rather wanted you to. And you've been loyal to our interests when it was obviously very awkward for you to do anything of the kind. Because you began on our side you stuck to us. I thought I'd like to say thank you, that's all. . . . What's the matter? Why are you looking like that?"

Campion turned his hand and took her own in it. He held it very tightly for a long time. It was firm and heart-easing and very hard to have to lose.

When he looked up again he was laughing a little.

"When one kicks over a tea table and smashes everything but the sugar bowl, one may as well pick that up and drop it on the bricks, don't you think?" he said lightly. "That was the phone, my lost, my lovely one. I've been waiting for it all day."

He left her standing among the rose trees, a puzzled, frightened expression in her eyes.

Before he was halfway across the lawn Lugg came out of the glass door at the back of the hall to summon him.

The hall was empty as he crossed to the table and he paused for a moment before picking up the instrument. His face was blank and he felt breathless.

"Hullo," he said at last.

"Hullo. That you, Campion? Everything all right your end?"

To his surprise he recognised Stanislaus Oates at the other end of the wire. The Central Branch superintendent sounded quietly jubilant.

"Yes," said Campion steadily. "Yes. Quite all right."

"Fine. Are you alone?"

"I think so."

"I understand you. I'm being discreet myself. Country exchange, you know. Congratulations, son. Nice work. We'll be with you. Get that?"

"Where are you?"

"At the local station." Oates laughed self-consciously. "I couldn't keep out of it. I came down with the sergeant and we brought the necessary authorisation. Campion . . ."

"Yes?"

"I think I might tell you this. I'll wrap it up. The woman cracked at once. Yeo phoned us in town before noon. She gave him all he wanted to know. Seemed glad to talk. We went ahead at our end and found the church. It's in Brixton. The date in the register is 1920. Suit your reckoning?"

"Near enough."

"Are you still alone?"

"Yes. Why?"

"I thought you sounded a bit subdued. It's probably the line. Well, that was that. We had plenty for a pull-in on suspicion, but to be on the safe side I called up the P.P. But the publicity still scared him. He said wait. However, I'd hardly put down the phone when the Austrian stuff came through. Campion, it's magnificent! Just what we want. K. was actually under surveillance up to last week. . . . Eh? Oh, concealing arms. I ask you! The Austrians were more than civil. I'll show you the wire. Seven forms of it and all relevant." He chuckled. "You can't help being excited, can you?" he said happily. "It goes on too. I must tell you. Things began to move at once. Last night I sent a routine call to the hotels, and this afternoon, just as we were coming away, we had a reply from a little place in Victoria. We rushed down there and got everything intact. It was all there in K.'s luggage. We got the name again, the address—everything—all in a tupenny notebook. It was blackmail all right. Then we hurried down here and found this end busy. The railway people had started remembering things once they had the name. It was a childish trick on Friday. The same trick as Petrie's. The train wasn't used at all. Follow me? We found the spanner too. It belonged to the car, as we thought. The whole thing has dropped together like a puzzle running out. It's open and shut. We've got everything. Pleased with yourself?"

"Howlingly."

"You don't sound it. You've got nothing to worry about. You couldn't have done it more quickly. Yeo's here. He sends his regards and takes back all hard thoughts. He says he misunderstood you, but now that he sees what you were working up to he'll be happy to buy you a beer at the first opportunity. It's such a pretty case, Campion. There's not a flaw in it."

"How long will you be?"

The younger man's voice was very quiet.

"Half an hour at most. We're practically set. I just phoned to warn you and to make sure there was no hitch your end. We can serve the doings at White Walls now, can we?"

"Yes."

"You'll stay there with your eyes glued till we come?"

"I will."

"Right. Half an hour, then. Good-bye."

Campion replaced the receiver and looked down at the polished surface of the table, where a light film of summer dust had collected since the morning. A childish inclination to scribble in it assailed him and he wrote the three words which he was trying to keep in the forefront of his mind against the intolerable temptations which besieged him: "The porter's wife."

He regarded the inscription helplessly for some seconds before he rubbed it out with his handkerchief.

As he crossed the hall he kicked something small and round in his stride and stooped to retrieve it. It was a small yellow button with a flower painted on it. He recognised it as one of the six on Linda's yellow dress. He turned it over, hesitated, and finally dropped it into his pocket with a secret, comforted sense of acquisition.

He saw Sutane as soon as he stepped out into the garden again. The dancer was seated on the last step of the terrace outside the morning-room windows. He had his back to Campion, and in the tight black sweater which he had pulled

252

over his white flannels his body looked kite-shaped and angular, like a modern drawing. He sat with his knees pulled up to his chin and his head resting upon them. No other man in a similar position could have appeared so completely comfortable, at peace and at ease.

Far down at the end of the garden Linda was walking with Slippers. Their dresses flickered white and yellow among the leaves. Eve had returned. She was lying in the hammock couch at the far end of the lawn. Her hands were behind her head and her eyes, Campion guessed, were staring with dark resentment at the little skiffs of pink cloud floating so serenely in the painted sky.

Sock had vanished, but the sound of his voice, punctuated by squeals of delight from Sarah, echoed from the kitchen lawn on the west side of the house and indicated that the three-card tricksters had found a suitable mug.

Campion sat down beside Sutane. In the cool depth of the morning room behind them Mercer was still strumming. His new tune, "Pavane for a Dead Dancer," had grown from a motif into a completed thing, and he played it over several times, working a flight of spontaneous conceits into it before skimming off into other phrases, some amusing and others reaching that substratum of banality which has, at least, always the merit of provoking astonishment.

Neither of the two men on the terrace spoke immediately. Sutane sat very still. He had not altered his position save that he had turned his head and now sat watching Campion with his dull black eyes intelligent and questioning.

"Hello," he said softly at last. "Come to make your report?"

Campion regarded him gravely. His own gamut of sensation had been played through. He had heard the whole scale and knew the last thin flat note. He was emotionally finished and was strangely at peace.

Sutane stirred and the familiar bent smile passed over his wide mouth.

"I thought you had."

Campion looked at his own long brown fingers and spoke without taking his eyes from them.

"The police have a copy of Chloe's marriage certificate," he said slowly. "I told them about it. They got it from a church in Brixton. When she came down here and increased her

253

blackmailing demands on her husband he lost his temper with her and..."

Sutane stretched himself suddenly.

"Oh, it wasn't so simple as that, my dear fellow," he said, turning over so that he lay on his stomach on the grass, with his elbows resting on the low flat step. "He didn't know he *was* her husband, you see."

Campion stared at him in fascinated resignation and Sutane went on, his pleasant voice playing dreamily with the words.

"She was a strange woman when she was younger. I don't know if you'll know what I mean, but she had that quality of recklessness which is the essence of passion. When the war was first over there was a feel for it. People talk of youngsters *drifting* into a life of good times. They don't know. There was energy, force, ecstasy, put into those good times. There was no drifting about it. We hurled ourselves into them and made them riotous.

"Here and there a particular woman was thrown up out of them like a bubble on the brew. She became not a leader but an embodiment of the spirit of the urge for enjoyment. The old anxiety to fill the day because of the death that was coming tomorrow had become a habit with our immediate elders and we caught it from them, but without their fear. We were young. We weren't tired. We weren't shattered. Our nerves weren't shot to pieces. We were repressed. We'd grown up in a world where there wasn't any fun. And suddenly, just when our blood was rising, it came.

"Chloe was a little older than the rest of us. She was successful and at the height of her looks. She married lightly in a fit of exuberance and a few months after, when she tired of it, she took another man. There was a row. The poor idiot of a husband thought he was in love with her and tried to hold her and she annihilated him by explaining cheerfully as she packed her clothes that he had no possible claim on her. She'd been married before, in the war, she said. Her husband was alive. She must be a bigamist and wasn't it amusing? She was not very sorry and he was not to be silly, not to be *vieux jeu*. It had been a rather jolly experience, she thought."

Sutane's voice ceased and he glanced down the garden to where the two women were still walking.

"The husband was brokenhearted, silly young ass, but he recovered," he added presently.

254

In the long pause which followed, much that had been dark to Mr. Campion became suddenly and painfully clear. He saw the garden again as it had been on that twilit evening a fortnight before when Chloe had gone down to the lake to dance to "Love, the Magician."

Sutane was waiting and Campion roused himself to speak.

"I had not seen that," he said.

"How could you?" the dancer murmured. "You never knew the real Chloe."

Campion took up his story again. He was acutely conscious that there was very little time and that there was much to be said.

"When she came to London this time she found it impossible to get hold of her husband alone," he began. "He was too busy, too closely surrounded. In despair she forced herself down to his home and begged or cheated him into meeting her in the garden at night. When the moment came and she actually had him before her in a lonely and romantic setting she must have played her trump card immediately. I didn't know how strong it was. She told him she was still his wife. Either her previous marriage had been a fabrication, invented on the spur of the moment when she wanted to be rid of him, or her first husband had died before her second marriage took place."

"There was no first marriage," said Sutane.

Campion felt intolerably weary. His bones were weighing him down and his head ached. He struggled on.

"She was alone, dancing, when he found her that night," he said, "and she must have talked to him with the gramophone still running. The whole interview couldn't have taken long because the last record of the set was still on the machine when I found it that night. I think she simply walked up to him and told him she had lied long ago and could prove it. Something like that?"

He paused questioningly.

Sutane nodded gravely. "Go on," he said.

Campion's precise voice wavered as he took up the tale.

"His first reaction was fear, naturally," he murmured. "Fear and then rage. He caught hold of her by the throat and, before he realised at all what had happened, her knees sagged and he felt her go limp. She was dead. The *status lymphaticus* accounted for that. He didn't know about that

255

then, of course, and he must have been terrified. He only saw that she was suddenly and unaccountably dead and the whole miserable secret must come out, with scandal and ruin in its trail.

"I think the gramophone must have finished about that time, for he turned the record over, not realising that the piece of trivia on the other side was hardly the sort of thing she would ever play. It was a natural thing for him to do. It was a subconscious effort to keep things as they were, you see, an instinctive attempt to delay the moment of disaster.

"After that I fancy he lost his head completely. He picked her up and carried her as far away from the house as he could. That was unreasoning instinct too. He was so careless that he left the gramophone running, trod on a record and dropped her red silk skirt, which had been tied tightly around her waist, and which he must have loosened in his first frantic efforts to revive her. The skirt fell on the grass, where someone else found it and danced on it.

"All this was done madly in his first terror, but when he came to the bridge his mind began to work again. The car was there and it put an idea in his head. He pitched her over into the lane and staged the accident. It wasn't murder the first time. That's the whole ghastly pity of it."

Sutane was still lying on the shallow steps, his eyes quiet and without expression.

"Why hadn't she come out with it before?" he demanded, bitterness in his voice for the first time. "Why leave her rotten story until now? Why give the poor beast years of peace and then spring it on him?"

Campion did not look up.

"Money, don't you think?" he suggested gently. "She came back and found—or thought she found—him rich. She didn't want the man. She wanted to be bought off."

Sutane laughed. The violent explosive sound echoed over the garden and startled the birds in the ornamental cherry trees.

"I never saw it, Campion," he said huskily. "I never saw it. It would have been so easy."

Campion passed his hand over his forehead and found it damp. It was a mad interview, a conversation in a dream, with nothing solid or static in the world, only a sense of inexorable disaster coming nearer and nearer every second.

"Konrad saw him," he said. "Or the husband thought he saw him. Konrad sneaked out about that time to telephone his accomplice and report the success of his surprise party. The following morning he began to talk wildly up in the dressing room. Then he appropriated the handbag. Then he threatened. The husband got frightened. He instigated a search of Chloe's rooms. The marriage certificate was found and burnt. Chloe was buried. He felt safe again, or almost safe. There was only Konrad to consider. But Konrad looked dangerous and in the end the husband committed the intolerable, incredible folly of deciding to shut his mouth.

"There was a man called Kummer in Vienna, a brilliant chemist with a crooked streak, the kind of person a young bohemian in Paris just after the war might easily have got to know. He was not hard to get hold of now, for a man with friends among the intelligentsia abroad. Need I go on?"

Sutane laid the back of his hand over his face. It was ballet rather than theatre and was oddly expressive.

"Those other people . . ." he said. "Oh, God! Those other people . . ."

The sun had sunk down behind the house and they were in the shadow. Linda and Slippers had passed out of sight. The kitchen lawn was silent, and in her swing couch Eve appeared to be asleep.

In the silence Mercer's little tunes came floating out caressingly, their sentimental meanderings flirting idly with the memory. An older melody than the rest caught Campion's attention. It reminded him vividly of his first arrival at the house. The name of the song slipped up in his mind—"Water-Lily Girl." He remembered Chloe playing it as she sat beside the disgruntled composer, and he saw again her raddled face, with the pale green, overbright eyes, turned archly towards the embarrassed man. He saw the scene clearly: Chloe playing the song all the way through, with obstinate insistence on each sickly phrase. Mercer was playing it like that now, almost as though he were caricaturing it.

As Campion listened to him a further memory returned to his mind. He went back to his undergraduate days and saw himself drinking coffee in a shabby teashop in a Cambridge back street where, behind a thin green curtain, an appalling gramophone ground out the plummy mouthings of a tenth-rate ballad singer.

> *"When the stars are wide awake, Water-Lily Girl,*
> *I'll be waiting by the lake, Water-Lily Girl.*
> *There's a beating heart at stake.*
> *Will you hide and let it break?*
> *For old times' sake—Water-Lily Girl."*

He sat up as the significance of the doggerel sank into his mind. That, then, had been Chloe's invitation to the meeting. There had been no note or hurried word during the flurry of the day, as he had supposed. The arrangement had been made then, under his nose. He understood at last her insistence on the verse of the song.

As the little piece of jigsaw dropped into place his mind jolted. A new thought clamoured at him. Sutane had not been there. Sutane had been out in the hall, rehearsing. He himself had not set eyes on the man before lunch.

As he sat stiffly, his eyes fixed upon the middle distance, his brain seemed suddenly to turn over in his head. It was a definite physical experience and was comparable to the process which takes place when an expected train in the underground station appears from what is apparently the wrong tunnel and the mind slips over and adjusts the phenomenon by turning the universe other side out, substituting in one kaleidoscopic second east for west.

Eve had been in the room that Sunday morning and so had Sock, but Chloe had been playing to Mercer.

Campion stared at the new vista.

Squire Mercer.

Mercer, who never considered anyone except himself, not only as a main rule but down to the smallest and most trivial circumstance. Mercer, who honestly thought himself all-important and, because of his gifts, was tolerated and encouraged by his friends.

Mercer, who had the one type of mind which was sufficiently ingenious and sufficiently devoid of humour to conceive the dreadful and ludicrous bicycle-lamp grenade, a notion quite as laughable and quite as horribly effective as the notorious Mr. Smith's recipe for murdering wife after wife in the cracked baths of second-rate boarding houses.

Mercer, who would not be particularly disturbed by the news that a number of strangers had met with an appalling accident on a railway station, so long as it took place twenty miles out of his sight.

Campion bent forward, his head in his hands. His mind had become very clear. He had the illusion of thinking very slowly.

Mercer had taken an overdose of quinine immediately after hearing on the 8:45 news bulletin the news of the disaster at Boarbridge. He had then developed, or said he had developed, severe cinchonism, which was a peculiar condition inasmuch as any doctor consulted had only the patient's word for the symptoms experienced—blindness, shakiness, headache, congestion of the middle ear. All these things could be simulated very easily by a man who was afraid his nerves might give him away during an awkward interview with the police.

Campion's mind travelled back to the night of Chloe's death. Mercer had been in the little music room with the window open. It was practically Mercer's own room. He certainly used it more often than anyone else. Campion remembered that window. He himself had slid out through it during his experiment with the weights from the kitchen scales. He remembered the hard turf below it and the straight path leading right through the garden to the lake. A man might slip out on to the dark lawn and back through that window a dozen times without being missed.

He thought of Kummer.

Kummer had come to London and had put up at a small hotel in Victoria. It had been assumed that the man had been in England for some time. But there was now the likelihood that he had only just arrived.

If Mercer's cinchonism was fictitious, why should he have gone to London on Friday to see a specialist? Suppose, instead, he had gone to see Kummer? Mercer could not or would not drive a car, but he knew where Sock kept his coupé, parked in the open street.

Suppose Yeo's piece of reconstruction had been the truth and Mercer had indicated the car standing at the end of the cul-de-sac and had asked Kummer to drive him back to his cottage on the White Walls estate. Suppose he had sat beside the man until the convenient moment had arrived and had then whipped the rug over his head and had killed him with

Sock's spanner, battering out his brains with all the frenzied terror of the man not naturally violent.

The superintendent's cautious conferences on the telephone returned to his ears. He had spoken of Petrie's trick. Suppose Mercer had pushed the car onto the verge after Kummer was dead and had then walked back to Boarbridge station and had waited there for his own chauffeur, who naturally assumed that he had come down by his ordinary late train.

Mercer had gone to Paris on the Tuesday after Chloe's death, when the bicycle was already in the house and Konrad had already made his threat. If to Paris, why not to Vienna, a few hours' flying distance beyond?

The whole series of murders had been so utterly careless. As Yeo had said, the man responsible was evidently blind to his danger. His crimes were the crimes of one who was a little god in his own circle. Who then was the little god of this circle? Not Sutane, who was the worker, the man who recognised his responsibilities and was secretly appalled by them, but Mercer, who was cozened, flattered and protected until his opinion of his own importance lost all touch with reality.

Campion scrambled to his feet.

The significance of Yeo's message through the superintendent had burst upon him. Yeo now knew the truth and erroneously supposed that he, Campion, had known it all the time. It was Mercer who had married Chloe, Mercer who had derived from the very briefness of his association with her the inspiration for his embarrassingly poignant music. It was Mercer's name in the tuppenny notebook, Mercer's name in the register at the Brixton church.

Relief burst over Campion, engulfing him, soothing him, comforting him with the old magic cry of his childhood—"It isn't true! It isn't true!" He was free. The load was lifted. Sutane was not the man. Linda—Sarah—Sock—Eve—the theatre—the house—the lovely excitement of those dancing feet—they were all miraculously saved on the brink of disaster. He had been gloriously wrong. It was not true!

He paused. Through the overwhelming flood which lifted him out of himself he heard the tinkle of the piano and with that sound came a new recollection, which stopped his heart.

There was an obstacle.

There remained the unanswerable consideration which had

struck Mercer from his list of suspects from the very beginning. Mercer had an alibi for the hour of Chloe's death.

All that evening he had been playing in the music room and the one man whose word on such a vital matter Campion would have taken without question had been sitting there listening to him—Uncle William, faulty but incorruptible, human but honest as the day.

Campion moved slowly across the terrace and stood looking into the house through the wide french window. In the shadow at the far end of the morning room he saw the crown of Mercer's untidy black head above the angle of the piano top. His glance travelled forward and he caught his breath.

In the deep armchair, his chubby feet crossed, his hands folded on his paunch, the empty decanter at his side and his crimson face immobile in the sleep of the happily drugged, lay Uncle William human.

A herd of buffalo in the room might conceivably awaken him within the hour, but very little else would disturb that deep and alcoholic peace.

Campion stepped back and turned abruptly at the top of the steps to find Sutane beside him. The dancer's angular and expressive body was relaxed and his arms hung at his sides.

"Keep Eve out of it," he said softly. "They were in the midst of one of those wild, impossible love affairs when it happened, you see. She was so jealous of Chloe at first and then after the woman's death he altered and she couldn't understand it at all, poor little beast. That's why she ran away. She couldn't bear to look at him any more. I hunted for her all over the place. I gave up the show on Friday night to go down and see her, once Sock found out where she was. I got it all out of her then."

He sighed and peered into Campion's face.

"They'd kept it a secret, knowing I wouldn't approve." Campion looked at the other man steadily.

"How long have you known the truth about Mercer?"

Sutane stared at him.

"I saw him," he said. "I thought you knew. My dear fellow, I saw him on the bridge. He pitched her clean under my wheels."

He came a step nearer and his deeply lined face was desperately sincere.

"I didn't dream he'd go on," he said earnestly. "I got hold

of the certificate and I burned it because I knew he'd never think of it. But I didn't dream he'd go on. After Boarbridge I had to have you here. I *had* to, Campion! Don't you see, you were my conscience. You had to find him out. But I couldn't direct you. I couldn't give him away. We were together in Paris after the war. I was his only friend and, oh, my dear chap, don't you see, I was the beggar who pinched his wife."

There was a whir of gears at the drive gates and as they glanced up two police cars crackled smoothly over the gravel towards the front door.

In the morning room Mercer was playing his little pavane.

Sutane took a long, slow, infinitely graceful step. In the midst of it he looked up. The crooked smile was on his lips and, surprisingly, his black eyes had tears in them.

"How could I, old boy?" he said.

ABOUT THE AUTHOR

MARGERY ALLINGHAM, who was born in London in 1904, came from a long line of writers. "I was brought up from babyhood in an atmosphere of ink and paper," she claimed. One ancestor wrote early nineteenth century melodramas, another wrote popular boys' school stories, and her grandfather was the proprietor of a religious newspaper. But it was her father, the author of serials for the popular weeklies, who gave her her earliest training as a writer. She began studying the craft at the age of seven and had published her first novel by the age of sixteen while still at boarding school. In 1927 she married Philip Youngman Carter, and the following year she produced the first of her Albert Campion detective stories, THE CRIME AT BLACK DUDLEY. She and her husband lived a life "typical of the English countryside," she reported, with "horses, dogs, our garden and village activities" taking up leisure time. One wonders how much leisure time Margery Allingham, the author of more than thirty-three mystery novels in addition to short stories, serials and book reviews, managed to have.

BANTAM MYSTERY COLLECTION

Kinsey Millhone is...

"The best new private eye." —*The Detroit News*

"A tough-cookie with a soft center." —*Newsweek*

"A stand-out specimen of the new female operatives."
  —*Philadelphia Inquirer*

Sue Grafton is...

The Shamus and Anthony Award winning creator of Kinsey Millhone and quite simply one of the hottest new mystery writers around.